# LITTLE SAIGON

Also by T. Jefferson Parker
*Laguna Heat*

# LITTLE SAIGON

## T. Jefferson Parker

St. Martin's Press          New York

This novel is a work of fiction. All of the events, characters, names, and places depicted in this novel are entirely fictitious or are used fictitiously. No representation that any statement made in this novel is true or that any incident depicted in this novel actually occurred is intended or should be inferred by the reader.

LITTLE SAIGON. Copyright © 1988 by T. Jefferson Parker. All rights reserved. Printed in the United States of America. No part of this book may be used or reproduced in any manner whatsoever without written permission except in the case of brief quotations embodied in critical articles or reviews. For information, address St. Martin's Press, 175 Fifth Avenue, New York, N.Y. 10010.

Editor: Jared Kieling
Production Editor: Amelie Littell
Design by Glen M. Edelstein

Library of Congress Cataloging-in-Publication Data

Parker, T. Jefferson.
  Little Saigon / T. Jefferson Parker.
    p.  cm.
  ISBN 0-312-02245-X
  I. Title.
PS3566.A6863L57  1988
813'.54—dc19
                                                    88-11586
                                                    CIP

First Edition
10 9 8 7 6 5 4 3 2 1

# Acknowledgments

I would like to thank the following people for their generous help in writing this book.

Many thanks to Wendy Asano, whose Saigon Cabaret in Garden Grove, California, served as a great inspiration—anyone who goes there will know why. I would like to thank Wendy, her daughter Rebecca, and son Jeff for hours of hospitality, good music, and good company.

Westminster Police Officer Dennis Gabrielli showed me the streets of Little Saigon and suffered my questioning presence in his patrol car more than once. I hope that his sense of humor and of fair play at least partially found its way into this story.

Detective Marcus Frank of the Westminster P.D., a specialist in Asian-American crime in southern California, was a candid and authoritative source of information.

Garden Grove Police Officer Mark Hutchinson showed me his beat in Little Saigon through the eyes of a young and capable patrolman.

I would also like to thank attorney Carolyn Malone of Immigration Law for taking me under her benevolent wing and introducing me to so many formidable and fascinating members of the refugee community of Orange County.

Thanks too, to the various workers of the National United Front for the Liberation of Vietnam, who spoke to me with openness and hope regarding their efforts to reclaim their homeland. One can only wish them well.

I also thank Donald Stanwood for his incisive reading of this novel in manuscript, and for his unfailingly good advice on what to leave out.

Last but not least, I thank Jared Kieling of St. Martin's Press, whose guidance was invaluable.

Whatever truth this book contains is theirs; the mistakes and misjudgments are mine alone.

—T. Jefferson Parker
April 1988
Laguna Beach

For my brother Matt

They of the west are appalled at his day
and horror seizes them of the east.

—Job 18

# LITTLE SAIGON

# CHAPTER 1

**C**HUCK FRYE, FORMER SECOND-best surfer of Laguna Beach, gazed through his windshield and saw no six-foot waves.

Instead, Laguna Canyon Road sped toward him in the darkness, its yellow stripe wavering, eucalyptus trees whisking past the beams of his skewed headlights.

Scenes from the last forty-eight hours played in his mind—fragments of a weekend abandon that was reckless far beyond the limits of common sense. It began as an epic debauch and things went downhill fast. It was exactly what he wanted. The time is nigh, Frye thought, to get myself together.

He sat up straight, took a deep and dizzying breath. How many motoring souls have met their maker on this road? he wondered. In his own lifetime it seemed like a million: busloads of tourists colliding with cement mixers, sports cars slamming into each other head-on, bikers wrapping themselves around power poles while their machines scattered fireworks across the hillsides. And always the orange outlines of the bodies, sprayed by the police to mark the final attitude of the departed.

Frye signaled contritely and made a left turn onto Canyon Oaks Drive.

The old Mercury rumbled past the nursery and body shops, then past the rickety little houses clustered in the darkness. The moon and a distant streetlamp shone on beat-up cars, toolsheds of odd design, drooping clotheslines. A cat ran through three gradients of shadow, then vanished under a pickup. A stand of plantain drooped with malarial laziness, while beside it a wall of honeysuckle gave off an aroma that made everything seem even warmer than it was. Laguna Beach—art colony, tourist trap, a piece of attempted Eden crammed between the hills and the ocean, hippies in the sixties, cocaine in the seventies, AIDS in the eighties, a representative Southern California beach town.

Nimbly executing a hairpin left, Frye gunned the Cyclone up a straightaway so vertical that the sky became a dashboard of whirling needles. Then the stars rushed back into place as he plopped level, narrowly missing the mailbox he had knocked over months ago and that now lay door-up in the ivy in front of his cave-house. He worked himself from the car, wrestled his mail from the box and advanced on his front door. "Home," he mumbled. "Frye one, Visitors zip."

The cave-house stood before him, a dark lump against a dark sky. It was built into a hill overlooking the city, facing west. Fumbling with his keys, Frye marveled again at the frankly weird history of the place—the gist being that one Skippy Sharp had paid a contractor to build a house in the great sandstone outcropping, then had run out of money when the project was only half finished. Skippy had lived in it for a few months before disappearing forever into Mexico, so the contractor himself took it over, then Sharp's mother somehow got control of the thing and rented it in succession to a painter, an architect, a fish breeder, a child-molester, a nurse, then finally to the former second-best surfer in Laguna. Not long after he had rented it, Frye learned that the land had been bought by his own father, the venerable Edison Joseph Frye, thereby adding this tiny piece of ground to the vast Orange County Frye Ranch. Mrs. Sharp still "managed" the property, raising Frye's rent often and with gusto, believing, he concluded, that his family fortune warranted such outrage. It was, in fact, a cave-house—with back rooms being nothing more than dark irregular caverns. But the living room, bedroom, kitchen and bath featured walls, electricity, and unimpeded views of the Pacific. Frye's friends said that the cave-house was like Frye himself: half-finished, prone to dark recesses. At any rate, it was home.

He stood in the living room and felt the floor rotating under him, an illusion he explained away as the spinning of Earth on her axis. He went straight to his answering machine. Frye attended to this gadget with devotion, hopeful that some huge improvement might be in the offing.

Linda called to say she had filed Friday.

Dr. Redken's office called: scan results in.

Bill Antioch at the MegaShop called to tell him about the Masters Invitational Surf Contest at Huntington Beach.

The last message was from Bennett. "Hope you haven't forgotten the birthday thing at the Wind. Li wrote a song for us. See you there about ten, little brother. Saigon Days is still going on—that civic party—so I'll save you a seat. That's today, *Sunday,* in case you forgot."

Frye checked his watch but it was gone. He fumbled for a light switch, knocked over a stack of résumés he'd just had copied, then consulted his MegaShop surf calendar. It was still turned to February because of the whopping Hawaiian wave pictured there, tubular and perfect as Jack Lord's hair. Flipping to August he confirmed that this was Sunday—Bennett's birthday and, of course, his own.

He gathered up the résumés, wondering if the *Register* would call him. The *Times* had turned him down for lack of five years' experience in daily-news reporting. He'd sent a résumé and a snappy cover letter to every newspaper in driving distance. He hated writing those letters more than anything on Earth.

Frye called time, made a cup of coffee, dumped in some milk and went outside. Feeling festive on this, his thirty-third birthday, he put down the convertible top and set out for Little Saigon.

Back out Laguna Canyon Road, up the San Diego Freeway, a warm summer night filled with redolent intervals of strawberries, oranges, asparagus, smog.

Thoughts of Linda—filing Friday—rushed his mind, but Frye

countered them with the radio news and images of his weekend bacchanal. His marriage had lasted five years. In the end it had shot downward with an almost ballistic velocity. He assumed he had asked for it. Linda, he thought, I can't face you now, love.

He pondered his family instead. Bennett Mark Frye, ex-second lieutenant, 3d platoon, C Company, 1st Battalion, 3d Marines. Bennett had made his bones and spilled his blood in Dong Zu, just north of Saigon, suffered the instant havoc of a Bouncing Betty, and returned to the States shortened and decorated. At thirty-eight, he was five years older than Chuck, to the day. Sometimes this shared birthday seemed all they had in common. Bennett, in his full complement, was shortish and thick; Chuck was taller, by far, and lean. Bennett was dark; Chuck light. Bennett was popular, a leader; Chuck was private and often even had trouble leading himself. Bennett was better at just about everything. Their father, Edison, took an almost sociological interest in the differences between his sons, which he concluded were generational and not genetic. As a decorated World War II hero, Edison believed military discipline had made Bennett what he was today, and that Chuck's lack of any discipline at all had made him what he was—and wasn't. Then there was Hyla, the peacemaker and source of whatever grace her sons had come to possess.

He got off on Bolsa, made a U-turn, and headed into the city of Westminster. The street signs were done in Old English lettering and the buildings sported hints of the Tudor—a grafting of English hamlet onto Southern California suburb.

Drinking coffee, he sped down Bolsa past the Brothers of Patrick Novitiate, which hovered quietly behind a stand of olive trees; past the Colony Funeral Home and its high stained-glass windows; past the subdivisions and trailer parks, the fast food stands, and auto shops. Everything closed at eight.

Westminster, he thought, just forty miles south of L.A. and fifteen north of Laguna, but a world apart. A suburb straining for identity, thus the Briticisms. The words "bedroom community" might apply, but always made Frye think of one huge mattress shared by people who did nothing but sleep, snack in bed, and mate. When the Indo-Chinese refugees arrived in the late seventies, Westminster got the identity it never had: it became capital of the largest population of Vietnamese outside of Southeast

4

Asia. The numbers kept changing, as numbers do. Last Frye had heard, there were three hundred thousand Vietnamese in California, and half of them lived in the south. Eighty thousand alone lived in Orange County—most of those lived right here.

Another block down Bolsa, and the suburban landscape suddenly changed. East of the Asian Culture Center, all the signs were in bright Vietnamese. Crenulated tile rooftops with ornate extrados winged off into the darkness. Storefronts and parking lots were cluttered with flyers. The shop windows were alive with hand-scrawled paint: Siêu Thị Mỹ-Hoa Supermarket, Thời Trang Fabrics, Bảo Ngọc Jewelry and Gifts, Ba Lẹ Café, Tuyết Hồng Service Center, Ngân Đình Sandwich. The warm inland air no longer smelled of citrus, but of cooked fish and frying vegetables and exotic, unidentified spice. Frye breathed it all in. Little Saigon, he thought, and a few years ago hardly a Vietnamese in the state.

He watched the cars bustling in and out of the lots, and the refugees—dark people with dark eyes and black hair and solemn faces—gathered by the storefronts, glancing about as if expecting the worst. The South Vietnamese flag—yellow and red—waved outside a fish market, and beneath it hung a banner proclaiming these to be City of Westminster "Saigon Days." An old man at the corner leaned on a cane and stared at the crosswalk. His wife stared too. A cultural pastime for some, Frye thought: waiting to leave. Three young girls skipped past the couple and weaved through the traffic.

He slowed and passed Washington Street, the first of the next half-dozen streets that—in a county called Orange but having few oranges, in a city called Westminster but having few English, in a place called Little Saigon but as far away from Vietnam as one might get—bear the names of the first six American presidents.

There seemed to be some lesson for the republic, but what was it?

He made a right at Brookhurst and kept his eye out for the nightclub, tucked in a corner and easy to miss. Then he spotted the neon green and orange with its bent palm tree, glowing against the summer night. ASIAN WIND CABARET—DANCING & DINING. The marquis said: CELEBRATE SAIGON DAYS . . . LI FRYE IN CONCERT

. . . HAPPY BIRTHDAY BENNETT AND BOTHER. Second billing again, he thought, and they spelled me wrong. Certain individuals would not protest that call. Looks like a sellout too—parking lot buried in cars and a crowd at the door.

Julie, the club owner, was working the ticket window. She looked up, smiled, and waved him in. Frye stuffed his wad of bills back into a pocket: six hundred and thirty-seven dollars, his total lifetime savings to date, not including a business account that had next month's lease payment for the MegaShop.

He stepped through the bead curtains and into the club.

It was jammed with refugees, all wanting to see their living legend. People were already looking for places to stand along the walls. Paper lamps cast an easy glow over lacquered tables and chairs, potted palms, and bow-tied waiters. The dance floor and stage were bathed in red light that glinted brightly off the microphone stand and guitars. The bass drum had LI FRYE emblazoned on it. Another banner over the stage announced SAIGON DAYS. A layer of smoke wavered in the beams from the spotlights. Frye scanned the ocean of Asian faces, all chopped into rotating bevels of shadow and light by a glitter ball hanging from the ceiling. The room seemed to be caught in some gentle, subaquatic swirl. Mirrored walls multiplied ever-diminishing replicas of it all.

He could see Bennett at a table near the back of the room, with Donnell Crawley and Nguyen Hy and a woman he didn't recognize. Burke Parsons was partially obscured, as always, by a cowboy hat. Bennett was holding forth: arms outstretched, head forward and canted to one side as he talked. Frye waved and headed backstage. Benny, always at the center of things.

Li was locking a silver Halliburton case when Frye walked into her dressing room. She glanced quickly to the mirror in front of her, then hopped up and came toward him. Full lovely face, waves of black hair, eyes dark and lustrous as obsidian. Her *áo dài* was purple, with black silk trousers. "I didn't hear you come in, Chuck. Happy birthday!" She tiptoed up, pecked his cheek, then wiped it with a pale finger.

He smiled. Something about Li always reduced him to appreciative idiocy, always made him smile. Maybe it was everything she'd been through. He had the feeling when he touched her that a fragile, priceless object was momentarily in his care. A smile was the least you could offer her. "Just wanted my kiss while Benny wasn't looking. And to wish you luck for the show."

She stood away and looked at him. "You are a sweet man, Chuck. My *chú*, my number one."

"You look great, Li. Break a leg." He kissed her. He watched her watch him. "What are these 'Saigon Days' all about?"

"That's the city, showing us off. Proud of what good citizens we've become." She smiled. "Have you heard anything from Linda?"

"Yes. We're history."

She put her arms around him and pressed close. Her perfume smelled good. Then she stepped back and took his hands. "Perhaps it was simply meant to be."

"Whatever."

"No one can kill your heart, Chuck." She looked at the Halliburton on her table. "Enjoy the show, *chú*. I have to finish my makeup."

"Sing up a storm, Li."

"I will. So many important people tonight. Lucia Parsons from the MIA Committee had to cancel, but she sent Burke instead. We can talk after the show, Chuck. There are a cake and presents at the house. I've written the most lovely song for Benny."

Frye picked his way back across the crowded room and sat down next to his brother. Bennett's face swam in the light of the glitter ball. His hand was dry and strong. "Happy birthday, Chuck. You're not even late."

"Wouldn't miss this," Frye said. "Happy birthday to you, too." He shook hands with Donnell Crawley, Bennett's dark and silent war buddy, who smothered Frye's hand and nodded. Nguyen Hy, looking dapper and frail as always, placed his cigarette in an ashtray and offered his thin fingers. Hy, Frye knew, was head of the Center for Vietnam, a local humanitarian group. He never missed a chance to solicit help or money. He introduced the Vietnamese woman beside him. Her name was Kim, and she worked as a fundraiser for Hy's CFV. "You don't look very much like Bennett," she said.

"Thank you," he said, elbowing his brother in the ribs.

"One surf nazi per family is enough," said Bennett. Frye saw him check his watch and glance toward the stage. "Five minutes and she'll be on, little brother."

"Surf nazi?" asked Kim.

Nguyen leaned forward to clarify. "A surfing enthusiast. Chuck is a former champion."

"Chuck is a former everything at this point," said Bennett, flagging a waiter. "What's the deal on your job?"

"I'm freelance now."

"Vodka?"

"Almost have to."

"That's the spirit," said Burke Parsons, tipping his hat to Frye. "I'll get this round."

Frye nodded, considering Burke: Texas-oil rich, quiet, generous. Another friend of Bennett's from the war. His sister Lucia got the headlines, as founder of an MIA Committee that was making genuine progress. Burke seemed to bask contentedly on her peripheries—rubbing shoulders, buying drinks, networking to no particular effect. Every time Frye saw him, Parsons was wearing the same moronic hat.

Bennett ordered for everyone. "Billingham won't reconsider?"

Frye sighed and looked out to the crowd. He had been a good, if sometimes overimaginative, reporter of the facts. He covered restaurants for free food, movies for free tickets, and boxing at the Sherrington Hotel for a free ringside seat. On three hundred twenty dollars a week, and negative cash flow from his surf shop, he'd learned to forage. But the fact of the matter—try as he might to forget it—was that Frye had been canned exactly sixteen days ago for writing an article about a boxer who obviously took a dive in the fifth round of a Sherrington semi-main event. When Frye tried to contact the young welterweight's manager for his side of the story, the man—one Rollie Dean Mack of Elite Management—wouldn't return his calls. Frye ran the story and said so. Mack's attorney then told Frye's publisher that either Frye or Elite's advertising would be removed from the paper, implying they'd sue for libel. *Ledger* publisher Ron Billingham had never much liked the boxing stuff anyway. Frye got his walking papers on a Friday, cleaned his desk out that evening, put in one last fruitless call to Rollie Dean Mack, then went out and drank at high velocity. That welterweight had gone down for pay, no doubt about it.

Frye shrugged; Bennett studied him. "Things will work out, Chuck. I know some friends of Billingham's, so hang tight."

Bennett pointed out the luminaries in the crowd: General Dien and his wife; Binh, a Vietnamese newspaper publisher; Tranh Ky, businessman and president of the Vietnamese Chamber of Commerce; Dr. Phom-Do, professor and author of nineteen books on Asian history. The mayor and some council members were here. "Miss Saigon Days" sat, banner-draped and hopelessly nervous, between her father and mother.

"Lucia couldn't make it, so she sent her idiot twin brother instead," said Burke. He smiled, sucking on his beer. "She had to meet with some senate folks out to Washington. Hated to miss this, I'll tell ya."

Frye noted how people were starting to speak of Lucia Parsons in tones of near reverence. She had made a dozen trips to Hanoi to talk about the MIAs—all lavishly chronicled in the press. Apparently, Hanoi was actually talking back. Rumor had it that she was eyeing a seat in Congress and the MIA Committee was paving her way. Frye had seen her on television. She was bright, articulate, beautiful. Burke, even with his cowboy hat, had the same dark good looks.

"Lots of good people here," said Bennett. "Then over there, some not-so-good ones."

He nodded toward a corner table populated by young male faces with gel-slick heads. Sharp clothes, quick eyes, an easy arrogance about them. "Gangs. That's part of Ground Zero." Bennett leaned close. "And right next to you is Eddie Vo, the leader. I don't recognize the guy with the sunglasses."

Frye watched Eddie Vo and Sunglasses pouring fresh beers over ice, bringing lighters to their cigarettes, ogling a young woman with sly enthusiasm.

"They are not bad people," offered Nguyen Hy. "Energy needing to be directed. They are fine, as long as the Dark Men don't show up. Ground Zero and the Dark Men are like matches and gas."

The waiter returned with a tray of drinks. Frye sipped his and watched the crowd, noting that Eddie Vo was fiddling with a cassette tape. A recorder sat beside it. Frye leaned over. "Chromium tape?"

Vo stared sullenly. "Five bucks, man, and it's already tangled."

Frye shrugged. Then the lights dimmed and a communal murmur rose from the audience, heads lifting toward the stage. Miss

Saigon Days was looking at him. She turned away before he could smile. The band came on, slender Vietnamese men in French-cut suits, followed by the backup singers, all in white áo dài, all lovely. Drums rattled, the bass groaned. The backup singers waited, looking down. The guitar player tapped the mike. Bennett adjusted himself in his seat, grinning in anticipation. Someone waved and Bennett waved back.

Li glided onstage, centered in a spotlight, her black hair shining through the smoky atmosphere, purple *ao dai* tight around her middle, silk pants loose and flowing. Frye could feel Bennett's hands pounding beside him, faster and faster. Li took the microphone. The stage lights focused her smile and brought a sparkle to her eyes as she looked over the crowd and found Bennett. She raised a hand and the spotlight angled to their table. "For my husband," Frye heard her say. "And for his brother, too. Happy birthday to you."

Then the light shifted back to Li and the band eased into its first song. Frye watched Eddie, still fighting with his faulty tape cassette. Sunglasses was staring at the stage, apparently transfixed. Li brought the mike to her mouth, and the first ripples of her voice settled onto the crowd as easily as foam onto a beach. Frye listened in rapt ignorance to the lyrics spilling out in Li's mother tongue: lilting, rhythmic, soothing. Kim scooted her chair close to him and translated in the caesuras:

> When everything is turned to night
> The leaves fallen from black branches
> I'm not alone, I have my song
> To you my brother, my love . . .

Frye watched the lights play off Li's smile and the embroidered lace of her blouse. Bennett's arms were crossed, a look of simple wonder on his face. Donnell Crawley tapped his glass to the beat and Nguyen Hy drew pensively on a cigarette. Kim leaned close again, her breath sweet against his cheek:

> When longing is my only life
> And the sky weeps rain of sadness
> I know that there is no end
> To you my brother, my love . . .

Frye could hear Eddie Vo cackling between the softly sung lines. "Just one night with her in my bed," he said. "I wouldn't be a brother to her!"

Sunglasses answered, "Stanley would be jealous."

"Stanley . . . *lại cái!* Goddamn this tape!"

Li finished the song with a note so high and pure that Frye feared for his vodka glass. She bowed, black hair cascading down. The applause seemed to force a gust of smoke toward the ceiling. Bennett shot Chuck a proud look as the spotlights found their table again.

Before he knew he was doing it, Frye had gotten up and hugged his brother, patting him on the back. The applause got louder. Then the light reapplied itself to Li, who had turned to her band to count down the next tune. Strange, thought Frye, as he sat back down, how in the middle of everything you find yourself just plain happy. Bennett was nodding at him. Kim leaned close again. "This is a new song, Chuck. About our home, and being heartsick for what you cannot have."

Li looked out over her audience, then spoke over the oddly syncopated rhythm of her band. "Vietnam, where are you? We must learn the language of getting you back."

The guitar opened, mournfully high and lonesome.

"I'm sorry for you people," Frye blurted past a wisp of black hair and into Kim's ear.

She looked at him in assessment. "You tried."

"No, I didn't. Not me."

I didn't do a damn thing, he thought: Bennett paid the family price. I didn't argue with draft number three-fifty-one. He drank more, guilty again that it was Bennett who had gone, Bennett who had lost. But he had won, too: a wife, and a life among the people for whom he had given so much. Chuck looked at his brother, wondering for the thousandth time if the trade was worth it. Half a man now, roughly—head, torso, arms, and two stumps. He looked at Donnell Crawley, the grunt who had carried Bennett back to safety, jammed his helmet onto one of Bennett's gushing thighs, and gotten shot in the head for his trouble.

Frye glanced around for Eddie Vo, but Eddie Vo was gone. So was Sunglasses. The tape recorder sat by their beer bottles, a gutted cassette on the table beside it.

Weird-ass time to go outside and smoke one, Frye thought.

Miss Saigon Days' father stood and came toward their table, smiling.

When three hooded figures walked to the front of the stage and lowered machine guns at the crowd, Frye thought it was part of the show. For the shortest of moments—between the fall of the drumsticks, between Li's melancholy lines, between the beats of Frye's heart—the Asian Wind went quiet.

Then gunfire shattered the submarine light, splashing mirror glass as if it were water. There was a collective heave, the crashing of bodies on furniture. Li hurled her mike at one of the intruders, then grabbed her stand and lifted it high above a gunman in a ski mask. But he jumped the stage, slipped inside her blow, and clenched her around the neck. Another, wearing a black hood, grabbed a backup singer, then let go, whirled around, and helped the man in the ski mask grapple with Li. Her hair splayed in the spotlight and a pale curve of shoulder flashed where the silk ripped apart in gloved hands.

Frye reached out and grabbed the beauty queen's father by his necktie. In the unbelievably long moment that it took to hit the floor, all he could think about were the people he should have treated better before he died.

Bennett landed beside him, rolled over and righted himself. Up on his fists now, with his stumps swinging between his thick arms, Bennett charged the stage. Shards of glass sprinkled down like rain. Frye saw the machine gun fix on Bennett and thought: All the way to Vietnam and back, and he's going to die crawling across a barroom floor.

For one blessed second, the gunman hesitated.

Frye jumped up and dove for Bennett. So did Burke Parsons, his Stetson flying off. With his arms locked around his brother's chest, Frye looked up through the stampede to see Li being dragged toward the rear exit. Her feet flailed uselessly above the floor—one shiny black shoe flying off.

Beside them, General Dien raised a pistol and fired. The gunman on stage jerked as a bright crimson halo burst behind his head. His weapon pumped bullets into the stage until it finally fell from his hand and clattered to the floor.

Frye fought to his feet, lunged through the crowd and through the back door. A blue Celica ripped from the parking lot in a puff of tire smoke and sped around a corner.

He jumped into his old Mercury, started it up, and slammed it into gear.

His headlights raked the lot, and for a brief illuminated second he saw what looked like Eddie Vo's wide-eyed face staring back at him from the front seat of a parked station wagon.

Then Frye was screaming for Bennett against the wail of his own tires, in a voice he could hardly hear. Just as he skidded up to the rear door, Donnell Crawley burst out, carrying Bennett in his arms.

# CHAPTER 2

E WAS OFF, BENNETT NEXT TO him on the big bench seat, Crawley riding shotgun. Bennett yelled in his ear. "Get on it! *Go!*"

He bounced the Cyclone onto Brookhurst and floored it. Police sirens started to wail. Up the broad, busy street, the Celica slanted into the slow lane and swung right onto Westminster Boulevard. Frye steered around a lame Volkswagen, ate a hundred yards of asphalt in one gulp, then slid through the corner gas station, pumps and astonished attendants flying past his ears. "Faster," screamed Bennett. "They're going left, they're going left!"

The big V-8 rush pinned them to the upholstery and Frye cut the distance—a hundred yards . . . fifty—but the Celica waited until the oncoming traffic was bunched and heading toward them before it lurched across and disappeared down Magnolia. He skidded to a stop in a chorus of horns. Two police units howled past him, sirens high. Six cars . . . seven . . . ten and still coming while they waited there, staring down Magnolia as if willpower could slow the escape of the Celica. Frye finally gave up and punched it in front of an OCTD bus, which lowered heavily like some great animal amidst its own brake lights and tire smoke as they shot by.

Far ahead of them, the blue Celica turned left again.

Bennett reached out and turned the wheel, jumping the Cyclone into the left lane. "Left on Green Flower, next light. They're heading for the plaza!"

Frye jumped the median, clipped a street sign, and barged past the cars lining up in the turn lane. When the oncoming traffic broke, he lumbered onto the street again and swung left onto Green Flower. In the distance Frye could see the lights of Saigon Plaza, the archway at the entrance. Two beams of light funneled up and crisscrossed in the sky overhead. "They're going to the plaza, I *know* it. Get on it, Chuck, goddamn it, *move."*

They came into Saigon Plaza from the back, squeezing along the narrow alley between Thanh Tong Fabrics and the office of Dang Long Co, M.D. Streetlamps lined the sidewalk. The shops and buildings with their bright signs and painted windows sat behind them. Cars filled the parking lot, flyers glided along the asphalt in the warm breeze. To his left Frye could see the huge archway and the two marble lions standing guard at the main entrance off Bolsa.

Bennett reached over and took the wheel, guiding them to the right. His voice was quiet, almost a whisper. "Go slow and hug the perimeter, Chuck. She's in here somewhere. Donnell, call the cops and give them the car make."

Crawley jumped out and ran toward the shops.

"Someone must have seen them," said Frye.

"They won't tell us shit," Bennett said.

Frye cruised. Crowded sidewalk, windows, groups of refugees looking on with curiosity. Hãng Du Lịch Bát Đạt Travel, Bồng Loi Seafood Company, Tài Lợi Donuts and Hot Food. Banners everywhere: FINAL SALE! CLEARANCE SALE! CELEBRATE SAIGON DAYS—THE CITY OF WESTMINSTER. Pop music came from Tranh Cafe, a group of young men hanging around in front.

At the far end of the plaza he eased left, following the sidewalk and streetlamps. Bennett leaned forward against the dash—his right hand spread to the vinyl, his left a fist that gently pounded the padding above the radio. Frye could still hear sirens heading for the Asian Wind. Two big searchlights shot their beams high into the night. The sign on the building said Phở Hạnh Café— GRAND OPENING! The outside tables were almost full. Drinkers sat, contemplating the convertible and its two passengers. They passed Rendez-Vous Fashions, Dry Cleaning and Art Gallery, its windows filled with silk dresses and lacquer paintings. They passed Kim-Thinh Jewelry and Masami's Needlecraft and Thời-Trang Fabrics and Tour d' Ivoire Restaurant. They passed Thúy's Hồng Kông Video and Phượng Fashions. They passed places with signs he couldn't hope to read.

It's too normal, he thought. Too business-as-usual. Why bring a kidnapped woman to a shopping center, anyway? "We guessed wrong, Benny. They'd never come here. It's too—"

"Shut up, Chuck. There it is!"

Bennett hurled himself out of the car before Frye even stopped. Crawley ran from Thời-Trang Fabrics. Frye squeezed into an open space beside the Celica and got out. He watched Bennett climb to the hood, swing across it, and peer through the windshield. Crawley cupped his hands to a side window. Frye touched the hood: still warm. He noted the odd paint job—the way that the grill and the chrome and the trim had all been painted the same dark blue as the body. Bennett slid off the car and landed with a thud on the sidewalk. For a moment he stood there, as if sinking in the cement; his fists down for balance and his face washed pink by the light of the nearest sign. Frye read it:

ĐOÁN MỘNG
DREAM READER
ĐÚNG-ĐẮN, CHÍNH XÁC
Giá Đặc Biệt
*Accurate, Specific*
*On Special*

Frye could see a woman inside the shop, watching without interest. Bennett pivoted toward the door; Crawley moved ahead of him and pulled it open.

The woman was big and old, with gray hair twisted back in a severe bun, and wearing a tight black *ao dai.* Sitting behind a small table, she looked at each of them in turn, her eyes half suspicion and half amusement. Black lights cast a violet glow over two chairs, a Chinese calendar hanging from one wall, a brush painting of a mountain with waterfall. Incense burned from a small brass pot in one corner. Bennett pushed a chair close to her, climbed in, and braced himself on her table. "That blue car, right there. Where are the people who were in it?"

She placed a small enamel box before Bennett. She looked at Crawley, then Frye. Crawley opened it, put two bills inside. Frye saw her glance at the money, then back to his brother. "I saw no one."

For a second it looked as if Bennett would end up in her lap. "The hell you didn't, lady. Two men and a woman. Li Frye! *Li Frye,* lady, you know who that is?"

"Everyone know Li. I was in the back."

"Look me in the face and tell me you didn't see that car come in."

She considered Frye, and for the briefest moment he was sure what he saw in her eyes was fear. "I did not see that car come in." She brought out a tape from a drawer and placed it beside the box as if it were the final card of a straight flush. It was one of Li's—"The Lost Mothers." Her face filled the front, photographed against a single strand of barbed wire. The Dream Reader crossed her heavy arms. "I know Li Frye. She was not here."

Bennett looked at her, then at Crawley, then went into the back room through a bead curtain that swayed and rattled in his wake. For the next few seconds Frye stood there and listened to his brother—a door opening then slamming, a grunt, curses. The incense burner shook, its brass lid chiming quietly. The Dream Reader stared at him. Frye had the feeling that she was memorizing his thoughts. Crawley's face was deep purple in the black light. Bennett heaved back in, beads flying, then trailing over his shoulders as he came through. "Let's go."

They spread out to cover the shops. Next door, the jewelry store owner told Frye he'd been with customers—didn't see the car arrive, very sorry. He hadn't seen Li since last month, when she sang a benefit here at the plaza. She look beautiful. He mentioned big savings on Seiko diver's watches, waterproof to two hundred feet, no tax. "That is a gang car," he said. "You can tell because they paint it all one color."

The woman in the flower shop spoke no English at all, but nodded and smiled when he said Li's name. She pushed the play button on a portable tape machine, and Li's voice creaked from the tiny speakers.

"Li Frye?" he asked, pointing to the blue Celica.

"Li Flye," she said, pointing to the tape player.

"Thanks."

Two young men drinking outside Tour d'Ivoire said they'd seen the car pull up, but it was empty. Frye pressed, and the story got changed to another car pulling up at another place at another time. When he thanked them, they said no problem, we always help police.

Up the sidewalk he could see Crawley coming from a noodle shop. Beyond him Bennett worked himself from a door with some difficulty, then slammed it shut. He went back to the Celica, stared for a moment at the eye-level license plate, then crashed his fist onto the hood. The dent showed like a cut, catching the pink light of the Dream Reader—accurate, specific, on special. Frye could see her, still sitting inside, plump and silent as Buddha. Bennett waved him toward the Cyclone. He's coming apart, Frye thought: he's blowing up like the mine that got him in Dong Zu.

Using a crowbar from the Mercury, Bennett pried his way into the Toyota trunk in less than a minute. He sat on the pavement when he'd finished, drenched in sweat, his chest heaving and his eyes definitely not right. He wasn't tall enough to see inside. "What's in there, Chuck?"

"Nothing, and you're wrecking evidence."

Bennett hurled the crowbar back into the Cyclone, then glowered at Frye. "We're going over every *inch* of this goddamned place. Don't come back to this car unless you've got Li with you."

Frye looked out at Saigon Plaza. People stared from the windows and doorways. The searchlights crisscrossed in the darkness above.

He went into every shop, stopped people on the sidewalk, and talked to everyone who would talk back. No one had seen a thing. When he returned to his car half an hour later, Donnell and Bennett were waiting.

Cops were all over the Asian Wind. Light bars pulsed, flashing against the building. Radios squawked. Two officers strung yellow crime-scene tape between sawhorses. An ambulance sped away. A potbellied sergeant stood, hands on hips, at a loss for some meaningful chore. An officer at the door let them in when Bennett told him who they were.

The cabaret had become a different place. The stage lights were off, the glitter ball stilled, and instead of music came the echoing murmur of police as they conferred, shot pictures of the body on the stage, roped off the back exit, nodded, and pointed like battlefield visitors reimagining some hopeless stand or bloody offensive.

Frye crunched across the glassy dance floor, righted a chair, and sat with his back to what was once a mirrored wall. Crawley stood beside him, arms crossed. Burke Parsons talked with an officer, pointing toward the stage with his hat, then stepped forward and knelt. With his free hand he indicated the exit route of the gunmen. Bennett climbed into a dinner booth, where a plainclothes cop joined him, pen and notepad poised.

Frye took a deep breath and leaned his head back, staring up at the bullet-sprayed ceiling. He tried to slow his mind, to organize his memory, but it swarmed him in undisciplined waves. It struck him that he had a true scoop here, a first-hand story, a big one. A week's worth of front-page news, he thought, and nobody to print it.

Julie came across the littered floor, her face tight, eyes quick and angry. She sat beside him. "They got away from you?"

"They got away."

"Did you get close enough to see them?"

"Someone at the plaza must have. Not us."

Julie lit a cigarette. They watched the police photographer snapping away at the body on stage.

"General Dien shot him," Frye said.

"I was under a table."

"He must be seventy years old."

"Seventy-six. I should never let gang people in here. This is what happens. In Saigon I was a singer. I open this cabaret so I can have music, but I get guns instead."

Julie rose when a cop waved her over. Her eyes were hard and dark as she looked down at Frye. "She will be all right. No one would hurt Li."

*Just one night with her in my bed.*

Frye stood and worked his way to the back of the room. Their table was flipped over, chairs scattered outward. A pair of sunglasses lay twisted amidst the napkins and stir sticks. The tape recorder was crushed. Had they planned on coming back?

He touched the recorder with his toe, and behind him someone yelled. "Hey!" Frye turned: it was the big-bellied sergeant, arms swinging as he approached. "Get the hell out of there."

Frye stood, frozen like a rabbit in a headlight. Authority figures were never his specialty.

The sergeant's face was now in his own. "Get back to that chair and sit there until Detective Minh wants you. Otherwise, out."

"Whatever."

" 'Whatever' don't cut it. *In the chair.*"

He sat down next to Crawley, put his face in his hands, and tried to think. His ears rang from the shots. The air still smelled of gunpowder. Julie brought him a cup of Vietnamese coffee—strong, black, and sweet.

Burke Parsons walked up a moment later, adjusting his cowboy hat. He shook his head, took a breath, but said nothing. At first he seemed nervous, but a closer look showed Frye that Burke was close to furious. "People don't mess with my friends. I told Bennett and I'll tell you too. You need something, call me. Anything you need. Anything." He swallowed hard, appeared ready to say something else, but didn't. He gave Frye a fierce look, then turned and strode toward the door.

Frye wandered over to the stage and watched the crime scene investigator doing his ballistics. He knew his face from an interview a year ago, but the name wasn't attached. Three feet away lay the body. They'd taken off the gunman's mask. He was a small Asian man with a slick of blood leaking from his head and a look of mild suprise in his eyes. He stared up at the stage lights.

The investigator pulled a roll of string from his case and looked at Frye. "You wrote that crime lab article for the *Ledger,* didn't you?"

"Sure did. Chuck Frye."

"I'm Duncan. Good job. It helped our budget." The CSI pointed toward Bennett. "Your brother?"

"Right."

Frye watched as Duncan pushed a tack into the floor near the dead man's head, then tied the string and walked off ten steps to a table. He looked at Frye. "Forty feet away and he gets it in the skull with a .22. Not his lucky day."

"More like fifty. The general was next table over."

Duncan stepped around a chair, string held high, and brought it down to where Frye was pointing. He tacked it down, along with a yellow tape measure.

"Dien leave?" Frye asked. "I didn't see him giving a statement."

"He took off. We had three people say he was the one who fired. 'Course the Viets change their minds about every five minutes. Worst witnesses in the world. You see him shoot?"

"Yeah. One shot."

Duncan paced back to the stage, trailing the tape. "Then what?"

"This one stood right there and sprayed the floor."

"Well, if you want to look on the bright side, there was a miracle here tonight. A couple of hundred rounds fired in a place full of people, and the only one hit is a bad guy."

"What's that tell you?"

"That they were more into shock value than slaughter."

Frye saw in his mind that second—that one blessed second—in which a gunman seemed to have singled out Bennett, but held his fire. "Me too. But I won't quote you on that."

"Don't, I'm just the CSI." Duncan eyeballed the tape, then looked at Frye. "Fifty-two feet, four inches."

In the far corner of the room, the plainclothes was still talking to Bennett. Frye looked across to Donnell Crawley, who sat mute and solid as an Easter Island statue. From below him, the dead gunman burped. Frye considered his dark face, the thick black hair, the trace of mustache. White cotton shirt. Black pants. Two black leather bracelets with silver studs. Black shoes with a crust of dried gray mud on the sides and bottoms.

"Where do you think he picked up that mud, Duncan, in the middle of August?"

The CSI set down his clipboard, walked to the aft end of the body. He touched the mud, smelled it, and shrugged. "CDL gave him a Westminster address. Nothing from Sacramento on him. Probably a local gang punk."

"What's his name?"

Duncan tasted the mud. "Sorry. If you really have to know, ask Minh. Our new dick for Little Saigon."

"Vietnamese?"

"Half. Half American. He's supposed to be the perfect recipe for down here." The CSI sounded doubtful.

When the sergeant wasn't looking, Frye picked his way across the dance floor, then drifted over to the backstage door. Leaning against the wall a moment, he watched the cops work. No one seemed much interested, so he went back into Li's dressing room, closed the door behind him, and flicked on a light.

Her perfume still lingered. The makeup containers were stacked neatly on the table. The chair was pushed away. Her street clothes still hung in the open wardrobe: jeans, blouse, a light silk jacket.

The Halliburton case was gone. In its place were three bottles of French champagne. The mirror had *"BẠN—You Have Lost"* scrawled across it in bright red lipstick.

Frye sat down in Li's chair and looked at the words, then the bottles. Taunts from the kidnappers? What's *bạn?*

The top drawer contained a hand mirror, a couple of brushes and combs, a new package of emery boards, three black elastic stretch bands that hold hair without pulling it out. There were several pencil-like items of various color and utility. Something to do with the eyes, he reasoned. The second drawer had tissue, creams, ointments, unguents, oils, astringents, powders—a beauty blizzard.

Drawer three contained five cassette tapes still in their boxes, a small sixer of V-8 juice and, beneath a clean white towel, a large caliber two-shot derringer.

Frye dropped the towel back, slid shut the drawer, and stood up. One side of the wardrobe held a few bright dresses and blouses, a half-dozen *áo dài,* a coat or two. The bottom looked like a bargain bin—shoes piled high, all colors and shapes. The other side was almost empty, except for Li's street clothes. He brought a chair over and stood on it. The top shelf held only a portable radio—the kind with detachable speakers—and a small bundle of cassettes tied with one of Li's black hair bands. Frye examined the radio, put it back.

He was about to step down when he saw the buzzer attached to the far corner of the shelf. It looked like the mounting of an old doorbell, with a tarnished brass base and a black button. Looking under the shelf, he saw the wires disappearing through the back of the wardrobe cabinet. He leaned closer, blew off some dust, wondering. A call button for service? Then why put it way up here? An alarm? Again, why here, where it's hard to get to?

He pushed it. Below him, on the wall beside the wardrobe, a rectangular section of the wall panel slid quietly away. A window appeared, looking into a small room that was closed off from the main part of the club. One table set for four, chairs, paintings, a dusty arrangement of silk flowers. A mirror directly across the room gave him no reflection of his own face. One-way glass, he thought. Private dining, with a not-so-private window. To keep customers from stealing chopsticks?

He pushed the button and watched the panel slide back, then stepped down and replaced the chair at Li's makeup table. Then he hit the light switch, opened the door and walked straight into the sergeant's belly. A big hand pushed him against the wall, his head hitting hard. "I told you to sit, asshole."

"I got bored."

The sergeant—his nameplate said Marxer—spun Frye around, handcuffed him, patted him down, then spun him back. "You're interfering with a felony investigation. *Walk.*"

Frye moved down the hallway and into the big room. Crawley stood up. Bennett looked over and shook his head. Detective Minh approached, pocketing his notepad. Frye studied the smooth thin face, the wavy black hair, the feminine mouth, and pale blue eyes. Marxer yanked him to a stop. "Kid's been prowling around all night," he said. "He was in the dressing room just now."

"What's your name?" asked Minh.

"Charles Edison Frye."

"What were you prowling for?"

"A bathroom."

Minh glanced at Marxer, then back to Frye. "Let him go, Sergeant. He looks the type who couldn't find a bathroom, and he can't piss with his hands behind his back."

Marxer twisted him around. "Stay where I can see you."

Bennett padded up to them, fists down, arms taut for each pivot, angling his way through the debris. "Try to cooperate with these guys, Chuck."

Marxer took his time uncuffing Frye, giving his wrists a good jerk. Minh took out his notepad. "Over here in the booth, Chuck. I've got some questions for you."

23

During the next hour Frye answered questions, answered them again, then answered more. What struck him most was that Minh wrote for a while with his left hand, then with his right, then with his left again. And he seemed to keep changing faces: he'd look Vietnamese, then American, then like a man, then like a boy or a woman. *He's supposed to be the perfect recipe.* There were only a few cops left in the cabaret when Frye was finally pointed to the door.

Five minutes later, half a mile from the Asian Wind, Frye walked up the ramp to his brother's house. It was just after two in the morning. The lights were on. Figures moved behind the curtains. Donnell Crawley opened the door.

Crepe paper hung from the ceiling, a little stack of presents sat on the coffee table, in the dining room was a cake and a pyramid of bright red party hats. Bennett slammed down the phone and started pacing. He looked at Frye with an unmistakable darkness to his face. It always means fury, Frye thought. Kim sat on the couch, with a notepad open on her lap. Nguyen Hy hovered near the dining room, dialing a cordless telephone. Near the door sat two large pieces of leather luggage, and a silver Halliburton case. "I just called Pop and Mom," Bennett said quietly. "They're . . . okay."

Frye sank onto the couch, suddenly tired. In the long silence that followed, he realized what a gaping hole Li had left—in the house, in his brother, in himself. So much of her here, he thought, so much to extrapolate the loss from. "Li taking another trip, Benny?"

"She was."

"Where?"

Bennett kept pacing, fists clenched, pivoting his stumps between his big arms, landing with muffled thuds. Frye marveled for the millionth time at this odd locomotion, which reminded him of apes, bar-dips, pain. But with Benny it's all grace and strength. Like a bumblebee, he doesn't know he can't do it. Bennett's van was the only thing he had configured for his loss— hand levers for brakes and gas. But his home and office, the entire rest of his life, denied that Benny was different.

No one had answered Frye yet. Finally, it was Kim. "She was going to Paris, Chuck. To see friends."

---

**2 4**

Frye gathered from this exchange that he was clearly not to be in the know. Bennett never told him much. It had always been that way. For a moment, Frye could see the child in his brother's haggard face, the child who was always making the plans, starting the projects, and gathering the information that made up a boy's private world. Benny, he thought, always up to something. When Frye had discovered the hole dug near the beach at Frye Island, hidden under sheets of cardboard that were sprinkled with a light layer of sand, it was days before Bennett admitted that he was digging to China. When Frye had been blamed for the disappearance of certain bedsheets, it was weeks before they were discovered stretched and stapled to form the wings of Bennett's "pedal-craft." Bennett had emerged from the boathouse on the contraption, peddling furiously to lift himself and the stolen sheets to freedom. The aircraft dropped like a brick as he steered it off the dock, leaving Bennett to gasp in the center of a spreading ring of percale cotton and cold Newport Harbor water. When Bennett developed a little limp that slowly got worse—Frye had imitated it convincingly—it was days before Hyla found out that he'd stepped on a nail that had gone straight through his foot. Benny hadn't told her—he knew a tetanus shot was called for, and he hated needles. When Bennett enlisted in ROTC, he'd called from Tucson to say he'd done it. When he joined up early to fight in Vietnam, he'd called from Florida to say good-bye. When he'd married a Vietnamese peasant named Kieu Li, he'd phoned from Hong Kong to announce that he was now a husband.

Always his own agenda, thought Frye. Benny's the kind of guy who'd call from the moon to say he'd become an astronaut.

When he came home from the war, Bennett told him even less, but since then, Bennett had become a minor public figure. He'd started out with the Frye Ranch Company in property management, graduated to development, become a vice-president in the commercial division. The press had always loved Bennett: disabled war hero, business wiz, and half of an interracial marriage to singer Kieu Li. His awards piled up, his civic involvement deepened and his fortune grew, though he lived modestly. With the rumors of Edison's retirement, Bennett had become heir apparent to the biggest real estate empire in the state. Frye could remember one night at Bennett's house when his brother had confided that he and Li couldn't have children. It was typical of Bennett: a short statement followed by no explanation. Frye had managed to deduce that Bennett was impaired. He assumed that his brother's sterility at least partly explained his ceaseless energy in business, his deep involvement with the refugee community, his silent intensities. From the first time Frye saw Bennett after the war, it was apparent to him his legs were not all that his brother had left in Vietnam. It was something in his spirit, in the depth of focus in his eyes, in the smothered pain that shone from them. It was the look a man who had lost something even more precious than flesh, and knew it. Frye had seen it in some of Benny's friends. It was a look of loss, a look of regret, a look of longing.

But even now, Frye thought, it's Benny's style to never announce his plans. He just does what he does, and tells you later if he feels like it. Two years in Vietnam, and he rarely speaks of it. He told about meeting Li, falling in love, marrying her in Saigon. He told about some of his patrols, about the Vietnamese friend who'd go down into the tunnels when nobody else would. He told about the drinking and the drugs, the freaks and the killers. But somehow, Bennett himself always seemed to slip into the background. The rest of it stayed locked inside, privately tended.

Frye looked at the case again. "How'd that Halliburton get from Li's dressing room to here?"

"Don't worry how," snapped Bennett.

Frye watched a quick exchange of glances, a flurry of eye talk that included everyone but himself. Kim brought him a cup of tea, delivered with an understanding half-smile. He leaned back into the soft couch. The fuck do I care, he thought, it's just a case that moves around on its own.

"Someone left three bottles of champagne on her dresser. And wrote the word *bạn* on the mirror, with her lipstick. Then it said 'You Have Lost.' Is *bạn* Vietnamese for something?"

Bennett looked up, some dark ceremony going on inside him. "The cops didn't say anything about champagne."

"Maybe they thought it was there before. It wasn't. I saw her just before the show."

"Chuck, come with me. I've got a favor to ask you."

Bennett led the way to his bedroom. Frye followed down the

hall, feeling again the great non-presence of Li. Her absence was everywhere. Bennett took a cigar box from under the bed and handed it to Frye. It was light, wrapped in layers of duct tape. Bennett's voice was low. "I want you to take this and put it somewhere out of sight, Chuck. About as out of sight as you can make it, is what I mean. Just for a day or so. That's all."

"What's in it?"

Bennett put a finger to his lips, then shook his head. "Doesn't matter. Don't open it. Don't fiddle with it, don't do anything but hide it and forget it."

"Why me?"

"Because you're my brother." Bennett clamped a strong hand to Frye's wrist. "I can trust you, Chuck. And right now I'm not sure how many people I can say that about."

"Sure, Benny."

"Chuck, I'm going to ask you to do one more thing for me. It's important. Be at the island at eight tomorrow morning. Have a full tank of gas and be on time. Can do?"

Frye nodded, feeling the pride of the enlisted man. "What do you think? Who'd take Li? Why?"

Bennett looked down a long time, lost to something in the carpet. "I don't know."

"Did you have any idea—"

"Hell, no, I didn't."

"Do you know who might—"

"What is this, a goddamned interview?"

"You've got no ideas at all?"

"We're only the richest family in the county, Chuck. You figure it out."

"What about the singing? The political songs? I know tempers get short up here."

Bennett hesitated, then swung toward the door. "She's a hero to these people. They'd die for her. But you know how it is— you try to help somebody and somebody else thinks you're after their ass. Now head out the back, Chuck. I don't want anyone to know you've got that thing. Not even the people in my living room."

Frye followed down the hall, glancing again at his brother's citations and awards displayed on the wall. They stopped in a small utility room, and Bennett pushed open the door.

Frye stepped out. "I'll be there at eight with a full tank. One more thing, Benny. What's *bạn?*"

Bennett turned toward the door. "It's Vietnamese. It means friend. Are you sure that the champagne wasn't there when you went backstage the first time?"

"I'm sure."

# CHAPTER 3

**H**E COULDN'T SLEEP. HE couldn't sit still. He couldn't concentrate. Every time the breeze rattled the blinds, his heart flew up and hovered like a bird. He kept hearing sounds. So he paced the cave-house, still seeing Li as she was pulled offstage, still hearing her last shriek above the screams in the Asian Wind.

He kept calling Frye Island to talk to his parents, but both lines were busy. Just before four in the morning, he got through. Edison told him to be at the island at eight, then put him on with his mother. Frye could hear her summoning strength, forcing her voice into rigid optimism. "I just know she'll be okay," said Hyla. "I just know it. Pray, Chuck. It works."

"I'm going to be there for you," said Frye.

Hyla hesitated. "Oh, Chuck, that's so good."

"We'll get her back, Mom. I know it too."

He hefted the cigar box, shook it, held it to his ear like he would a Christmas present, set it down. Solid. One pound. Animal, vegetable, mineral?

With Bennett's orders not to open it ringing in his mind, Frye opened the thing anyway, layers of silver duct tape rasping off, sticking to his fingers. He lifted the top, looked in, then spilled the contents: one video cassette, black case, rewound.

He slipped it into his VCR, turned down the volume, and watched. Bad color, jerky camera work. Then Nguyen Hy, the young refugee leader, sitting alone in . . . a restaurant?

He checks his watch. He sips from a tea cup. Fifteen seconds later a man in a tennis shirt and chinos strides in, briefcase in hand, sunglasses on. He's tallish, well-muscled, with a no-nonsense look when he takes off the shades. His mustache is heavy, drooping, red. They shake hands and talk silently; Nguyen accepts the case. More talk; Red Mustache leaves. Hy lights a cigarette, waits half a minute, then squares the briefcase before him, lifts open the lid and displays to the camera neat stacks of twenty-dollar bills. Nguyen smiles, shuts the case, leaves.

The screen goes blank, then Nguyen again—or someone who looks just like him. He's far from the camera, standing under a tree not far from the Humanities building on the UCI campus. It must be early morning. No students. He's being shot from above, from an office, or maybe the fifth floor German department.

Frye recognized the place because he'd flunked out.

Hy smokes, waits. Red Mustache arrives shortly, wearing a coat and tie this time, and a pair of professorial glasses. No mistaking his hair; his erect, athletic posture. The briefcase looks the same; they talk; he leaves. Again Nguyen waits, then walks toward the camera, stops on a walkway below, and, with a grin, opens the case.

Money again.

More than I make in a week, Frye thought.

He hit the fast forward to another scene with Nguyen. This time, the video tape showed still photographs of a drop near the carousel at South Coast Plaza. Nguyen sits alone on bench; Red Mustache arrives with the briefcase and leaves without it. Hy doesn't show off his booty this time, he just looks into the camera without smiling, then grabs the handle and leaves.

That was the grand finale.

Interesting theme, here. The only thing Frye could come up with was: If you get something you gotta give something. Especially if you're getting a briefcase full of money.

He stuck the tape back in the box and took it to the far dark region of the cave-house, where he stashed it deep down in a cardboard box of Christmas ornaments.

He stood there for a moment, feeling the eerie proximity of the cave walls, the solid darkness encroaching just outside the beam of his flashlight. In the old days, he thought, I liked this cave. It was a little corner of mystery right in my own house. Now, it just scares me. Just like the surf when I go under. He felt a wave of vertigo wash over him, thick, warm, tangible. His scalp crawled and his heart sped up. He followed his light beam back out.

Benny, what did you get yourself into?

And who wants this tape so bad you can't even keep it where you live?

He went outside. From his patio he could see the Pacific—a dark, horizonless plate with a wobble of moonlight on it. High tide at five-forty, three-to-five foot swell from the south, warm water, strong waves. Hurricane surf due soon, spawned in Mexico. What'd they say her name was—Dinah, Dolores, Doreen?

The trouble with five in the morning is Linda's ghost. It's her time, Frye thought, she's got the run of the place. Ought to charge it rent. Eight o'clock in New York. She's up . . .

He went back inside and pulled on a short-john wetsuit—one of his own MegaSuits—and ground some fresh wax onto a board. Then into a pair of red MegaSandals for the steep walk down the hill and into town. Where are you now, Li? What have they done with you? Red tennis shoes. *The man who dragged you out was wearing red tennis shoes.*

Forest Avenue was deserted. The morning air was cool but already he could feel warmth building inside the wetsuit, and smell the biting, high-pitched smell of rubber and sweat wafting up.

He thought about the ocean and saw himself going down, swirling with dizziness and vertigo, thrashing in panic. Will it happen again, this time? Next?

He walked past the leather shop and the flower stand, boarded up for the night. Then past the post office, where a bum was sleeping under the wanted posters, his shopping cart standing guard above him.

*I'll tell Detective Minh tomorrow: The man had red tennis shoes.*

A painting in the Sassone Gallery stopped him cold, a giant

blue swirling metallic thing that seemed spring-loaded, ready to act. The longer he stared into the dense psychedelia the more he saw forms of Li's last show: bodies in mass exit, glass falling like rain, pockets of light marching the walls, a halo of red mist suspended in the stage glow over a dying man's head.

On the kiosk outside the gallery hung a poster for the MIA Committee—Lucia Parsons' group for getting American prisoners out of Vietnam. Frye studied the stylized graphic of the silhouette of a man's head, with a strand of barbed wire behind it. Lucia Parsons, he thought. The *Ledger* society-page pet, and Laguna's local heroine: rich, educated, willing to speak her mind. A former U.N. translator, fluent in four languages. She'd worked briefly for President Carter. Since coming to Laguna three years ago, she'd scaled down a bit: delivering food and money to earthquake victims in Guatemala, stopping offshore oil drilling, mobilizing the city to build shelters for the homeless. Then, two years ago, her MIA Committee began quietly getting attention. Now, she's all over the place again, he thought. Always in the news, in the spotlight, rallying for support, money, publicity. A dozen trips to Hanoi in the last two years and, after each one, more "positive developments" on the MIAs. In last week's papers she claimed she had evidence that American soldiers were still alive in Southeast Asia. She hadn't delivered the proof. Frye wondered why. Lucky you missed the birthday concert tonight, he thought, would probably have wrecked a good cocktail dress.

Beside the MIA poster was a "no nukes" poster, below that, something for the whales. There was also a poster for the free clinic. Laguna, he thought, so rich and sated, but so hungry for a cause.

He jaywalked across a barren Coast Highway and arrived at Rockpile with the first light of dawn. The waves slapped the beach hard, indicating size and precision. To the north he could see the cliffs of Heisler Park, the profile of its gazebo, Las Brisas restaurant and a stand of palm trees, all outlined in lazy relief against a lightening sky. The rockpile began to materialize before him, whitewater surging on boulders where the pelicans stand eternal guard: observant, stoic, crap-happy. He plopped down his board and sat on the sand beside it. Looking to the water he could see the sets forming outside, shadows within shadows, and feel the frightened beating of his heart.

Frye had once loved being in the sea, and she had loved having him in her. But things had changed since the accident, since Linda. When he went down in her now, he could feel her cold fingers reaching for him with dark intent, trying to hold him there forever. Frye understood, on some primitive level, that he had disappointed this ocean. He wasn't sure how or when or why. Now she was unforgiving of error, poised for vengeance. To Frye, hell was a small, dark place.

There's only one path to atonement, he thought.

*Try.*

In the hissing tube of his first wave, Frye kept seeing himself going under, swimming down through darkness but thinking it was up, his head crunching against the rocks or the bottom. At least it looked like himself, but his hair was longer and his eyes were different. Himself, but not himself.

It was a right—top-heavy, cylindrical and adamant, the sweet-spot rifling toward him as he shot through, rose to the lip and aimed back down for a bottom turn of such velocity that thoughts of disaster peeled from his mind and he finished in a balls-out rush that sent him and his board rocketing skyward, then down with a splash. For a moment he tred the dark water, heart thrashing like a kitten in a gunnysack.

One is enough. Don't press it.

He sat on his board for a while.

As always, the fear left him hungry for something to hold onto. Something actual. Something warm. Something that won't go away.

He paddled back in.

A young woman was standing on the beach as he came up. Jeans, a sweater, no shoes. Good face. Frye caught her eye and got an evaluatory glance that measured and classified him in one instant. A big dog with a red scarf sniffed around her, then pissed on a mound of sand for lack of anything more vertical. "You're Chuck Frye."

"I am."

"I saw you in some contests. You were real good."

"Thanks. Any chance you'd like to go to bed with me?"

"Not a chance in hell."

"I see. What's your name?"

She yanked the choke chain, and the dog snapped to her side, red bandana trailing.

A moment later she was gone, blending with the sunrise, her dog a minor blotch of red moving across the sand.

He watched her go. There was always in Frye a yearning for the unlikely.

Newport Beach is six miles up the coast from Laguna, and is rightly considered to be a stronghold for conservative high-rollers. Their children drive Carerras and BMWs, purchase their educations at USC, marry each other, then head into solid careers. Basically, Frye had flunked out. To his mind, Newport Beach was a pain in the ass anyway, though it does have a couple of great breaks.

Frye Island is the smallest island in the Newport Harbor, but the only island with just one house, a helipad, tennis courts, and servant's quarters on it. When Frye was a child, it was his entire world. Driving up Coast Highway, he wondered at the distance he had come since those days, about the life that had developed. From Frye Island to the cave-house in thirty-three years, he thought. Is this growing up?

According to his father, it was not. Edison considered him prodigal and had abandoned hope that Chuck would, in any Biblical sense, ever come home. Frye grew up with his father's disappointments like some boys grow up with bicycles: one model always on the way out, another forever on the way in. He had let Bennett carry the family banner. Flagrantly, though often accidentally, Frye had besmirched the family name. As a child, he had been indifferent to adults, given to odd enthusiasms, and always seemed to get caught. A school psychologist had termed him "troubled." He was the kind of kid who drinks highball remnants at his parents' cocktail parties, then falls into the punch bowl. Frye knew that Edison had hoped for vindication in his university career, at which he had failed miserably. Instead, he opted for the pro surfing tour, the MegaShop and his line of surfing gadgetry, all a shameful demerit to the Frye name. His high status as a surfer was his nadir with Edison, something on par with sodomy or treason. His marriage to Linda Stowe had been "a dot of light at the end of one helluva dark tunnel," as Edison had once quipped, but was now coming to a screeching official halt. His stint as an Orange County *Ledger* reporter—his first real job—was over.

Long ago, Frye had abdicated success to Bennett, to whom it came more easily, upon whom it sat with a certain grace that Chuck could never muster. After a point, it was expected.

Turning onto the Newport Peninsula, Frye mused on his latest sin against the family name: an alfresco sexual event that took place at his own Halloween party and was found so shocking by neighbors that they called the police. The foreplay was duly photographed by one Donovan Swirk, a photojournalist of the lowest order. The picture, which ran front page of Swirk's *Avenger,* showed Frye in an ape costume—without the head— chasing a woman dressed as a maid toward a hedge of blooming hibiscus. Frye was leering wildly. The maid's minidress danced up to reveal her naked buns, which caught the strobe flash just so. But her face was turned from the camera. The caption read: HALLOWEEN DREAM—LAGUNATIC CHUCK FRYE GOES APE OVER MYSTERY MAID! What actually transpired behind the hedge was hinted at. Swirk had made an offer of one hundred dollars for the maid's name, which was to be announced in his next issue. Edison and Linda's father—Laguna Mayor Ned Stowe—had run Swirk out of business with dispatch. Frye punched Swirk in a restaurant one night, but the damage was done. He wouldn't give up the name of the Mystery Maid, and that was that. He was released on his own recognizance, charges pending—disturbing the peace and indecent exposure.

Frye remembered the angry visit from Ned, demanding to know how Frye could pull such a shit stunt while married to his daughter. Every few weeks since then, the Laguna cops had called him in to say that Mayor Stowe would press charges unless the Mystery Maid was identified. Frye sensed a bluff here: Every- body feared they knew the girl. This civic interest was, to Frye's thinking, prurient beyond belief. On some primitive level, he had cuckolded the entire city.

As he drove over the peninsula bridge and watched the yachts bobbing at their moorings, he realized with a sharp sadness that Swirk's photograph had doomed his marriage long before he even knew it was doomed, an invisible turning point, an imperceptible pivot. How had he been so deaf then, he wondered, only to hear it now, like the report of some distant pistol? The beginning of the end with Linda, he thought: and I was too dumb to know it.

The Cyclone eased off of Balboa Boulevard, then through a series of short side streets. He crossed a narrow bridge, regarding the canals and homes crowded onto the precious sand-spit peninsula. The road shrunk to one lane and took him over another bridge that left him facing a black iron gate with a brass plate that said FRYE ISLAND. He got out and called on the intercom. A moment later the gate swung open on silent, well-oiled hinges.

Home.

The driveway leading to the main house was wide and lined with stiff, pungent junipers. Edison preferred masculine flora. Frye guided the car around a curve, bringing into view the big antebellum house, sprawling lawn, a sliver of swimming pool, the helipad and copter at the far west end, the servant's house, and his father's cottage. Two new Mercedes and a red Jeep sparkled in front of the white colonnade of the house. Bennett's van was there, with two more cars Frye didn't recognize. Beyond the orange trees that surrounded the entire island, ocean glimmered on pale sand. Motor yachts heaved slowly at the dock—Edison's *Absolute* looking like a skyscraper turned on its side.

Hyla met him at the door. She hugged him and he pressed gently back, feeling the stiffness of her aging body, smelling her hair, thinking that she seemed a skosh shorter than the last time he'd seen her. Mom. Straight shoulders. Strong face. Eyes blue and clear as bottled water. Her hair was cut short, in New Wave fashion. She stepped back and looked at him. "All I can do is thank God you two are alive," she said. "And all I can tell you is that Li will be all right. We'll get her back. I know it."

Frye nodded. Then Hyla was crying, but her face never lost its composure, just big tears rolling down her cheeks. "I keep thinking about her, about what I could have done . . ."

Frye held her close, saying what he could about not worrying, thinking positive, faith, and a dozen other ideas that seemed pitifully outgunned by actuality. It was the first time since she learned about Benny that Frye had seen her cry.

She took a deep, quivering breath and stepped away again. "They're in the cottage. Breakfast is ready when you are. And happy birthday, Chuck. We'll have a proper dinner on Thursday, okay?"

He walked across the lawn to his father's cottage, a squat, one-level affair on the far north end of the island. A kennel built onto it teemed with springer spaniels, who bounced and yapped as Frye ran his hand along the chain link. It's useless to try for names anymore, he thought: There must be a dozen dogs now, maybe more.

As usual, the cottage was locked. He knocked, and a moment later Edison swung open the door: gray hair slicked back over his big patrician head, shirt-sleeves rolled up, eyes hard, his face heavy and lined. "Well," he said. "Look what the tide washed in."

Bennett was sitting behind the desk. Donnell Crawley leaned against one wall, arms crossed. A man that Frye recognized as Pat Arbuckle, head of Frye Company Security, stood beside the fireplace, smoking a cigarette. Two of his men were with him, at semi-attention. A bulky man in a pale suit sat on the sofa, with the telephone to his ear, concentrating.

"You stash that box I gave you?" Bennett asked.

"Stashed."

Edison reintroduced Chuck to Arbuckle.

The man with the telephone stood up and gave it to Edison with a frustrated shrug. Edison listened a moment, then barked into the mouthpiece. "I don't give a damn what any lame-ass senate committee thinks it's doing this morning. Get me Lansdale out of that meeting and do it now." His bushy eyebrows raised and lowered. "Of course I can wait, but not for very goddamned long I can't!" He slammed down the receiver and wiped his forehead. *"Politicians.* Okay, Bennett, we've got Nguyen and his Vietnamese out on the pavement, digging for a witness who doesn't have lockjaw. We've got Minh and the Westminster cops looking for this Eddie Vo. I'll get Lansdale to light a fire under the FBI. What in hell are you doodling there, anyway?"

Bennett looked up at Edison, then back down at the graph pad before him. Frye looked over his shoulder. A simple schematic of Saigon Plaza, the parking lot and shops, the place where they'd found the blue Celica marked by a square with an X in it. "Somebody at the plaza saw her."

"Maybe they'll talk to Nguyen."

Arbuckle stepped forward, flicking his cigarette into the fireplace. "Apply pressure."

"Pat's good at that," said Edison.

Arbuckle's men nodded gravely.

Bennett leaned back in the chair. "Apply lots of it. That fat Dream Reader sat there and watched the car pull up. I know she saw them. Cops searched her place but they found the same thing we did. Nothing. Bring me that phone, Chuck. Maybe Minh's got something on Vo."

Edison took Arbuckle by the arm and aimed him toward the door. "You're wasting time and oxygen, Pat. Go apply pressure to the fat madam."

Bennett finished dialing, looked up. "Money talks with her. And get one of Hy's people to interpret."

Arbuckle was still nodding when Edison pushed him out the door, his assistants in tow.

Frye looked at the heavy man in the suit. "Chuck Frye," he said.

"I know," said the man. "Phil Barnum. I'm the congressman for the Westminster district. Friend of Bennett's."

Edison glanced at Chuck, then to Bennett, who was still waiting for his call to go through. "You'll get a ransom demand today. And you ought to be home where those bastards can find you. Fucking Lansdale. Where's the FBI anyway, those goddamned blue-suit Boy Scouts?"

Edison now marched to a far wall, onto which he had stapled several sheets from a large desk pad. He had written the main headings in black felt-tip: POLICE (MINH), FBI (LANSDALE), HOUSE/SENATE (BARNUM), FRYE COMPANY SECURITY (ARBUCKLE), COMMITTEE TO FREE VIETNAM (NGUYEN), BENNETT, EDISON. Under each he had noted the exact time and whatever progress each had made, or whatever assignments he wanted them to carry out. Frye saw that his own name was not included. Beneath (LANSDALE), Edison now scrawled "8:12 A.M.—STILL OUT!"

"Bastard," he muttered, then dropped the pen, which swung on a string tacked to the blotter.

Bennett raised his hand, leaned into the phone. "Minh . . . Bennett Frye. Was that Eddie Vo's Celica I chased all over hell last night, or not? The word I get from the street is it was." Bennett pressed the speaker button and put down the receiver. Frye heard Detective John Minh's clear voice come back over the line.

"Eddie Vo drives a dark blue Celica, painted out like the one at the plaza. He reported it stolen two days ago."

"You bust him?"

Minh paused. "We approached him for questioning early this morning. He escaped."

"What do you mean, escaped?"

"We'll find him. We now consider him our prime suspect."

"I sure as hell hope so. What about fingerprints, hair? Got an ID on the dead man yet?"

"That's all I can tell you right—"

" 'Cause that's all you have!" bellowed Edison. He began a verbal assault and Minh clicked off. Edison stopped mid-sentence, sat down, stood up again, and looked at Chuck. "What you hear in this room stays in this room."

Frye nodded. "Fine, but Eddie Vo didn't do it."

They looked at him. Edison raised an eyebrow. "The hell's that mean?"

"He was in the parking lot, sitting in a car. I saw him. Minh knows it—I told him last night."

"Then he's obviously found out something you don't know. He's the prime suspect, son. You heard the detective."

"I don't care what he is, Vo wasn't even inside the Wind when it happened. Bennett, listen to me . . . I saw him sitting—"

Edison shook his head and turned to Bennett. "Minh isn't going fast enough on this. Gimme that phone, I'm trying Lansdale again!" Thirty seconds later he was swearing out the senator, demanding an elite FBI team in Westminster before evening. Frye listened to Lansdale, pausing, evading, placating.

"She could be at the bottom of the Pacific by then!"

"They'll find her, Ed. Just hang tight."

Edison pounded down the receiver, stared at Bennett's notepad for a moment, then marched to the intercom and demanded breakfast immediately. He looked at Chuck again, then at Bennett. "What do you want him to do?"

"I need you to drop off Kim at the LAX, Chuck. She'll have the Halliburton case with her. You got some gas in that clunker?"

"It's ready. Shouldn't I do something a little more useful?"

"Like what?" asked Edison.

Frye looked at his father, then at Bennett. "There are plenty of things I could—"

Edison stood up and went toward the door. "What you can do is what Bennett tells you to do and no more, Chuck. It's a case of too many cooks."

"While you and Minh chase a guy who didn't do it? Come on, I'll go out with Hy's people, work the neighborhoods . . . something. I know a little bit about asking questions."

Edison shook his head. "This isn't the time for that."

"You better go," said Bennett. "Kim's plane leaves at eleven, and I want you there plenty early. Call me as soon as you get home, okay? And one more thing, if Kim says there's been a change, there's been a change."

"Of what?"

"Do what she says."

Frye pushed through the door and headed back to his car. Bennett padded up behind him. "Chuck . . . there is something else you can do for us. It's not easy, but your contacts with the cops might help. If it gets sticky, back off. But find out what you can about John Minh."

Tough assignment, thought Frye. Cops don't talk about other cops. Especially to reporters, ex or not. "What's in the case that Kim's taking to the airport?"

Bennett looked at him matter-of-factly. "Li."

# CHAPTER 4

"TAKE INTERSTATE FIVE, CHUCK. We're not going to Los Angeles airport."

They headed up the Santa Ana Freeway toward the city, late enough to miss the Monday morning traffic. The suburbs marched by, divisionless and vast. A blanket of tan smog hung ahead of them, while above it the sky gradually reasserted its blue.

Kim sat beside him with the air of someone awaiting diagnosis. She fingered a red handbag and stared straight ahead through dark glasses. She had smoked four cigarettes in a row and was now lighting her fifth. Every few minutes she turned to look behind them. "I could not sleep last night. All I could think of was Li."

"Me, too. What's in the case, Kim?"

She worked the combination and opened the top. Frye looked down at thirty odd cassette tapes, neatly arranged, surrounded by foam.

"What's on them?"

"Li's songs. Some messages to friends. News from the United States. Gossip from relatives."

"Why not just mail them?"

Kim drew on the cigarette and looked at Frye. "Some places the mail cannot go."

"Paris isn't *that* far away."

She locked the case and turned to stare back at the traffic again.

Frye looked out to the Los Angeles skyline: overpasses and buildings and palm trees floating in a warm, tangible light. "Did you see her before the show last night?"

"We ate dinner together."

"How was she?"

"She was tired and anxious about her trip. She had no idea of what was to be."

"Did anyone?"

Kim glanced behind them again. "There is always a feeling in Little Saigon that things may happen. You read the newspapers. There was the shooting last week. Before that, the fire. Robbery. There is activity." She tossed the cigarette and drummed her fingers on the seat. "North of the city, take Highway Fourteen."

"I'm wondering if it was someone who knew her. A friend. Someone she thought was a friend. *Bạn.*"

Kim's fingers stopped moving. She ran them through her long black hair. "That is possible, Chuck."

Past Burbank, he took Highway 14 to Palmdale. The traffic thinned, the air cleared, the high desert landscape was rugged, parched. It was hot. Frye felt his shirt sticking to his back, his legs damp against the seat. "Where we going, Kim, Death Valley?"

"Go through Palmdale, all the way to Rosamond."

Frye noted that the temperature needle of his car was creeping to the hot zone. He wiped his face and looked out to the flat, unforgiving desert.

State Highway 14, wide, fast and in good repair, took them north. It shimmered ahead of him and vanished in a clear, acrylic hallucination. A faded sign announced the next city: WELCOME TO ROSAMOND—GATEWAY TO PROGRESS. Rosamond Boulevard led them east. Five miles past the town, Kim guided him north on a wide dirt road. Then west on a smaller dirt road, marked by a rotting wood sign that said Sidewinder Mine. Two hundred yards later, the road ended in a sliding chain-link gate. Wind had driven

**4 2**

tumbleweeds against the mesh. She got out into the heat, dug the keys from her purse, and opened the locks. The breeze caught her hair as she leaned into the gate and pushed it aside, loose brush and all. Frye proceeded. In the rearview, he watched her check the locks.

"One-half mile, then right," she said. A slight smile crossed her face. "It's very hot today, Chuck."

The Cyclone rolled down the road, fan belts squeaking, gravel popping against the tires, a dusty cloud forming in its wake.

The Lower Mojave Airstrip was two swatches of bleached, cracked cement held together by liberal patchings of tar, a quonset hut hangar and one low square building that once might have been a terminal. The tower was boarded up. A sign slouched, its words faintly visible after years of sandstorms, vandals' bullets, neglect. "Cheaper fares?"

Kim studied the place. "Better movies. Park by the tower."

Human life materialized in the dust as Frye pulled close. A mechanic in overalls stood outside one of the huts. Two young men—both Vietnamese—stood on the far side of the tower and squinted Frye's way. The door of the terminal opened, then shut. At the far end of one runway, Frye noted a Piper, an old Fokker replica, and an ancient transport prop. It was repainted a beige that blended with the desert around it. The words "Liberty Transport" were stenciled below the fuselage. The left cargo door was open and a ramp led up from the runway, where a dozen or so wooden crates waited for loading.

"Stay with me," Kim said, pushing open her door against the growing wind.

Frye followed her to the two men by the tower. They spoke briefly in Vietnamese. The shorter man seemed to be indicating the Halliburton, then the terminal. Kim squared her sunglasses and led the way to the squat building. Inside was a counter, a desk, a clock, two chairs, about twelve hundred square feet of nothing, and the father of Miss Saigon Days. The last thing Frye remembered of him was the bulging shock on his face as Frye yanked him to the floor by his necktie. He now sat at the desk, in front of a small computer screen. "Thank you, Mr. Frye," he said quietly. "You saved my life."

"Any time."

"My name is Tuy Xuan. It is pronounced swan—like the bird."

"Chuck."

Xuan looked at his screen, then at Kim. Frye heard the wind howl, then die, leaving only the low drone of the transport engines behind it. A stinkbug wobbled across the dust-caked linoleum.

"Has our friend been here?" she asked.

"No. But there's no reason to wait. You are ready, Kim?"

She turned and kissed Frye on the cheek. "Thank you. I know your brother will want to talk to you soon."

As I will to him, Frye thought.

Xuan was coming around the counter when his daughter appeared in the far recess of the empty terminal. Frye watched her approach: hair back in a ponytail, a yellow cotton dress, pumps. She carried a silver case, like Kim's. She looked once at Frye and averted her eyes, just as she had at the Asian Wind. She brought the Halliburton to her father. They spoke in Vietnamese. Xuan opened the case—well away from Frye's line of sight—touched something inside, then shut it and spun the lock. "Nha, this is Chuck Frye, the man who saved me."

"Thank you," she said. "I'm honored."

"I didn't do much but half choke him."

"I read your articles before you left the newspaper," Nha said.

Frye tried to catch her eyes with his, but they slid off of each other like magnets of the same polarity.

Xuan held open the door for Kim. A hot puff of air blew in. "Please wait here," she said to Frye. "When the plane takes off, you can go. Nha will escort you to your car."

She blushed, turned away and busied herself with the computer. The door slammed.

Frye went to the opaque, sand-scratched window and looked out. Kim's hair swirled as she moved up the loading ramp with the silver cases. The wooden crates were gone. The two Vietnamese men closed the door behind her and pushed away the ramp. The pilot was obscured by headgear: All Frye could make out was his pale, Anglo nose and mouth. The overalled mechanic untied the ropes from the ground cleats, ran forward, and motioned the pilot toward the runway. A tumbleweed rolled across the tarmac and came to rest against the defunct tower. In the shimmering middle-distance, Frye could see the gaping entrance of the Sidewinder Mine—old struts leaning precariously, boulders covered by black spray-paint. When he turned, he caught Nha studying him. He smiled at her. "Paris, my ass," he said.

Nha's expression didn't change. "Talk to Bennett."

Like talking to a rock, he thought. "Pretty bad last night. You and your family okay?"

Nha nodded slightly. "Frightened. I stayed beneath a table with my hands over my head, holding one of my sisters."

The droning of the plane engines rose to a higher key. Frye watched it crawl onto the runway and straighten into the wind. Tuy Xuan hustled across the tarmac and disappeared behind the tower. A moment later, *Liberty Transport* sped down the runway and lifted into the air, wings rocking, engines torquing, flaps extended.

Frye stepped outside with Nha. Her father joined them, a satisfied smile on his face. "Chuck, you have helped us. Would you honor our house for dinner tomorrow night? We all wish to thank you."

Nha looked at him, then out to the runway where the cargo plane lessened into the vast blue sky.

"I'd like that," he said. "What was in the crates?"

Xuan touched him lightly on the shoulder and smiled. Then his face stiffened and his eyes focused on something past Frye's shoulder. He muttered something in Vietnamese. "Come in here," he said, leading Frye and Nha back into the terminal building. Looking back over his shoulder, Frye could see the white car parked on a rise in the dirt road a hundred yards away. Someone was standing beside it. Xuan produced a pair of U.S. Government binoculars and kicked open the door. He gave the glasses to Frye.

The man was leaning against a white Lincoln, apparently at ease. A camera with a huge lens lay on the hood of the car beside him. Frye recognized him immediately, half expecting him to step forward with a briefcase full of money, as he had so often for Nguyen Hy. Red hair and mustache, polo shirt, thick arms and neck. Red Mustache lifted his camera again. Frye shrank back into the doorway. Xuan and Nha were talking again in Vietnamese. The camera lowered; Red Mustache got back into his town car. Xuan dialed the telephone.

"Who is he?"

"A writer . . . and a former friend." said Nha.

"He doesn't look like a writer. Who does he work for?"

"I don't know."

"What do you mean, 'former friend'?"

"Attitudes change," Nha said. "Sometimes quickly."

"What was in the crates?"

"Food and clothing for the camps in Thailand."

Frye watched as the Lincoln backed down the road, rose over the hillock, and vanished.

"Vo couldn't have done it." Frye was looking at the oddly androgynous face of Detective John Minh. Minh had an office in Detectives, a desk buried in reports and Vietnamese business directories, a poster of Li on one wall, and a phone that kept ringing.

"Why not?"

Frye explained again how he'd seen him, sitting in the car.

Minh studied him. "He disappeared before the shooting, according to ten witnesses. No one saw him after, except for you. You were speeding past his car in the parking lot?"

"Not exactly speeding."

"But you were looking through two windshields, late at night, driving?"

"I told you that."

"You were certainly thinking of other things, weren't you? Your heart was pounding. Your ears were ringing. But you now claim to identify a man you had seen exactly once before in your life?"

"That's true."

"We know he left before the shooting. We know it was his car used in the getaway. We went to his home to question him this morning, and he ran away. Why? He hasn't gone to his record store all day. He's a fugitive. He could easily have planned it and watched the execution. Did you ever think of that? Did you ever think that you may have seen his brother, or a friend who looked like him? How many Vietnamese gang boys have hair like that? A dozen at least, maybe more. Don't sit there and tell me who did it, and who didn't. It insults me and makes me angry."

"I saw him."

Minh smiled bitterly. "It doesn't change anything right now.

We need to find him, either way. Do you have anything useful for me?"

"The gunman had mud on his shoes. Gray. Dried."

Minh nodded and checked his watch. "It's in the CSI report. It wasn't hard to notice, Chuck."

"I took a walk downtown late last night. I remembered a few things I didn't tell you before. First, two of the gunmen wore ski masks. The one who got shot had a hood, with the eye holes cut out. Looked homemade. Second, the one who dragged her out had on a pair of red tennis shoes. High tops."

"We didn't know that."

"And the hooded guy grabbed the wrong woman. He went for one of the backup singers first. Then he helped drag Li off, jumped back on stage and started shooting. That's strange."

"Why strange?"

"Who in Little Saigon wouldn't know Li?"

Minh brought out a tape recorder, nodding. "That's true. Tell me again, exactly what you saw."

Frye made his second deposition in two days. His account was interrupted by three phone calls and a visit from the chief, who told Minh that the press conference was set for seven o'clock. He looked at Frye with sleep-starved eyes, and tossed a stack of afternoon papers on Minh's desk. "We got the search warrant ten minutes ago, Detective."

Minh looked pleased.

"Press is hot on this one, John," he said. "Do your best to cool them off. We've had half the department in Little Saigon the last ten hours, and I don't want that fact unpublicized." He walked away, sighing, checking his watch.

Minh regarded Frye placidly. He tapped his pen against the desk. He looked at the poster of Li, then back to Frye. "Did Kim get into the sky okay?"

"Huh?"

"Kim, the woman you drove to the airstrip this morning. You know, the airstrip out by the old Sidewinder Mine."

Frye just sat there, feeling stupid. He felt his ears turning red. "Is this one of those deals where I tell you everything and you don't tell me jack?"

Minh switched off the recorder and offered a thin smile. "What did you come here to find out?"

"Was the dead guy a local?"

"We haven't decided yet. It's difficult. So many of the refugees don't carry proper identification."

"Eddie Vo's friend talked about Stanley last night. Stanley who?"

"Smith. He's connected to the university, popular with the gang boys. He's one of those academics who thinks he knows everything—useful at times. We've already questioned him."

Frye hesitated. "Then yeah . . . she got into the sky okay."

"With the usual assortment of tapes?"

"I don't know how usual they were."

Minh considered. "Your brother is a difficult man to deal with. He offers us little; his answers are short and often unsatisfactory. He behaves, in my opinion, like a man with things to hide."

I've got things going backwards here, thought Frye. *Find out what you can about John Minh.* "I wouldn't know."

The detective dumped his pad and pen, answered the phone, listened, and hung up. He scribbled something on his blotter.

"What's *lại cái?*"

"Homosexual."

"What about the writing on the mirror?"

Minh's pale-blue eyes narrowed. "That's tampering with a police investigation."

"I didn't touch it."

"You were a reporter once? That's about what I'd expect from one of you."

"I go with my strengths."

"How would you like to take them to jail with you?"

Minh leaned back in his chair, an expression of appraisal on his face. He answered his phone, listened again, said he would be right there. "You don't spend much time in Little Saigon, Frye. I know, because I do. I'm there. This is the situation. Everything in Little Saigon can be dangerous, every whisper and every move. People get shot for saying the wrong thing. There is much extortion and robbery. My personal opinion is that you should stay out of the affairs of the Vietnamese. My American half tells me you're a nice guy. My Vietnamese half tells me that you are easily taken advantage of. If you have something to prove, you should prove it somewhere else. The best thing you can do for Li is to keep out of the way of my investigation."

I've heard that before, Frye thought. He rose, feeling impaled by Minh's sixth sense, glad to be free of his calmly prodding eyes. "My sister-in-law got kidnapped, and my brother's hurting bad. Sucker or not, I'm going to do what I can to get her back. I learned a long time ago what happens when you do nothing."

Minh stood. "I appreciate your coming here. If you have more information, please come again. It's possible that I might be able to pass certain things back in your direction. I find your brother almost impossible to deal with, but you are not like him. We both want the same thing here."

Frye stepped into the hallway. The man waiting to see Minh stood up and took a briefcase from beside the chair. He was bigger than he looked in the video, or through the binoculars at Lower Mojave Airstrip. He walked past Frye like he wasn't there.

When Red Mustache was inside Minh's office, Frye came back down the hallway, took a seat, bent down, untied his shoe and listened.

"Paul DeCord."

"John Minh. You have about two minutes."

"I have as long as I need, Detective."

Minh's hand appeared from the doorway. Frye didn't bother to look up. The door closed. He finished with his shoelace, stood and walked out.

From a pay phone at the station he called his brother's house and got nothing. Bennett's secretary at work said he hadn't been in all day. Hyla said he'd left at four.

Ronald Billingham was underwhelmed to see Frye walk into the *Ledger* offices. The editor eyed him from his glass-encased office. Frye grabbed a fresh copy of the day's paper. The reporters acknowledged him with caution: such is the aura of the once-employed. Fingers tapped keyboards, monitors offered their dull green glows, a wire machine chattered in the one corner. Frye waved like a politician to no one in particular, then ducked into the morgue. He was halfway through the MASTER CHORALE—MUD-WRESTLING file when Carole Burton burst in, all silk and perfume. She gave him a robust hug.

"Ronald's going to kick you right out," she said.

"I know."

"Sure is good to see you, Chuck. How's the family taking it?"

"Oh, just fine." He slipped Minh's clip file into a his morning paper and folded it shut.

"Good God, I didn't just see that," Carole said.

"See what, Carole?"

Billingham strode in, shook Frye's hand, and asked him to leave. He was a soft, fungoid man who always seemed ashamed of himself, especially when he smiled. He made the most of his minor authority. "You don't have any business here, Chuck. I'm sorry." Billingham reddened, looked down.

"As am I. I was just in the neighborhood and wanted to say hello."

"To the morgue?"

"The memories still run deep."

"Would you give one of our reporters a comment about last night?"

"No."

"Get out."

"Can do. 'Bye, Carole."

Billingham watched him leave with a proprietary air, victory written all over his face.

Frye drove down Bolsa and parked a block from Saigon Plaza. So, he thought: Paul DeCord hands Nguyen Hy a briefcase full of money, and DeCord goes to Minh. Who is it, then, that I'm hiding evidence from? DeCord, Minh—or both?

Benny knew the cops would come to his home sooner or later. FBI too. If the payoffs are illegal, that explains why I've got the tape. Then where'd the money come from? And where is it going? Maybe Paul DeCord got burned. He wants his money back. But he wouldn't go to Minh if the payoffs weren't legit. Did Nguyen rip him off?

The afternoon had begun to cool. He stopped to consider two marble lions, white, snarling, and heavy-maned, guarding the plaza entrance. Each stood on a black marble pedestal, with one paw resting on a ball. Behind them were four thick red columns supporting the elaborately crenulated archway. Two Vietnamese women hustled by, pushing a cart, then paused to read a CELEBRATE SAIGON DAYS banner hanging from a balcony. Outside the Bồng Lai Seafood Company, a rubber-booted worker hosed pungent, unspecific waste into a drain. In the window of Tăng Fashions, a woman arranged a red silk dress on a mannequin. Two uniformed police came from the store and headed into the next one.

Outside Tăi Lợi Donuts and Hot Food, two more cops confronted a group of gang boys. Words were passed. A bulky officer spun one kid around, then handcuffed and pushed him into the back of his black-and-white. A man in a rumpled suit appeared from nowhere with a camera and started snapping pictures. The other cop moved in. Frye saw a press pass flash, watched the officer muscle the photographer off the sidewalk. The photog kept shooting. Give 'em hell, Frye thought. It's all front-page stuff.

As if there wasn't enough of it already. He stood in front of the news rack and read the headlines through the smudgy plastic: VIET SINGER KIDNAPPED IN 'MINSTER NIGHT CLUB . . . CABARET SHOOTOUT LEAVES ONE DEAD . . . POP SINGER TAKEN AT GUNPOINT . . .

There were pictures of Li, pictures of the Asian Wind, pictures of Bennett hobbling out with Donnell Crawley behind him. He bought copies of everything and took them to Paris Cafe, where he sat outside and ate a heaping plateful of chicken and noodles. Looking out to the plaza, he saw another team of policemen going door-to-door. A network news crew was taping outside the Buddhist pagoda, a colorful establishing shot.

Did Arbuckle crack the Dream Reader? *Apply pressure . . . The best thing you can do is just stay out of my investigation . . . Paris, my ass . . . Everything in Little Saigon can be dangerous . . .*

He slipped out Minh's clip file and read the articles. The *Ledger* reporter on the Westminster beat was Rick Ford. Rick had an in-depth interview with Minh, a "day in the life of" ride-along deal, even a "detective at home" article. Rick Ford, Frye thought, is a good reporter.

Minh had joined the Westminster force just one year ago. He went through training at the L.A. Sheriff's Academy, graduating high in his class. He was born in Saigon to an American employee of the CIA and a Vietnamese woman from a diplomatic family. During the war, he was commissioned, made lieutenant, and served in Intelligence Corps. He was evacuated during the fall, with his wife. They now lived in Westminster. During the eleven years since leaving Vietnam and joining the Westminster PD, he had earned a bachelor's degree from Cal State Los Angeles, worked a series of odd jobs. His parents settled in Washington,

D.C., where his father now worked for a political study "consortium."

All fine and dandy, Frye thought, but how had Minh gone from officer to detective in less than a year?

He found a pay phone and called the *Ledger.*

"Easy," said Rick Ford. "The department wanted to show him off. Call it extra equal opportunity. Vietnamese cops are tough to find, so Minh shot right up the ladder when they put him in Little Saigon. He's the only guy on the whole force who speaks a word of Vietnamese."

"What do the other cops think of him?"

"Not much."

"That's what I gathered from Duncan."

"He's gotten a lot of press. They're jealous. He's not a bad cop, I don't think. He's just kind of over his head. Why?"

"Just curious."

"I would be too, if he was working that kidnapping. How's your brother taking it?"

"He's concerned."

"Shit, Frye, I could have guessed that much. How about the FBI? Rumor has it some high-powered team is on its way from Washington."

"That's news to me."

"I could go for an eyewitness description of what came down last night."

"That's my exclusive."

"Got a new job?"

"I'm working on it. One more thing, Rick. Did you get the feeling that Minh keeps in contact with his dad?"

"He said he did."

"Thanks, Rick."

Frye went back to his table and read Minh's file again. Why doesn't Benny trust him? Does Benny trust anyone?

Suddenly, he felt his scalp tighten and a jittery flash of nerves run up his back as he heard Li's voice, lilting and echo-ridden, passing through the atmosphere of the plaza.

It hit Frye like a ten-foot wave at Rockpile. He could see her standing in the spotlights, smiling down at Bennett. He could see her that last time at Frye Island, when she stooped in the flower-bed and placed the marigolds in the holes, then flattened herself against the ground when a car backfired coming onto the bridge. He could see her that first time, standing in the hallway outside Bennett's room at the San Diego Naval Hospital while staff and patients strode widely around and pretended to ignore her. She hadn't lowered her eyes one bit when Frye introduced himself, but looked straight at him and said: "I am Kieu Li—your brother's wife. Beg pardon, man, but I faint." She had, crumpling into his arms as her purse slid from her shoulder, a Coke clunked from her hand, and her hair—the longest, blackest hair Frye had ever seen—spilled across his elbow and dragged through the bubbles before he could hoist her to his chest and carry her outside. He could see her that one Christmas, playing a lovely version of "Fire and Rain" on the old D-28 that Bennett had given her, with the capo way up on the fifth fret to accompany her high and flawless voice. He could see her studying the television with intensity, adding to her English with ease, trying out words on him like "reparations," "documentary," and "amortization." She had been horrified to learn that, according to all the major networks, the same word applied both to the item you wiped your face with at dinner, and the one used—as she put it—to "defeat" menstrual flow.

He could see her in the recording sessions he'd watched, earphone to her head as she stood in the booth and did her takes, time and time again. Twenty, thirty versions of the same song, and she never lost her composure, never lost her drive. He could see her at his parents' parties, elegant but demure, the kind of person who draws interest like a magnet draws steel. He could see her as a girl just over from Vietnam, then as a woman of style and class, and as he did so, she seemed to grow from one to the other in a single brief second.

Sitting in the late afternoon sun of Little Saigon, he could see her face as she looked up at him the day he'd told her Linda had left him and said simply, "Forgive her."

Li.

Five phone calls later he had gotten the office number for Dr. Stanley Smith, UCI Professor of Social Ecology. The professor answered his own phone. His voice was soft, rounded.

"Why do you want to talk to me?"

"The cops say you know everything."

He could hear Smith's flattered chuckle.

"I'm afraid, Mr. Frye, that this isn't a good time for me at all. No, not at all."

"Last night wasn't a good time for my sister-in-law to get kidnapped either."

Smith paused. "No. I wouldn't think so. I . . . can make just a few minutes for you. I'm working off campus, at the Ziggurat building. Floor three, room three-forty-one."

# CHAPTER 5

**F**RYE TOOK THE SAN DIEGO Freeway south. He watched clouds coloring above the tan hills, a herd of cattle raising silent dust, a magnificent smog-charged day atmospherically impossible in another age.

He got off at El Toro Road and wound through the south county pastureland. Islands of new homes floated on the dry hills. Half of these are Edison's, he thought: Rancho Cay, The Oaks, Club Niguel. Nickel and dime stuff for the Frye Ranch—under two hundred grand apiece.

Off La Paz Road, the Ziggurat loomed into view, a Mesopotamian extravagance built by Rockwell, then never used. The offices were now let to various organizations: IRS, Federal Records, the university. The lofty pyramidal structure stood out against the hillocks with a hallucinogenic air, a temple waiting for worshippers.

The parking lot was a continent of asphalt, with a few cars clustered near the entrance. Frye parked and went in, heading for the elevator.

A wall plaque outside 341 read DR. STANLEY SMITH—DIRECTOR—

CENTER FOR ASIAN COOPERATION. The reception room was cluttered with bookshelves, but no receptionist was in sight. Behind the closed door to the office came the muffled sound of a woman's voice.

Frye opened the door and stepped in. A man at a desk was nodding to a woman who sat across from him. She was talking fast, in Vietnamese. A tape recorder sat between them, reels moving. Smith was fifty-ish, plump, balding. He wore a pink polo shirt and a gold chain. His cheeks were rosy and his eyes a pale, sad blue. Frye sensed an unsuccessful boyhood here. Smith raised a finger to the woman, drove it downward to punch off the tape recorder, then smiled. "You must be Chuck Frye?"

Frye nodded.

Smith spoke to the woman in Vietnamese. She turned to Frye and smiled. She was gaunt, early seventies, he guessed, her long gray hair trailing over a dark leather face, her teeth stained dark from betel juice. He sat down. Smith introduced her as Bakh.

"You know where Li Frye is?" she asked.

"Not yet," he said.

Frye surveyed the office: big messy desk, file cabinets, an old wooden wardrobe, a poster of Li on one wall, a gruesome photographic blowup of a man's face beside it. There was another door beside the wardrobe, closed and plastered with fifties travel posters of Vietnam.

"Last night's event is absolutely ominous," said Smith. "There are no other words. The police told me nothing this morning, except that they want Eddie Vo. Have they any substantial leads, anything to go on except that poor frightened boy?"

"I'd be the last to know."

"Ah . . . I understand."

Frye looked again at the horrible portrait, noting that its subject wore sunglasses. "What do you do here, Doctor?"

Smith looked around with an air of pride. "I'm a professor, and Little Saigon is my area of expertise. My current project is for the Vietnamese archive—collecting oral stories and translating them for publication." He went on for a moment about his work-in-progress. It dealt with the "acculturation process" of the refugees, the "impact of cinema and television on the youth," and the "problems of village culture meeting mass culture in this crazy melting pot we call America." The book would be called *By War Displaced: A Modern Narrative of the Vietnamese Refugee.*

"Sounds good. What I'd really like to talk to you about is Li's kidnapping, Dr. Smith."

"I imagine." He rose and politely guided Bakh from the room, chatting all the time in Vietnamese. A moment later he returned and sat down again.

"This kidnapping has tragic proportions . . . may I call you Chuck? Li Frye has done so much for her people. She deals with the Thais, getting refugees out of the camps and into the States. Her music, of course, is a great inspiration. In some circles, as I'm sure you know, she is called the Voice of Freedom."

"Who would want to take her?"

Smith pursed his lips. "That's just it, Chuck. No one I can think of in the Vietnamese community would do that. The young respect her. The old adore her. In my opinion, we are looking at economics here, not politics. Your brother is rich. The kidnappers will want money."

"What about the gangs? They might respect her, but they'd love to get their hands on ransom money."

Smith shook his head. "The youth gangs of Little Saigon are much exaggerated by the press. They are a loose structure, with no formal organization or 'turf,' as we see in the Hispanic and black gangs. They form, extort money or sometimes commit robbery, then break up, disappear, and form again. By all indications, Chuck, this could hardly be a gang crime. Automatic weapons? The organization and planning that went into it? The target itself? No. The police are on the wrong track, in my opinion."

"What about organized crime?"

"*Gậy Trúc?* The Bamboo Cane? Now they are a possibility. Several of the top leaders have been seen in Little Saigon in the last six months. I've personally identified two of them."

"How good are they at kidnapping?"

Smith glanced casually to the closed door, then looked at Frye. "With organized, professional criminals, seeing the leaves on top always implies the roots below. In my opinion, it's conceivable that *Gậy Trúc* knew about the kidnapping, perhaps was involved."

"Where can I find them?"

Smith shook his head, pressed his lips tight, and leaned forward in his chair. Again, he looked at the door, then back to Frye. "I certainly wouldn't tell you where, Chuck. They wouldn't be there *now,* for one thing. And for another, these are very dangerous men. Besides, I'm not making accusations, I'm outlining possibilities."

"Minh says that you're . . . popular with the refugee boys."

Smith blushed a little. "I take that as a compliment. I have an affinity with them. They are a gentle race, so misunderstood and so confused in this new country. I myself feel misunderstood at times, feel . . . outside the mainstream. Many of them had no childhood. In some sense, we are kindred souls."

"When's the last time you saw Eddie Vo?"

Smith adjusted himself behind the desk and looked at Frye. "Three days ago. Are you looking for him, too? Like the police?"

"No. I know he didn't do the job on Li. He was in the parking lot."

Smith looked at Frye incredulously, blushing again, his eyes widening. "You saw him outside the cabaret?"

"That's right."

Dr. Smith smiled. "Ah . . . then the police have no solid reason to suspect him. Chuck, this makes me very happy. Eddie Vo is such a . . . mixed-up kid. He's terrified."

"How do you know, if you haven't seen him in three days?"

Smith swallowed hard, pursed his lips again. "I know him well enough to understand what he's going through. He disappeared, right? He knows the police are after him. He is afraid. That's all I meant. But if you saw him outside the Asian Wind . . . it means he's innocent."

Frye looked at Smith, who looked down at his desk.

"Where is he?"

Smith looked up again, feigning surprise. "I . . . are you willing to tell the police he was outside?"

"I already have."

"Then Eddie really has nothing to fear?"

"They want to question him."

Smith sighed, then cast Frye a furtive glance. "This is an impossible situation. I really . . . don't have the disposition to do this."

"Do what?"

Smith stood, blushing again, brows furrowed. "This is stupid. He must talk to the police and clear himself." He walked to the door, unlocked it with a key, and swung it open.

Eddie Vo sat in the other room, his feet up on a desk, hair still gelled into a top-heavy Elvis kind of deal, reading *People* magazine.

"Come out here, Eddie. I won't lie for you any more. We have a witness."

"Fuck you," he said. He glared at Frye. "Fuck you, too."

Frye looked at him. High cheekbones, smooth dark skin, eyes deeply set and suspicious, their narrowness less epicanthic than fearful. Something like the Vietcong lieutenant in the famous news photo, with the pistol at his head and the first breeze of death blowing through his hair. Frye regarded Eddie Vo with some wonder: These people are harder than us.

"I remember you from the show, man," Eddie said.

"Li's married to my brother."

"I know that. I know everything about her, except where she is. I split before it went down, man. I'm innocent."

Smith implored Vo to turn himself in, bear the interrogation and clear his name. Eddie listened with a glacial look on his face.

"If you go to the police, it will look good for you," Smith continued. "If you make them find you, it can only be bad."

Eddie stood up, walked past them into the main office and looked out the window. He sat down and looked over at Frye. "With him?"

"You don't have a car, Eddie. He can take you back home to change your clothes, then to the police. It's your only choice, really. The police will look until they find you."

"They'll shoot me. When they came to my house, they had their guns out. So I ran."

"American police are not gangsters, Eddie."

"I watch TV. I know what they do."

It took Smith another ten minutes to convince Eddie to ride back to Little Saigon with Frye, and turn himself in for questioning. Frye saw that Vo, despite his petulance, was bright enough to know that his professor was right. Smith finally sighed and sat back in his chair. "I feel a lot better now. Please, Eddie, tell them you came to me *after* the police did. Say, noon. I don't want to be arrested for harboring a fugitive."

"I'll lie. I'm good at lying." Eddie stood up, went to Smith's wardrobe and threw open the doors. Frye could see the clothes inside: black leather vests and jackets, studded pants and belts.

Smith looked from the wardrobe to Frye, his pink cheeks going a shade brighter. "Thank you. I'm glad you came." He reached into his desk and brought out a thick manuscript. "You might like to read a draft of my book. There is a section told to me by Li. Any comments you have might be useful. I'm aiming for a lay audience."

"I want these!" said Eddie. His back was to Frye.

Frye took the padded envelope and thanked the professor. He looked again at the chilling portrait. It looked less like a man's face than some special effect. What's so compelling about the horrid, he wondered, and why does the horrid wear sunglasses? "What's that?"

Smith appraised the face. "Colonel Thach. It is proper that his name rhymes with 'attack.' He's part of Hanoi's Internal Security force. He is in charge of crushing the tiny pockets of rebellion in Vietnam. I thought his ruined face was the perfect counterpoint to Li's beauty."

"What happened to him?"

"Some say napalm, some say white phosphorous. Some say he was left to die and that rats . . . partook of his flesh. He spent years in the tunnels around Saigon, so his eyes are ruined. He must wear dark glasses in daylight."

Eddie slammed the wardrobe shut. "Man, these are cool!" He made two fists and held out his arms, brandishing two new silver-studded bracelets on each wrist.

Exactly like the dead gunman's at the Asian Wind, thought Frye. He looked from Eddie back to Smith. "You give away a lot of those?"

"Oh, of course. Gifts of goodwill. Would you like a set?"

"Did you give away any recently?"

Smith considered. "Well, yes. To some friends of Eddie's, in fact."

Vo stared sullenly at Smith. "The Dark Men aren't my friends, Stanley. Get your facts right."

"Loc was practically a brother to you for ten years."

"I hate him. I hate you. Let's go, Frye. I'm sick of this place."

"Thanks for the book," Chuck said.

"You're welcome. Are you sure you wouldn't like a set of bracelets?"

"Gee, I really would."

Smith nodded, then went to the wardrobe and pulled out a pair. Frye took them. "Thanks for everything."

"Tell me what you think of the manuscript." Smith rose and placed a hand on Eddie's shoulder, but Vo turned away and walked out.

Eddie was at the radio of the Cyclone before Frye even got the engine started. He pushed the knobs, found a Pretenders song, turned it up loud, and started tapping the dashboard. "I love music, man. That's where I got my name. After Eddie Van Halen."

"What's wrong with your real one?"

"It's Dung, man. How come you don't have a tape deck? You poor or something?"

"Guess so."

Frye headed back down the 405 freeway while the sunset gathered above the hills, turning the exit signs to mirrors of gold. Vo lit a cigarette and stared out the window.

"What do the cops want?" he asked.

"They want Li."

"I don't have her! I'm innocent of all things. Hell, man. Shit."

"Where'd you polish up your English?"

"UC Irvine. My grades were bad, so I dropped out and opened the record store. I was getting Cs. This country doesn't like Vietnamese who get fucking Cs. You're not smart, or a beauty queen like that Tuy girl, you're just a gook."

"I don't know about that."

"You don't know about shit, Frye."

"I know I saw you in the parking lot after the shooting. What were you doing in that station wagon?"

Vo looked at him, then blew a mouthful of smoke out the window. "Getting a new tape, man. The one I had got all tangled up. I took my friends for protection. I love Li Frye, man. I'm her biggest fan. I got a lot of her stuff. I wrote her love letters, but I knew she'd never write back."

*Just one night with her in my bed. I wouldn't be a brother.*

"Did you know something like this would happen?"

Vo glanced at him. "No."

"The gunman who was killed had the same bracelets that Smith just gave us. Who is this Loc guy?"

Vo looked at him again, turned down the radio. "He's just a punk I used to know. But Loc would never touch Li Frye. He knows I would kill him if he did. I am her official protector from the gangs. Ground Zero is devoted to her."

What I need from Minh, thought Frye, is a positive ID on the gunman. "What do you know about John Minh?"

"That he's a cop and you can't trust cops. Especially the ones that don't wear uniforms. They're all gangsters, like me."

"You deal with him before?"

"He's new. He's trying to be powerful. They say the cops here are different than in Vietnam. I don't believe it. They're all gangsters, just like in Saigon."

"How long have you been in the States?"

"Ten years. I was in Saigon when the war ended. Then the camps in Thailand. That's where Ground Zero started. I was six, and we were small thieves. Where were you, Frye?"

"Flunking college."

They got off the freeway in Westminster. Eddie's house was a mile from Saigon Plaza. When Frye turned onto Washington Street, Eddie leaned forward to stare at a white Chevy parked along the curb. Frye could see someone behind the wheel.

"The Dark Men?" Frye asked.

Vo shook his head, but continued staring as they passed.

Eddie's place was an old two-bedroom home with a dead lawn, a starving orange tree out front, and weeds everywhere.

Frye pulled into the driveway, got out, and followed Eddie to the door. Vo looked again at the Chevrolet parked down the street, but said nothing.

The living room was furnished with thrift-shop stuff—nothing matched, or was less than a decade old. But Vo's stereo was state-of-the art: big flat speakers, a CD player, and a reel-to-reel. A poster of Eddie Van Halen hung crookedly on one wall.

Vo stood for a moment, as if beholding his own home for the first time. "Something's wrong," he said.

Frye looked into Eddie's bedroom: a lamp, a pile of Vietnamese magazines and papers, a mattress on the floor with a sleeping bag tossed over it—one of the old thick ones with pheasants flying over red flannel.

Eddie walked in, fingered some items on his dresser. "Someone's been here," he said. He shot back into the living room and peered through the drapes, then checked his door lock. "Loc, probably. I hate the Dark Men, no matter what Stanley Smith says."

Eddie went to the kitchen, produced a pistol from one of the cabinets, and waved Frye into the other bedroom.

Frye's face went cold. "Be careful with that thing, Eddie."

"I'm a great shot. You're lucky you're with me. Look at this."

Vo flipped on the light. The room was a temple of Li. Signed posters, an *ao dai* on a hanger nailed to the wall, about thirty snapshots crowded in a big frame, clippings from magazines, a collection of covers for albums Frye had never even seen, a blurred blowup of a photograph of Li and Eddie at the Asian Wind. There was a microphone with a card leaning against it that said "Li Frye's microphone—4/7/88."

"This shit's all hers," Eddie said quietly. "I collected it over the last seven years. I got more in the closet." He looked through the window and drew the drapes tightly closed.

An icy little wave rippled down Frye's back. "Nice."

"Beer?" Eddie tossed the gun on his bed.

"Sure."

He went to the kitchen and came back with two cans. Frye watched Eddie contemplate the *ao dai.* Beneath the hardness of Vo's face, he could see the worry.

Frye noted a framed photo next to the snapshots, the only picture in the room that didn't have Li in it. It was Eddie with his arm around another young man. Same height, same age. Eddie's hair was gelled to perfection. The other's was cut into a flat-top that must have been two inches high. They were the two happiest haircuts Frye had seen in years. They were made for each other. The boys smiled at the camera.

"Loc," said Eddie, staring at the picture.

"So you were friends once."

"In the camps we survived. I came over first and formed

Ground Zero. He came over later and joined me. Later, he split to form the Dark Men. He betrayed me. I will take down the picture when I feel like it."

"Is that who's out there in the white Chevy?"

"No."

"Who is?"

"If I knew I wouldn't be nervous, man."

They went to the living room and Eddie put on a Li Frye tape. "You've never heard this," said Vo. "I made it myself."

Eddie went to the bedroom while Frye listened. A moment later he came back wearing fresh clothes, his hair carefully sculpted. He had the gun again. "I want you to take me to my store before we go to the cops. I want to lock up this piece, turn on my burglar alarm, and get some money to bribe my way out of jail. Man, you can't trust nobody anymore. Not even the gang you used to be in."

As Frye steered the Cyclone down Eddie's street, he watched in his rearview mirror as the Chevy pulled from the curb and followed. One block down, another car fell in between them. "Dark Men behind us, Eddie?"

"I told you Frye. I don't know."

Saigon Plaza was Monday-night quiet. The rows of street lamps sent their glow over the parking lot, the marble lions at the entrance, the big archway. As always, colored flyers lay scattered across the asphalt.

But as soon as Frye turned in, he saw the fire units outside Ground Zero Records, the police cars, the little crowd huddled to one side. Two men in yellow, legs spread, supported a hose heaving white rapids of water into Eddie's burning store.

# CHAPTER 6

THE FIRE WAS A BRIGHT, VAS-cular thing, big flames roaring behind the windows. Frye skidded the Cyclone to a stop, and they jumped out. Eddie dodged two patrolmen and ran for his shop.

Detective John Minh materialized from the white Chevy that had followed them from Vo's house. He drew his revolver, took a long look at Frye, then pointed the officers after Eddie. The firemen lifted the hose, sending a bright arc of water over the lamps and into the darkness.

The cops caught Eddie at the door of the store, then hustled back with the slender kid pinned between them. They were all soaked. Vo glared at Frye, then at Minh. "Dark Men," he said.

As soon as they got a cuff on one of Eddie's wrists, he broke away, and ran a zigzag pattern down the sidewalk. One cop drew down. One slipped in the water and fell.

Minh leveled his revolver and yelled for Eddie to stop.

Frye could see Vo look back over his shoulder, eyes big, legs pumping, the silver handcuff shining as it trailed and snapped behind him.

Before he was aware of deciding to, Frye took two steps forward and shoved Minh hard. To his left someone opened up, six shots in a frightful instant. Minh pistol-whipped Frye, sending him to his knees. Through his blaring vision, he saw Eddie make the corner and disappear.

When Frye finally caught up, Eddie was out of sight. The row of shops sat neatly, odd customers lifting themselves from the sidewalk, peeking from behind doors, scrambling for their cars. The cops were already dodging in and out of the stores, under the frantic direction of Minh, whose high-pitched shouting echoed through the plaza. The smell of gunpowder blew past Frye, then gave way to the hot stink of fire. He stood there, ears ringing, dizzy, waiting for them to drag Vo out, dead or alive.

Minh ran back and handcuffed Frye to a street lamp. He cinched the cuffs tight. "If you happen to get loose, I'll shoot you."

Frye watched them search. Echoes of last night, he thought: into one shop where nobody tells you anything, then onto the next where they tell you it again. His head throbbed where Minh's pistol had hit him. A few drops of blood hit the sidewalk below. Minh sent three officers to the back of the building. Two more units skidded up, sirens on, lights whirling.

Five minutes dragged by. Frye watched. Like kids on an Easter egg hunt, he thought, but nobody's finding anything. The cops went in, only to emerge moments later with grim expressions of wonder and defeat. When they'd tried every place that Eddie could possibly have gone, they gathered outside the jewelry store with an air of communal bewilderment, making notes, hypothesizing.

Minh finally marched from the Dream Reader's door and waved his men back to their units. Frye watched him approach: short and slender, a perfectly cut suit, face pale and angry. He stopped a few feet away. "Simple answers. Why?"

*"Why?* How can you blow away a half-crazy kid who's just had his store burned out? How the hell can you—"

"Shut up!" Minh backhanded him, quite hard. Drops of red flecked the lamp post. He told Frye his Miranda rights. "You're under arrest for obstruction, aiding and abetting a fugitive, interfering with an investigation, tampering with a crime scene."

Minh unfastened Frye from the light pole, then cinched the cuffs even tighter. He dragged Frye into the parking lot while a crowd of Vietnamese looked on. The flames in Eddie's store were dying down.

They stopped at the white Chevy and Minh unlocked the trunk. He found a flashlight and flipped the top off a shallow cardboard box beside the spare tire. Li's purple *ao dai* lay inside, covered by a dry-cleaning bag. Beside it were her silk trousers and one shoe. There were dark drops of something on the blouse, and it was torn. "We found an earring, too, and underwear."

"Where?"

"Eddie Vo's garage. This afternoon. Think about it while you're counting the roaches in jail tonight."

The police bagged his possessions and fingerprinted him at the Westminster station; the Sheriff's deputies booked him and sprayed his ass for lice at Orange County Jail; the inmates whistled and offered to fuck him as he was led down the cellblock in blue overalls with the cuffs still so tight that his fingers bulged with pain. He looked at the taunting faces and doubted John Waters was really right when he wrote that everyone looked better under arrest. Sometime during the nightmare, he was allowed to call Bennett. After that, a burly doctor poked five stitches into the side of his forehead.

He lay on his cot and stared at the ceiling. The man in the bunk below gave him a chew of Skoal, then told him about the bum rap he'd gotten for aggravated assault. When the man began his fifth version of the same story, Frye told him to shut up and go to sleep. His other two cellmates kept to themselves, lying on their beds, faces to the wall.

He was exhausted. As he lay there, Frye conceded that this is probably just where he belonged. *The best thing you can do is keep out of the way.* It's hard to believe, he thought, that I was close enough to Eddie Vo to strangle him, and I let him go.

Li's *ao dai,* spotted with blood. Her trousers. Her shoe. Her earring. That's why Minh staked out Vo's house. That's why he didn't take Eddie as soon as we got there. He was hoping Eddie and I would lead him to Li. Maybe he would have.

Instead, he's gone.

Frye dozed off. Sometime after midnight a deputy led him to the checkout room. He got his clothes back. His money was still there.

He met his new lawyer, Mike Flaherty, dispatched by Bennett. Bennett himself didn't show. Frye stepped outside into the cool early morning, and Flaherty led him to his Mercedes.

"Your brother wants to see you," said Mike. "I'll drive you back to your car."

Bennett, Donnell Crawley, and Nguyen Hy were in the living room, each with a stack of handwritten notes in front of him. A .38 lay on the coffee table in front of Nguyen. Two men that Frye had never seen before were connecting a tape recorder to the telephone. Both wore suits, both studied him intently as he walked in. Crawley introduced them as Michelsen and Toibin, FBI. The windows were open and the night was warm.

Bennett looked at Frye briefly and told him to go out to Donnell's cottage in the back.

Frye moved down the hallway, noting again the pictures, decorations, and awards. He stopped at the war photos—shots of his brother and Li at the Pink Night Club in Saigon. Benny with two good legs under him, looking fresh-faced and happy, a little giddy with war, a foreign land, romance. Li stood beside him, her hair wound monumentally upward in the prevailing Western mode, her face oddly girlish. It seems so long ago, he thought: it must seem like centuries to them. Then Bennett's citations and awards, both military and civic—two Purple Hearts, a Silver Star, the *L.A. Times* Orange Countian of the Year, the Vietnamese Chamber of Commerce Helping Hand Citation—dozens more. Even a couple of new ones since the last time he'd looked. Benny, he thought, never happy unless he was the best.

Frye glanced into Bennett's studio: bookshelves, a drafting table, and a model of the Laguna Paradiso development on a stand in the middle of the room. He looked at the tiny hillsides, the blue enamel water, the miniature boats in the marina, the homes, and stores.

The Laguna Paradiso, he thought, the biggest Frye Ranch project yet. Bennett's baby. Edison's parting shot.

He went through the utility room, then out to a back porch. A spotlight on the garage illuminated the yard—a brick patio, an awning, a good expanse of lawn. The hedges were neatly trimmed, the grass freshly mowed, the plants along one side perfectly spaced and tended. Donnell kept the grounds. Nestled at the far end, under a big orange tree, stood his cottage. Frye let himself in: a bed, a Formica table, a tiny television set. Ten years, he thought, and I've never been inside. He sat on the bed and waited, his stitches hurting and the lice spray making him smell like a pet hospital.

Bennett came in a few minutes later, braced himself on his fists and looked up at Frye.

"You all right?"

"I'm okay."

"Get down here to my level, would you, Chuck?"

Frye knelt on the floor in front of his brother. Bennett's eyes weren't right. Even as a kid, he would get that look.

"Chuck, what were you doing?"

"Trying to help. See, Vo—"

"I see."

Bennett's fist slammed into his chest before Frye could react. His breath ripped out of him as if gaffed, something wailed in his ears, and Bennett toppled him over and fastened his thick hands around Frye's throat.

Bennett's face loomed over him. Pressure throbbed in his eyes. Two thumbs locked into position against his windpipe. The voice that came from the clenched mouth above him was hard and cool as the stainless of Minh's revolver. "Never do that again. Never do anything I don't tell you to do. Don't move. Don't think. Don't breathe without my permission again. *Ever.*"

Frye believed he was nodding. Everything was red, just like when he was under the water, fighting for direction. The next thing he knew, he was gasping. The ceiling was turning from red to bright white, then back again. He could hear his breath—rapid on the exhale, deep on the inhale. He sat up dizzily and let the room spin around him. As soon as he caught his breath, he started coughing.

Bennett returned from Crawley's kitchenette, pivoting on one hand, bearing a glass of water in the other. "Here, drink."

Frye swatted away the glass, which shattered against a wall. When he stood over Bennett, he was as close as he'd ever gotten to kicking the living shit out of him. Bennett's gaze was impartial, measured. Frye could already see the arc his foot would take, a short upward swing, off the floor, weight shifting, straight into Bennett's jaw.

It was too easy.

It was too hard.

He sat back onto the bed.

"Good soldier, Chuck. Calm down. We've got business to do now and we need to do it right. Are you with me?"

Frye nodded, coughed again.

"First, tell me what in Christ's name you were doing with Eddie Vo."

Frye sputtered out the story.

"Any hint at all as to where he took her? *Any?*"

"Benny, I just thought he was crazy. He took me right back to his house. He didn't act like a man who'd just kidnapped someone. He showed me his collection of Li stuff. He looked at a poster like it was really her. He's nuts. He named himself for Eddie Van Halen, for God's sake."

Bennett swung from one end of the little cottage to the other, then back to Frye.

"Next, what about Kim?"

"We ended up in Mojave. She got off. A guy named Paul DeCord took pictures of us from the road."

"DeCord took pictures of *you?* Are you sure?"

"I think so. Who is he? And don't tell me he's a goddamned writer."

Bennett shook his head. "How did Kim behave?"

"She was nervous. What was in those crates, Benny?"

"What did she tell you?"

"Damn it! What's going on? She didn't tell me anything."

Bennett tapped his fingers on the floor, staring at Frye. "And what did you gather?"

"Kim isn't going to Paris, and neither was Li. The music is going to Vietnam, and so are those crates. Li couldn't take them, so Kim did. And Minh knew I took her to the airstrip. He knew. When I was leaving his office, Paul DeCord was walking in."

Bennett nodded, looking down at the cottage floor. "Okay. Okay."

Frye took a deep breath and got his right fist ready to slam into Bennett's face if he had to. "What the hell is going on out there, Benny? What's in those crates and how come Paul DeCord's taking pictures and running to Minh?" Frye stood up and put about three feet between his brother and himself. "I watched the video. DeCord paying off Nguyen. What are you guys doing?"

Bennett looked long and hard into Frye's eyes. But the spark of violence was gone, replaced by assessment, caution, control. "Chuck. Brother Chuck. I wish you'd just believe in me the way I believe in you."

"What shit."

Bennett's face took on a softness now, the same expression he had last night at the Asian Wind when Li glided on stage and smiled into the lights. He climbed onto Donnell's bed and leaned against the headboard. For a long moment he closed his eyes, breathing deeply. When he spoke again, his voice was quiet.

"It's amazing how simple people can make simple things so complicated." Bennett crossed his thick arms. "We're trying to help people who don't have a country anymore, Chuck. We send them recordings of Li's music, because it feeds their hearts. It helps to keep them going. It reminds everyone over there of the way things used to be. They listen to it. The people in the refugee camps listen to it. The villagers listen to it. It'd be like us ending up in Vietnam, Chuck. What would you want to hear—our music, or theirs? But it's not just music, Chuck. There are other voices on those tapes. A son's birthday wishes to a father still in the camps. A wife's love to a husband who never got out and lives under the Communists now, too afraid to move. Greetings. Gossip. News from the refugees here. Encouragement for those still over there. Plans for bringing them out. Li always felt like she wanted to help the ones who weren't as lucky as she was. I always felt the same. Is that so hard for you to understand?"

Frye shook his head.

"You saw these crates. How long were they, Chuck, how many feet long?"

"Three, four."

"They're forty-inches long, exactly. What would fit in a case that size, Chuck? Be honest now, tell me what would fit perfectly in a forty-inch wooden crate?"

"Guns. Arms."

"Ah, somehow I thought you'd say that. Arms, sure. But what about legs?"

Frye didn't get it.

Bennett looked down, grasped one of his stumps in both hands and lifted it up. Frye looked at the dirty padding on the bottom, a kind of special wad that Li sewed into the Bennett's pants to protect the tender ends of his legs. "What do you see besides a stump?"

"Nothing."

"That's exactly what a lot of those people over there have to stand on. That's why we send those crates over. Legs. They cost almost a thousand dollars apiece, but we buy a lot of them and get a good price. It's not the hardware that costs so much, it's the doctors you need to fit them and show those crippled people how to use the damned things. They're better than nothing sometimes, Chuck. Believe me. Yeah, there are arms in there too, and feet and hands. There are hooks and crutches, bandages, antibiotics, pain killers, vitamins, cortisone, and enough tape to wrap everybody in the country from head to toe. Any of that meet with your approval?"

Frye nodded.

"I'm happy to hear that. Now, why am I giving you a tape of DeCord paying money to Nguyen? Simple, Chuck, part of the money for those supplies comes from DeCord. I'm just keeping the accounting clean. If it's ever necessary—and I hope it won't be—I need to be able to prove where it came from. There is a lot of money involved. You must understand that."

"Where's DeCord get it?"

"Foreign sources, Chuck. Sympathetic to a free Vietnam. It's nobody's business, especially yours, who those donors are."

"Why's DeCord taking pictures of the airstrip?"

Bennett's gaze shifted past Frye to the window. He looked at the black pane as if trying to read an answer there. "I don't know yet. That's why the video is important. It's insurance. That's where you come in. That's why I'm asking you to trust me now. That's why I'm hoping and praying I can trust you to take care of it. Have you?"

"It's safe."

Bennett smiled. "Things are pretty simple, when you slow down and look at them correctly. Aren't they?"

"It's just kind of embarrassing to be the last one to find out what your own brother's doing."

"I had to bullshit you a little, Chuck. The longer you thought she was going to Paris, the better. Chuck, what Li does—what we do—is outside official channels. It isn't illegal, but sometimes it isn't approved, either. There are some uncharted areas out there, and that's where we work. But we have to keep things quiet."

Frye got up, paced the tiny guest house, looked out the window to the back yard. *I had Eddie Vo in choking distance. And I let him get away.* "I'm sorry about Eddie. I was just trying to do something . . . something goddamned right for a change."

"I know you were."

Frye sat down on the bed. "I'm sick of being a liability to my own family, but you punch me again, I'm going to tear you apart. I mean it."

Bennett reached out and touched Frye's head, near the stitches, then placed his hand gently on his neck. "No one believes that, unless it's you. I know what you're thinking. Don't blame yourself for Debbie. It wasn't your fault. I know that, even if you don't."

"I don't want to talk about her, Bennett."

Bennett looked down to the floor, ran his fingers through his thick dark hair. "Can't you just understand, Chuck, that there's some things you can't do anything about? You can't do anything about our sister. You can't do anything about Li."

"I can. I will."

"You're right. You can keep an eye on that tape I gave you. You can find out about John Minh. You can help me out when I need you, Chuck. I need you to be there for me."

Frye looked at his brother. Somewhere just behind the skin, just inside those dark blue eyes, he could see Debbie: her spirit, her face, her blood. "I can't do nothing, Benny. Don't ask me to sit there again and do nothing."

"Then tell me what you found out about John Minh."

He told him everything.

Back in the living room he sat with Crawley and Nguyen, organizing the notes that Hy's people had collected. Michelsen and Toibin looked on. One hundred and fifteen interviews, and basically it all boiled down to nothing.

Edison called and Bennett put the telephone speaker on. The sound-activated tape recorder started up.

Edison cursed the slowness of the FBI for a moment, then

presented Pat Arbuckle's first solid lead: He'd found a young lady who'd seen Eddie Vo's car arrive outside the Dream Reader Sunday night. Inside were three men—she didn't know them—and Li. According to the witness, Li wasn't struggling at all, but standing up straight, head high, apparently part of a fortune-telling excursion. Arbuckle had determined that two of the men had stayed quite close to her. "With a gun to her back is my guess," said Edison.

"Her blouse was torn and she only had one shoe," said Bennett. "Didn't the lady think that was unusual?"

"Apparently not. Maybe they gave Li a coat."

"But they didn't go into the Dream Reader?"

"The lady didn't bother to watch them. They must have been switching cars, before they delivered her to Vo."

"Did Arbuckle lean on the fat madam?" Bennett asked.

"Affirmative. But she really must not have seen them. Chuck out of jail yet?"

"He's here. He's okay."

"I talked to the D.A. five minutes ago. He'll drop the charges if I ride him hard enough. Tell Chuck to do us all a favor and stay the hell out of this mess from now on."

Bennett hung up.

A minute later the phone rang again. Bennett punched the speaker button. The tape recorder started up. "Bennett Frye."

A short pause. Then a quiet, distorted voice that sounded long distance, even though the connection was flawless. "I know. Hello, *bạn*. I have a greeting for you."

Bennett turned up the speaker. Crawley stood. Nguyen straightened and checked his watch. Michelson and Toibin rose together and moved toward the phone.

Frye's stomach tightened.

The next voice was Li's. She was sobbing. "I love you, Benny. I'm all right. You're number one. I am being taken care of."

Bennett leaned toward the phone, hands out, as if to embrace the machine, the voice. "Li. Li!"

"Benny, I love you."

The line went dead. He swung off the couch and started pacing the room. When he stopped, an odd smile came to his face, as if he were finally realizing something he'd overlooked too long. "She's alive," he said. "She's alive."

Frye felt a huge weight being lifted, a weight that, on some deep level, he had already prepared himself to carry for the rest of his life. All he could do was smile.

For a brief moment, they all looked at the phone again.

"She's alive!"

Michelsen had already placed the cassette in its plastic box and headed out the door with it.

The cave-house was totaled. He just stood there in the doorway, his finger still on the light switch, his heart pounding like a dryer with a load of tennis shoes. Television crashed from its stand, stereo speakers ripped apart, couch cushions slashed open, wet-suits and surfboards everywhere, surfing posters crumpled and tossed to the floor, coffee table overturned, guitar smashed, lamps crushed, rug bunched and tossed in a corner, Linda's oak credenza toppled and its doors pulled off. You name it, Frye thought, and it's wrecked.

His hands were shaking. He didn't have to look very hard to know that the videotape was gone.

# CHAPTER 7

THE KITCHEN LOOKED AS IF had been bombed; the bedroom was worse. His box of Christmas ornaments had been dragged from the cave region to his living room. Through the carnage, strings of Christmas-tree lights blinked on and off, multi-colored, gay. A wreath hung from a nail that used to hold up a *Surfer* magazine photograph—framed, thirty bucks, now broken on the floor—of Frye dazzling the locals at Pipeline.

He toured the house with an unhealthy voltage roaming his nerves, alternating currents of rage and helplessness, feeling the need to reach out and break someone. His worst instincts gathered, brooding like demons. I've done some dumb things in my life, but this is off the charts.

He stood in his room for a moment, Christmas lights twinkling around him. Truly, he thought, the best thing I can do for anybody is just stay off their side. He thought of calling the Laguna Police, but the last time they were here was to bust him for indecent exposure at his own Halloween party. Hard feelings still lingered. He thought of calling Minh, but that was out of the question. He thought of calling Bennett but Bennett's fury was simply too much to even think about at this point.

He thought of calling Linda but lost heart.

Instead he called the Newport Beach surf report, the recorded daily message that had comforted him in trouble spots all over the globe. Air sixty-eight; water sixty-five, visibility six miles; swell from the south at eleven-second intervals and a height of two to three feet; for skin and scuba divers underwater visibility is considered fair.

He listened twice, then finally decided to call the Laguna cops anyway.

The two officers who showed up half an hour later—Simmons and Kite—looked about nineteen years old and carried impossibly loud radios. The sight of their uniforms made him nervous. Frye wondered why cops were always turning down their radio volume but it never got quieter. They scribbled the vital statistics with an air of gravity befitting funeral mourners. Kite inquired as to the identity of the "Mystery Maid." The officer attempted something jocular with his eyebrows. Frye referred him to his lawyer and Kite backed off.

Frye answered questions. Kite wrote with diligence.

Half an hour later came the detective, a middle-aged gentleman named Pavlik. He took one look around, sighed, and set down his case.

It was then, for the first time, that Frye noted the faint, muddy footprint on his floor. From the cave region, he figured, where they found the tape. Looks the same as the light gray stuff the dead kid at the Asian Wind had on his shoes. Mud. In the middle of August in Orange County, these guys find mud to walk in.

"What'd they take?" Pavlik asked.

"Nothing," said Frye.

"What were they looking for?"

"No idea."

"Got someone mad at you?"

"Not that I know of."

Pavlik studied Frye through his thick lenses. "You're the surfer reporter guy. Frye. Married the mayor's daughter, right?"

"I'm not sure how right it was, to tell the truth."

Pavlik surveyed the scene, pushed his glasses snug to his face with a forefinger. He looked disappointed. "I'll try to lift some prints."

Kite and Simmons left to question the neighbors, turning down their radio volumes, trails of official static following them into the darkness outside.

Pavlik already had his brushes and powder out, arranging them on the opened case lid with myopic intensity. Then he erected a tripod lamp, plugged it in, trained it on the door. "These bastards trashed your place here pretty good."

"Bastards?"

Pavlik shrugged, dipped a narrow brush into a vial of black powder and went to work on the doorknob. "Just an expression. One could have done all this, I suppose." He pointed to the footprint. "The one with the muddy feet."

Frye looked at it, the wisp of gray on his wooden floor. "The guy who got shot the night they took Li. He had muddy feet too."

"Not my jurisdiction."

Pavlik held out a piece of white tape with a partial, black thumbprint on it. "Gimme your right thumb," he said. Frye held it out. It was still black from the booking ink. Pavlik raised his eyebrows, passed the brush over it, then pressed it to the tape, which he finally held close for inspection. "They either wore gloves or wiped the knob. This is you. We'll try the TV. You fingerprinted recently?"

Frye nodded but offered no explanation.

Pavlik dusted patiently, more black powder for the silver face of the television set. "Anything on your sister-in-law?"

"A suspect at large."

Pavlik looked at Frye over his glasses. "Vietnamese?"

"Yeah. A gang kid named Eddie Vo."

"Those gangs are bad news. The thing about the Viets is they don't trust anybody. Keep it all to themselves. That's what I hear anyway. Interesting that Lucia Parsons and her MIA Committee think they can deal with them, when our own government can't. We don't have many refugees in Laguna, 'less it's from the IRS. So I don't really know."

The television was clean, and so were the lamps, the light switches, the picture frames and the Christmas bulbs, still glowing red and green and blue all over Frye's living room. Kite and Simmons later returned to report that the neighbors hadn't seen a thing. The detective took a few pictures, examined the lacerated couch cushions, and made some notes.

He finally packed up his things and leaned in the doorway, beaten and apologetic, like a man about to abandon his wife and family. "They wore gloves."

"What kind of gloves?"

"Hard to say. We could run a fiber sample through county, but it takes lots of time, and lots of money. Chief wouldn't approve it, I can tell you right now."

"But I'm important. I'm the former second-best surfer in this entire metropolis. This is a glamour crime if I've ever seen one."

"It's not even worth taking a sample. Nothing was stolen. For all we know it could have been Linda Stowe coming here to make your life miserable."

"Tell the mayor that."

"Not in my lifetime."

"If they'd murdered me I'd be better off."

"Anyone would be, evidence-wise."

When the cops left, he repaired the major damage, putting the television back on its stand, rearranging the speakers, stuffing some of the foam back into the cushions. He played back his phone messages, finding a dinner confirmation from Tuy Xuan. He thanked Frye again, three times, for saving his life.

The Christmas lights actually pleased him in some unspeakable way, so he left them blinking brightly around the living room. He knew he couldn't sleep, so he poured a rather colossal vodka over ice. Linda's ghost threatened from the shadows. He sat for awhile on his patio, watching the traffic below, listening to the throttled buzz of electricity in the power lines overhead.

The vodka disappeared at a truly astonishing rate. Evaporation, he concluded: a real problem here at sea level. He made another, which vanished immediately.

Half an hour later he was illegally parked near the Hotel Laguna, wondering at the dire motive that had propelled him here. He jaywalked Coast Highway to the Sail Loft Restaurant and found a seat, ordered a double and let the loose-jointed jazz rattle his bones. He asked the bartender if he knew a blonde who walked a dog with a red scarf around town. "I've seen her. Killer legs.

Don't know much about her, Chuck. Cristobel something or other. Why?"

"I owe her an apology." I'm after her now, he thought. On a mission from God.

It seemed critical to keep moving.

Coast Highway was thick with walkers. He fell into a slipstream of perfume, letting two women pull him along like tugboats leading him to ports north. Their hair swung in the night breeze, riots of gold breaking out under the streetlights. Then everybody seemed to know him: Hi, Chucky; Hey, Chuck, big contest coming up and Bill says you're gonna surf it; Chucky, my MegaSkate broke in half; Radical sandals, Chuck; I got an eightball of the flakiest, Chuck; *Chuck . . . Chuck . . .*

He suddenly longed for a remote island, a big city, for blinding motion or invisible stillness; but the cave house with its ruined rooms was all that called, where Linda's succubus beckoned from the bed, an apparition warm and tactile as the woman herself. Why does everybody know who you are, he thought, just when you want to be somebody else?

He paused for a moment at the corner of Forest and Coast Highway, where the street people hang out in summertime. A poster showing the outline of a man's head and a strand of barbed wire was hanging in a storefront window. On top it said:

## MIA COMMITTEE
THE CITIZEN'S COMMITTEE TO FREE OUR PRISONERS OF WAR
RALLY AT MAIN BEACH, LAGUNA
TUESDAY 1 P.M.
*All Freedom-Loving Citizens Invited*

Her third rally in the county this month, thought Frye. He wondered if Lucia Parsons had bitten off more than she could chew. She keeps promising proof that they're alive. Good luck to you, he thought. Bring them all back home, each and every one.

The nearest bar was dark, hopeless and comforting. I am blending with my habitat, thought Frye, I am camouflaged. He felt like a perfect jungle lizard, hidden here amidst friendly branches. He ordered a double he was determined to nurse, which knocked another five bucks from his life's savings. He took a stool and watched the pool balls roll around the felt. Sounds of contact from the table reached him late, like distant pistol shots, and the balls weren't moving fast enough. His drink disappeared ahead of schedule. The TV on the wall kept falling down, then levitating up again, but no one seemed to notice. The physical world was a tad off tonight.

Try as he did to concentrate on the billiard balls, all he could see was Li being dragged offstage, the curve of flesh under her *ao dai* as it tore away, her screams amplifying through the Asian Wind. He could see her struggling through the back door exit. He could see her bloody blouse in the trunk of Minh's car.

And most of all, perhaps, he could imagine the looks of disappointment on Bennett's and Edison's faces when they found out that he'd helped Eddie Vo get away.

The really fun part, he thought, is when I tell Bennett that his tape is gone.

He paid, veered off the stool, and headed back outside. Snap out of it, he told himself, melancholy is the nurse of frenzy. You tried. If you don't make mistakes it means you're not doing anything.

He walked south now, past C'est La Vie and Georgia's Bistro to the Hotel Laguna, where he stopped to contemplate—with a thrill beyond delirium—the dog sitting dutifully beside a bench. The red scarf looked freshly arranged, John Waynesque.

Cristobel Something or Other. Eureka.

She wasn't in the bar or on the patio. He marched through the dining room, horrifying the maître d', nearly taking out a two-top, apologizing profusely and promising a free bottle of wine, seeing her nowhere. He made a quick pass through the women's restroom, calling her name. Someone screamed. The hotel security chief intercepted him forthwith, threatening police. "You can do that in Manhattan," Frye protested. "I read *Bright Lights, Big City.*"

"Then move to Manhattan, creep."

The man was still glaring at him, arms crossed, as Frye headed for the door. At the desk he secured a pen and a sheet of hotel stationery. Sitting on the bench outside, he wrote: "Apologies for a bad opening line. Things get better from here. Charles Edison Frye requests the honor of an introduction." He added his phone number, then approached the dog. Dogs had always loved him, which he felt reflected poorly on his character.

"Hey, mutt," he said. The dog's tail thumped on the sidewalk as a police siren ascended in the distance. The dog smelled his hand and the folded note. When Frye intertwined the paper with the bandana, the dog licked his arm. The cop car was nearing now, drawing a bead on him, of that much he was certain. The security man regarded him with malice from the doorway. "This animal belongs to my long-lost cousin," Frye explained. "Until tonight, we believed her dead."

Someone he didn't recognize hooted at him from a car, the war cry of the Southern California surfer, loud enough to match the fast-approaching siren. The thought occurred to Frye that he had just disturbed the peace, that he would fail any sobriety test, that he had a morals rap pending, that he had just spent far too long in jail, that he was, in short, poorly positioned to deal with our criminal justice system again.

He bolted around a corner, down a sidestreet, and into an alley. The Cyclone waited at the far end, 390 cc's of freedom. He sprinted for it, dove in and was about to start the engine when the dog hurled in after him, barking its fool head off. It licked him with zeal, note still locked around its scarf. Frye started up, easing from alley to street in time to meet the cop car speeding his way. He nodded officiously—pursue the criminal element, gentlemen, you have my total support—barely making a yellow light at the signal, then turning south, and gunning the Mercury down Coast Highway toward Linda's house. It was a short blast to Bluebird Canyon, his heart pounding far too hard, the dog ricocheting from back seat to front then back again, shrieking with delight. He punched the car up the steep incline.

The city fell away below. Then they were high in the hills, rich with the narcotic aroma of eucalyptus, heavy sea air, the faint scent of brush from the canyons to the east.

Linda's house was a big shady affair off of Temple Hills. Frye pulled up near a huge bougainvillea aflame with purple bracts that shifted in the darkness. In a vague technical sense, he considered this to be their tree: they had made love under it in a sleeping bag one summer night that now seemed ages ago, and the purple discs had stuck to her back and her hair. Odd, he thought, that when she left the cave-house she moved here, right behind our tree. Was it a declaration of independence, or nostalgia?

In the upstairs bedroom a light shone, and for a moment he saw her behind the curtains. With a burst of optimism he commanded the dog to stay, then jumped out of the car, crunched across the leaf-strewn yard, hurdled a low white fence and hailed her from below the window. "Linda! It's Charles here! Chuck Frye, inventor of the MegaSkate, joy to millions of skateboarders across the world!"

The curtain parted.

"Linda's not here, Chuck. She moved out three weeks ago, just like I told you last week and the week before that."

This was all wrong. This was not the woman he was expecting. From somewhere back in the narrow lanes of his memory came the message that he had been here before. "I'm prepared to hang myself for you. I've brought a belt to do it. Right here on our tree, where we made love."

The face above him laughed. The curtain swung open. "Chuck, you know she's in New York, so why do you do this? You've got her number, for heaven's sake. You put the poor woman through enough. Really. You kinda give me the creeps when you're like this, to tell you the truth."

Frye tried to take off his belt for the self-lynch, but he wasn't wearing one. This is getting gothic, he thought.

"Sleep it off, Chucky." The curtains came back together, and Frye heard a window slide shut and lock. Glad she set me straight before something stupid happened. What are friends for? He tore a branch off the bougainvillea shrub.

Back in the Cyclone now, Frye sped up Coast Highway, past the hills of the Laguna Paradiso, past Crystal Cove to Corona del Mar. The night was clear and the stars dense and he could see the ocean stretched like a jeweled blanket to the horizon. He parked on top of the bluff and found the marker. The grass was freshly cut. Someone had brought flowers. Hyla, probably. He set the bougainvillea branch on the granite, closed his eyes, and started a prayer he couldn't finish. Things just kept unwinding. Everything was a blur: the moon, the city lights below, the paths among the stones. The dog wandered, apparitional. Frye wiped his eyes.

He brushed the smooth granite with wet fingertips and tried his best not to remember.

The trip back to town was a blur of steering wheel and brakes, the stink of rubber, of close calls with large objects positioned specifically to cause him death. The dog sat beside him, bandana lifting in the breeze, tipping left and right, barking with insane happiness.

The dog followed him into the house. Frye stopped in the doorway and felt a shot of adrenaline coarse through him. Inside, his neighbor, Denise, was sitting on his couch, pulling at the loose foam, watching his TV, which miraculously still worked. "Hi, Chucky. I was lonesome so I let myself in. Mind?"

"No," someone said. "You scared me."

Denise giggled. "Sorry. What a beautiful dog. Is he yours?"

"We're brothers."

"That's what this lady on Letterman says too. Look."

Frye regarded the lovely face of Lucia Parsons. She was speaking of governments getting us into war and the *people* getting us out. Letterman swallowed his gap-toothed smile and mustered a look of sincerity. "This is a grass-roots movement of *people,*" she said. "Our Committee is Americans working with Vietnamese. There is no direct government involvement. The governments simply can't get the job done—look at past efforts. We'll get our prisoners back, working with the Vietnamese *people.* My counterpart over there is a man named Tran Tanh—he's a wonderfully open and generous man. He has the support of Hanoi, but he isn't a politician. In fact, he teaches school."

"But *are* there any POWs?" Letterman asked.

Lucia Parsons smiled. "I have some very strong evidence. It isn't something I can make public yet, but I will. I can tell you, David, as surely as I sit here, there are American prisoners alive in Vietnam. And I can tell you we're going to get them out. We need money, we need time, and we need the support of the American people."

Letterman alluded to the support of his sponsors, and the program cut to some deal on Nissan hardbodies.

"She lives right here in Laguna, Chuck. Isn't that neat we've got a national movement in our own back yard? There's a meeting tomorrow and I'm gonna sign up. Think of all the good-looking guys around if someone like her is running it."

"The mind reels."

"You look bad tonight, Chuck. How come your house is all busted up? What happened to your face? This couch here is really fucked, you know that? Salvation Army's got a good one for seventy-five bucks, some rich lady died but it's got cat pee all over it. I love cats, so for me that pee isn't a negative thing at all. Want some homemade acid?"

"God please no."

"You need something. Come here and lay down. I'll give you a rub since I'm drinking your wine."

The dog leapt to to take his place, and Denise shooed him away. Frye nosedove to the couch, then worked himself over to his back. He looked up at Denise, who from this vantage point had implausibly large nostrils. Lucia Parsons was saying that the Vietnamese government had entirely approved the basic concept of working with the American *people*. Denise kneaded his shoulders with strong fingers. "Poor Chuck. Linda ditches him so he drinks too much. It's lonely at the bottom."

Looking up, Frye wondered how Denise made thirty look like sixteen. A pale little woman without fat or wrinkles, a wonderfully preserved pixie. Amazing, he thought, considering her appetite for abuse. Might drugs and relentless fornication promote age-abatement, a pickling of youth in its tracks? Worth looking into. "Who's the squeeze this week?"

"Week nothing, Chuck. I've been seeing Simon for almost a month straight. He's a chemistry student at State, and makes this great acid. I'm tripping right now. Your face looks like wax, except for the beat-up part, and that looks like, well . . . something geological."

"What happened to Dick?"

Denise's fingers moved to his neck. "Went back to his wife."

"Billy?"

"Turned out to be gay."

"It makes you think."

"Yeah, but not that much. Life is reflex. Want me to take you to bed?"

Frye looked up, considering Denise for the thousandth time.

She was pretty and willing, but her legion lovers implied venereal realities of the worst kind, crippling viral bummers with cures still centuries in the future.

"No. Thanks."

"You really look bad, Chuck. Want some coke?" She produced a heap and held a loaded fingernail toward him. He turned away.

"God please no."

Then she was off on a detailed account of today's colonic enema, how clean you feel when it's over, how pure and new. "I'll give you one sometime," she offered.

"You certainly won't, young lady." Frye felt the first waves of sleep tilting over him, let out a groan.

"You're no fun anymore, Chuck."

"The trouble is, Denise, I just keep messing things up."

"Today's problems are tomorrow's jokes and yesterday's worries. God, that's stupid."

"It really is."

Frye shook his head, patted the dog's. He liked how round and smooth it was. "I had one little thing to do. Keep something for a few days. That's *all* I had to do. Then they come in here today while I'm gone and take it."

"Those little boat people?"

Frye sat upright. Below him, the dog's ears shot up: full alert. "Who?"

"Those Viet Cong-style guys who came to see you. Kinda cute. One was tall with a great flat-top and the other one was short and extra skinny."

"Flat-top?"

"Like a totally bitchin' one—two inches high at least. I'd just come onto this acid when they drove up so I figured I was seeing things. They knocked and went in. Then they came out half an hour later, waved good-bye to you, and drove away. Did they tie you up or something?" Denise's eyes glittered with excitement.

"I wasn't here."

She blushed a little, retreating. "I just figured you knew them. I mean, they turned around and said something and waved when they left. Little dark guys. Gosh, Chucky, maybe I kinda like blew it."

Little Dark Men.

"What kind of car?"

"Beats me. Just a car. The only car I know is a red Champ, 'cause that's what I've got."

"What time?"

"Four maybe. Or five. Something right in there."

Frye lay back down. The ceiling moved on its own. So, he thought, while I was at Smith's, the Dark Men were here bagging Bennett's tape.

"I knew I should have called the cops, but I can't deal with authority when I'm high. Some came around a couple of hours ago, but I played nobody home."

Frye groaned.

Long after she had left, he was still on the couch, staring at the darkness and listening to the pounding in his chest. *Eddie's garage, this afternoon.* He could hear the dog roaming his house and at times see the outline of its head as it stopped by the couch to pant hot loyal dog breath into his face. *Chuck, you know she's in New York, so why do you do this?*

Lucia Parsons was gone, replaced by the dizzying effects of Letterman's Monkey-Cam.

He could sense Linda's ambassador in the far corner, looking on.

"Keep that bitch away from me," he told the dog. "She thinks she owns the place."

He dreamed of Debbie, going under.

# CHAPTER 8

S THE SUN CAME UP, FRYE was sitting cross-legged in his living room, drinking coffee, and contemplating the dry mud footprint on his floor. The Dark Men got it in the cave, he thought: but where did the gunman get his? The stitches in his head hurt. Cristobel Something or Other's dog sat beside him, relaxed, witless. Frye named him Dunce.

He stood, hovered his foot over the print and guessed a size eight. *How did they know I had that tape?* Bennett knew I had it. But no one else did, according to Benny. Crawley? Nguyen? Kim? No. They're the inner circle. Is it Paul DeCord? Possibly. He's the co-star. How would he know? A lucky guess, instinct?

As he poured more coffee, Frye knew that the only way to redeem himself here was to find the Dark Men and get back the video. What other choice was there? He couldn't go to Minh because the tape was supposedly a secret; he couldn't go to Bennett because Bennett had given it to him.

The Dark Men. I'll find you bastards, he thought. Tonight, if it's the last thing I do. In Little Saigon, the last place I'm supposed to be.

You're wrong, Benny. I can do *something.*

He got Smith's manuscript from the coffee table and sat back down. The first chapter was called "Kieu Li", and the introduction was short and to the point.

> Kieu Li played a fascinating, if minor, role in the Vietnam-American conflict. In 1970 she was seventeen years old. She was a singer. While entertaining the Viet Cong at night—often underground in tunnels, or in other makeshift "theaters"—she gathered information. By day, she would go into the village of An Cat to her work as a seamstress. There, she would meet her "contacts," an eighteen-year-old man named Huong Lam, and an American lieutenant. During these secret meetings, taken at great risk to herself, she would pass to them the intelligence she had gathered while among the Communists. When Kieu Li's secret spying became dangerous, she simply failed to return to the Viet Cong one night, and fled to the American base in Dong Zu. There, she continued to work in an intelligence capacity for the South. In a fascinating ending to Li's story, she later married the American lieutenant—Bennett Frye—and now lives in Westminster, California, where she is active in helping refugees become settled in their new home. She is a popular singer. In this excerpt from a lengthy taped narrative, Kieu Li describes how she went from being a simple peasant girl to living the perilous life of a spy.

Frye knew the basics of this story. They had come from Li one hot summer night when they'd sat at Frye Island and fished off the dock. Li had told him about her first meeting with Bennett, her strange feelings toward him, his plan to use her as an informant. Bennett had contributed a few details. As always, he was more willing to talk about his patrols, his rooting out of the Viet Cong, his carousing at night, his friends and their drinking, than about the particulars of his romance. Still, Frye noted, when Li told of their meetings and the slow love that developed, Bennett listened intently, as if hearing it for the first time.

## Kieu Li (Li Frye)

An Cat, a village twenty miles north of Saigon, was my home. I had a hut outside the village. It was small but the thatch roof was good when the monsoons came and there was a garden in the back. I wove material on a loom that I sold in the market place and I was a seamstress. This, I traded for other goods. I played my guitar during the slow market days. My mother died in 1964 of fever and my father disappeared in the spring of 1966. I believe the Viet Cong were responsible.

An Cat was supposed to be safe from the Viet Cong. But we all knew that was not true. No one could be trusted unless it was your family or best friend. The Viet Cong would put your head on a stake if you supported the South. Americans and ARVN would kill you if you supported the north. Trying to remain neutral was like remaining completely motionless in a stormy sea. It could not be done.

I saw Huong Lam one morning at the market. I was playing my guitar because no one was buying. I had known him ten years before, when we attended school together. He had left the village. Since then, I had not thought of him often. He was on a bicycle and he had grown from a boy into a young man. He seemed nervous as we talked. He said he had work for me. Two days later he came back with a small bundle. Inside I found the green cotton uniform with the patches on the shirt. It needed to be mended. I knew then that he was with the Americans. He told me one evening as we walked to the road from An Cat that he was a scout.

Huong Lam was a shy man, but very strong. I could see his courage in the set of his jaw, in the clear and unwavering gaze of his eyes. He would stand by my table in the marketplace occasionally. When there were no others around, he would become confidential. He admitted to me that for a year, he fought for the Communists. This was shocking to me. I learned that he felt betrayed by them. He feared their ruthlessness and believed that their promises were empty. He said that they were killing the Vietnam he loved.

But he spoke of the Viet Cong with a quiet respect and I began to wonder if he were secretly still with them.

We became friends.

Eight weeks later, he became very sad and serious as he walked his bicycle beside me down the road. He proposed that I express my sympathies for the Communists and offer myself to them. The Viet Cong were always in need of morale boosting—and perhaps I might sing for them. They were scattered throughout the Iron Land, just north of my village. *[Editor's Note: The Iron Triangle was an area of concentrated Viet Cong influence, the southern tip of which lay some thirty miles from Saigon. It was among the most vigorously bombed, shelled and defoliated areas of the war. The triangle's points were the villages of Ben Cat and Ben Suc, and the junction of the Saigon and Thi Tinh Rivers.]* Some of the people of An Cat, I know, were Viet Cong by night. Lam told me that I was risking my life to spy on the Viet Cong. He seemed both eager and afraid for me. With the disappearance of my father still fresh in my heart, and the stories of murder and torture by the Communists, I agreed to try. Even as a girl, I always felt the need to support one's beliefs with action. It may have helped that I was seventeen and rather naive. If more of the Vietnamese had felt that way, our homeland would not be under the Communists today.

To become sympathetic with the Communists was easy. A word here, a comment there, and soon, I was approached by a young man who began to share his ideas with me, to "educate" me. This was over a period of weeks. I accepted his theories with eagerness. The inevitability of Communist victory was easy enough to feign. I made a point of letting him hear me sing and play. In modesty I will say that I had a very lovely voice.

Months later, he first offered to lead me into the Iron Land. There was a need, he said, for singers in the tunnels. I believe he regarded me as a lucky catch. He said I might meet the great poet Pham Sang, whose troupe of actors was famous for its underground performances. I would have my own theater and my own audience. One part of me was very flattered and nervous and one part of me knew that I could aid the cause of freedom by playing this dangerous game.

It was long after dark that I met him by the creek and we rode bicycles along a trail that led back to where the trees were dead and the bomb craters looked like volcanoes under the moon. I had my guitar strapped to my back. We rode and rode. When we were perhaps ten miles from An Cat, I began to wonder if this man was deceiving me. Would he go to such elaborate lengths just to rape a village girl? The trees naked from defoliation stretched their bony branches toward us. The trail became too bad to ride on. Walking my bicycle behind him, I realized that he had simply seen through my own deceit and was taking me out here to be tortured, raped, and murdered by the Viet Cong. And me, innocent enough to have brought my guitar! Still, I followed, because escape was not possible.

We left our bicycles by a twisted *tram* tree and hiked up the steep side of a hill. Two men watched us. They wore black-and-white checked scarves, so I knew they were the Viet Cong. I could sense people around us, but could not see anyone else.

From the top I looked down into the huge bomb crater below us. And there was my stage!

The audience sat in this natural amphitheater, along the sloping walls. There were no lights or sets but people all around to hear me! And a band of musicians! I was led past the Viet Cong by my guide. At the bottom was the small, earthen stage. The musicians said they knew some of the songs I asked them for. We played ten in all.

The guitar player played with a green stick so as not to be loud. The drummer had an old snare drum with tent canvas on it, which made a dull *thump-thump* when he hit it with his sticks. For one cymbal he had an American helmet, and for the other a canteen. There were watchmen all along the perimeter of the crater, with their backs to me, looking for the enemy.

I sang love songs. Our performance was well-received. The audience was not permitted applause, but a low humming sound of approval came after my first song.

After the show, the Viet Cong colonel in charge told me that I was to sing no more songs of love, only songs of struggle and victory. He was a twisted, angry man. But he smiled before he dismissed me and said I had the lovliest voice he'd ever heard.

I met the poet Pham Sang that night, and he told me very quietly to damn the Communists and sing whatever I wished. He said we artists must be free from all tyranny of thought. He was a thin, sad-faced man and I liked him.

For a few minutes I sat with other performers and a few Viet Cong soldiers. We talked of the war and drank bad tea.

Early that morning I returned to An Cat, my heart filled with contradictions. I did not like the Communists' ideas, but the people seemed good people. They liked me. I loved to sing to an audience, but they were an audience of enemies.

It was one week later, after performing three more nights, that I passed along my first information to Huong Lam. It was about new tunnel work near Cu Chi, the exact place that an underground munitions shop was being constructed. Sympathetic villagers were helping move the fresh earth by hiding it beneath the false bottoms of their water baskets. It was good intelligence. And with those words of betrayal my life was set. The only thing more intimate than betrayal is trust. I was now an enemy of the Communists, and that first secret I told guided my life from that point as surely as a rudder guides a boat.

Frye closed the manuscript and looked again at the dried foot-print on his floor. Amazing, he thought: after all that Li went through in the war, she's kidnapped from a stage in California. He looked out the window to the pure blue sky outside and wondered how it must have been. For Li. For Bennett. In a lot of ways, they purchased that window right there, they purchased that sky—for me. They paid.

Cristobel Something or Other's dog thumped his tail against the floor and looked at Frye with an expression of total under-standing. Frye read on.

One day Lam said it was time for me to meet with his commanding officer. This was the man to whom my information was passed. It was unwise for me to be seen too often with Lam, and very dangerous to be seen with an American. So, his friend, known to me only as Tony, was to often serve as my contact. Tony was a Liaison Officer, a loyal man who followed Lam everywhere and did all that Lam wished.

Toward evening we left the marketplace. We walked the road toward my home as we sometimes did together. But when we were out of sight of the village, we cut through the jungle on a small trail that I had never known about. The foliage was dense but the trail was good. Lam was ahead of me and I followed his back. For a Vietnamese man he was large and his back seemed like a powerful ally to me. Every few seconds he would turn to look back at me. In his eyes I saw strength and purpose. I also—for the first time—believed that I saw doubt. I told myself there was kindness there too, but I suspected that I was only Lam's tool, his spy—not truly a resident in his heart. That was how it should be. Always with Lam I had the feeling that his true thoughts were kept from me. Yet I believed in him.

We walked the trail to where it intersected the road to Saigon. We crouched in the bushes for nearly five minutes. Three American vehicles went by, going south toward the city. Then three more. A moment later, a jeep came slowly toward us and stopped. It had a blue scarf tied to its antenna. Lam rushed me into it and jumped in behind me. We went down the highway only half a mile before turning into the jungle on a small road. I recognized it as one of the roads to the rubber plantation. Tony pointed the way.

I was sitting next to an American soldier with dark hair and thick, strong arms. I could tell because his sleeves were rolled up as he drove. Like most Americans, he seemed large, but later I found out he was actually shorter than the average GI. He looked at me once, nodded, and said nothing. A necklace bounced around his neck along with his dog tags as we bumped over the road. It was an ocean wave inside a circle, made from silver. Squeezed in the back with Lam and Tony was a huge black man, very frightening, who neither looked at us, nor spoke.

We drove toward the plantation house. I could see its old majestic walls through the trees as we approached. The walls were covered with flowering vines and all the *tram* trees around it were healthy and full. A hundred yards from the main house we stopped at a smaller house with a courtyard in front and an old fountain that did not work anymore. There was a statue in the fountain, stained black from the rain and weather, of a man and woman embracing. It was French in attitude. Here we parked and sat on stone benches around the fountain.

Lam introduced me to Lieutenant Bennett Frye. I could

not say his name properly and when I said "Flye," both of
the men smiled. He pronounced my name perfectly. His
Vietnamese was good. My first impression of Lt. Frye was
that he was a hard man and very intelligent. His eyes held
none of the doubt that I often could see in Lam's. When
he looked at me, it was with a mixture of aggressiveness
and respect that I found strange. But I had the feeling
from him, even stronger than from Lam, that I was only a
tool and not really a human. This was all right with me.
He had none of the recklesss energy that we often
associated with the Americans. Lt. Frye's energy was
controlled.

The black man was Private Crawley. He said nothing
during that entire first meeting, but he listened very
intently to everything that was said.

Lam was strange at this first meeting. He attempted a
level of familiarity with me that he had never shown
before. He sat a little closer to me on that stone bench
than he had sat at any time. He interrupted me often,
explaining to Lt. Frye my loyalty and intelligence. He
seemed proud of me.

It was agreed that we would meet here once a week to
pass the information I was to collect. If Lam was not able
to join me, I should wait for Lt. Frye alone in the clump
of trees by the highway. His jeep would always have a
blue silk scarf tied to the antenna. At this first meeting, Lt.
Frye told me of several things the Americans were very
interested in. These involved enemy strength in the village
of Ben Cat, and any specific information I might get on a
suspected Viet Cong headquarters in the Bo Ho Woods.

Once, when he interrupted Lam, I saw a moment of
anger in Lam's dark eyes. It was then I understood that Lt.
Frye did not trust Lam in all things, as I did not. Huong
Lam had once been a Viet Cong himself. Could anyone
fully trust a man who had once been the enemy?

It was obvious by the way that Lt. Frye looked at me,
that I was not trusted either. I had not expected to be. But
when you trust yourself, no suspicion from another even
matters. At one point, as his doubting eyes bore into mine,
I returned his gaze with the arrogance that only the
innocent can have. Many weeks later, I learned from him
that I had won his respect that day, if not his trust.

We drove back to the place in the jungle where he had picked us up. Before we left, Lt. Frye flattered me immensely by saying he would like to hear me play and sing, if I would be willing. You can imagine how inflated by vanity I was—a seventeen-year-old girl with an important American as a potential audience! He was a very handsome man.

For a moment, Frye imagined them sitting there in the plantation courtyard, that first meeting between a man and a woman who would eventually fall in love and marry. Did either of them have an idea, a feeling? Much later, Li had told him that she did. Bennett had told him that his affection for Li developed slowly. When he described those early days with her, it was always with an intelligence officer's air of detachment. Just the facts. Still, Frye could sense the passion in his brother's calm voice, sense the heat beneath the cool when he spoke of Kieu Li.

He closed the manuscript and found an old tape of Li's songs. He tried to play it, but his smashed speakers just hissed and crackled. He fetched a small tape recorder he'd used for interviews and slipped in the tape. The dog cocked his head at the commotion, then walked outside to the patio. Frye read the English translation:

> In my nightmares hands reach out
> But I will not return
> Fingers tear my heart away
> But I will not return
> In the courtyard you betrayed me
> By the fountain with the lovers
> I will not return, old love
> Until the fountain flows.

He addressed and stamped two more résumés. He called Rollie Dean Mack of Elite Management, but Rollie Dean was out. He got through to Nguyen Hy, who feigned ignorance as to where the Dark Men congregated.

"There is no reason for you to see the Dark Men, Chuck. Unless there is something you haven't told us."

Frye mumbled about something Minh had said—just following up a lead. "What's the progress on Li?"

Nguyen hesitated. "The FBI examined Eddie's place after he got away last night. We are not supposed to know this, but now they don't believe she was actually inside his house or garage."

"But what about her clothes?"

"He . . . removed her clothing somewhere else. The agent who talked to Benny found that her blouse had muddy earth on it. Her shoe, too, but the earth was found on top of the shoe as well as on the bottom. Even her earring had mud on it. It was as if she was stripped in a yard or a lot of some kind. But there was not a single print or smudge or hair to indicate that she was inside the house. Chuck—we are not supposed to have this information. Your father managed to . . . get it out of Senator Lansdale. The FBI still regards Eddie Vo as their prime suspect."

"If Li was never at Eddie's, then that stuff could have been planted there. Eddie could have been framed."

"That is exactly what your brother and I thought, too. Keep this information to yourself, Chuck."

He called Julie at the Asian Wind, who told him that the Dark Men gathered at Pho Dinh Restaurant on Bolsa, a block east of the plaza. The leader, of course, was Loc—the tall thin boy with the high flat-top, Eddie Vo's former friend and gang mate. Julie said that he was known to carry a gun. When Frye asked her about seeing Eddie Vo that night, just before the shooting started, Julie sounded angry.

"The police say he was involved in the kidnapping. They say that I must be mistaken. I'm sure I saw him out there, in a car, but I don't remember when. Not *exactly.* It must have been before the shooting, but how much before? And could it have been a boy who only looks like Eddie? I don't know. I wish Minh would leave me alone. I hate the way he tries to trick me into agreeing with him. Now the city threatens to take away my entertainment license. I get the feeling that the more I say what Minh wants to hear, the easier the city will be on me. I am being manipulated."

Everybody, Frye thought, wants to lean on Eddie.

"Tell them the truth, Julie. Let them worry about it."

"Thank you, Chuck. Be careful with the Dark Men. They are very unpredictable people."

Dunce bounced back into the room with that look of hopeful expectancy found in only dogs and children. This was clearly an animal with a mission in mind. Any mission.

"To the doctor," Frye announced, picking up his résumés. "To check on my condition. And after that, we'll mail these and try to get you home."

He took one more look around his semi-demolished home, locked the door, and headed downtown on foot.

# CHAPTER 9

**H**E CLIMBED ONTO DR. RED-
ken's examination table, aiming for
the sanitized tissue runway. The doctor—of ears, nose, and throat
fame—affixed a rubberoid gadget to the end of a light and drove
it deep into Frye's ear. The doctor moaned. "Interesting," he said
finally. "Your spells of imbalance persist?"

"Only when I'm in the water. Or sometimes in a dark, closed-
up place. I get them then, too."

Redken moaned again, probing afresh from a new angle. "And
you've been taking it easy?"

"Yeah."

"No superhuman efforts out there in the waves?"

"No. I'm just scared shitless, Doc."

Redken retracted his light with an air of finality, clicking it off
and sliding it into a coat pocket. Frye shifted on the table, tissue
clinging noisily to his legs. Redken brought a set of X rays from
a folder, then a collection of gray, unfocused photos of some
kind.

"These, of course, are the X rays from two months ago, when
the injury took place. They show now what they showed then—

no damage to the inner ear bones." Redken consulted the murky film. "And the CAT-scan done two months ago shows the ruptured tympanum. I'm still surprised that the surfboard didn't break bone. Now, the scan we did last week shows no fluid build-up at all, no indications of labyrinthitis or Ménière's syndrome." The doctor fixed Frye with an oddly pat stare. "In other words, Chuck, you're healed. A recovered patient of nature's own slow therapy."

Frye watched his feet crossing and uncrossing below him. The truth was that he had been hoping for mildly tragic news to justify his dread of the water, not some toast to mother nature's skill as a doctor. This, he thought, is a whole new ballgame. "Then how come I get the spells?"

"Fear. Worry. It could be that you anticipate them, thereby bringing them on."

"I was hoping for something nasty but curable."

"Well, you've been struck by a hard object about the face and head. That cut is curable. What happened?"

"Slipped in the shower."

Redken eyed him with professional resignation, sensing limits. "Water seems your nemesis these days, Charles. Tell me, are you quite afraid of the ocean?"

"I'm afraid of not coming up. You haven't lived until you've swum to the bottom of the Pacific to get a breath of air."

Redken leaned against a cabinet, nodding. "Describe these feelings of confusion again for me."

"I take off, I get a ride, I get wiped out. Or sometimes it's just TOADS."

"Excuse me?"

"Take-Off-And-Die-Syndrome."

Redken made a note. "And?"

"Sometimes I'm at the surface where I'm supposed to be, and sometimes I get all mixed up. So I swim for the top. I can tell it's there and I can see the sunlight. Then I'm running out of air and ready to hit the surface but I'm at the bottom instead. I swim up, but go down. Sometimes I'm watching myself go through it. Or I'm watching someone who looks a lot like me. Like me, but longer hair. Sometimes I'm just dreaming and I wake up standing there looking down at the bed."

"Interesting, Chuck. It sounds like a new disease. A combination of vertigo and claustrophobia."

"Can you name it after me?"

Redken tossed the folder to the cabinet and crossed his arms. "Chuck, you have been living with a great deal of anxiety about this. You didn't know you were all right. My advice is to go easy, to get your confidence back one wave at a time. Come in next week and we'll talk again. And for heaven's sake, don't go out in the hurricane surf that's coming. That's enough to shake up anybody."

Frye pondered the irony of not knowing he was all right. "Can do, Doc." He slid off the table and stood.

Redken clicked his pen shut and slid it into his pocket. "Chuck, tell me something. Have you been thinking of Debbie recently? More than . . . usual?"

Frye nodded.

"Her birthday is this month?"

He nodded again.

"There was nothing you could have done," he said quietly.

"I know." *There was. Something.*

Redken sighed. "Let go, Chuck."

"I try."

Redken forced a nod. "It's tragic about Bennett's wife. Any . . . positive developments at all?"

"They've got a suspect but can't find him."

"I suppose that's a start. Your entire family has my support." Redken hesitated, pursed his lips, and shook his head. "I miss your boxing articles. You're one of the few writers who refused to portray prizefighters as idiots."

"Write my ex-publisher. Ronald Billingham. Tell him if I don't get my job back you're going to die of depression. From a leading doctor in Laguna, it could mean a lot."

Redken checked his watch. "Are you going to the big MIA rally at Main Beach today?"

"Hadn't thought about it."

"You should. You should donate a little money, too, if you can spare it. Yesterday at the Laguna Chapter meeting, Lucia Parsons implied she has proof that some MIAs are alive. She stopped short of saying what exactly it is, but said she would show solid evidence by Thursday of this week. That woman is powerful, and practical too. She gets people to believe. That's a gift, in times as cynical as ours."

"I'll think about it."

Frye counted out sixty-eight dollars for the receptionist, who said she could bill him. He said next month he'd probably be broke. She took the cash with offended dignity, gingerly as a specimen, and placed it in a drawer.

He stepped outside and into the languid morning optics of summertime Laguna. Dunce was waiting where Frye had left him. Downtown, things seemed muted, slightly airborne. As Frye walked down Forest Avenue, shoppers floated by on a radiant sidewalk, mouthing silences, dazed by the harsh economics of looking for bargains in a town where none exist, burying their woes in two-dollar ice-cream cones, dreaming of air conditioners, Bloody Marys, naps. The traffic had already slowed to a crawl, and the tourists weaved slowly between the overheating cars as if protected by force fields. A mother stopped her stroller in front of an idling Mercedes and adjusted her baby's bonnet. Her husband waited in another dimension, ice cream melting down his wrists, gazing to the Pacific with some unfocused longing. Paying customers, Frye thought, endure them. He dumped the envelopes in a mail box.

A fresh batch of MIA Committee posters had sprung up around town—on the trees, the storefronts, the lamp posts. Frye could see the crowd starting to gather on Main Beach.

Organize, he thought. Organize all this, just like a newspaper piece. The inverted pyramid. Who, what, where, when, how, and why?

Eddie leaves early.

Li gets kidnapped.

One gunman has muddy shoes and bracelets on his wrists—gifts of Stanley Smith.

They get away in a blue Celica, Eddie's car.

They vanish in Saigon Plaza with people everywhere.

I get a tape with DeCord paying off Nguyen Hy.

DeCord shows up with Minh.

Minh finds Li's bloody, muddy clothes in Eddie's garage. Or says he did.

The tape of DeCord and Nguyen gets taken by Eddie's rivals, the Dark Men. They total my place. More muddy shoes, in the middle of August.

The whats and the whens. But not enough whos, or hows . . . and no whys.

*And who knew I had that tape, besides Bennett?*

Maybe I can find out—tonight.

He headed down Coast Highway, bought a *Times,* then took a deep breath before ducking into the MegaShop to see Bill Antioch. There was a sense of duty here, because Bill had been his partner for eight years in the only venture at which Frye had been even mildly successful.

It smells the same, he thought—rubber wetsuits; new cotton shirts; leather MegaSandals; fresh resin on new boards; the sweet, sexy smell of MegaWax, concocted with essence of coconut and an expensive dash of musk.

He took visual stock. Plenty of boards left, sandal boxes scattered around the floor, wetsuits stuffed onto hangers, Mega-Skates stacked in a corner, MegaLeashes dangling everywhere, posters fading on the walls, and all of it covered with the same sad coat of dust that had settled here months ago and never left, like some new product that refused to move.

"Don't say it, Frye. You wanna know why this is, like, a total dive, just ask yourself why you don't give a shit anymore."

Antioch sat behind the counter, reading *Guitar Player,* slurping a health shake of some description. Tanned perfectly, a properly faded Hawaiian shirt, a shell necklace around his neck just low enough to flirt with his golden chest hair. Bill. Frye smiled, regarding the unsold lumps of MegaWax still displayed with the warping sign: MEGAGREAT STOCKING STUFFERS! STOKE YOUR SURFER THIS CHRISTMAS!"

"Hello, Bill. How's business?"

"Radically bad."

"Thought I'd check in."

"You checked out from around here a year ago, man."

"I'm on a rebound."

"Glad to hear it, Chuck, but if you want to rebound this place you got a throbbin' long way to jump."

Frye turned to assay his shop again, and the closer he looked the worse it got. Windows blighted with dirt, carpet littered, stacks of magazines piled behind the counter, product marked down to giveaway prices but still unmoved in almost a year. And the goddamned dust. Dunce nosed a three-hundred-dollar surfboard with some curiosity and lifted a leg. Frye cuffed him and the dog looked up woefully. "Well, I'm ready to try, Bill. Either that or sell the whole thing. What can we do?"

Bill's eyes glimmered for a moment, the spirit of free enterprise still kicking. "First, you owe the help for last week."

Frye counted out three hundred and fifty dollars and handed it over. Simple arithmetic suggested that his life's savings were now right at one hundred and eighty-two dollars, plus change. Maybe Billingham will go for a freelance piece on Li's kidnapping. Maybe the *Times* would pay better.

"Thanks, Chuck. Money well spent. Now like I've told you before, we got to do like four things before this place can throb again. First is the women's wear. Bikinis, one-pieces, shorts, shirts, the whole deal. We still get half a dozen chicks a day—*superior-looking chicks too*—asking for Mega. I tell them we have no Mega for women, as such. So they head right down to Stussy or Gotcha. *Gotcha?* Those South Africans are killing us, right here on our native shore, and Chuck, that hurts." Bill sucked on his straw, gaining momentum. "Second is we gotta go with kneebusters. I know they're butt-ugly, but they're big now. Supply and demand. Then I've got to get off my ass—I'm not blaming this whole mess on you, not even. Fourth, bro, is you gotta get back in the contests and dust off your name. The buying public is a fickle animal, and if you're not out there in the water, at the parties and surf films, they just forget about Mega. You gotta get visible, man. Frye, the last thing you did public was when you dressed like the ape at your party and chased the chick through the bushes and got your picture in the paper. Great photo. Great stunt, but you gotta follow up. You gotta be apparent. Hell, Chuck, you gotta *surf.*"

Frye nodded, considering this four-point plan. Bill was contagious in his own way.

"You forget how to surf or something, Chuck?"

"No."

"Good. Getting fired from the paper was the best thing that could've happened for Mega. Now you can win contests again

and put us back on top. In fact, I just entered you in the Huntington Masters Invitational next month. Great exposure. All the
Aussies and Hawaiians will be there and you can blow them out
of the water. Totally."

Frye wondered if drowning in a contest would boost sales.

"And one more thing, Chuck. Your hair. I mean, it's like way
too long. Kids now got it kinda fifties-like, you know, Tab
Hunter or something. Modernize, Chuck."

"I like my hair okay."

"You're a chop."

"And I don't know the first thing about bikinis."

Antioch choked down more shake. "You don't have to! We just
get a designer. You didn't know anything about sandals either,
did you? But look how they sold! Two years ago everybody on
earth had those things on. Who else can say they sent the *president*
a free pair of MegaSandals to wear at the White House Beach
Boys Concert?" Bill's countenance fell; he grew pensive. "You
know, we made 'em too good. I *still* get people in here wearing
MegaSandals from years back. They don't ever wear out. Bikinis,
Chuck. The future is a string bikini. MegaKini. There you are. It's
all out there for the taking."

Frye tried to reconcile the kidnapping of Li, the death of his
marriage, and his fear of the water with a future of string bikinis.
He thought, something has to give. Haven't I known that for too
long? He looked at Dunce, asleep now in a rhombus of sunlight
inside the door. He watched the cars on Coast Highway, droning
past the bleak windows. Back in the old days, this was quite the
place. Parties. Linda. Profit. A little attention was all she needed.
Like everything else, there comes a point when you put up or get
out. How come it took me so long to realize that if you do
nothing, things fall apart? "Okay, Bill. Let's get this place going
again. Find a designer for women's wear and I'll get back on the
surf circuit. We'll make it work."

Bill finished his shake with a last desperate slurp, then swung
out his hand, smiling. "We can get back on top, Chuck. I swear.
We'll kick everybody's ass, like totally. You miss the contests
anyway, don't you?"

"Oh, yes."

"Linda?"

"She split."

"What a drag. There was a girl in here looking for you yesterday. Real nectar. Cristobel Something or Other. Matter of fact, she had a dog with her, just like that one."

Frye regarded the brute, body bent and one leg up now in the patch of sun, chasing a flea around his balls with a fervent snorting and clicking of teeth.

She came here looking for me, he thought. This could be the start of something long and beautiful. Erotic in unprecedented ways. Eventually a family of adoring children, all with genius IQs. I will teach my son to surf. Maybe she changed her mind about my offer. On the other hand, maybe she just came by to tell me I'm an asshole. "She leave a message?"

"Here's her number."

"Okay, Bill. Clean up this dust, will ya? Mega is on the comeback trail."

Antioch eyed Frye's stitches. "Radical face. What happened?"

"Shaving accident."

"What with, dude, a chainsaw? Hey Frye, you mind if I close the shop for an hour today? I wanna go see that MIA rally. Every time I look at Lucia Parsons, my prick gets hard as a surfboard."

"Do what you feel is best, Bill."

Frye called Cristobel Something or Other's number. Her voice was kind of low and she sounded tired. He explained that he had found her dog. She gave him her address—on Coast Highway, just two blocks from the MegaShop—and asked him to bring him back.

Outside, he found an empty bench and opened the *Register* to the Orange County section. Eddie Vo's face stared back at him, sullen, dark and inward. GANG LEADER SOUGHT IN KIDNAPPING. The piece said that "articles belonging to the kidnapped woman were found in Vo's rented Westminster home." Vo was "at large," and the cops were looking all over the county.

Li smiled in the photo beside him, serene, goddesslike.

Below the fold was a shot of Ground Zero Records, little more than a black cavern now, gutted by fire. The caption posited that a rival gang may have set the blaze.

The rival gang that took Bennett's tape.

And broke into my house, wrecked my stuff, strung my room with Christmas lights and generally shit in my mess kit. While I was out helping Eddie Vo get away.

1 0 6

# CHAPTER 10

**C**RISTOBEL'S PLACE WAS A washed-out, once-blue, and now rickety apartment just past Fahrenheit 451 Books. The dog, sensing home turf, led Frye down a walkway. The buildings seemed to slouch in lazy angles, a patternless surrender to time and gravity.

He stood on a big patio, surrounded on three sides by railing. Dunce nosed the door to Number Seven. Through the Dutch door, Frye could see her sitting with her back to him, shoulders forward, head down a little, right elbow held outward.

For a moment he watched as she worked a big pair of scissors through some material, her left hand spreading it flat. Through the picture window she worked behind, Frye noted the blue glitter of the Pacific and the sun high in a flawless sky. Her reflection rode across the water, mingled with the sun—a truly special effect, Frye concluded. He moved closer.

Dunce barked and jumped at the door, and Frye watched Cristobel turn. He was getting a smile ready when a dark shape suddenly blotted her out and he found himself looking at a large black man who wiped out the ocean and sun: no shirt, muscles bunching and sweat glistening off his chest, his hair planed flat in the manner of Carl Lewis, a not very friendly look on his face. The man moved from the window and the door swung open. Dunce slipped inside with a series of whimpers that told of abduction, torture, escape. The black man offered his hand. "Jim Strauss," he said.

"Chuck Frye."

"Find our dog?"

"He kinda found me."

Frye stepped in, aware of the commotion at the far end of the room—woman and dog in a homecoming scene. Dunce barked at him. Cristobel turned. Same face, he thought—full, pale skin, good mouth. Dark eyes, light hair. Off the charts. She gave him a contraceptive glare.

"Well, hello, Mr. Frye."

"Hello, Miss . . ."

"Strauss."

He forced a smile at both of them. "Oh, you two are . . . great, super."

Jim smiled at him without mirth.

"Cristobel will do," she said. "Blaster latch onto you?"

"He did."

"He's like that. A social animal." She looked at Frye, shaking back her hair, hands on her hips and fingers spread against her jeans.

"Good to meet you," said Jim. "Thanks for bringing back our dog." Frye watched him disappear into a hallway. A door closed, music started up.

"He's not rude," she said. "He's just working out."

"Olympics?"

"Model. Everything has to be perfect."

"Looks like he's getting there." Blaster's head slipped under his hand. "I was putting a note on your dog's scarf last night and he followed me to my car. I was in a hurry and he just sorta jumped in. The note said I was sorry for a bad opening line and wanted a proper introduction. Anyway, I apologize for what I said, and I'm sorry I kidnapped your dog."

"That was a crappy thing to say to a girl you don't even know."

"I know."

"You didn't really expect me to say yes, did you?"

"No."

"You Southern California guys are so damned arrogant sometimes. You think it's cool. Some women must like that, but it just makes me think you're a bunch of narcissistic queebs."

"If you've got a blindfold and rifle, I'll shoot myself."

She stared at him for a long moment. "Okay. Truce. Beer?"

"Sure." He watched her go to the kitchen with an adulterous guilt, very much tuned in to the way she filled her jeans. Full-bodied but light on her feet, a gold chain around her ankle. He glanced toward Jim's room, from which a series of odd huffing noises came, timed roughly to the music. When she came back, he was looking at the material she'd been cutting. It was a light blue background with yellow slices of moon on it. "Nice."

"Kind of a sun dress," she said. She held up a swatch of cloth. "Good silk. I liked those little moons."

Frye sat on the couch and Cristobel took a chair. He looked out to the sand, the sun, the ocean glittering like a tossed handful of diamonds. "Nice place here."

"Thanks. We rented it a year ago. Cheap and a good view. Hard to find in Laguna. What happened to your head?"

"A cop hit me with his gun."

"Are you in trouble?"

"Not exactly."

"I've been following the story about Li. She's been missing since Sunday, right? Any suspects?"

"There's a suspect but I'm not so sure he's solid. The cops think so."

"My experience with cops is you get good treatment if you're high-priority, and bad treatment if you're not. I'd think that Li Frye is pretty high."

Frye wondered just what this experience with the cops was, but it didn't seem time to press it. He looked at Cristobel, feeling a sour regret that she was married, that he was married—technically, at least—that he had put his worst foot forward, kidnapped her dog, and now sat here with his pecker coming up like a garden gopher while he drank her beer.

"Don't get discouraged," she said. "They'll find her."

Through the picture window, Frye could see the people gathering on Main Beach. Bleachers and a stage had been set up, banners proclaiming the MIA Committee rally.

Cristobel fiddled with her anklet. The sun lit up her hair from behind. She has eyes that seem to see a lot, Frye decided. She picked up a framed picture from the coffee table: a young man in a flight suit, and his F-4. "I lost my brother Mike over there," she said quietly. "Somewhere over Quang Tri." She handed him the photograph.

"I'm sorry."

Cristobel nodded, drank from her glass, shook back her hair and looked toward Jim's room. "You got a job besides that surf shop?"

"I was a reporter for a while. Got fired."

"Looking for another one?"

"Kind of. I'm trying to help Benny right now. I'm trying to find Li. The cops and FBI are all over the place, but nothing's happening."

"Sometimes when nothing seems to be happening, that's when everything really is." She looked straight through Frye with a curious air of resignation, as if he were a window and she a passenger gone one stop past her destination.

"I'm done with my work for the day," she said. "Like to walk over to the hotel, have lunch?"

Frye listened to the music still throbbing from Jim's workout room. This woman can turn on a dime, he thought. It makes me a little nervous. "Sounds like a good way to get my face really creamed."

She smiled. "We have an understanding."

"I've got the sore face."

"Don't worry."

They found a table at the far end of the patio, pads on the chairs, great view. Cristobel wanted a bottle of Cabernet and Frye could find little wrong with the idea. He looked down at the whitewater easing toward shore, a few kids splashing around, a couple standing in the surf for a kiss that lasted until the wine arrived. A hundred yards up the beach he could see the MIA Committee banner and a huge American flag. The public address system squawked over the hissing waves. They touched glasses. "To the safe return of your sister-in-law," she said.

Frye nodded and drank. "Good wine." He drank more and leaned back, letting the sun and the alcohol mix, using the privacy of his sunglasses to study the person across from him. The wine loosened him a little and he babbled: surfing, the Mega-Shop, contests, growing up on Frye Island, college failures and his several years of aimlessness that ended in his first real job as a reporter for the *Ledger.* His words seemed to come out under their own power, and as he listened to his voice he wondered about this woman. There's something oddly real in her, he thought, or something really odd. But which?

He pondered this, poured more wine, and glanced again at the water. A little west swell at Rockpile, not much shape, cool water. Hurricane surf due soon, according to the papers. A big round of applause eased its way through the breeze. Frye looked to the rally stage. He could see Lucia Parsons, positioning herself behind the podium. The applause got louder. She thanked her audience. Her voice was clear, if a little faint. *It's always good to be here in Laguna. It should be. It's my home.*

Frye looked at Cristobel and whipped up a quick theory. The facts were thin, but that had never stopped him before. Cristobel Strauss. My age. Skin isn't wrecked by now, so she probably grew up somewhere else. A few major secrets, none good. No surprise at that, though: beauty always gets the worst offers, and who can say no to all of them? Aware of her effect on the male. How to use it, how to enjoy it, both in moderation. Prone to misgivings about God, country and family, but has the good sense to change what she can, shine what she can't and know the difference between the two. Level-headed in all respects except the really big ones, but who can brag that? Still, something is not quite right about this. Something doesn't fit.

*I'm here today to tell you I want our soldiers back from the jungles. I want them back on home soil. I want them here, with me and you. And I'm here today to tell you there's a way to do it.*

He smiled, poured more wine for them, laughed.

"What's so funny?"

"You're not married to Jim, are you."

"I never said I was. It's kind of an IQ test, how long it takes a man to figure it out."

"How'd I do?"

"A little above average."

"What's the point?"

She looked at him a little placidly, but he sensed the wall just behind her. "He cuts down the flak from jerks, and I deter some of the ladies. He doesn't care for them, in general. Jim likes men, and I like to be left alone. The last name's a coincidence, and an occasional source of fun."

"It was really a gas."

"I could have strung you along."

He looked at her and realized she was right. This puts things in a new light. Just what light is it? "True. I must be wearing a little thin on mysteries these days."

"Well, you figured out this one and no one hit you in the face with a pistol."

Frye listened to Lucia Parsons describing her rapport with the Vietnamese people. The MIA Committee not only had their support, but had enlisted thousands of Vietnamese as members. "Day after tomorrow, we will be able to provide positive proof that American soldiers are still alive in Vietnam. What we need now is to meet Goal Three—our third and largest fundraising plateau. When the days come to negotiate for our men, we will need money to finance our travel, to support our volunteers, and perhaps to deal with the people of Vietnam. The day is coming soon when we will hear the good news," she said. "On that day, we must be ready to start bringing those men home!"

"Lucia Parsons is doing good things," Cristobel said. "If I had someone over there—a husband, or a brother, or a son—I'd do anything in the world to get him back. Anything. She's great."

He smiled, touched her glass with his. She told him about growing up in the wine country of Mendocino, a hundred acres of Cabernet and Zinfandel; college at Berkeley, masters in art at UCLA; a stint at fashion design that didn't work out; ditching L.A. for Laguna Beach and a chance to design on her own again. Almost married once but changed her mind. She looked at Frye, then out to the water. "I'm waiting tables at the Towers mornings for money. It's a good restaurant, gives me time to myself."

"Ever think about designing for a company again?"

"Not really. Why?"

"Just curious."

"Anyway, I guess I'm in a holding pattern right now. L.A. ended bad."

He waited for some clarification but she offered none, choosing instead to wrap herself tightly in the light coat she'd worn, tug-ging the collar up close, then shaking back her hair in a riot of golden waves that struck Frye as feloniously lovely. Call nine-one-one, he thought. In his mind she shed her clothing and wrapped him in a splendid coital knot right there on the patio while outraged drinkers ran for the exits, all sweat and golden hair stuck to her shoulders and breasts, mutual shrieks of love challenging the surging surf below. But he saw as she gazed out to the bright ocean that her eyes held an entirely different vi-sion—anger maybe, or a disappointment too major to air, or some deep and unitemized sorrow, or perhaps nothing at all he could understand. A group of young Mexicans took a table next to them, restaurant workers done with the lunch shift. Cristobel looked at them, then at Frye, an odd confusion on her face. "Well," she said, standing. "Time for this one to go home."

"What about lunch?"

"I'm not hungry."

She led him down the steps to the sand and headed toward the blue apartments, a disheveled outline to the south. He checked the waves again, gazing down to Brooks Street, water splashing the boulders with a faintly purple tint. The color of Li's *ao dai,* he thought. Where is she now?

*. . . Good people, there are only three things we need to make this happen. You—each and every one of you—and your money. And you've got to write your representatives in this government, and get them to support our House Bill eight-eight-two-three-one, which will establish a modest relief fund for the people of Vietnam.*

Cristobel looked toward the Rockpile, a silent seascape of rock and foam in the distance. "Going to surf that place tomorrow?"

"Maybe. You going to be out with your dog?"

"Maybe. I usually am."

"I'm glad you were there that morning, Cristobel."

"I'm in the pageant this year. Susanna and the Elders. I'll leave you a ticket at 'will-call' if you want to come see me Thursday night."

"I'd like that."

"Be there by eight or they'll sell it to someone else." She stopped, looked up to her apartment, crossed her arms against the breeze.

Frye moved a stray strand of hair from her face and thought seriously about kissing her. Something mannered, he thought, a skosh formal. The hell?

She stopped his hand with hers. There was a struggle in her eyes as she regarded him. He sensed some contest being fought. Fear versus something he couldn't quite identify, and fear seemed to be winning. "The last guy to do that's in the slammer now. His three friends are too. You should know that about me. They kind of show up at bad times, you know?"

Frye looked at her, the sundry data falling into place like a ton of cold bricks. It had been a while since he'd felt like such an ass. Several hours, in fact. "I'm sorry."

"You didn't do it." For a moment, she looked a thousand years old. "There's just a whole lot of bad precedent staring you in the face."

"I'm sorry. I—"

"That's one thing I don't want from you right now." She looked long at him.

"What do you want?"

"I don't know yet."

"Let me know when you do."

"One thing you ought to understand up front is I'm not like anybody else. I've got some territory there aren't maps to."

"You're not the first one who got lost."

"I suppose not. But I'd feel a little better if I could call you."

Frye thought this one through. "As in, don't call you?"

"It's got something to do with control."

"Suit yourself."

"See you at the pageant, maybe." She turned and disappeared up the rickety stairway, shoes thudding against old wood as she climbed.

The MIA rally was breaking up by the time Frye got there. He was just in time to see Lucia Parsons getting into a limousine double-parked on Coast Highway, and to pick up a flyer that listed private and corporate supporters, along with a form for joining and giving money.

Edison and Hyla were donors. So was Bennett. So was the Frye Ranch Company.

Frye looked up to see Burke Parsons, hat in hand, slogging through the sand in his cowboy boots.

"Haw, Chuck."

"Burke."

Parsons wiped his brow, and looked out to the water. "Seems like everybody I know's trying to get somebody back."

Frye nodded, assessing Parsons. He was tall as Frye, thicker, ten years older. Same curly black hair as Lucia, just shorter. Something about the eyes seemed slow. They focused lazily, then bore in.

"Any news on Li?"

"Bits and pieces."

"Well, I did what I could to help Benny, but he ain't much in the mood for help these days. Kinda like told me to take a hike, is what he did."

"The pressure's getting to him."

"I guess. Any luck on a new job? I miss your boxin' stuff in the *Ledger*."

"I'm working on it."

Parsons turned to watch the limousine roll up Coast Highway. "I go to these rallies when I get time off work. I like to sit back with the crowd and just listen. You know, this'll sound dumb, but being proud of your own blood is just about the best—well, second-best—feelin' there is. My goddamn twin sister. She gets another ten grand raised for her and her assistants, and it's back over to Hanoi next week. She's just real sure the government's about to break down and admit they've got some of our boys. Admit they've *found* some of our boys, is what they'll do. And if she gets Congress to pass that aid package for Hanoi, that'll make the dealings go real smooth-like. They want those dollars, same as anyone else. That's why she was telling everyone to write their reps. I don't know where she gets the energy, Chuck. I really don't. I'm just proud as all get-out."

"You ought to be."

Burke wiped his brow again, frowned at the water, then looked at Frye. "Benny keepin' you busy looking for her?"

"I'm doing what I can."

"Well, if there's anythin' I can do to pitch in, just say the word. I'm busy, but I got time for friends. Benny has my number, and I live right down here in Laguna."

"Thanks, Burke. It means a lot, all of you pulling for her."

Burke nodded. "Fuckin' gooks. Ought to just ship 'em back

where they belong. Let 'em eat their dogs and grow their rice. Li and Hy can stay. They're real Americans, if you ask me. But the rest don't bring much to the party."

"I don't know about that."

"Me neither, Chuck. I'm just a little bit out of kilter about all this. But Li's a great gal. See ya around. Call if I can help now, hear?"

# CHAPTER 11

H E WAITED UNTIL EVENING TO find the Dark Men.

Pho Dinh was a simple noodle shop on Bolsa, a block east of the plaza. From the outside he could see rows of tables filled with young Vietnamese, a big white panel behind the counter with words and prices on it, and a slender man behind the cash register. The young men were dressed well, as always—loose jackets and sharply tapered pants, collars turned up, thin neckties, pointed shoes. So were the women—tight jeans and pumps, short coats, their hair teased and sprayed. Music blared. A group of boys clustered around a video game, heads bowed, silent and intense.

Frye walked in, feeling about as out of place as one can get. Heads turned; a pane of quiet seemed to insert itself between the din of the music and the low hum of voices. The air was hot and heavy with a sweet, oily presence. Sesame, he thought, and mint. The locals are not overly friendly tonight. People stared. He started back, searching for Loc.

When he finally saw him—at a corner table with three other boys his age—Loc had already spotted Frye. He simply sat there and looked through him, then turned back to his friends. He had on a dark gray shirt, a black coat and tie. Frye stepped to the counter, ordered five beers for the table, paid up and walked over. He sat down. "I want my cigars back."

Loc spoke to his friends in Vietnamese. No one had acknowledged Frye yet; he had the odd feeling that perhaps he wasn't there, that he had become an invisible man. "Some people saw you go in. I've got sworn statements. I've got pictures of you. I'll go to Minh if I have to," he lied. "But I'd rather not."

Loc stared at him. "Who are you?"

"I live in the house you wrecked yesterday afternoon."

The four consulted quickly again in Vietnamese; Frye sensed a genuine puzzlement here. A waiter delivered the beers and five glasses filled with ice. When he left, Loc leaned forward and spoke quietly. "Do you know where they are? My brother, Duc, and my friend?"

"No. I just know you've got my box."

Loc poured his beer into the glass without looking at it. The boy next to him, wearing a black leather necktie, lit a cigarette with fingers thin as fork tines. Loc leaned back. "What do you know about Duc?" he asked.

Frye reached into his pockets and dumped the bracelets that Stanley Smith had given him onto the table. "Not a thing. But maybe I can help."

Loc studied them like a poker player with two pair would study a winning straight. Then he handled the bracelets lightly and looked at Frye. One of the other boys stopped his beer glass halfway to his lips, and stared. "We can't talk here."

Frye stood.

He trailed them out of the noodle shop, then across the parking lot to a beat-up station wagon. The lights of Saigon Plaza glowed in the near distance, and Frye could see the elaborate archway posed against the darkness. Loc ordered his three friends into the back seat of the car, then headed for the driver's side. "We ride around and talk," he said.

This looks like a real bad idea, thought Frye. "Just you and me," he said, pointing to the back. "Get rid of them."

Loc offered a wry smile. "You don't trust us?"

"No."

Loc brought out a cigarette and lit it. He hesitated, then spoke to the boys. They climbed back out, staring at Frye with insulted dignity. Loc said something; they mumbled apparent approval.

Frye walked to the driver's side and stood in front of Loc. He could feel his chest thumping against his shirt. "Leave the gun."

"I have no gun." Loc held open his coat, then grasped each side pocket in a hand and squeezed the material together. "Clean."

Frye got in.

Loc backed out of the lot while his two friends stood and watched. The big car heaved onto Bolsa, heading west. "Let me see the bracelets again," he said.

Frye put them on the seat between them. Loc picked up one, rubbed it, set it down. "These belong to Duc. Where did you get them?"

"They belong to me. And I got them the same place Duc did. How long has he been missing?"

Loc glanced at him, his hands on the steering wheel. The big coat dwarfed him. "You're from Lawrence. You try to trick me."

Frye wondered who Lawrence was. It wasn't the time to ask. Play along, he thought. "I'm not. I just need that box back, Loc. That's the truth."

Loc drove past Saigon Plaza. Frye looked out at the big lions guarding the entrance, the archway, the streetlamps. When he turned back, Loc was staring at him. "If you're not from Lawrence, how do you know my name?"

Frye explained the photo in Eddie Vo's room. "My name's Chuck."

Loc remembered. "I need my brother back, and that's the truth. You're from Eddie, aren't you?"

"I told you, Loc. I'm not from anybody. You took my box and I need it back." Even if they've made a copy of it, Frye thought, at least I'll have something to give back to Bennett. "I'll give you a hundred bucks for it."

Loc steered the wagon north on Beach Boulevard, running a red light on the turn. At a break in the traffic, he turned left into Westminster Memorial Park. Frye looked out at the trees, the gently sloping grounds, the picnic tables, and barbecue stands.

Loc pulled into a parking spot and killed the engine. "Let's walk," he said, reaching for the door.

"Let's stay right where we are," said Frye.

Loc turned back to Frye with a huge revolver in his left hand.

He cocked it—Frye could hear each part moving into place, followed by the definitive, lower click of the trigger locking—and placed the barrel against Frye's ear. "You don't understand anything," said Loc. "Now we will walk."

"A little fresh air might be nice."

Loc followed him out the passenger door, the gun pushed hard into Frye's side. "That way."

They moved down a path, past the park's restrooms. Frye's legs felt like old wood. A young Vietnamese couple passed them, moving off the walkway when they recognized Loc. Frye could see a table and benches in the dim lights as they cut across the park toward the north end. When they got to the picnic area, Loc pushed him onto a bench. He stepped back and with one hand produced a cigarette and lighter. The other one stayed in the pocket of his coat. Frye watched the orange flame illuminate Loc's thin, hard face.

"Where is he?"

"I told you, I don't know. How long has he been gone?"

Loc puffed on the cigarette. "Since Sunday. Where did you get his bracelets?"

"They're not his. Smith gave them to me."

"You are a friend of Smith?"

"Not exactly."

"But you are a friend of Eddie Vo."

"No more than you are."

Loc stepped forward, grabbed Frye's hair, and jerked back his head. The gun barrel found his neck. "Why did you go to him then?"

Frye looked up at the fierce face. Loc's flat-top seemed a foot and a half high. A cloud of smoke lowered into his eyes. Frye could feel his stitches yawning. He realized now that if he played his cards just right, Loc would kill him. "I was looking for Li Frye. I went to Stanley and found Eddie, too."

Loc cinched up on Frye's hair. "What do you care about Li Frye?"

"She's my sister-in-law."

Loc stared down at him, cigarette dangling. He released Frye's hair and stepped back. "You are Bennett Frye's brother?"

Frye nodded.

"What's this shit about a box I have?"

Frye looked at Loc, wondering if this boy would give an inch. "Some friends saw you go into my house, Loc. Nice job—you creamed it pretty good. I don't care about the house. I need the box back. It means a lot more to me than it does to you. Name your price."

"What's in it?"

"Shit, Loc, you don't even know?"

"It was just a job, man."

"For Lawrence?"

Loc studied him. "That's right."

"Did you already give it to him?"

Loc nodded.

Frye groaned. That video tape keeps getting farther away, he thought.

"What was in it, Frye?"

"It was personal. It doesn't mean anything to anybody, except me. And whoever in hell Lawrence is." Frye looked out to the darkened park. An older couple walked a tiny dog down the sidewalk. "Nice job with the Christmas lights, Loc. A very festive approach to residential burglary."

"Christmas lights were the first thing about this country I liked. You're really Li Frye's brother-in-law?"

"Really." Frye watched Loc pocket the big weapon, then light another cigarette.

"Man, I wouldn't have ruined your house, if I knew that. I love Li Frye."

"Me too."

"Ever heard 'Lost Mothers?' "

"Of course I have."

"That's my favorite."

"I'm glad you're such a fan, Loc. It's really doing me a lot of good."

Loc sat down on the bench. He called something toward the trees and his three friends materialized from the darkness. Frye turned to watch them approach.

"I believe you, Frye. Now what do you know about Duc?"

"I told you already. Nothing. The deal was that Lawrence would locate your brother, if you got that box for him?"

Loc nodded. "Duc disappeared Sunday afternoon. He and another Dark Man went out. They missed a party I had on Sunday night. They did not come home. They missed work on Monday . . . and lunch. He never misses lunch. He is like a dog. If I don't find him soon, he will do something. He can be talked into anything. He's a fool."

"When did Lawrence talk to you?"

"Yesterday afternoon. He came to the restaurant. He said that it was Ground Zero that took Li Frye, and my brother and my friend, too. He said Eddie Vo would kill them, but he could prevent that. But he wanted something in return. Something that would save Duc's life. It was easy to get. And Lawrence promised that Duc would be free soon."

"That's a pretty thin proposition, Loc."

"Lawrence wasn't asking much, in return for what he promised. I knew right away that he was dangerous. What choice did I have?"

"You could have gone to Minh."

"I don't trust Minh. Then Duc would die and Li would be gone and it would be my fault. Li helped bring Duc over from the camps."

Frye watched Loc toss his cigarette. The boy seemed to diminish into his big black coat. What Frye saw now was a scarred, skinny kid—a hundred and thirty pounds of anxiety under a wild haircut. "How did you get the box to Lawrence?"

Loc eyed him sullenly. "No."

"Where is he? I need that thing real bad."

"Lawrence said that Duc would die if I talked."

"When was he supposed to get Duc free from Eddie?"

Loc sighed and looked down. "This morning."

"Then you got screwed, Loc."

Frye stood up. Loc's friends sprang back, hands moving inside their jackets. Loc snapped something at them and they edged away.

"Loc, you know Eddie. If he even has Duc and Li, where would he keep them?"

Loc shook his head. "I've looked everywhere I know. Twice. Now Eddie has vanished, too."

"Do you really think Eddie arranged the kidnapping? Do you think he could have done it?"

"Eddie is crazy enough to do anything. Minh would have him now, if not for you."

If not for me, Frye thought. "If we can find Lawrence, maybe he can lead us to Duc. And Li."

"He'd kill you. I could see it in his eyes."

"What's he look like?"

"Tall as you, but stronger. Dark hair and mustache. Very handsome, like a movie star without the smile."

"Where can I find him, Loc?"

"I don't know."

Frye sat back down. "Okay, you won't go to Minh because you don't trust him. What *are* you going to do?"

"I was going to ask General Dien. He is the most powerful man in Little Saigon."

"And?"

"He is . . . not to be trusted."

"And what's happening to Duc while you wait? Or to Li Frye?"

Loc stood glowering above him. "You insult me."

"I'm trying to get my box back, for chrissakes. If I can find Lawrence, I can get it. Maybe he doesn't know squat about your brother and Li, but maybe he does. It's worth a try, isn't it? He used you, Loc. Use him back."

The look in Loc's eyes was half terror and half hope. He looked at his friends, then back to Frye. "You will help me find my brother."

"I need Lawrence."

"I put the box in a brown grocery bag, as he told me. I brought it to the restroom here and left it. I got in my car and drove away. But I drove to another place and watched with binoculars. A few minutes later, a limousine arrived. It was General Dien's. I am sure of it. Then a man went to the bathroom. When he left I went in and the bag was gone."

"Did you see the general?"

"No."

"What time?"

"I delivered the box at yesterday night. A few hours after I broke into your house."

"Did Lawrence put you up to burning out Ground Zero Records, too?"

"No. That was my own idea. Frye, I would not have disturbed your house if I knew it belonged to Li's relative."

"Where can I get a hold of you?"

"Call the restaurant. They will know."

They took the same path back to Loc's station wagon. The other Dark Men vanished into the trees. Loc dropped off Frye a block from Pho Dinh.

Frye leaned into the window. "Was Duc wearing a pair of red tennis shoes on Sunday?"

Loc nodded. "I bought them for him. Who cares?"

"One of the kidnappers wore the same thing."

Loc glared up at Frye. "Duc is a fool, but he wouldn't hurt Li."

"Where was he going when he disappeared on Sunday?"

"To see the Dream Reader."

"About what?"

Loc shrugged and lit a cigarette.

So, Frye thought, someone else went near the Dream Reader and never came back.

Like Li and her two escorts.

Like Eddie.

Like how?

Michelsen and Toibin were sitting in a car outside Bennett's house when Frye drove up. Crawley was in the living room, sitting by the telephone. "He's at the office, Chuck. Be home in an hour. You can wait here until he's back."

"This can't wait."

Frye was scrutinized by the FBI men as he went back to his car and started it up.

The commercial division of the Frye Ranch Company had been moved to Westminster at Bennett's insistence, to the displeasure of Edison. The suites were on Bolsa, in the Cal-Asia Building, a block from the heart of Little Saigon. Frye parked, looking at the huge glass facade. A fountain gurgled in front of the main entrance, surrounded by pine trees carefully pruned to offer an oriental bonsai effect. He could see the shops and restaurants through the glass walls. Bennett's van was in the space reserved for it.

He took the stairs to the Frye Ranch lobby on the third floor. Almost eight, he thought, but still bustling like always. Bennett was notorious for working his people late and paying them well. Erin, the receptionist, looked at Frye while she talked to one caller, punched another call through, and tried to get to still another blinking light at her switchboard.

He nodded in sympathy and walked past her. The property management suite still hummed with activity. Middle management types cruised past with the long strides of the indispensable. As he walked past Development—Industrial/Commercial, Frye noted three shirtsleeved architects hovering over a drawing that was spread out on a table. The division flack, Pincus, blew around Frye and into the executive wing. The walls were decorated with seascapes and occasional full-color photo blowups of Frye surfing choice breaks around the world. He stopped to consider a shot of himself casually executing a risky off-the-lip maneuver on a Sunset Beach monster. He stopped, admired his handiwork for a moment, then walked down the hall toward Bennett's suite.

The door was shut but he went in anyway. The receptionist's desk was neatened and vacated for the night. Strange, Frye thought, Benny's always the last one here. Stepping down the hall, he could hear his brother, speaking loud and clear, as if over a very bad, or very long connection. Frye paused just outside Bennett's door.

*"Yes . . . that's exactly what we need to know . . . is Xuan's itinerary still valid? What about kilometer twenty-one?"*

Frye leaned closer.

*"It will leave tonight and be through Honolulu by morning . . . tell Kim to listen to the goddamned tapes, will you? Give her my love and courage . . ."*

The shipment, thought Frye, the supplies from the Lower Mojave Airstrip.

Bennett hung up and Frye pushed through the door. His brother sat on a stool at a drafting table, hovered over a model of the Laguna Paradiso. At work, Bennett dressed in a suit, wore his prosthetics, and used his crutches. Frye looked from his brother to the tiny Laguna Paradiso with its miniature homes, retail centers, hotels, marina, and the trolley designed to take residents down to their own beach without having to walk.

"We're going to get her back. I can feel it."

"We got a problem, Benny—"

"It can wait. Now this is from Lansdale again. Michelsen and

Toibin won't talk to me, but Lansdale leaks it to Pop. The gunman wasn't a local, Chuck. He was from San Francisco. He left there two weeks ago; told his wife he had work in Garden Grove. He was a cook by trade, so I've got Arbuckle trying to find a local employer. So whoever put this together used some out-of-town talent. And we've finally got something from Eddie's car. They found one of Li's fake fingernails under the seat, and she got hold of someone pretty good with it. It had torn skin under it, and type O blood. They're still looking for medical records on Eddie to type him. Mixed in with the skin were a few splinters of wood. It was ebony, and it was finished with a good lacquer. They think from a club maybe, or a knife. Maybe a gun handle. You see anything like that in his house? Anything at all?"

"No."

Bennett paused. "Chuck, I need the box I gave you. Bring it by in the morning, before eight."

Frye took a deep breath. "I don't have it. It was stolen out of my place yesterday afternoon."

"No. Say that isn't true."

"It's true."

Bennett looked at him. Frye could sense the rage percolating inside his brother. Then Bennett took a deep breath. "Of course it is. Explain."

Frye told him of the Dark Men, Denise's drug-hazed account, how it had been corroborated by Loc. "He's sure it was General Dien's limo. Do you know a Lawrence who looks like that?"

Bennett shook his head. For a long moment he stared down at the miniature replica of the Paradiso. Then he climbed off the stool, steadied himself on his crutches, and swung past Frye into the hallway. He stopped and looked back. "Come on, Chuck," he said. "Go home. Stay home. Just stay away. You can do that much for me, can't you?"

# CHAPTER 12

THE TUYS' HOME WAS SMALL and neat, on a quiet cul-de-sac two blocks north of Saigon Plaza. A hedge of hibiscus ran along the front. Frye thought of his ill-fated tryst with the Mystery Maid, which culminated beneath just such greenery outside his own house. He thought too of the Lower Mojave Airstrip, and of the quiet presence of Tuy Xuan as he sat in the barren terminal with his computer. Cases of tapes. Crates of arms and legs. DeCord taking pictures of it all, and Bennett tracking it from his office phone. Frye went through a gate and down a walkway to the front door.

Tuy Xuan greeted him with a controlled smile, and offered his hand. His eyes were magnified by thick glasses. "I am very glad you are here," he said. "Please come into my house."

When Frye called him Mr. Tuy, the man shook his head. "You call me Xuan," he said.

Madame Tuy and the four daughters were sitting in the living room. Xuan introduced them from the oldest down: Hanh, Tuoc, Nha, and Lan. Nha brought Frye a beer, stared straight into his face for a brief moment, and then looked away. He could see a little of the parents in each girl, the fine skin and lovely deep eyes. Nha was the tallest and most assured. Her grace was easy—half a woman's, half a girl's. Lan was toylike, diminutive, perfect. The two older sisters, Hanh and Tuoc, had permed their hair and wore blouses and jeans. Nha joined her father and Frye while the others disappeared into the kitchen. Their living room was sparse but tasteful: a lacquer painting of Saigon by the artist Phi Loc, an American sofa, a black enamel coffee table in the Chinese mode. An upright piano stood along one wall. Beside it was a small Buddhist shrine—a red altar loaded with fruit and prickling with sticks of incense.

Xuan was about to turn off the TV when the newsman announced that the FBI had joined the search for kidnapped singer Li Frye. The agent-in-charge was Albert Wiggins, a blandly handsome man of about forty, who said that finding gang leader Eddie Vo was of foremost importance. He held up a picture of Eddie: big smile, thin neck, a swirl of hair. He pleaded for community involvement. For a moment they all stood, watching in silence.

"Eddie Vo," said Xuan, "could not do this alone. It is beyond his capacity. He could have been used—he writes her love letters, he is improper—but he takes his boys and storms the Asian Wind like a commando? Your FBI is naïve."

"It is impossible," said Nha.

"He is a performer," said Xuan. "He behaves like a scene from MTV. Our young people, they are so eager to imitate the worst in your society."

Nha turned off the set at the next commercial. "They'll find him. Eddie Vo can't stay invisible for very long. Not in Little Saigon. He will talk. We will be one step closer to Li."

Frye nodded. "If Eddie didn't set this up, who did?"

Xuan eyed him placidly. "Enemies of freedom."

"Enemies of the shipments you make from the Lower Mojave Airstrip?"

"Yes, that is correct."

"Why?"

Xuan looked at Frye through his thick glasses, then stood. "Please come with me to my study. Nha, help your mother."

Frye followed Xuan down the hallway and into a small den. For the first time, Frye noticed that he walked with a slight limp.

Xuan shut the door behind them. There was a desk and reading lamp, a sofa, a bookshelf, and a large map of southeast Asia on one wall.

"Some things are best discussed in private, Chuck."

"I understand."

Xuan smiled. "When did the war end?"

" 'Seventy-five."

"Then you really don't understand at all."

Xuan stooped in front of a tall gray safe and dialed the combination. The door opened with a squeak. He squatted, reached in with both hands and removed a wooden board. He leaned it against the blotter on his desk. Frye looked at a second map of Southeast Asia, dotted with colored pins—blue, red, yellow.

"For many, Chuck, the war still goes on. There are freedom fighters in Vietnam, there are resistance leaders in Kampuchea, there are many refugees here in the United States, working for the day they can liberate Vietnam. The war is not over. Not until they accomplish their goal."

Frye sat down. Xuan pointed at his map. "The yellow pins are pockets of resistance. The blue are actual locations of the Secret Army. The red show the areas in which Colonel Thach is most active. You have heard of him?"

"I saw a picture of his face."

"He is an enforcer of state security, a brutal and clever man. He fought in the jungles during the war, and he continues. Do you know what he does to suspected resistance leaders? He decapitates them and places their heads on stakes for the local people to see. During the war, he did the same thing to those sympathetic to the West."

Xuan, his arms crossed, looked at the map as if it might offer some new discovery. "But what are colored pins on a map? What we cannot show is that Colonel Thach's influence reaches far into Kampuchea and Thailand—that he is feared and hated throughout Southeast Asia. When the Vietnam resistance became active in Paris, two of our leaders were murdered. In Australia, two more. Last year in San Francisco, a patriot was found slaughtered in his car. His name was Tranh Hoa, and he was a deep friend to me. We grew up together outside Saigon. He was closer to me than a brother. These are unsolved crimes, Chuck. No one was caught. They were organized by Colonel Thach. He was kind enough to remove the heads of his victims. It was the same as signing his name."

Xuan brought an envelope from the safe, sat down beside Frye, removed his glasses, and wiped them with a handkerchief.

Then he pulled out a small collection of newspaper clippings. An article from Melbourne told of the grisly discovery in some detail; *Le Monde* carried a picture of one victim before his death; the *San Francisco Chronicle* piece was surprisingly small, considering the horror of the crime.

"Do not look for the name Colonel Thach," said Xuan. "To connect him is beyond the authorities. His men are well-trained and financed."

"Would he send his men to Little Saigon?"

"That is my belief."

"To take Li and choke the supply line to Vietnam?"

Xuan nodded. "It is not terribly complicated, when one looks at it from this angle."

"But why send his men to California when she goes into Vietnam—with the supplies?"

Xuan nodded. "Colonel Thach is out to crush the resistance, Chuck. To do that, one must crush the spirit of freedom. When terror reaches into Little Saigon, Hanoi is achieving its goal. Consider this from Colonel Thach's perspective. Here is Li Frye, a beautiful and talented singer. A woman who has the hearts of the refugees. A woman who dresses in fine Western clothes, who wears jewels and perfume. A woman married to an influential businessman. Thach imagines them going to lavish parties together. He imagines them being written about, photographed. He sees her walking in the shoes of privilege. What greater statement of power than to tear her from her own home?" Xuan leaned forward, put out his hands, and slowly clenched his fists. "What greater power than to crush her in front of her people? And remember, Li grew up in the jungle. She is popular in the countryside and difficult to catch. One of the sad realities of your free society, Chuck, is that people are easier to kidnap or assassinate. Look to history for proof."

Frye considered. Slowly, what Tuy Xuan was saying began to sink into him. "If it was Thach's men—then Li will be . . . she's . . . dead."

"We are prepared for that possibility, but no, that is not certain. I believe Thach's men will always sign his name. They want us to know that they will pursue us to the ends of the earth. That Li has not been heard from is, in a way, positive news. It means that they have . . . other plans for her."

"Like what?"

Xuan folded the clippings back into the envelope. "I cannot guess, Chuck."

"But why? You send supplies, medical stuff, arms and legs. Why send killers thousands of miles to stop that?"

"What we send is not the point. You don't understand the tactics of the Hanoi government, or the methods of Colonel Thach. More important than the supplies is Li herself. Her music. Her stature and reputation. She is a symbol of freedom, Chuck. To remove her is to remove hope. Imagine the heaviness of heart, when innocence and hope are destroyed. When our leaders in Paris were murdered, the community shrank back in fear. Afraid to show their faces. What breaks the will of a people faster—to have their soldiers killed, or their towns and cities ruined?"

Frye considered. "Have you gone to the police, the FBI?"

Xuan nodded and pointed out the window to the sky. "To them, mine are the theories of an old man. They think my head is in the clouds. Besides, what evidence can I provide, except for what I've told you? None. They are doing what they can do to find local men who may have helped. But the true instigator is many layers, many thousands of miles away right now."

"Local men, like Eddie Vo?"

"Oh, yes. The young people are so easy to influence. So easy to manipulate."

Frye considered. "What does Nha do for the resistance?"

"Many things, Chuck. Her English is nearly perfect and she is good with numbers. She helps me account for shipments, helps me deal with suppliers. At the university, she attempts to educate her peers." Xuan sat down. "In my best dreams, I see her doing for our people what Li has done. A symbol of hope. She has the fierceness of the cause behind her. I did not indoctrinate her. It is her spirit. There are few of her kind among the younger people. They are our future."

"Like Nguyen Hy?"

"Yes. His Committee to Free Vietnam is a good thing."

"What about General Dien?"

Xuan shook his head slowly. "He is like a branch gone bad. He sucks nourishment from the soil and turns it into more disease. For years he collected money in the name of freedom, and little came of it. He is a wealthy man now. You can do the mathematics yourself."

"Why hasn't he been busted?"

"The people's faith in him turned away over a long period. For a while, he was our apparent hope. The donations, the support? No one would accuse the general of being a thief. He made small advances for a short time. He always has a new plan about to be executed. The people cannot admit he is dishonest, it would demonstrate that they themselves are fools. The Vietnamese people are proud, Chuck. We will go to . . . unrealistic lengths sometimes, in order to save face. You should know that about us. The general is like your national debt. If we ignore Dien, our foolishness is not exposed. Slowly, people have seen that Nguyen Hy is the true expatriot leader. Support has gone to him. Now, only the very old still believe in Dien. But it is a fact, he is very powerful."

"He did what he could to stop that kidnapping."

Xuan nodded. "I am thankful for that. At heart, he is not evil, he is just greedy."

"Why have you told me all this?"

Tuy Xuan looked at Frye, eyes magnified by his thick glasses. "Because you saved my life, and I want you to know what it is you saved. And because the more people who understand our struggle, the better. You are a fine young man. I am an old man with a bad leg. But to tell you about my tiny, insignificant battles does my heart good."

"I never really knew that Benny and Li were involved in this. They never said one word about it to me."

"And now you can see why. Things in our arena are dangerous, Chuck. They wanted nothing but to protect you. Bennett has two lives. In one, he is a businessman, a man of money and influence. But does he live in a great home? No. Does he wear expensive clothing or drive big cars? No. The other Bennett is a soldier and a patriot. Much of the costs of supplies, he bears himself. He will be angry, when he knows I've talked to you." Xuan gave a little laugh, then placed his hand very lightly on Frye's shoulder. "I believe that you should know. And Chuck, I know what it is to be . . . outside."

"Outside of what?"

"Your family."

"What makes you think I'm outside mine?"

Xuan folded his hands and smiled. "It is something that I see in your face. In the way you behave with your brother. In the way you looked at him at the Asian Wind and stood up to hug him. In the way you go to him and he does not go to you. You come from a powerful family, Chuck. But you are not among them. You are outside." Xuan wiped his thick glasses again. "I mean no offense. I was outside my own family. I was considered too political. There came a time when I had to choose. I chose my country."

And what is it that I've chosen, wondered Frye. A surf shop? A cave-house? A wife I couldn't keep?

"No," said Xuan. "You don't have to choose. You are a country at peace. You are a generation of peace. Enjoy the fruits of that freedom."

I've done some of that, Frye thought. Maybe too much. "Benny paid for it, I know."

"Then make good with what he bought for you. Someday, I hope my people can say that. It will not be in my lifetime though. Peace and freedom are as far from Vietnam as the moon is from the earth."

"We got to the moon, Xuan."

Tuy Xuan smiled. "Yes, we did. What I've told you is for you, Chuck. Forgive my presumption about you and your family. Old men love the business of others, because their own is fading so fast."

"If Thach's men took Li, where are they now?"

"I think they are holding her. Where? Who can say? My guess is nowhere in Little Saigon. We are a close community. We talk. I believe they are somewhere else."

"Thank you, Xuan."

"Shall we eat?"

Dinner was immense and unending. Frye took instruction on mixing the proper ingredients: easy on the fish sauce, use the greens to make your own soup, plenty of mint and cilantro and bean sprouts, stretch the rice paper just right and it will stick to itself and make a perfect roll. The rice cake was thick and sweet; Frye ate three helpings.

"Nha is a writer," said Xuan. "She was very interested to talk to you about journalistic work."

Nha explained that she was finishing her senior year at Cal State Fullerton, with a communications major. "I do enjoy the reporting," she said. "But only when my heart is in the material. It's difficult to care about football games."

"Wait until you hit the rewrite desk on your first job," Frye said. "You don't know what boring is yet."

"If I get a job I'll be pleased," she said. "It's an overcrowded profession, I know."

"Well, there's one less reporter on the *Ledger* now," he said. Nha and Xuan both blushed and looked away. "Anyway, it's a good job. You'll like it. You'll learn to write fast and ask lots of questions. Think you have the personality for that, Nha?"

She smiled. Frye studied her creamy skin, the perfect red lips, her black hair tied with a white ribbon in a ponytail. "I can adjust. I've very good at that."

Xuan, fortified with wine, told of their escape from Vietnam, the long days on the boat, the near-starvation and final rescue by an Australian fishing crew. Frye watched the daughters glance anxiously among themselves, then lower their heads as Xuan mentioned the pirates who had attacked their leaking escape boat. "There were things too terrible to describe," he said quietly, and that was that.

Nha excused herself and returned with an empty champagne bottle. She explained that while her family floated in the Pacific, nearly dead from thirst, they found this bottle floating past the ship. They'd prayed that it contained something drinkable. She shook a tiny scroll loose from inside and gave it to Frye. It said "To Whoever Finds This Note: We Hope You're Having As Much Fun As We Are! Lance and Jennifer Gentry—Honeymooning in Hawaii—6/82."

Xuan went on to say how they had arrived in California with no money, no work. Only a few friends and Li Frye were here to help them get started. Frye considered the nice house, the new dining room furniture and the lacquer paintings of Vietnam. A trade, he thought: your country for your life.

The girls all spoke English well; Xuan's was fair, and Madame Tuy's wasn't good at all. They've come a long way, he thought: further than I'll ever go. Xuan thanked him again for pulling him down at the Asian Wind, for saving his life. An exaggeration, thought Frye, but I'll go with it. Dinner ended with a toast to him. It was Frye's turn to look down, and he caught Nha's steady gaze from the corner of his vision.

Something hit him as he sat there with this family, some glimpse of what his own was like when they were together, all those years ago. He wondered if they might be like this again, together without the swells of disappointment, without the unspoken battle lines, without the sharp memories of how it used to be and could never be again.

He excused himself, went into a bedroom, and called home. Hyla answered. She had entertained Mrs. Lansdale all day and tried to get Edison out of his cottage long enough to eat. "He's been there all day, poring over that big chart on the wall. Filling in things, putting question marks in the little boxes. How are you, son?"

"Okay. I just wanted to call and tell you . . . that I love you and I know this is going to be all right."

"I know it is too, Chuck."

"I'm doing what I can, Mom. I'm not gonna mess anything up."

"Chuck, don't be that way."

"I saw your flowers last night."

"When this happened to Li, it made me think of Debbie."

"Me too . . . put me through to Dad?"

Edison sounded like a linebacker breaking huddle. *"Edison Frye!"*

"Chuck."

"Sonofabitching FBI is all over the place and they still haven't found Eddie Vo! I got Lansdale with me here right now, and I told him he's a hostage until we get Li back safe and sound. Bastard's drinking all my gin."

"You've got news on my case?"

"They'll drop the charges. It took some leaning on my part, Chuck, I'll have you know that."

"Thanks."

"For chrissakes, just mind your own business for a while, will you?"

"I'm trying."

"You can die trying, son."

"There's no better way to go."

Edison barked something to the senator. Springer spaniels howled in the background. "What do you have on Minh for us?"

"His father was American CIA and he's still alive. One popular notion is that Minh gets information from him. The other popular notion around the department is that he's a lousy detective and got the job because he's a minority."

"Half a bloody minority. It's amazing we've got a flag left to salute in this country."

"Anyway, I just wanted to call and say I'm doing what I can. I'm doing that." Frye paused while his father told Lansdale to pour him another drink.

There was a moment of silence. "Pop . . . I want back in."

"Back into what, son? Jail?"

"Back into my family."

Another pause. "What the hell's that mean?"

"If we could all like . . . pull together."

"Been drinking again?"

"We'll talk later, Pop."

Edison slammed down the receiver.

Frye sucked in his breath and called Bennett, but one ring later, he hung up.


After dinner, Madame Tuy and two of her daughters rushed out to go to the movies. Xuan said he had work to do.

Nha took Frye on a walk around Little Saigon. The night was warm and filled with the smells of the restaurants, the chiming rush of Vietnamese.

The shop signs glowed brightly, the cars bustled in and out, and everyone seemed to know Nha. She introduced him diligently, but Frye was bad enough at American names. It was a pleasure just to watch her, this woman-child, filled with a beauty she scarcely knew she had.

Frye noted that she kept her distance from him, and that when their arms brushed against each other, hers would shrink away. But in the shop windows, between the flyers and posters, he could see her looking at him. Curiosity, he wondered—gratitude, interest? She told him of her studies, the books she was reading, the friends she had made. She kept asking about newspaper work. He told her what he knew, and insisted that she never write about boxers or fixed fights. When she smiled, Frye felt happy. "I could never do that as well as you," she said.

"Don't even try."

Nha bought him a red silk rose in thanks, she said, for saving her father's life.

"I didn't do anything but yank him down, Nha. Really."

"It was enough. He could have taken a bullet. We've come too far for that to happen."

For a brief moment, Nha put her arm in his. When a friend drove past them and honked, she took it out. "I'm not sure what to do with myself," she said finally. "In Vietnam, young people who are not married do not expose themselves."

"It's a little more liberal here."

"Are you ashamed?"

"I'm proud."

They stopped at Paris Cafe. The coffee was strong and black and sweet. Nha studied him over her cup. "American women are so confident. So . . . aggressive." She looked at him and, under the table, touched her hand to his. "What am I? I don't know. I'm not sure who I am or what I am."

Frye saw a young man hustling down the sidewalk, a shopping bag clutched in his hand. He was wearing sunglasses and a fedora, moving fast. "You're Tuy Nha. That's enough, if you ask me. You know that guy?"

Nha looked, shook her head. "You Americans are so simple sometimes. Kind. But simple. And bold."

"We've got home field advantage." Frye watched the kid move past the cafe, shifting his bag from left hand to right. The hat was pulled down over his face. Where have I seen that walk?

"Can I say I desire to know you?"

"Only if you mean it."

"Then what do I do?"

"Shit."

"What?"

*"It's Eddie."*

As Frye stood, he saw the Eddie's fedora rotate briefly in his direction. Vo broke into a run.

Frye jumped up, over the railing and ran through a crowd on the sidewalk. The hat weaved ahead of him.

He veered into the parking lot for a clean line of pursuit and was nearly flattened by a Oldsmobile. Ahead of him, Eddie cut through the shoppers, his left hand raised, steadying his hat. He dodged into a gift shop.

Frye ran in, took one look around and barged his way past a protesting clerk to the back room. The door was open. Vo fled down the alleyway, knocking over a trash can, looking back over his shoulder.

Frye jumped the trash can and watched Eddie sprint through the back door of another store. He followed. Two steps into the shop, he realized he'd been had.

Whatever it was that Eddie had picked up now slammed into the back of his head. Frye lurched forward and caught himself on a cleaning bucket with wheels, which rolled away and left him face-down on a hard floor. Water sloshed out, splattering over his arms. He rolled onto his back in time to see Eddie jumping over him, the police handcuffs still locked to one wrist.

Frye reached up and caught an ankle. Vo crashed down, twisting and kicking like a roped calf. His hat flew off.

Frye tried to right himself and drag Eddie toward him, but there was no purchase on the wet floor. Vo struggled and kicked harder. Frye clamped onto Eddie's leg as hard as he could, but he could feel it slipping through his hand.

He got a handful of sock, then a pinch of cuff, then nothing but his fingers digging into his own palm as Eddie scrambled up and hurled himself toward the store front.

Frye finally righted himself in the soapy water and wobbled to the storefront. Out the door and back into the plaza, he could see Eddie making an all-out dash across the parking lot. Straight— Frye guessed—for the Dream Reader.

He followed, turned a corner, and burst through her door a few seconds later.

She just sat and looked at him, apparently bored.

"Where's Eddie?"

"Eddie who?"

Frye threw open the door and went into the back room. A bed. A refrigerator. A Chinese calendar, a poster of Li, a small radio.

Vo wasn't under the bed, and he wasn't in the tiny bathroom. He looked up, he looked down, he went back to the front room and looked at the Dream Reader.

"Where'd he go?"

"Eddie who?"

*"Eddie Vo, goddamn you!"*

"Eddie Vo. He run fast by the window. I saw him. That way."
She pointed.

Nha spilled in, her eyes wide.

Frye kicked open the door and ran along the shops. Nha trailed behind him. When he came to the end of the sidewalk he jumped the cinderblock wall and looked out to the drainage ditch that ran behind the plaza. Moonlight wavered on the brackish water. The field was laced with power poles.

There was silence and darkness, and nothing moved.

He climbed back down, panting. "It *was* Eddie."

"Are you all right?"

"Goddamn that little prick. How can he just disappear like that?"

"He's just faster than you are."

"You're one helluva big help, Nha." Frye's breath came in gasps.

"If he's gone, he's gone. Come with me. Minh will be here soon and you'll be in trouble again."

"No."

Frye went back to the Dream Reader and asked to use the telephone. She was sitting at her small round table, as always, it seemed, watching the people pass her storefront.

Frye couldn't get Minh, so he told the Watch Commander that Eddie Vo was back in Saigon Plaza. He called Frye Island and told his father, who rang off immediately to call the FBI and Pat Arbuckle. There was no answer at Bennett's house.

The back of Frye's head was moaning in pain. He felt the lump with his fingertips. "Let's get out of here, Nha."

"Climb the wall and we'll cut through the field. You don't want to be around if Minh comes."

Nha unlocked the front door of her house and let them in. Standing under the bright kitchen lights, she examined the back of Frye's head, which she termed "battered." She wrapped ice in a towel and held it to his throbbing skull. "No one is here but my father. Let me see if he'll look at it—he's knowledgeable about wounds."

Frye sat in the living room while Nha went to the study.

A second later, he heard it.

The scream was high, full of comprehended terror. It was loud enough to sink into his bones.

He burst into the study to a vision so obscene he could only believe that he was dreaming.

Nha was on her knees, bowing to the floor and rising as if in worship. Her scream had risen in pitch to a keening that could come only from the darkest region of her heart.

Xuan sat on the couch, just as he had a few hours before, hands crossed on his lap, knees apart. His head was six feet away, resting on the desk blotter, glasses still on and eyes barely open, as if trying to read the small print. It looked as if his body had been dipped in a vat of blood.

Frye was sure that Nha's screaming and the sirens wailing in his own eardrums were enough to bring down the walls. Come down, he thought, come down and bury us and make this all untrue.

He stood there for a moment, blinking, married to Nha's screams. Nothing would go away.

# CHAPTER 13

FOR THE NEXT TWO HOURS Frye controlled events from over his own shoulder, a hovering, objective, third party to himself. It was just after one in the morning.

He got the other Frye to answer questions and control his urge to vomit. He tried to counter the other Frye's drowsiness and the constant grinding of his jaw. He watched with detached interest as CSI Duncan finally walked from the study, bearing a plastic garbage bag, tied and tagged. The gurney slid by silently a few moments later. The other Frye just stood there in front of him with tears running down his cheeks, and he thought: The kid needs a break.

The other Frye dealt with Minh rather admirably, he thought, answering his questions patiently, then finally standing up and telling the detective to go fuck himself and talk to someone else. The other Frye bummed a smoke from someone and went outside.

The other Frye watched as the FBI descended and Special Agent Wiggins in his lawyer's suit took charge. He nodded when Wiggins took him into one of the girls' bedrooms and explained that no one, repeat, no one must know that Xuan was beheaded. This, in order to catch the perp. He refused to sign whatever it was they asked him to sign.

The other Frye saw the horror in Madame Tuy's eyes as an agent escorted her and her daughters into a waiting car.

Both Fryes watched as they wheeled Nha to the ambulance on a stretcher, her body cold and pale as ice, a shock so deep that the faces of the paramedics said she really might not make it.

Then it was two o'clock. The two Fryes slowly joined again and melted into the bucket seat of the Cyclone. The car either moved, or the road slid under it—he wasn't sure of the mechanics—but Bolsa Avenue began to pass along the windows.

Little Saigon crept by on either side, a tunnel of lights and shops. First there were two of everything, but he wiped his eyes and then there was only one.

Outside the Committee to Free Vietnam headquarters, Bennett's van waited in the parking lot.

Frye pulled in and parked next to it. For a long while he just sat there, wondering why he was just sitting there.

He found himself outside the well-lit lobby. The door was cracked open. Frye tried it—locked, but not pulled shut. He went in. Posters of entertainers—Li among them, maps, three desks and typewriters, three phones, and a collection of cheap patio chairs. A South Vietnamese flag hung against the far wall. Another wall supported a military shrine of some kind: a glass case containing an empty uniform pinned to a backboard as if still occupied by its owner. The boots, medals, holster, pistol, and belt were all in place. A dark walnut door leading into further into the building was shut.

Frye stood there, trying to quell the visions that kept swirling before his eyes.

But displayed in a case beside the uniform were three photographs that brought them on even stronger. In the first picture a naked man was being led by two soldiers. Behind them were thatched roof bungalows and jungle. In the second, the man was kneeling before a man with a sword. In the third he was still kneeling, but his head lay on the ground beside him and dark streams of blood ran down his chest.

Colonel Thach stood above his victim in post-pivotal grace,

legs bent, arms and sword extended, like Reggie sending one out of Yankee Stadium. His face was a hideous grimace. Below the photographs was a simple card, thumbtacked to the wall, that said IN MEMORY OF GENERAL HAN, RESISTANCE LEADER—1935–1986.

Frye slumped into a patio chair, staring into the horrible face of the colonel. I'd give just about anything in the world, he thought, to make this all go away.

A muffled thud issued from somewhere beyond the lobby. Frye wondered why his heart didn't beat faster, why a surge of adrenaline didn't break loose inside him, but all he felt was numb. Another thud, voices.

He stood up, turned off the lobby lights, and cracked the wooden door.

The back room was a warehouse, expansive and tall, with open rafters and industrial lights hung from chains. There were shelves stacked with pamphlets and literature, rows of books, boxes and cartons of indeterminate content. A portable podium with microphone, a public address system, and a couple of television monitors were placed along the near wall. At the far end of the big room Crawley and Nguyen loaded crates from a pallet into a red van. Coffin-shaped, but shorter, Frye thought. Legs and arms. Hands and feet. Heads are not replaceable.

Bennett stood nearby, watching, a short automatic weapon in his hands. He held it up, sighted on some target in the rafters, pulled the trigger. Frye heard the dry ping echo toward him. Bennett placed the weapon into a crate and Donnell hammered on the lid.

Frye wondered at how unsurprised he was. Deep down inside, he told himself, I knew he was lying all along.

"That's the end of it," said Crawley.

Nguyen swung shut the van doors, wiped his hands. "We shouldn't worry. DeCord will change his mind. It's his job to be reasonable."

"He just followin' orders," said Donnell. "You shoulda seen his face when Benny told him it was all down on tape."

"Well, the fucking tape is gone, so hurry up," said Bennett.

He swung across the floor opened the door of the van. The special platform rotated out, and he climbed into the seat. Frye watched Crawley point in his direction. "Gotta lock it up?"

"I already did," said Nguyen, checking his watch. "Let's go."

Frye saw the big aluminum door rise, folding back into its runners. Bennett's van started with a roar and a puff of white smoke. When it was outside, the door came down and a moment later, the lights went off.

From the darkness of the lobby Frye watched Bennett's van emerge onto Bolsa and head west, toward the freeway. The invisible man in the uniform watched from beside him. Frye did what Nguyen should have done: closed the door all the way.

You lied to me, brother.

He walked to the Cyclone, unaware of what was around him, watching the van roll down Bolsa. He felt drawn to Bennett now like a moth to light, like a junkie to the needle, like a tightrope walker to the heights.

He wondered dully just how bad this could get.

He steered down Bolsa, Bennett's van mixing with the traffic ahead.

Traffic was light on the San Diego Freeway south. Frye stayed four cars back and in another lane. His head ached and his hands felt cold. Things kept jumping into the periphery of his vision— ugly things, things disassembled, shapes within shapes. He looked down and realized how hard he was gripping the wheel, tried to relax.

Westminster gave way to Fountain Valley, Huntington Beach, Costa Mesa, Irvine. Frye started shaking, so he rolled up the windows and turned on the heater. At Jamboree Road, Bennett signaled and got off. They headed toward the ocean. Corona del Mar was busy and the lights all wanted to blur together so Frye just let them, thinking—go ahead fuckers, blur all you want because all I have to do is follow the red taillights, the bouncing red taillights, there's too much red in this world, if everything was blue or green it would be a better place, no doubt about that at all.

Then south on Coast Highway along the hillsides and pasturelands belonging to the Frye Ranch, future site of the Laguna Paradiso—three hotels, twenty clusters of custom homesites, riding trails, an equestrian center, a yacht marina, and a shopping plaza the size of a small Central American republic.

Frye looked out his window. Shouldering moonlight, the hills stooped like peasants, humble, uninformed of their future. He read the sign as he passed it:

FUTURE SITE
## LAGUNA PARADISO
EDISON & BENNETT FRYE
A FRYE RANCH DEVELOPMENT

Bennett had stopped in a left-turn lane. Frye moved to the far right and sped past. In his rearview he saw the van wait for the traffic to clear, then ease across the highway toward the development entrance. Nothing more than a dirt road, he thought, winding back into the country. I'll just get on it, wind back and keep winding until the road disappears, then I'll get out and walk until the continent ends, then I'll swim until the water dries up, and when the water is gone I'll move through the air, like a vapor, a hawk, an angel . . .

He watched Bennett's taillights bounce toward the gate. A moment later he yanked his wheel hard and spun a U-turn. By the time he came to the gate and another big sign announcing the Laguna Paradiso, the van had disappeared over a hillock.

He killed the headlights, got out, and tried the lock. The dust from the van settled around him. The lock wouldn't budge. Just as well, he thought, they'd spot the Cyclone anyway. He backed the car up the highway, nearly out of sight around a curve, then wandered back, jumped the gate, and started down the dirt road.

The Coast Highway traffic was soon behind him. He looked ahead in the darkness for Bennett's van, but all he could see was the pale strip of graded earth blending into the hills. The smell of dust hovered over the road, along with the scrubbed aroma of sage and eucalyptus, a hint of oranges from the east, of ocean from the west. He stopped, turned his ear away from the onshore breeze: an engine died in the middle distance; doors opened and closed. The road climbed steeply over the next rise, leveled, then rose again. Frye stopped at the top and surveyed the meadow, wide and touched by moonlight. The van sat in the middle.

Beside it was a dark transport helicopter, rotor blades drooping. Crawley and Nguyen had swung open the van doors and started moving the crates into the cargo bay of the waiting chopper. Bennett stood nearby, with two men that Frye couldn't recognize.

He squatted behind a small oak and watched. It could have been fifteen minutes, or two hours. He counted the cases as they were loaded.

A family of skunks waddled past, not ten feet away, a stinking mom and three perfect miniatures. Frye held his breath and kept counting: twenty-six cases in all, heavy enough to require two men, even when one was Donnell.

When he turned to watch where the skunks had gone he saw the form on a ridge behind him, a kneeling hump with a large mirror of moonlight where its eyes should be. It was still as a rock. It gave off a series of softs clicking noises. Paul DeCord focused one end of the long lens.

Frye almost shot through the oak branches when the helicopter started, an earth-shivering whine that set the blades slowly into motion. Donnell was closing the van doors. Nguyen had already climbed in. The man that Bennett was talking to lowered his hand and Bennett shook it, then swiveled toward his van. Frye turned slowly back to DeCord, but only the ridge was there. Not much choice, he thought, but to stay put.

The helicopter engines accelerated, the blades slowly straightened, the meadow grass whorled and flattened beneath them. Bennett's van backed away without sound. When the machine lifted into the air, Crawley ran over and kicked up the flattened grass where the tires had rested. The van circled, headlights spraying light onto the meadow.

Frye knew he should press himself against the earth and put his face to the dirt. Avoid detection. Protect his night vision. But he just sat there while the chopper roared over, shaking the tree, raising leaves and debris. He closed his eyes.

Then the pounding of the engines gave way to the minor workings of the van as it lumbered up the road toward him. A moment later it was past, a set of red taillights in the dust.

He leaned against the oak tree and finally opened his eyes again.

A road. A meadow. The muted hiss of traffic on Coast Highway. The future site of Laguna Paradiso, Edison and Bennett Frye, a Frye Ranch Development.

He turned on the television and every light in his house.

Cristobel had left a message that said: "Didn't mean to freeze you. I'm still touching the water with my toes. Cold sometimes. Thanks for bringing back my dog. See you soon. How about lunch tomorrow?"

He poured a huge glassful of vodka.

The nurse at Westminster Hospital would tell him only that Tuy Nha had been admitted that night.

He dragged his old typewriter from the cave region, set it up on the kitchen table, and started writing the story of Tuy Xuan.

He told about the killings in Paris, Australia, and San Francisco. He told about the arms and legs that Xuan and his daughter helped to ship to Vietnam. He told about Colonel Thach's vengeance and the tiny war the refugees waged against him, the kidnapping of Li, the secret photographers, the FBI, the flat-footed cops, the gangs that hated each other, the kids that loved Li.

An hour later he read it over, and all he saw were holes. What evidence is there that some distant colonel ordered Xuan's murder? That said colonel had orchestrated murders around the world? What witness could testify that the supplies Xuan sent weren't legs but guns? What did it matter that stubborn refugees who'd already lost the war were still at it in their pitiful, impotent way? What connection was there between the kidnapping of Li and the politics of Little Saigon? She was part of the richest family in the county, wasn't she? Who cared that people loved her and looked up to her—people loved and looked up to Jimmy Swaggart for chrissakes. And Tuy Xuan's study was torn apart, wasn't it? Who's to say that vicious thieves hadn't taken his savings—Vietnamese don't put their money in banks, you know—and signed Thach's name to divert attention from them? And how much money did Xuan take in, to purchase his "prosthetics"? Did a little get into his pocket, perhaps? And who knows what kind of shady deals the Vietnamese here really make, anyway. Maybe the old man had it coming. Maybe in the war, in his patriotic fervor, Xuan had rolled a few heads himself.

Frye could picture Ronald Billingham hovering over his desk, tossing the copy back to him and saying, "You can't accuse a man of murder when nobody saw him do it and he was halfway around the world when it happened. This is America, Chuck. You're a little too close to this one, buddy. I've got an art museum fundraiser tonight—cover it with a photog and don't drink all the champagne."

Besides, a story like that would expose Bennett.

Frye tossed the sheets to the lacerated couch.

Bennett called at quarter of four. "Wiggins just told me about Xuan, Chuck. I was out tonight or I'd have—"

"I know. You were at the Paradiso."

"Who told you that?"

"I watched. And so did Paul DeCord. With a camera."

"It's real important, Chuck, that you don't say anything to anyone at this point. I can't stress how—"

"I figured that."

The silence seemed to go on forever before Frye spoke again. "Do you know about Colonel Thach?"

"You can't spend much time in Little Saigon and not hear about Colonel Thach."

"Did Wiggins tell you what they did to Xuan?"

"They shot him."

"Wiggins made me swear I wouldn't say anything, but Xuan wasn't shot. He was beheaded."

"Jesus, Chuck."

"Thach could have engineered this, couldn't he?"

"I've been praying since Sunday night that he didn't."

"You've suspected since then?"

"You saw what left the Paradiso tonight, Chuck. Colonel Thach and I have been making war on each other for ten years now. I never thought he'd bring it to me."

Frye just stood there, part of him surprised at what his brother had been doing, part of him not even surprised a little. "What if he has?"

"Then we'll never see Li again—alive. And more people in Little Saigon are going to die."

"Who could stop him?"

Bennett waited. "Nobody has been able to yet."

"What about the Feds?"

"They won't even talk, not to me."

"Dien?"

"He's looking after his money and his reputation. I don't think he could touch Thach's people if he wanted to."

_____

**1 4 8**

"What about you?"

"I'm working on it. I have been for ten years. That's all I can say."

"I figured as much."

"Chuck? Do one thing for me. Be careful, very careful, about where you go and what you do. I've asked you to stay out of this, now I'm ordering you."

"I don't work for you, Bennett."

Bennett was silent. "No, I guess you don't."

Frye hung up. Who might know if Thach's men had come here? Who knows all the comings and goings in Little Saigon? Who talks to the people, has his finger on things?

Who?

*He is the most powerful man in Little Saigon.*

Now I've got another reason to see the General.

More exhausted than he'd ever felt in his life, Frye fell into bed.

# CHAPTER 14

ENERAL DIEN'S HOUSE WAS A big two-story brick affair, half a mile from Saigon Plaza. It was American Colonial-suburban, with a black iron fence around it, a video camera at each end of the semi-circular driveway, and two men in suits and sunglasses standing outside the gate.

Frye stepped from his car and walked toward the guards. They spread their feet and crossed their arms. Frye came up close enough to see his face reflected in the dark lenses. "I'd like to see the general. It's important."

One guard looked at the other, then shook his head. "General not home."

"Where is he?"

"With his people."

Frye introduced himself and offered his hand, but got no takers. "Do you know where I can find him?"

"What is your business?"

"I'm Li Frye's brother-in-law. I want to talk to the general about . . . the case. And thank him for what he did that night at the Asian Wind."

Again, the two conferred. The shorter one produced a telephone from under his coat and punched some buttons. A moment later, Frye heard the crackling report of a connection. The guard talked in Vietnamese, waited, said something else, then pushed down the antenna and replaced the unit on his belt. "The general is an extremely busy man, but he will see you now. He is in the Paris Cafe, in the back room, through the curtain."

The Paris Cafe was lunchtime-crowded. Frye angled through the tables, led by a slender maître d' in a tuxedo. Everybody stared at him. His guide held open the bead curtain for him. Two men in suits stood just inside. It was a small room, with four tables, a long lacquer painting on one wall and a stack of unused chairs by a service door.

General Dien sat at the corner table with three Vietnamese men. The general put down his bowl and looked at Frye. His face was leathery and dark, his mouth tight, his eyes brown and moist. The polo shirt was too big for him. It was buttoned at the top, but scarcely touched his thin, weathered neck. "One moment, please," he said with absolutely no change of expression. His flat eyes beheld Frye a beat longer, then he looked to his men by the curtain. He motioned irritably with his chopsticks. One stepped forward and offered Frye a chair.

Here, thought Frye, is a man who wears power as comfortably as a pair of mucklucks.

The general's guests excused themselves in humble voices, and disappeared through the rattling beads. When they were gone, except for the bodyguards, Dien offered a strong thin hand.

"Mr. Frye, finally."

"My pleasure, sir. I know you're busy."

Dien nodded, pulled out a silver cigarette case, and offered Frye a smoke. The waiter approached quietly, lit the cigarettes, and disappeared again. "Your brother is a brave man, and his wife a courageous woman," said Dien. "You have much to be proud of."

"Thank you. And thank you for doing what you could to help that night. We're grateful."

Dien nodded slightly. "Old soldiers are never too old to shoot straight. Li is more than a woman to her people. She is symbol of everything we were, and hope to be again."

Frye studied the flat, dark face. "It was carefully planned, wasn't it? The gunman on stage had a chance to shoot Benny and didn't take it. They were in and out in less than two minutes."

"In the confusion," Dien said, "it seemed like hours."

"Sir, I came to you for help. First, for something . . . general. Second, for something specific."

"What can I do?"

"First, do you think that Colonel Thach could have planned it?"

Dien leaned back and looked toward the curtain. The waiter came through a moment later with tea for both of them. Dien drew on his cigarette, old cheeks hollowing. "That is a very sensitive question, Mr. Frye. You see, there is no act that happens alone in Little Saigon. We are a close community, so one thing inevitably touches others. You will find no people on earth as strongly anti-Communist as the Vietnamese refugee. They have seen the horror. So, everything is seen as political here. Every whisper and every breath. Last year, a newspaper publisher was burned to death for running an advertisement believed to be pro-Communist. Before that, a community leader was shot for what he said in an interview about recognizing Hanoi. His words were misinterpreted, but that didn't prevent the bullets from entering his stomach. Not long ago, an editor in San Francisco and his wife were both killed because of the socialist leanings of their magazine. Things in Little Saigon, Mr. Frye, can be extremely volatile, when you mention the name Colonel Thach."

"I understand that."

"I explain it to show you why I am moving very cautiously so far as Li and Xuan are concerned. We are confronted now with a terrible dilemma. If one believes that overseas agents are creating terror here, and says so, those words can be explosive as bombs. If one believes that Li's kidnapping was done by elements wanting to . . . divert attention to the Communists, then words of skepticism can get one killed. So, you will find a difference here between what people believe and what they say."

"What do you believe?"

"Am I being quoted for your paper?"

"No."

Dien sipped his tea and tapped out his cigarette. "I believe that Hanoi has done this. I believe that they have organized their terror to break our spirit. I believe that Colonel Thach is behind what happened."

Frye considered. "But that's not what you've said on TV, or in the papers."

Dien nodded. "I would never say that. For one thing, it is too incendiary. It creates more fear. Second, it is not something I can prove. Third, if the true kidnappers are using Thach's . . . methods, to make it appear as if he is behind it, then I would be falling directly into their plan."

"But what if you don't say anything, and Thach *is* behind it?"

Dien lit another cigarette. "To my people here, I must remain moderate. I try to . . . mollify, to comfort, to prevent passion from boiling over. At the same time, Mr. Frye, I have my resources. I have twelve men very loyal to me—trained men, intelligent men. With the exception of the two at my home, and the two standing by that curtain, they are on the streets all day, every day, looking for Li. They are asking questions, interviewing. They report everything to me."

"What have you gotten?"

The general looked at Frye in irritation. He pointed at Frye with his cigarette. "I cannot tell if you are offensive, or simply tactless."

"Just tactless. And impatient. Have you gotten anything solid on Li, or Thach?"

Dien sat back and nodded. "Solid, but . . . distant. My people in Hanoi tell me that Colonel Thach has been especially busy and secretive lately. Trips at odd hours. Many days in his apartment, with only a few assistants around him. These are the marks of a man running an operation."

"Have you gone to the FBI?"

"And received their insults for thanks. The FBI has no jurisdiction in Asia, and no expertise. And one cannot help a fool like Albert Wiggins—he only resents it. But the fact that the FBI will not consider Thach is actually beneficial, for the moment. In their own way, they are doing what is best. It would be an act of folly to inflame Little Saigon. I only wish that they would bring in more men here, work harder in California. With enough people looking, it is only a matter of time until we find Li. Wiggins and four others, plus a couple of field officers talking with the local police? It is simply not enough. Not against Thach's men."

Frye looked at the two guards, still as statues, beside the curtain. Dien poured more tea. "And your brother? Has he made progress?"

"Some. He doesn't have much more than you do."

Dien looked toward the curtain, then back to Frye. "I deeply regret your brother's disrespect for me."

"He has his blind spots."

Dien sighed. "For years I financed the resistance in Vietnam. From my own pocket, mostly. Three years ago, my tiny band of freedom fighters over there was slaughtered by Colonel Thach. One of the boys was my son-in-law. Thach put their heads on stakes. He sent photographs back here to Little Saigon. It was then I decided my war was really over, Mr. Frye."

The general sighed. He seemed to diminish still further into his shirt. "I left Vietnam in great bitterness and with little hope. Here, in this country, my people gathered around me. They said to me, 'Give Vietnam back to us.' They asked me to fight. They asked me to be their savior. For a moment, put yourself in my position, Mr. Frye, and imagine what your answer would be. I can truly say I tried. I can truly say that I love Vietnam with all my heart. But you cannot fight forever. At some point, if you live, you simply accept exile and, once you have done that, you must begin again. For the last three years I have tried to strengthen my people from within. To Bennett and Li Frye, I am perhaps a coward. But in my heart, I have fought well and long and now I fade into peace. America is our future. I am trying to sink new roots here. I am not defeated, merely tired. Your brother's arrogance toward me is a thing of pain."

"We haven't discussed it."

Dien waved his hand. "I am too old to let the opinions of young men arouse me. I help my people as I can. I am at peace with myself. War is for the young. And truly, Mr. Frye, there can be no victory in Vietnam. The resistance is too small. There is no support. Hanoi is far too strong. We have lost. Now, we have the life that goes on around us. Do we participate, or live for days that will never come? I choose to help here, where I am needed."

Frye saw that the old man was trembling.

"I talk too much. Another affliction of the old. Now, you have my theories on this embattled city. You mentioned something more specific I could help you with? You need only ask."

Frye looked at the weathered face in front of him, the sad, wet eyes. The feeling he had now was of being poised at the top of that wave at Rockpile, looking down from a gut-softening height. You're committed. You're scared. You wish you could close your eyes. But you go for it. "There was a man, an American, hanging around Little Saigon on Monday, the day after the kidnapping. Dark, curly hair. Mustache. Good-looking. Did you notice him?"

Dien smiled wanly. "I don't know everything that happens here, Mr. Frye, despite what you may imagine. Please, go on. What did this man do?"

"He went to Pho Dinh in the afternoon and found Han Loc and the Dark Men. He asked to talk. He told Loc that his brother, Duc, was in some trouble. He told Loc that he could make sure Duc stayed . . . healthy . . . so long as Loc did him a small favor. Loc was frightened. He agreed. The favor was to steal a box out of my house. Loc stole it and delivered it, but Duc never got out of the trouble he was in. In fact, I wonder if he's still alive. Does any of this make sense, General?"

"I can hardly judge that, Mr. Frye. I know only what you tell me. But go on, it is interesting."

"It gets even more interesting. Now Loc has the box from my house, and he takes it to Westminster Park to hold up his end of the deal. He's supposed to leave it in the bathroom for the man to pick up. Oh, General, I remember his name now—it's Lawrence. Lawrence. Does that sound familiar to you?"

Dien's face showed no expression. Frye locked eyes with him.

"I know many men named Lawrence. What is his last—"

"I don't know yet. He never told Loc. Can you guess what happened next?"

Break point, thought Frye.

Dien shook his head. His thin lips pursed; smoke poured from his nostrils. He glanced toward his men at the curtain.

"Do you want me to go on?"

"Please, Mr. Frye. Tell me everything you know."

Inside, Frye laughed without mirth or joy. Tell me what you know, little boy, so I can figure out if I should have you for lunch or save you for dinner. "Let me explain a little something about myself, General. I used to be a reporter. I'm nosy. You see, I watched Loc rip off my house. I came home right in the middle of it, hunkered at my neighbor's place, and watched through a window while they totaled my home. I called the cops, but do you think they could get through the tourist traffic in time? So I followed Loc and his boys myself. An old station wagon. Loc drove. Straight to Westminster Park, where I watched him drop off a box I happened to recognize as belonging to me. He put it in the men's room."

Frye studied Dien, but there wasn't much to study. The leathery face had locked. The eyes looked amused.

"And did you go in and collect your precious box?"

"I didn't have a chance to."

The general smiled. Frye could sense the relief coming off the old man. Dien lifted his tea. "I'm sorry, Mr. Frye. I truly regret the criminal inclinations of some Vietnamese youth. I do not know this man, Lawrence. Your tale is interesting, but it goes nowhere."

Frye leaned forward, speaking quietly. He didn't have to act sincere, because he meant his next words as deeply as he'd ever meant anything in his life. "I was thinking you might help. It's extremely important, sir, that I get that box back. No questions. Nothing. Just the box. It isn't for me. It's for Li."

"What was in it?"

"That only matters to me."

Dien smiled. "But, Mr. Frye, I told you. I know no Lawrence."

Frye waited and watched. If Dien won't budge, he thought, I'll give him the final push. "The story has a twist ending, though. See, it wasn't Lawrence who made the pickup."

For all the general gave away, Frye thought, he might have been listening to a radio ad.

"I must tend to business now, Mr. Frye." Dien folded his hands and gave Frye a look of regretful closure.

"I guess you do."

"Thank you for confiding in me. I will keep my eyes and ears alert for this Lawrence. Perhaps something will come of it after all."

The general stood.

Frye stood too. "General, I just have one more thing to tell you. Li got kidnapped Sunday night, and I'll do whatever I have to to help get her back. Anything. I happened to like Tuy Xuan quite a lot. When I saw what happened to him, it scared me first, then it did something else to me. It made me mad. You're a big important man, and I'm squat. But I'll tell you this: I won't quit. Ever. I know you're a tough old bastard, but, General, you don't know what tough is until you've tangled with Charles Edison Frye."

"You are arrogant and a fool. You are worse than your brother."

"That's the nicest thing I've heard all week." Frye looked at the guards, who were now looking at him. He shrugged and walked out.

Two minutes later he had found Loc at Pho Dinh. He was with the Dark Men, five of them. "Dien knows we talked. He isn't happy with me, and he won't be happy with you."

Loc stared at him for a moment, then nodded. "Duc has still not come back."

"I wouldn't bet he will. Be careful, Loc. You can come stay with me if you want, get out of Little Saigon."

Loc shook his head. "I will wait for Duc. I have my friends. The general cannot surprise me now."

"You know where to find me."

"Thank you, Frye."

He picked up three newspapers at the stands outside. They all carried stories on Tuy Xuan, killed by intruders in his Westminster home. They all said he'd been shot. No suspects. Motive: robbery.

He tossed them into a trash can as he headed back to his car.

# CHAPTER

# 15

THE FBI OFFICES WERE IN THE
Federal Building in Santa Ana. Frye
waited in a nondescript lobby for thirty minutes before anyone
was ready to see him, while a receptionist answered the phone,
channeled calls, took messages.

She finally showed him to a back office. It was spacious, with
a view of downtown, an overactive air conditioner, and cool gray
carpet.

Special Agent-in-Charge Albert Wiggins shook Frye's hand
with federal authority, then pointed him to a chair. He was thin-
ner in real life than he looked on Xuan's TV set, with eyes a little
too close together and an undentable layer of confidence about
him. His coat was on, his tie was knotted tight. "I'm glad you
called this morning, Chuck. In fact, I was about to call you. There
are a few things I'd like you to think about. You feeling okay
today?"

Frye nodded.

Wiggins sat back. "First, what can I do for you?"

"I think you ought to pay some attention to the Thach angle.
I know General Dien has been trying to tell you the same thing."

Wiggins smiled. "What angle is that?"

"That Thach has engineered things like this before."

"What are you referring to?"

Frye told him what he knew of Paris and Australia, the beheadings, Thach's mission to obliterate the resistance. "I had a long talk with Xuan about three hours before he was killed. He more than suspected Thach's influence in Little Saigon. When he died that way, it was too much of a coincidence to ignore."

Wiggins nodded along with the whole story, as if he'd heard it just a few minutes before. "Yes, well, you can be assured that we've not been ignoring it either. Despite what your Vietnamese friends tell you. It's a fact that Hanoi has its eyes and ears in Little Saigon. We kicked a few loose back in seventy-eight, more in eighty. All small-time people. They were encouraged by Hanoi to send reports about what was happening, and to send dollars. You might know that Vietnamese currency isn't negotiable outside the country. The dollars are extremely valuable."

"I imagine."

Wiggins leaned back in his chair and linked his fingers behind his head. "You're a reporter."

"Used to be."

"You know, we're extremely cautious about this Thach angle, as you call it. Any mention of Colonel Thach is enough to stir up the refugees. They're terrified of him. You wouldn't be contemplating an article, a piece on him, would you?"

"I'm contemplating how to find Li, is all."

"I understand. We'll find her. But you have to know that by implying Thach's influence here, you would be creating a great amount of fear and causing a potentially dangerous situation in Little Saigon. In fact, we believe this is what Xuan's killers, and Li's kidnappers may well want."

"Who are they?"

"If I knew, I wouldn't be here talking to you, now would I?"

"You must have some ideas."

Wiggins nodded, leaned forward. "I might. And you, Chuck, are the last one I'm supposed to share them with."

"I know that."

Wiggins stood, crossed his arms, gave Frye a governmental stare. "But I'll do it anyway. I think—and this is purely a personal opinion at this point—that we're not looking at a political situation at all. We're not even looking at two related crimes. Listen. I think the kidnappers will come through with a big ransom demand, once they've sweated your brother long enough. God knows, between him and your father, the resources are there. When they do, we're ready for them. That's what Michelson and Toibin are there for. They're the two best ransom men we've got. The second those kidnappers try to pick up the money, we'll have them. I guarantee it."

Wiggins took a deep breath. "Coffee?"

"No thanks. I'm listening."

"I'll admit it, Frye, when I first heard about Xuan, I thought the same thing you did. Two prominent resistance leaders . . . removed in the same week. But I did my homework on Xuan, bless his heart. He's one of those Vietnamese who sees a Communist behind every bush, and remember this is the FBI talking. He organized his own secret police back in 'seventy-eight, to screen the refugees coming in. People were beaten. People disappeared. You know what he was saying then? Thach. Thach is behind it all. Guy had a regular fixation, Frye. And I've got evidence now that Tuy Xuan may have been involved in some questionable dealings with the local gangs."

"What kind of dealings?"

"He's an activist. He enlists support in Nguyen Hy's so-called Committee to Free Vietnam. They fund a 'resistance' over there. I'd speculate he got some funding from the gang kids' families, and the gang kids went to get it back. It's damn easy to throw suspicion, if you want to leave a signature. Look at yourself, it worked on you, didn't it?"

"Who? The Dark Men? Ground Zero?"

"I don't know, at this point. I'm not sure it matters. Let's just say we've got early indicators that Xuan and the criminal youth element were tied. So we're not talking politics here. We're talking plain old dollars and cents. You know something, Chuck? The refugees are smart. They know that they can point fingers at Hanoi and we good Americans will go along with them. We hate Communists in this country, don't we? Well, the refugees know that. They play on our own fears, and every time someone gets their pocket picked, they blame Hanoi. The gangs know that. Eddie Vo knows it."

"Gang kids beheading an old man? Hard to swallow."

"There was a gang working here in the early eighties. Their leader was infamous for doing just that. His nickname was Chop, for God's sake. So it's not hard for me to swallow at all. Unless, of course, you know something about Li or Xuan that you're not telling us." Wiggins sat down, looking at Frye innocently.

"Something like what?"

"The pipeline to Vietnam. The 'prosthetics' that Bennett and Li send over there." Wiggins smiled. "He told me he was sending over plastic limbs, and I laughed in his face. Which isn't easy to do to a man who hasn't got any legs."

Frye said nothing.

Wiggins smiled. "Hey—I don't care. I think it's great. Send all the guns and ammo he can afford. That's the question, though. How does he afford it? Where's he get the money?"

"You got me."

"Knew I would, Chuck. Just knew I would."

"Funny how we got back to politics again."

"Fleecing money from homesick refugees isn't politics. It's theft."

"General Dien is the master of that game, from what I hear."

"And Nguyen Hy is a close second. Bennett and Li are just a little too close to Hy's CFV for the . . . contact not to rub off. You know—sleep with pigs, you pick up their smell. And sooner or later, the suckers find out and what happens? Heads roll. So, if you've got any information on how that pipeline is financed, I'd sure like to know. I might be able to keep something like this from happening again. Talk about good copy, Chuck. You help me, and I'll help you on this one. We could show just who's taking money out of Little Saigon and where it's going—or not going. But if you've got any ambition to write about some Vietnamese colonel cutting off heads in California, Chuck, I have to ask you to run it by this desk first. Would you do that?"

"No. I'd end up with my byline on the same kind of lies you let the other papers print today."

Wiggins face darkened. "Chuck, let me put it another way. Stay the fuck out of Little Saigon and forget about Colonel Thach. I'll give you the first tip for your big exposé. The main reason we didn't release the MO on Xuan's murder isn't because we're afraid of starting a riot in Little Saigon, though that's a possibility. The main reason is that Colonel Thach can't even leave his apartment in Ho Chi Minh City anymore. He's in protective isolation—a better term for it is house arrest. The new Hanoi Politburo doesn't trust him. He's an old war machine and they know it, and they also know they can't control him. They've been sitting on him since June. His ice is too thin for the kind of skating you're talking about."

Frye considered. "That's exactly what Hanoi would tell you, if Thach were running an operation like this, isn't it?"

Wiggins sighed and looked at Frye as if he were a moron. "Hanoi didn't *tell* us that, Chuck. We've got more reliable sources than those lying bastards. So lighten up. Let the FBI do its job and you do yours. What the hell *is* your job anyway? Besides hustling Tuy Nha?"

"I don't have one, exactly."

"Well, you're so hot to trot, why don't you go find one?"

"I'm working on it."

Bill Antioch presided over the empty MegaShop, drinking his ever-present health shake. "Got you all signed up for the Masters at Huntington, Frye. Okay?"

"Okay."

"I'm also telling everyone you'll be at the showing of *Radically Committed* Saturday night. At the Surf in Huntington. Any truth to that rumor?"

"It's my movie, I guess I ought to be there."

"Gnardical." Bill gave him four comp tickets.

"How are we doing today, Bill, from a sales angle?"

"We've sold one bar of wax."

"Large or small?"

Frye surveyed the shop. Bill had straightened things, dusted, arranged the boxes and boards, taken down the faded Christmas signs, put the wetsuits back on the rack by size. MegaT-shirts were marked down to three for ten bucks. This stung, but Frye said nothing. The windows were clean. The first inklings of retail hopelessness crept over him as he reached behind the counter for the phone.

He called Elite Management and got the usual put-off from the receptionist. She said that Rollie Dean Mack would return his call, but Frye had heard that one before. He tried again to get the address.

"It's like no way, unless you have an appointment," she said. She sounded like a certified surf-bunny, about age eighteen, loose-jawed, heavy on the schwas. "We don't give out our business address unless we're expecting you. Elite isn't, like, geared to the *publuck.*"

Frye slammed down the phone. Then it hit him. "Advertising."

"Can't afford it," said Antioch.

"No. Elite ran advertising in the *Ledger,* on Wednesdays, so that means someone had to go over the veloxes with them on Tuesday morning."

"Cool."

He called the *Ledger* and asked for display advertising, Dianne Resnick. Dianne once liked Frye, who occasionally wrote puff pieces to make her advertisers sound better than they were. Frye did this because Dianne had great legs, and because exaggerating the virtues of hopelessly third-rate companies was just plain fun. He brought a desperate, manic enthusiasm to these pieces, which read like a cross between Hunter Thompson and Alexander Haig. The all-seeing Ronald Billingham had edited the hell out of them.

Dianne answered the phone in her sales voice, soothing and eager to please. Frye explained that he needed to know where Dianne sent the ad proofs for Elite Management. The pulling of these ads was understandably a sore spot with Dianne, who was now out fifty-six dollars and seventy-eight cents a week in commission. "You still make ten times a week more than I did, Di," he said.

"That's because I bring money to this paper. Any nerd can write copy."

"I did my best to tout those greedy mutants passing themselves off as businessmen. You have to admit that. It would mean a lot to me if you could give me that address, Dianne."

She sighed. He heard papers shuffling. She put him on hold for a full minute. "Okay, Chuck, here it is. For a company called Elite, they sure didn't seem to have much going for themselves. The receptionist proofed the ads, a little beach tart is what she sounded like on the phone. Anyway, it's Number Eighteen Palisade, up in Newport Center. I'm sure the receptionist will just love you."

"Rad."

"Like, woah. Any chance you're coming back? I really did like piece you did about my rug dealer being a Persian prince, and his a family held hostage by the Ayatollah."

"That one was true. Just nobody bothered to ask him. Put me through to Billingham, would you?"

"I think he misses you, Chuck."

Frye asked Billingham for his job back and Billingham said no. Frye told him he had a Pulitzer winner on a Little Saigon patriot who finally got tracked down and beheaded by Hanoi. Bill Antioch looked on with horror.

Billingham waited. "I read the papers, Frye. Nothing at all about anybody's head rolling. This kind of like watching that welterweight go down and calling it a dive?"

"It was a dive, and I can substantiate every word of it. Now this murder piece is already written. The slug at the top says Frye/*Ledger*. Cost you my spindly salary for a look at it."

"No can do. I've replaced you with a J-school girl already."

"What do you pay her, two-seventy-five a week?"

"Two-fifty."

"There should be a new rung in hell for editors like you."

"Give us a quote about how the Fryes are coping with the kidnapping."

"Get fucked, Ron."

"Go to another paper. Our circulation's dying anyway."

"I just may do that, and you'll be sorry I did."

"How come you need an address for Elite Management?"

He guided the Cyclone through the long thin shadows of the Newport Center palms. The palms were newly planted, a hundred feet tall and there were millions of them. Everyone had a different story of what they'd cost: some said three thousand per tree, some said twenty thousand. The idea was to make the place more attractive to shoppers and the palms were brought in, like relief pitchers, after twenty years of so-so consumerism.

On the afternoon that he was fired, Frye had sat in his car for an hour and watched them plant a few. The root systems, carefully bound in wet burlap, were the size of living rooms. Now the emerald grass of Newport Center had been rolled right up to the trunks and the trees looked like they'd been there all along.

Number 18 Palisade was on the west side of Newport Center,

in a building that housed a bank, a beauty salon, and a jewelry store. He climbed the stairs, looking in, each of the clients in a different state of beauty improvement. The hairdressers hovered over them, all elbows and chatter.

Elite Management was next to the restrooms. The door was locked, so Frye pushed the intercom button. The surf-bunny sounded half asleep when she asked who was there. Frye said he was UPS. The lock buzzed open and he walked in. The girl's desk plate said SHELLY—RECEPTIONIST. Frye smiled and watched her face turn sour at his lack of packages and brown uniform. She had long blond hair, a denim dress, and skin rich and dark as teak wood.

"You're not UPS, no way" she said.

"That's true."

"There's no reason for you to be here."

"Why not?"

She picked up an index card and read Frye the blurb about Elite not being geared to the public. He studied the office: a small room with two chairs, a desk, a Hockney litho on one wall, and a door behind Shelly. The door was shut. She had been brushing her hair. The brush lay on her desk blotter, trailing golden scraps. She finished the reading and looked up at him. Her face changed. "You're Chuck Frye, aren't you?"

"I am. And you're Shelly, right?"

She smiled and put her hairbrush in a desk drawer. "I heard you'll be at *Radically Committed* Saturday night."

"That's one of the reasons I'm here."

"Woah!" she squealed, "Like what's the deal?"

"The deal is I want to see Rollie Dean Mack."

"Oh, that's going to be hard, Chuck."

"Is he in?"

"No."

"When will he be?"

"Beats me."

"Must be in sometime."

"I've worked here all summer and I've only seen him, like, three times. I usually say he's in the field, 'cause that's what I'm supposed to say. But I wonder what a millionaire like Mr. Mack would be doing in a field. Think about it."

"Come on, I really have to see him, Shelly."

She brought out her brush and ran it through a couple of times. Her hair gave a static crackle, lifted out, and hung a moment. Her teeth were white as typing paper. "I'm telling you, Chuck. I sit here eight hours a day. I do my nails, then my hair, then my makeup, then I listen to the radio, then do it all again. I'm not allowed to talk on the phone to my friends or this would be great. Daddy got me the job. Anyway, I take calls for Mr. Mack and Mr. Becwith. I write the messages on this." She held up a one of those three-color memo pads that make a different color copy for each person.

He sighed.

Shelly kept brushing her hair and smiling. She shook her head. "Sorry."

This chick's no dummy, he thought. Harder to get past than a free safety. "Damn it, Shelly, I surf all morning and it isn't easy, you know? I gotta work at it, like everyone else does. I come in here to see your boss about a job and all I get is a run-around."

"I'm real sorry, Chuck. I love the way you surf. And the way you moon the camera in *Committed.* Can't wait till that part."

"So you're not going to let me see him?"

"I told you. He's hardly ever here. Neither of them are."

From the utter blankness on Shelly's face, Frye could only conclude she was doing her job and that was that.

"You know, Chuck, I was in Mega looking for a board the other day. I looked all around. Gotcha has good boards but too expensive."

"My stuff's better. How much you want to spend?"

"Not much."

"Shelly, we can work a deal. You let me see Mr. Mack and I'll give you a board at cost."

"Can't do it, Chuck. I *told* you what the deal here is."

"I'll give it to you for free."

Shelly's eyes glittered. She laughed perfectly. "I'd love a Mega board."

"Get me Rollie."

"I'll get you as close to him as I can. How's that?" She stood up and opened the door behind her. Frye walked into the larger room. Two desks and chairs, two round wastebaskets, two blotters, a couple of lamps. The office was a mess. It looked like the *Ledger* newsroom. Piles of paper on each desk, trashcans full, notices and bulletins thumbtacked to the walls. The blotters were scribbled upon. The desk calendars were on the right day. He flipped through Mack's, but found no hint as to where he might be. In fact, there was no hint as to where he'd ever been. Not a single note in eight months. His finger came away from the desk top with dust on it.

"Oops," said Shelly. "I'm supposed to dust every morning before they get here, but I forgot."

"Before they get here? I thought you said they don't come in."

"They don't. You know, like, dust before they got here if they ever did. But they never do. That's what I mean."

He noted the pile of yellow message slips on each desk. Shelly said they never told her to put them there, but she did anyway just in case they came in, and to cover herself.

"Who's your boss?"

"They both are."

"But you've never seen them?"

"Well, I've seen Mr. Mack like a couple of times. He was here when I came to interview. He asked me what I wanted to do for a career and I told him be a model or be in advertising, then he said I was perfect and hired me. After that, he's come in a couple times with little beat-up guys. I think they're wrestlers or something, but they're kind of small for that. He doesn't show up much. He's like independently wealthy, so why bother?"

"How do you know that?"

Shelly giggled. "Why else would you never show up at your job? And Mr. Becwith works nights."

"Yeah. So when you take the messages, how do you pass them along?"

"Mr. Mack calls in at nine, one, and four. Every day."

"From where?"

"Beats me. Why all the questions, Chuck? You must really need that job."

"You have a number to get him, say for an emergency, or a real important call?"

Shelly looked at him for a long moment. "I really think what I'm doing here is, like, getting myself into trouble. Daddy got me this job, ya know. I don't want to—"

"—Give me that number, Shel."

"Gawd, Chuck. Be cool."

"Sorry. I mean it, I'm sorry."

She smiled. "Okay."

"You've been a real help, Shelly. I promise I won't say anything to anyone about what you told me." He looked around again at the empty office, then helped himself to a business card from a holder on each desk. Shelly eyed him from the doorway, a little red-faced now, a little fearful, a little like a girl who's just been seduced. Frye felt bad.

"Thanks. One more thing, Shelly. Don't tell Mr. Mack I've been here asking questions."

"You don't have to worry about *that.*"

For a brief moment Frye wanted to hug her and apologize. "You come to Mega any time you want and pick out a board. Take whatever you want, and a MegaSuit too. No charge. Bill gives you any trouble, just have him call me. I'm in the book."

She brightened, started brushing her hair again. "Me too. Shelly Morris. Thanks for the board, Chuck! I always liked Mega the best, except you don't have any girls' stuff."

"We're working on that." He gave her a couple of tickets to the Saturday movie. She took them in a smooth dark hand.

"Will you tell him I was here, about the *Ledger* advertising? Just the advertising, not all the questions."

"I may be an airhead, but I'm not like completely stupid. I'll write on that pad that you came by about ads. That's all."

"Come get that board sometime, now."

"Thanks, Chuck. You really want to know if Mr. Mack comes in here, don't you?"

"I really do."

She deliberated. "I could maybe like sneak you a call when he's back in the office or something."

"Be careful."

"See ya Saturday night. If you act like you know me, my friends will think I'm cool."

"You're a good friend, Shelly. Does Elite have a fighter on the Sherrington card tonight?"

"We have *two.*"

"Mr. Mack be there?"

"He always goes when one of his guys is fighting, Chuck." She smiled and the phone rang. The wall clock said one o'clock. "You better go now."

Frye nodded and headed down the stairs. At a gas station he called Dianne Resnick to see if she'd ever actually laid eyes on Mr. Mack of Elite Management. She hadn't.

Neither had Ronald Billingham, who had taken Elite's advertising cancellation over the phone.

# CHAPTER 16

CRISTOBEL WAS STANDING ON Frye's patio when he drove up to the cave-house. She had an immense spray of flame-orange gladiolas in one hand and an envelope in the other. Her dress was short and her legs were lovely, and she stood like a woman who knew it. She had a purse slung over her shoulder. Frye's heart surged.

She watched him come up the walk. "I'm busted," she said. "These are for you. For bringing back Blaster."

As if on cue, the dog nosed around a corner, pissed on Frye's mailbox stand, and looked at him with absolutely no recognition whatsoever.

"Your dog's a moron. I love him."

"Careful. He's my main man."

"Wish I had one just like him. Thanks. Beautiful flowers."

Frye opened his door and let them in. When she walked past him he could smell the alcohol.

Cristobel sat on his couch while Frye put the flowers in a vase. He watched her while he trimmed the stalks. "You've got a choice between tea and straight vodka."

"Tea."

They sat in the living room. She took off her sunglasses. She looked at Frye, then at the flowers, then outside for the dog, then at the coffee table in front of her. "So, this is it."

"You nervous?"

"Not a bit. Why?"

"Your eyes are. Don't worry, I'm done with bad opening lines."

"I'd prefer to stay off that topic just now."

"Can do."

She drank off half the tea and checked her watch. "How's the case progressing? Any news about Li?"

Frye shook his head. "Just a lot of strings that don't make a rope."

"Like what?"

"Stuff that she and my brother were into. Things that . . . don't look good on a résumé."

"Cops have a way of finding out."

Frye wondered what kind of bureaucratic rack the cops had stretched Cristobel on. Four men. Inside, Frye shuddered. "I hear the cure's worse than the disease, sometimes."

"I wouldn't go that far."

Frye looked at her, wondering just how you handle a case like this. "All I feel qualified to say is the wrong thing."

"How about saying nothing?"

"Is that best?"

"I'm afraid so."

"What if at some point, just say for the sake of argument, that I wanted to get to know you better?"

"Skate over the silences. They're hard as ice."

Frye nodded. "I found this bird once that blew out of a tree in a Santa Ana. I couldn't find the nest, so I kept the bird. Little fleshy guy with no feathers and big eyes, like something from outer space. Anyway, I kept him in a tissue box and fed him with and eyedropper every two hours."

"What happened?"

"He died after the third feeding."

"What's the moral?"

"I'm not sure. It's been a bad couple of days."

Cristobel smiled, but it wasn't happy and she didn't seem amused. "I'll go now. I just wanted to say thanks."

Frye walked her to the door. She stood in front of him with her arms crossed and her sunglasses back on. "This isn't easy for me. I've never been in this position before. I hate it."

"You know where I live."

"Is that an invitation?"

"Yes."

She reached out and touched his face, then brought her mouth to his. Frye felt her purse fall off her shoulder and tug down on her arm. It was one of those kisses that seal off the outside world and make a better one, just between the two of you. His brain rang. His ears got hot. She was there, but tentative, willing but controlled. She sighed into him, then stepped back.

"I'm sorry," she said.

"Don't be."

She touched his face again. "You don't understand."

"Maybe I don't."

"It's quite a way from point A to point B," she said. "But I like long, straight lines."

Frye smiled. "I'm going to the fights tonight. Want to come?"

She looked at him uneasily. "I was going to see Steve Martin's new one. But, well, okay."

"Pick you up at seven."

Cristobel nodded. Blaster bounded to her side and led her down the driveway toward her Volkswagen.

He sat at his kitchen counter and opened the card. It had a picture of a wave on the outside, and Frye could readily imagine himself tubed in the thing. It looked African—Durban, he thought, or Cape St. Francis. Inside it said: "Thanks. You asked me on the beach what I wanted. I want a reason to believe in anything. Best—Cristobel."

He sat on the patio with Stanley Smith's manuscript in front of him. He checked his watch. Two hours until fight time at the Sherrington. I'll explain to Mr. Mack that I can retract the article, print an apology, anything he wants. A man needs work. And I could use a press pass, a WATS line, and some movie passes.

He found his place in Li's story and began reading.

Huong Lam, Lt. Frye and I began to meet once a week in the courtyard by the plantation. Often, Private Crawley would attend. Sometimes Tony, Lam's liaison officer,

would be present. The lieutenant always brought a
notebook but rarely wrote anything in it. He always
seemed pleased by my information. Sometimes it was
specific, such as the names of Viet Cong leaders, the places
they could be found, the exact location of new tunnel
entrances, which were always being built. Sometimes all I
had was a feeling that something was about to happen.
More than once I was correct. I would sense from the
nervousness of the fighters I entertained that something
large was to happen.

At the end of our fourth meeting, while Lam was
walking ahead of us to the jeep, Lt. Frye put a piece of
paper from his notebook into my hand. When I read it
later that night by my candle, it said: "Li—You are
beautiful to me."

I thought of him as I lay on my plank bed that night. I
could see his eyes, blue as the feathers of a *chai* bird.

About this time, Lam began to make advances toward
me. On our walks to meet the jeep, he would attempt to
take my hand. He would often arrive at my hut before the
scheduled time. He looked at me in certain ways. A
woman knows. He brought me a bunch of lilies once and
they were quite lovely, but I took them under a feeling of
obligation. My feelings toward him were good, but not of
love.

Soon, we began to bring food to our meetings. I would
bring red yams, tender bamboo, and eggplant. Lam would
always bring French champagne—two bottles—and he
never would say where he got it. I know he spent a lot of
money for it on the black market. It gave him pride to
provide such a luxury. Lt. Frye brought fresh bread and
often a meat of some kind I know was expensive. Then
Lam started bringing three bottles. He saw this as a
competition with Lt. Frye. We would spread a canvas tarp
on the ground if the weather was good, and if it was
raining we would go into the cottage.

Frye saw the three bottles of French champagne sitting on Li's
dressing room table. He wondered.

There was always a time when they would ask me to sing.
I wrote songs for these occasions. They were the

sentimental love songs that the Viet Cong no longer allowed me to perform. These songs, at the beginning, were written to no man in particular, but I could see they brought great pleasure to both Lam and the lieutenant. That brought me pleasure too. Sometimes I could see a very quiet but deep love pass between these men. They each seemed to be aware of the thin string from which life dangles in war. They were far apart in many ways, but the war, just as it tore so many apart, brought some together. I'll always remember the way that, after we drank all our champagne one afternoon, Lt. Frye put his silver-wave necklace around Lam's neck and hugged him. They were alike in one important way. Each man was silent and deep and would never tolerate even a tiny betrayal. They were like oceans. With Lt. Frye and Huong Lam, you were either an enemy or a friend. You either floated on their calm surface, or you sank under terrible waves.

Entertaining the Communists became easier. They responded well to me. The "theaters" were always makeshift and often underground. The caverns were small and poorly lit, and I was limited to three-minute songs so that the ventilation shafts could be opened in silence to give us air. Sometimes the sound of artillery or bombs would drown out the music. One time I remember the famous American, Bob Hope, was performing for the troops above ground, while I sang underground, not a half mile from him. There was great glee in the tunnels at this situation. But life was hard and dirty there, and my audiences could never applaud or sing with me. I resented being given material to sing, but the longer the war went on, the more I was forced to perform songs that would rally the Communists to victory. The good thing about being an entertainer was that I was moved from tunnel to tunnel, from camp to camp, from crater to crater to perform. I was always able to gather new information. I never worried that I would be found out, because by the time the Americans could take action on my intelligence, I was gone and not suspected.

One day Lam did not come to my hut. I set off alone through the jungle and came to the road to wait. When Lt. Frye came, he was alone, too. Private Crawley, he said, had another task at the base.

We went to the plantation courtyard and ate our food. Then the rain came and we ran inside. I sang over the rain and Lt. Frye lay on a cot and smoked. Then, for a long time, we talked of our families and our past, our hopes and our fears about the war. For the first time I saw a gentle spirit in the lieutenant that he never showed before. He touched my cheek and I wanted to run, but I knew there was no place to go. He seemed ashamed to have frightened me. We rode back to the turnout point very quietly.

Lam was waiting there when I got home. He was obviously drunk, leaning against my hut like a palm in monsoon. His eyes were fierce and heavy from the drink. He said he loved me. He accused me of terrible things I will not repeat. He grabbed my arms, and I hit him very hard. Finally he let go and stumbled off into the rain.

In the morning there was a bough of holly and some lilies outside my door. Lam had written a note that expressed his deep sorrow and apology for his behavior, and said he wished only to be forgiven. That day in the marketplace he stood while I spun cloth, and I told him I forgave him. He was happy and ashamed still, but he walked away with his head up and I felt good.

Even Lam had his woman problems, thought Frye. He could still taste Cristobel; still smell the faint, dark perfume she wore; still feel her cool, hesitant fingers on the backs of his arms.

There's so much inside her that wants to come out.

*Skate over the silences. They're hard as ice . . .*

It was two months after our first meeting that things began to go wrong for Lt. Frye's operations. First, he and his men were ambushed by Viet Cong in Hien Phu, which they believed was friendly. Later, when they had fought off the attack, they found several of the villagers dead nearby, and the rest they never found. How had the Viet Cong known they were coming? Then a tunnel entrance that I had told them about—a new one—was found just where it was supposed to be. It was booby-trapped, and one of Bennett's men lost his eyes. Then a trip wire was found by Lam, who was walking the trail first. There were other incidents.

As we sat in the courtyard of the plantation one day, he told us that information was leaking from his men to the Viet Cong. Lam agreed. For a brief moment I felt Lt. Frye's suspicion hover in the air around me like a silent bird. Then I saw Lam looking down to the ground, and I knew that he felt it too.

For two weeks nothing happened. Then, on a night patrol near the Michelin Plantation, Lam became lost and the men were ambushed again. Two of them died, and Lam became separated from the platoon. It was an hour later that he found them, still lost, and managed to lead them back to the base. Later, Lt. Frye told me that this was the point he became sure that Lam was the traitor.

It was while we sat in the courtyard one day, and Lt. Frye told me of his suspicions, that I fell in love with him. It had been growing inside me like a seed, but this was the first green sprout reaching above the earth. I said nothing. But I knew then that I would do anything for him and that in some small way I would show him my affections. When I look back on that moment now, I can only remember what a warm, large feeling it was. Love has its own mind, and sometimes the lover cannot read it. I did not question.

I wrote for him the best songs I could. My heart was so full and pure that my music was beautiful. I wrote simple songs in English to please him. A few of them were too strongly worded for Lam to hear, because I knew of his affections for me. These I wrote onto small sheets of paper and passed them to Lt. Frye in secret. I know now that my young girl's eyes were filled with love for him, although I believed I was being very secret.

The next week our meeting went as usual, but I noticed a coolness between Lam and Lt. Frye. Private Crawley sat behind us, silent as always, with his gun nearby.

At the end of the next meeting we had alone, Lt. Frye told me that he had fallen in love with me. I told him my feelings. He told me he wished me to move onto the base in two weeks. He did not want me exposed to the enemy any longer. He said he could not forgive himself if shells directed by his Intelligence were to land and kill me. He said that my value to him as a spy was now second to my value as a woman.

I was happy. I was terrified, too. I told him I needed to

think. One cannot imagine the contradictions of heart when one falls in love with a man during war—a man of another race and religion, of another place, another world. I knew that if I were to move into his base, I would be leaving my life forever. I had seen the girls taken advantage of by the soldiers. Words of love, drunkenly spoken. Or sometimes less than that. And I knew that a Vietnamese woman who went to an American was scorned as a prostitute by her own people. These women became neither Vietnamese nor American—they were outcasts. But never once did it enter my mind that Lt. Frye would be using me in that way. The woman inside me yearned for him. The girl yearned to run away.

The next day I didn't go to market. Instead I walked to the pond near my hut and thought for many hours. I sat and tossed sticks into the water. I was afraid of what going to Lt. Frye would mean to me, yet I wanted to go to him. I was afraid to bring the wrath of my own race upon me, yet I knew that if I went to the lieutenant, I would be hated.

Lam must have followed me to the pond. He was quieter and more brooding than usual. He sat a few feet away from me. Finally, he looked at me with his dark eyes and said that he loved me. He wanted to be with me and help me. He said we were of one blood and destiny. He said the war would be over soon, and the Communists would win. He asked me to marry him, so that we each would have something to hold onto when the dark days came.

All this, when I had gone to the pond to think!

I told him that I was thinking about moving to base with Lt. Frye. Lam stood and hurled a branch into the water. He said things about the Americans that were not good. He said to mix blood was evil, and that our race was not to be one with the Americans. He stormed around the pond, then came back to the stone where I was sitting and brought his face close to mine. He said that Bennett Frye would use and discard me like a basket. He said that I must learn to survive without him. He said that if I went to the lieutenant I would be murdered immediately when the Communists overran us. He said to go to Bennett was to choose death.

All I knew at the time was that I did not want Lam.

Our next meeting was heavy with tension. Lam and Lt. Frye showed no love for each other. At the end of it, Lt. Frye told me he had changed his plans. He wanted me to meet him at the base that very night, with my belongings. I would be provided a hootch and safety. He told me too, in secret by the plantation wall, that he believed it was Lam who had betrayed their plans and cost some of his men their lives. He asked me not to say anything to Lam about his desire for me, but it was too late.

When Lam and I walked back through the jungle toward my home, he told me he knew of Lt. Frye's proposal. He stopped me on the trail, put his hands gently on my arms, and asked me not to go. He pleaded with me to pack my belongings and bring them instead to his hut, which was between my home and the base. He would love me and protect me. We would be what we were—Vietnamese.

I was shaking with sorrow. Lam saw this, so he let me go. He told me that whatever I decided, to please come to his hut that night—either to say good-bye or to say yes to him. He made me promise.

It was the honorable thing to do, so I agreed.

That night I packed my things. There was not much to carry: a few cooking baskets and pots, my clothes, my guitar. I said good-bye to my home forever and walked out into the night. In my heart, I knew what I would do.

I could see a candle burning in Lam's hootch. He was inside, sitting alone on his cot. He could see what my decision had been by the look on my face. He did not say any of the things I thought he would. He was very serious. He told me he loved me and wished me success. He hugged me. Then he gave me a pack that he had prepared and slung it over my back. It was small, but heavy and hard.

"This is for you and Lt. Frye to open together," he said. His face was full of bravery and defeat. "Open it when you are together. And be very careful not to drop it or hit it hard. It has a fragile content. Good-bye, Kieu Li."

Tearfully, I said good-bye and started out again.

I knew what Lam had done to me.

It was the last time I saw him.

When I got to the base, Lt. Frye was waiting as he said he would be. I was trembling, and I told him what Lam had put on my back. That he wanted us to open it together. That I feared it. Very carefully he removed it and carried it away. Later I learned that his demolitions experts had detonated the bomb, which was strong enough to kill ten men.

I stepped into my new hut and my heart was wailing. I was relieved. I was sad. This was my new life. Lt. Frye looked at me with kindness and I felt better. I was then able to acknowledge to myself how close to being killed I had come, not just that night but during all the nights and months before.

I lay in my new home and wept. Lt. Frye came after midnight. Lam had only made it one kilometer north before he was intercepted by a patrol. When he would not stop, they killed him. I gave myself to the lieutenant on the plank bed. He was the first man I had known, and the only man I have ever known. We were married two months later. Two weeks after that, he stepped on a mine and lost his legs. I knew that if he died, I would, too.

We live in America now. When I look back on those times, they are clear but distant, a dream that I cannot forget, a nightmare that I will always remember. We went to war and found love where most found only death. When the Day of Shame came, I watched on a television in California as Saigon fell. So many things have ended, so many have begun.

Frye closed the book and took a deep breath.
Li.

After all that, he thought, they take you offstage at the Asian Wind. He saw her struggling again, saw her blouse rip in their gloved hands, heard her screams through the amplifiers.

He remembered her, sitting at the dinner table on Frye Island, dressed in Western clothes, looking like a princess who had never slept in anything but silk sheets. He pictured her standing in Bennett's living room one night, with her guitar strapped to her shoulder, playing a new song she had written. He thought of her on his own wedding day, lovely in that dress, standing in the row of women beside Linda, looking at him in absolute joy. And later, at the reception, dancing with her, when she had said into his ear, "The love shows on your faces, Chuck. You should never let it go and never let it die. It is not an easy thing to find, but it is an easy thing to lose."

Champagne, three bottles.

He checked his watch. It was almost seven. He put on some good clothes and shaved twice. He brushed his teeth vigorously, thinking of Cristobel.

# CHAPTER 17

THEY GOT TO THE SHERRING-ton Hotel in time for the first fight. He flashed his press pass at the door. The attendant checked his list and told Frye it wasn't good anymore. Frye mumbled apologies, went to the ticket window, and came up with two ten-dollar seats way in the back.

The door man took their tickets with a sigh.

"Where can I find Mr. Mack?"

"Never heard of him. Try the directory."

On fight-night the ballroom houses the ring, and rows of chairs pressed all the way to the walls. Frye stepped inside. His stomach fluttered a bit, and he felt good at the lights and the ring and the ropes and the general carnival atmosphere. Cristobel took his arm.

He worked his way to the third-to-last row, from which the ring looked like a bright sugar cube. He checked his program. Stinson was in the white, out of Bakersfield; Avila in the red, out of Sonora, Mexico. At the bell they moved toward each other with the slowness of men wading through water.

Frye stood. "I'm going to find Mack."

"Yes, *sir.*"

"Sorry. I'll be back in just a minute."

He found the Elite listing in the lobby directory, and took an elevator to the eighth floor. Suite 816 was at the end of the hall, just across from the stairway. A small brass plaque said ELITE MANAGEMENT—PRIVATE. Frye knocked and waited; knocked again. The door was locked. He waited a moment longer, then headed back to the arena.

Cristobel smiled at him. "When you said a minute, you weren't kidding. No dice?"

"None."

He lifted his Bushnells and focused on the ring. Avila was a sinewy Latin, pesky, hard to hit. Stinson looked Irish, with heavy hands and thick calves. The kind of fighter who'll run out of gas about the tenth, Frye guessed, if he hasn't put his man away. But if he catches you with the right, you eat canvas. He'd seen Avila last year: The kid couldn't be more than twenty.

He turned the binoculars ringside to see who'd gotten his old seat. It was Edison.

On one side of him was Lucia Parsons. On the other was Burke and his cowboy hat. Next to him was Paul DeCord. They all held gigantic beers.

Frye said nothing. He just looked through the binoculars and wondered what in hell his father was doing with Lucia Parsons and a man who kept spying on Bennett. He gave the glasses to Cristobel and looked down at the floor for a moment, thinking.

When he looked at the ring again, Stinson caught Avila with a right cross, then a left to the chin. Avila folded in the middle and plopped butt-first to the canvas. Frye could see he wouldn't be getting up soon.

"Want to meet my dad?"

"A little early for that, don't you think?"

"I didn't know he'd be here tonight."

She gathered up her purse and beer. "I didn't know I would either. But why not?"

The ringside crowd thinned between bouts. Edison spotted him, blinked, then smiled. He gave Frye a Mafia bear hug and kiss, his standard public greeting. "The hell you doing here? And what's this?"

Frye introduced Cristobel. Edison eyed her like a jeweler might a diamond. Frye was introduced to Lucia Parsons, who looked prettier and more substantial in real life than she was on TV. Burke grinned, said "Haw, Chuck," and flagged the waitress to get Frye's drink order. Paul DeCord remained in his seat, lost to his program.

"I didn't know you covered these things anymore," said Edison.

"I'm free-lancing tonight."

"Gotta make a buck, I guess. You familiar with Lucia's work?"

Frye regarded Lucia Parsons. Dark wavy hair, cut just above the shoulders. Green eyes, good skin. Conservative suit. Just enough jewelry to imply more at home.

"I heard your speech yesterday," he said. "Are you planning another trip to Hanoi now?"

"We met our Phase-Three goal at that rally," she said. "I'll be going over again very soon."

Frye noted that Lucia's private voice was exactly like her public one: calm, confident, unassuming.

"I was impressed," he said. "I'll be even more impressed if you can get some solid proof that there are MIAs still alive over there."

Lucia smiled. "You and the rest of the world. When Phase Four begins, I think a lot of people will be impressed, Chuck. But thank you. I'm a real fan of your articles, by the way. Your boxing pieces are actually superior to those in the *Times*."

"Their only fight writer hates the sport. Papers don't pay enough attention to boxing anyway."

Burke tipped back his hat and shook his head slowly. "You can say that again, Chuck. It's the only game around that amounts to much fun anymore. I read every one of your ditties. You gave a damn about the sport, and it showed."

"Well, thanks."

Burke took off his hat and smiled at Cristobel. Frye watched his eyes stray to her neck, then back up again. "Cristobel. Spanish name?"

"My father was German, my mother Mexican."

"One helluva interesting combo," said Burke.

Lucia was about to say something to Frye when three women closed in around her, offering their hands, introducing themselves.

Edison shook his head. "Everywhere she goes it's like that. They mob her."

How do you know? Frye thought.

"I got to thinking about your job, Chuck," said Burke. "Your pop here filled me in. And I'll be damned if I don't know that Mack character. I come to so many of these fights, I couldn't help but run across him. Tough little pecker. Didn't surprise me at all he got his panties in a bunch like that."

"I'd sure like to talk to him. That's why I came."

"Well, he's here most of the time. Don't see him tonight, though. Might try his office up on floor eight. Elite something."

"What's he look like?"

"Rollie?" Burke smiled, first at Frye, then at Cristobel. "Shorter than you, gray hair, fifty or so. Just a regular sort of fella."

"If you see him, tell him I'd really like to talk."

"Sure enough."

Lucia introduced Frye to Paul DeCord, who offered a friendly smile as they shook hands. Frye saw an alertness in the eyes, behind the glasses that sat crookedly on his nose. But there's something about that face, Frye thought, that tells you it's got nothing to hide. Not the same face he wore to his drops with Nguyen Hy. Or the one he brought to the Lower Mojave Airstrip.

"You're a writer, I hear," said Frye.

DeCord chuckled. "I'm doing some research on the refugee community for Health and Human Services. So I do my share of writing."

"Photography, too?"

"Occasionally."

Frye considered. "I guess you know Stanley Smith."

"I'm familiar with his work. My own has a completely different focus."

"Are you interested in the MIAs?"

DeCord looked over Frye's shoulder, then refocused on his face. "On a personal level only. Burke and Lucia are just good friends. Are you?"

"At this point, Li's my main MIA."

"I can understand that," said DeCord.

Frye watched his father watch Lucia. Something like pride showed on his face, something like dumb admiration. The last time Frye had seen Edison look that way, it was at his favorite spaniel.

Edison caught him, mid-study. He smiled, a little sheepishly. "Take a walk with me, will you, Pop? We should talk."

Frye excused himself from Cristobel, already the target of Burke Parsons's attentions.

They left the ballroom and took the walkway toward the swimming pool. Edison held open the gate. The pool was huge and elaborately shaped, with deck chairs around it and a bunch of kids splashing in the shallow end. Frye watched branches of light and shadow spread and wobble along the bottom. Edison sat on a chaise longue.

"Well, I guess that was one helluva scene you and Tuy Nha walked in on last night."

"Right up there with the worst of them, Pop. Is there any more news about Li?"

Edison shook his head and loosened his necktie.

"Would you tell me if there was?"

His father looked at him, checked his watch. "I see what happens when you get involved in your brother's business, son."

"What do I have to do? Bring Li to Frye Island on a Rose Parade float?"

"You'd probably steer it into the bay."

"And let her drown, like I let Debbie drown. Right?"

Edison stood up. "That's horseshit, Chuck. Not me, not your mother, nobody ever said that."

"It's what you believed though, isn't it?"

Edison stood before him, nose-to-nose. "What in hell's wrong with you?"

"I'm locked out."

"You're nothing you haven't asked for."

"What I'm asking now is to be let back in."

"You got off in Chicago, Chuck, and the train kept going to New York."

Frye stepped back, looked out to the pool. "Who's Paul DeCord? And don't tell me he works for Health and Human Services. He's taking pictures of Benny, visiting Minh, and sitting with you."

Edison glared at him. "I just met the sonofabitch myself, son. He's a friend of Lucia's, and he's a Fed researcher, for chrissakes. What do you mean, taking pictures of Benny?"

"You know about the medical supplies Bennett sends over?"

"Of course I do."

"Well, DeCord's documenting it. What I'm telling you now is to be careful what you say. I don't know who the hell this guy is, and neither do you."

Edison shook his head, the same way he did twenty years ago when Frye had started up the family station wagon and driven it through the garage door. He checked his watch. "I don't want to miss the main event. Heavyweights."

"Where's Mom tonight?"

"She canceled last minute, Chuck. Wasn't feeling up to it."

"What are you doing here?"

Edison looked at him, a long cool stare. "Lucia's a major investor in the Paradiso, and this is a chance to talk strategy. I've got better things to be doing right now, but we made the date a month ago. You have a problem with that?"

"Yeah. You got my old seat. It's the best one in the house."

Edison turned and walked back through the gate, letting it slam it behind him.

In the main event, a Nigerian heavyweight lost a close decision to a big kid from San Diego. The Nigerian left the ring in a tiger-print robe. Frye was certain that no tigers lived in Nigeria. He watched the boy from San Diego parade around the ring after, toothlessly demanding Mike Tyson. Mike Tyson would knock you out before you got off your stool, Frye thought. He watched through the binoculars, but the fight seemed less compelling than Lucia, Burke, DeCord, and Edison. Just after the ninth round, they left their seats and trailed up the aisle. His father walked closely behind Lucia, and Frye thought: He looks like a dog.

"You got quiet after that walk with your dad," said Cristobel.

"You don't have much leverage on the topic of quiet."

"That's pretty romantic for a first date."

"You want a romance, buy one at the market."

"You can be a real prick, can't you?"

"It's genetic. Come on, I want to see if Rollie Dean Mack is up in his suite now."

They took the elevator to the eighth floor. Frye led her around the corner and down the long hallway. He knocked, tried the door, and knocked again.

"Not your night with this Mack guy," Cristobel said.

They had just started for the elevator when Frye heard Edison's laughter booming up the stairwell behind them. He stopped and peered around the corner. Lucia Parsons climbed the last few steps, Edison behind her. They made their way to the Elite Management suite and Lucia opened the door with a key. She took Edison by the arm and led him in.

"Not what you wanted to see, exactly?"

"No."

"Maybe it's not what it looks like."

"Nothing much is these days."

"Let's go home, Chuck."

They walked along the beach near Cristobel's old blue apartment. The moon hovered through the palms of Heisler Park and the black water was smooth and glittery. Close to shore, waves dissipated into phosphorous-purple suds.

Cristobel held his hand. "Is there another way to find this Mack character?" she asked.

"I've been thinking."

"I know it's none of my business, but maybe you ought to try something different. A different paper, maybe. Let that Mack guy have his way and just get yourself a better job. You know, like play in a bigger league."

"I got some résumés out, but it's tough when all the publishers know what happened. He made me look bad."

"Is that the only place he works? I mean, doesn't Elite Management have an office or something else somewhere?"

"Newport. He's never in. The girl who works there said she'd call me if he ever shows."

They walked north, toward Rockpile. Frye watched a steady stream of cars heading out of the city, climbing the grade on Coast Highway.

"Let me know if I can help," she said. "I'm good at résumés."

"It just really pisses me off."

"Your dad and Lucia?"

"Not so much Lucia, just . . . the whole thing."

"I take it there's some space between you."

"A whole lot of it. I guess it's been getting wider the last few years. Talking to him—it's like trying to yell across an ocean to someone."

"Have you done what you can to get through?"

"I suppose I could have stayed closer. More involved. I just kind of spun out for awhile, lost contact. I've never been interested in the family business. That's all Bennett and Dad now. Maybe Pop took it a lot more personal than I did."

"Well, when a father works hard, he likes to share it. If you had better things to do, maybe he felt . . . like you didn't need him."

They walked up the zigzag stairway to the park. The path was lined with rosebushes and the grass was trimmed neatly around them. Frye led her to the gazebo that looks to the west. "I got married here," he said.

"That's nice."

He looked down the ragged cliff to the rocks below, shining with ocean spray. The water hissed up the sand toward them, stopped just short, then receded.

"Miss her?"

"Yeah."

"Going to patch it up?"

"I don't think it's patchable."

"Things end. Things start."

"There was a lot of damage. I wonder why we beat up on the people we love so much."

"Our cages are too small."

They sat on a bench by a cypress tree. Cristobel lay her head on Frye's shoulder. For a while he thought she was dozing.

"It was a little over a year ago when it happened," she said quietly. "Went to a party, had a fight with a man, and stormed out. I was a little drunk. Three blocks to walk in Long Beach—that was all. Next thing I knew, it was four men, a gun, and a car."

Frye heard the waves crashing below.

"They took me out to a field. When it was over, I remember lying there and looking up at this big oil thing going up and down. One of those giant grasshoppers. It smelled bad. I hurt and I was freezing cold. I got my things back on and started walking. I found this workman in a shed. Big fat guy, smoking a cigar. He wrapped me up in some big towels and put me on cot. The cops came and did their thing."

"And they caught them?"

"Two hours later. They put one away and the others walked. The trial was bad. I felt unclean, and that made it worse. I got up to four showers a day, but they didn't help. You can't wash your mind with soap and water. Not a day goes by, not an hour, when I don't think about lying there with the oil machine pumping away over me. I wake up and the first thing I wonder is: Am I going to make it through this day without re-living that night again? Funny, because as soon as you ask that, you've already failed. And I swear, Chuck, I swear I've seen those other three. They're in the same car—an old Chevy—and they cruise Coast Highway in front of my apartment. I've seen them three times in the last month. I'm sure of it."

"You tell the cops?"

"They say there's no law against driving Coast Highway. They think I'm paranoid. The funny part is, I am."

"I don't blame you."

"So if I'm weird, please bear with me a little. If you don't want to, I don't blame you. But if you buy the ticket, you ought to know what the ride's like."

They stood for a while on the sand below her apartment. Frye held her close and could feel her heart beating against his chest. Her hair smelled like rain. Her mouth found his, and she was more assured now, eager. She put both her hands on his face and locked him in. She sucked out his breath. Frye gave her all he had. A moment later she was walking up the stairs toward her door. Frye stood and waited, but she never looked back.

Bennett was sitting on his couch when Frye walked in. Donnell Crawley stood in the corner, looking at one of Frye's surfboards. "Your security stinks, little brother. No wonder my tape got stolen."

"I told you I'm sorry about that—"

"Forget the tape, Chuck. We've got bigger problems now. I played a hunch on the black hood the gunman was wearing. I checked the yardgoods stores in town and found a lady who'd sold a piece of black cotton to a man, eight days ago. She was terrified. Donnell leaned on her a little. She'd seen the guy before. Twenty years before, near Nha Trang. He was Dac Cong—Communist Special Forces."

"Jesus."

"Pop got Wiggins to let her view the body. Bingo. It was the same guy who bought the fabric."

"From Vietnam to San Francisco to Little Saigon. One of Thach's men?"

"That's what I'm thinking. The FBI's doing a background check on him but it will take a while. They're not in any goddamned hurry to share with us."

Crawley sat down with Bennett. Frye went to the window and looked out. The traffic on Laguna Canyon Road hissed along, tourists heading inland with genuine Laguna art. "I talked to Wiggins about Thach. The colonel's a prisoner in his own apartment right now. His bosses don't trust him."

"I got the same intelligence."

"Do you believe it?"

"No. But my sources need a few days to look into it."

"Wiggins talked down the whole Hanoi angle anyway."

"No one in the government will listen to that, Chuck. Not with Lucia Parsons getting Hanoi friendly enough to talk about POWs. Not with a city full of refugees ready to panic at the mention of his name. They want to be real sure before that can of worms gets opened."

"Do you really think he's behind it?"

"I don't have any proof either. It's easy for people to make it look that way."

"Why do that?"

"Terror is a tool. I learned that well enough."

Frye considered this. "Has she called again, Benny?"

"No word. Nothing. The FBI ran the voice print yesterday and it was definitely Li on the phone."

"What about the other voice?"

"Male Oriental, middle-age. Not a native speaker. That's all they could say."

"Benny, I read the story that Li told Smith. About Lam and you and her. Three bottles of French champagne on your . . . picnics. And three bottles of champagne on her stand in the dressing room."

Bennett heaved off the couch and swung over to Frye. "Get down here, Chuck. Get down to my level."

"No way."

Bennett glared up at him. "I'm going to tell you something. These stumps I'm standing on aren't the worst thing I brought home from Nam. The worst is up in my head, and that's just where I'm going to keep it. You can't pry into me. Don't even try. The war is nobody's business but my own. Not yours, not Pop's . . . nobody's. Someone's fucking with my head, Chuck. Don't you start, too."

"They're trying to make you remember Lam, aren't they?"

Frye could sense Bennett, navigating his own fury now. Bennett stepped back and stared up. He spoke softly. "That's exactly what they're trying to do. What they don't know is that I remember him all the time, every day of my life. I don't forget traitors. Ever."

Bennett lurched over to Crawley, who produced a Colt .45. Bennett brought it over to Frye and held it out. "If Thach is behind this, you might need a friend. I got Donnell and more FBI than I can stomach hanging around my house. Now you've got this. The clip's full, no round in the chamber, and the safety's on. You know how to use it?"

"Pop showed me a long time ago."

"Well, the Colt .45 hasn't changed in fifty years. It shoots straight and slow, and hits like an elephant. Keep it close, watch your back and don't spend any more time in Little Saigon than you have to."

Frye took the heavy weapon. What mass has more finality? he thought. A tumor? A gravestone? "Thanks, I guess."

Bennett swung toward the door, stopped, then exhaled long and slow. He turned back to Frye with a curious look of pain and disappointment. "Wiggins finally caught up with Eddie Vo. About an hour ago."

"Where'd they find him?"

"Trying to get into his house. He pulled a gun, and they shot him six times on his front porch."

Frye leaned against his broken stereo speaker. "Eddie Vo was just a mixed-up kid."

"Wiggins talks like he just got Joe Bonanno. The FBI's happy now—they've got their prime suspect. Be careful, Chuck."

Crawley waited for Bennett to pivot past him. "Good night, Chuck. Anything not right, you call me. I be here fast as I can."

Frye got a flashlight and went into the cave. He dug through some old boxes and finally found the little pair of stereo speakers that he'd outgrown years ago but couldn't bring himself to toss.

In the living room, he hooked them up to his receiver and put on Li's *Lost Mothers*.

The sound wasn't great, but the music came through anyway. He read the translation of "Tunnel Song."

> Deep in this earth I sang to you
> You were many miles away
> I went to the enemy for you
> You were waiting for the truth I'd bring
> With the morning I'd leave the hell of earth
> And return myself to the sun
> And put in your hands the plans of death
> So you could plant flowers of freedom
> In the earth that held me down.

Frye looked at the fresh traces of mud on the floor, on his shoes. From the cave, he thought. From the cave.

Suddenly, obviously, like a shade being removed from his eyes, he knew where they had taken her.

And he knew where Eddie had gone.

And he knew where Duc had gone.

Mud in the middle of August.

He called information and got her number. The Dream Reader answered on the ninth ring. She sounded sleepy. Frye said he'd just had a bad nightmare and demanded an emergency reading. She said it would cost twice as much this late. They agreed on midnight.

The Westminster police wouldn't give him Minh's home number. After pleading with the watch commander, Frye left his own, then hung up and waited on a callback.

It took less than a minute. Minh was calling from Eddie Vo's house.

"Detective, I know you'd rather see me in jail than talk to me on the phone, but I know where they took Li. And I know where Eddie Vo went after I let him get away."

"Tell me where, exactly."

"I can't. It might take some finding. But I'll take you there if I can. You game?"

"Yes, I'm game."

"Meet me at the Dream Reader's in twenty minutes."

He rang off, dialed the prefix to Bennett's number, then hesitated. What if I'm wrong? What if I'm right and it doesn't amount to jack? Okay, brother, I'll stay out of your head. I'll do it your way.

He locked up and walked outside to the Cyclone, tapping the flashlight against his leg.

# CHAPTER 18

**L**ITTLE SAIGON WAS DESERTED until he came to St. Bartholomew's Church, where cars were still jamming into the overfilled parking lot. Caught in the stalled lane of traffic, Frye could see through the open parish doors hundreds of Vietnamese packed into the small church, more in the vestibule, more trailing across the lawn from the lot. The marquis said MIDNIGHT MASS FOR TUY XUAN—MONSIGNOR DINH HO HANH. There were two cop cars parked in front, an NBC News van, a station wagon from KOCE TV in Huntington Beach. A photog that Frye recognized as a *Times* staffer stood near the church steps, composing a shot of parents and two tiny boys in suits. The strobe raked them; the photographer waved them inside.

Another block down Bolsa he turned left under the archway of Saigon Plaza and passed the two snarling lions guarding the entrance. Both were plastered with posters of Li's face—announcements of a CFV "Freedom Rally" set for Friday. He slowed, pulled one off, and put it on his seat.

The parking lot was almost empty. A few small sedans were huddled near the noodle shop. The owner of Ban Le Cafe hosed off the walkway in front, where the outdoor tables were pushed against the wall and stacked with chairs. Frye parked in front of Siêu Thị Mỹ-Hoa Supermarket. The lights were still bright, and a few shoppers came and went.

Frye got the flashlight, stuffed it in his belt, pulled his shirt down, and locked up the Cyclone. He could feel the sticky sweat on his back and smell the high, thin stink of fear on his body.

Minh was waiting for him.

The Dream Reader's light still glowed over the sidewalk in a purple-pink wash. He pushed on the door but it was locked. Inside it was dark. He cupped his hands, looked through the glass and saw the wide, old woman making her way toward him. She opened the door and regarded with him with a suspicious, tired expression. "Bad visions?" she asked.

"Uncertain visions," he said.

She looked at Minh. "I am not open for business."

"You are now." Frye pushed past her and into the front room. The smell of incense hit him. Minh and the Dream Reader conversed in Vietnamese while Frye scanned the carpet. She took her seat and opened her box.

"Fifty dollar."

Frye counted out the money and handed it to her.

"Tell me of your dream."

"Mind if I walk while I talk? I'm nervous."

She eyed him, then Minh, who was standing against the wall with his arms crossed. She nodded.

"I have this dream over and over that I'm in a small dark place and I can't get out. I wake up sweating, and my heart's ready to blow up."

"Small dark places frighten us all."

Frye continued to walk the room, testing the floor for consistency, sound feel. I know it's here somewhere, he thought. "Sometimes I dream I'm in the ocean."

"The ocean can be a dark place when you're under the water."

"Exactly."

"How old are you?"

"Thirty-three."

"I see helplessness in your dream. You are dreaming of death."

How true, thought Frye. He tapped the floor with his foot.

"What are you doing?"

Minh spoke sharply to her, then to Frye. "What in hell *are* you doing?"

"Lighten up. I could have called the FBI. You'll see."

The Dream Reader fidgeted on her chair. "Have you lost a loved one to death?"

Frye looked at her. A chill rippled up his back. He felt the Dream Reader, sucking out his thoughts. "My sister."

"In the water?"

"Yes."

"You relive her death. You wish to join her."

He stopped, knelt down and rapped his knuckles on the floor. Nothing.

Where?

Frye moved to the wall, feeling along with his hands now, tapping, listening. He had covered every foot. Every foot of floor except . . .

He stood over the woman. She looked up at him with contempt. Her thick hands were folded on the table, her huge bosom tight within the *ao dai.*

"You may leave now," she said.

"Get up, please."

"I stay."

"Up, doll."

She sat back and glared at him.

He stepped around her, took the back of her chair and towed it away with her in it. She grasped the arms like a frightened airline passenger and cursed him in Vietnamese. Then he pushed the table aside and ran his hands over the carpet. Nothing but a scrap of string.

A loop.

He slid his flashlight through it and pulled.

The trapdoor rose. It was roughly square, the same size as the Dream Reader's table. The smell of earth wafted up. Minh jumped to his side. When Frye shined his light down he could see the rounded sides of the tunnel and a ladder made of rope. "I knew I'd get my fifty-bucks' worth," he said.

She stared at him, still and silent.

Minh smiled. "I've heard rumors of a tunnel, but no one could ever find an entrance. This is quite impressive, Chuck."

"That was the truth I was telling, about small, dark places, Detective. If I start to freak, I'm coming up."

"You've got the light. You first."

Frye considered the Dream Reader. "What about her?"

Minh snapped something at the woman. She talked rapidly until he cut her off. "She says she'd have told me sooner, but she was afraid of the gangs. She'll stay right where she is," said Minh.

Frye shoved the flashlight into his belt, then lowered himself down one rung at a time—nine in all—until he found himself stooping in a small earthen room. It was cool and damp, and the ceiling was too low for his head. His first instinct was to scramble back up and get the hell out of this place. He breathed deeply—a loamy, ancient smell, like the cave-house's, but stronger—and tried to slow his galloping heart. Above him the round shaft of light diminished, and he could see the Dream Reader's thick face gazing down before she shut the door. It was totally black inside. He held a hand in front of his face and saw nothing.

He could hear Minh breathing beside him.

Using the flashlight now, he saw that two tunnels led off in opposite directions, right toward Bolsa and left toward the inner part of Saigon Plaza. He looked at Minh, who shook his head. He went left.

The tunnel went straight for nearly fifty feet, then bent to the right. It was impossible to judge, but Frye had the feeling that he was moving deeper. With the walls close around him, he could feel the first quivers of panic spreading up his back, that feeling of being trapped, of never getting out, of losing direction. He stopped, turned off the light, and closed his eyes. Breathe deeply. *Control.*

"Are you still alive, Frye?"

"Yeah."

With his flashlight on again he went fifty feet to where the tunnel opened into another small room. A camping lantern hung from one wall. He found a pack of matches on top of it, worked the pump a few times, and lit the wick. The room coalesced in a soft orange glow. A sleeping bag lay on the earth, neatly flattened. He pulled it open. Inside, pheasants flew across a background of red flannel. "It's Eddie's," he said. "I saw it in his room.

When he was sneaking through the plaza, he had a bag with him. He'd gone home to get something to sleep on."

Beside it was a white sack with a half-eaten hamburger inside. Frye held it and felt a truly unpleasant coolness settle on his nerves. Next to the sack sat a white bowl filled with what looked like used napkins. Minh smelled them.

On the other side of the sleeping bag was a candle in a small brass dish. The wax had melted into a pool, now hardened. Frye reached out to touch it, but Minh's hand clamped over his. Propped up against the dish was a thin gold earring. Minh reached out with a handkerchief and picked it up. "It looks like the one I found in his house. He brought her here first. It explains the earth on her clothes."

"You don't want to hear this, Minh, but Eddie Vo never brought her here at all."

"How do you know that?"

"Because he wouldn't. That's all."

"Then who did, Frye?"

"I don't know."

A small stack of Vietnamese magazines and newspapers sat beside the candle. Sacks from fast-food restaurants were piled next to one wall: several days' worth of rations. Leaning beside them was a short, sawed-off shotgun. The barrel was rusted, the old wooden stock dark and beaten. The box of .20-gauge ammunition that sat beside it was brand-new. Frye examined the red plastic cylinders—high base, expensive. Next to that, another lantern and a can of fuel.

A trickle of sweat started at his neck and dribbled all the way down his back.

Something rumbled overhead; the floor vibrated. Cars, he thought—cars in Saigon Plaza. He could feel his pulse rising, a fresh wash of sweat break over his scalp. He checked his watch: ten minutes down. The lantern mantles glowed brightly, charging the room with clean, white light. Frye turned down the gas.

The tunnel continued, a neat hole in the far wall. He put the flashlight in his belt and unhooked the lantern. Thirty steps later the tunnel emptied into a concrete passageway with a dark sluggish stream moving slowly along the bottom. Spikes of old re-bar sprouted from the side walls, leaving brown stains and skewed shadows in the lamplight. From the darkness in either direction came liquescent echoes, intermittent splashes. Mud slid and shifted under his heels. He looked back and held up the lantern to see his footprints refilling with ooze.

It was then that he saw the man, maybe fifty feet away, crouched too, looking at Frye with a shocked, feral face.

"Halt! Police!" Minh pushed down on Frye's shoulder with one hand and aimed his revolver with the other.

The man never looked back. He just turned, loped down the tunnel into the darkness and disappeared.

Minh charged ahead. Frye stood there, listening to the splattering from the detective's shoes. Finally he commanded his heavy legs to move, the echoes of Minh's footsteps still sounding in his ears.

When he caught up with him a moment later, Minh was standing in the mud, gun at his side. "Gone," he said. "Like all the rest of them. Stay close, Frye."

"Don't worry."

A hundred yards down, the river narrowed and disappeared through a grate. The concrete walls and ceiling tapered to almost nothing. Frye could hear the constant rush of the water, spilling over to wherever it went. He stopped a few yards short, unable to go any further without wading. Holding up the lantern, he could see that the grating was stuffed with captured debris— branches, a dripping black tumbleweed, a car tire, something that looked like a patio chair. The end of the line, he thought, for everything.

He held up the lantern again, looking for a connection, a way in or a way out, but all he saw was solid concrete, an aging drain system doing its thankless subterranean job.

"What do you think, Frye?"

"There's got to be a way. Another trapdoor maybe, or a ladder. Something."

"Lead on. Your luck is good so far."

Frye turned and headed back out, still hugging the cool wall. Minh sloshed behind him. Frye tapped with his knuckles, about waist-height as he went, hoping. "Must be on the other wall."

Landing on a pile of trash that formed a small island in the middle, he made the other side in two jumps and worked his way back down the wall, tapping, lantern held high and casting its bright glow against the stained and pitted concrete.

His fingers found the trapdoor before his eyes did; it was hidden that well. But it gave a hollow thud when he hit it, and a bit of concrete dust fell from the plywood that had been cut to fit the opening, then smeared with cement to look like the rest of the wall. He pried it with a car key. It scraped toward him, then fell, dangling from the hole by a piece of rope.

Looking up the steeply angled, narrow tunnel, Frye shuddered. He pointed to the smudges the man had left.

"I'll go first now," said Minh.

Frye stood for a moment, eyes closed again, trying for confidence, or at least composure. He checked his watch: twenty minutes down. With a deep breath he gave Minh the lantern, then followed him inside.

Knees, elbows, concrete cold on the belly, not even enough room to raise his head all the way. Halfway in, he decided this was a big mistake. The lantern flickered and hissed ahead of him. Minh cursed.

Then Frye began to scramble, his elbows burning and his knees aching, but the harder he tried, the tighter things got. He finally had to just stop everything and listen to his own breathing for a moment and feel the precise thudding of his heart against the tunnel floor and try his best to think about something else. He thought of Cristobel, stark-raving nude, beckoning him. His face was hot against the cement. I hate this place, he thought, never again down here, never again. He inched forward, one calibrated movement at a time, putting his faith in the infinitesimal degrees of progress. He could see Minh, thirty feet ahead. The detective was on his back, pressing up with his arms. Something gave; his arms straightened. Frye heard a cover slide away.

Minh worked his arms and shoulders through the opening. He slipped through; Frye followed.

It smelled worse than anything he'd smelled in his life, unimaginably foul. When Minh settled the lantern on flat ground, the glow fell on rounded shapes that scurried into shadows and vanished. A high buzzing filled the air around him, a sense of motion in the upper reaches of the cavern. He choked down the urge to vomit and pulled the rest of his body into the chamber.

It was bigger than either of the first two rooms, with a high ceiling that glittered, Frye saw as he raised the lantern, with the shifting bodies of flies. A rat waddled before him and he kicked it. The rodent seemed to melt into a corner, tail disappearing, snakelike. The walls were earth, supported by a makeshift network of uneven beams laced with rope. Scrap lumber, he thought, tied instead of nailed, so no one would hear the construction from above. Three lanterns hung from the ropes. A cooler stood in one corner. He stepped over, stirring the flies overhead, and opened it. A couple of soft drinks floated in a few inches of water.

"Thirsty, Minh?"

"Shut up, Frye."

He almost gagged again. He closed his eyes and concentrated against it. He finally took off his shirt and wrapped it around his face, tying it snug behind his head. A few feet from the cooler lay a stack of announcements for the Freedom Rally. Li's hopeless face wavered in the lantern light.

"How do you get an ice chest into this hellhole, anyway?"

"I don't know, Frye. I don't care."

"You ought to. It means there's another way in here."

He picked up the lantern again, and the flies hummed louder.

Built off of the main cavern was a smaller one. Frye held the lamp before him, cinched up the shirt around his face and ducked in. On the ground was a large canvas tarpaulin, and something underneath it was moving. His hand shook with the lantern, quivering the bright light. Something scraped beneath the tarp, then moved. Frye knelt down, took one corner of the material, then stood, peeling it away. Rats turned from their meal and peered into the light, then wobbled across the two decomposing bodies and headed for the shadows.

Frye hurled away the heavy tarp, let it drop. The bodies lay face up, strewn with lye. Rats had eaten the good parts. The ski caps they had used at the Asian Wind lay beside them, removed so the lye could do its work. Their bellies had swelled. One exposed and non-eaten hand looked like a glove filled with water.

Duc, Loc's little brother, was still wearing his red high-tops.

Frye gave Minh the lantern and went back to the main room. The tunnels started tilting, and he braced himself against a damp wall. He couldn't get enough air. His skin was hot, and a throbbing pressure felt as if it was about to burst his head. His eardrums roared.

Minh's pale face looked around the corner from the other chamber. "Frye?"

What seemed important at this point was to get the hell out. "Frye!"

The next thing he knew, the Dream Reader was helping him into her den. He lay there on his back, chest heaving, the light burning into his eyes.

She looked down on him. "No Li?"

"No Li."

"You should listen to your dreams."

"I tried, goddamn it."

"The demons always win."

A few minutes later Minh crawled up, bearing the lantern before him. Frye recognized the fear in his eyes.

The detective talked to the Dream Reader in Vietnamese. Frye gathered that some deal was being made. She protested, then nodded, then nodded again.

Minh used her phone to call Duncan. "Just come to the Dream Reader's, I'll explain it when you get here."

He looked at Frye. "I'll have questions for you, but I need answers from our friends below first. I appreciate what you've done. Can you keep your mouth shut for the next forty-eight hours? Tell me I don't have to send you to jail again to make sure."

"If you send me to jail again, I'll get out and murder you. I promise." Frye stood shakily.

Minh smiled. "You okay?"

"I think so. Just got kind of mixed-up." He took one of the Dream Reader's business cards and wrote "Cristobel Strauss" on it. He handed it to the detective and explained what had happened to her. "I want to know who did it," Frye said. "I need to know who they are."

Minh looked at him with new suspicion. "Why?"

"Three of them are still following her around. I'd just like to know who I'm dealing with, and I don't want to get her upset. You can do it in one phone call to the Long Beach cops, or I can spend an hour at the courthouse. Either way, I'll—"

"Okay, Frye. I know you well enough by now to realize you don't give up. I'll find out who they are."

# CHAPTER 19

**T**HROUGH THE SCREEN DOOR, Frye could see his brother sitting on the couch. The room was dark, but a soft light played off Bennett's face. There was a tall glass in his hand and a bottle of gin on the table in front of him. A movie screen was set up in front of the TV. A carousel projector sat beside the gin bottle. Bennett looked up, his eyes all wrong. "It's late. Even Michelsen and Toibin are asleep."

Frye stepped in. "Need to use your shower."

"What happened to you?"

Crawley appeared from the kitchen.

"I found out where they first took Li. Where Eddie went. There's a tunnel under the Dream Reader's."

*"Jesus!"*

Frye plodded to the bathroom, stripped and showered, put on some clothes that Donnell brought in. He looked at himself in the mirror. He had never looked so pale and drained in all his life. Li. Xuan. Eddie. Duc and the third gunman. The smell of death was so strong on him he got back in and showered again. He stopped when the hot water ran out.

There was a glass of ice waiting when he came back to the living room. He poured on the gin, sipped, and sat back. He told them about footprints on his floor, the mud on Li's clothes, her song about the tunnel, his realization that she had been taken underground first. He told them of the trip down, every stink and horror still fresh in his mind. He told them he'd promised Minh to say nothing.

"Didn't you call Wiggins?"

"I thought Minh would handle it better. He'll tell the FBI soon enough, earn the points."

"Me and Donnell spent the whole night at the plaza, asking people if they'd seen any new faces in town. If one gunman was an outsider, maybe more out-of-town people are involved."

"Luck?"

"Zip. We'll try again in the morning."

Frye looked at the movie screen.

"I've been looking at some old stuff, Chuck. Absence doesn't make the heart fonder, it just fucks it up." Bennett drank from his gin. He looked at Frye a long while, then down. "I think about her every minute. Her face gets blurred and turns into something else. I'm trying to get a grip on it again, little brother. Pictures of me and Li. Want to see?"

Bennett had never once in twenty years showed him a candid picture from his seventeen months of war. A story here and there, a snippet, a recollection. A lot of nothing, Frye thought. Bennett slurped down more gin. He picked up the control. The projector fan eased on, and a slide rotated into place: Li and him standing outside a nightclub. She was dressed simply in a Western-style skirt and blouse. Bennett was in his dress uniform. It was night, and the club lights down the avenue were dense and bright. Bennett was smiling, his arm wrapped around her. "Saigon, March 'seventy. I'd been in-country for seven months. I'd known Li for four."

"You look happy."

"Weirdest thing in the world, Chuck, to be happy in a war. Here's some earlier shots."

He flipped back. Shots of the 25th Infantry Headquarters at Dong Zu—"Tropic Lightning," said Bennett—a sprawling complex of one-story buildings and quonsets. A swimming pool. A golf course. Jeeps and grunts everywhere. Pictures of Benny and Crawley playing basketball.

Bennett stopped at a picture of a plain quonset surrounded by DO NOT ENTER signs. A guard stood out front. "Interrogation Central," he said. "We called it Spook City. Between the CIA guys, the PSYOPS flakes and the civilian 'reps' who came and went, it was one weird fuckin' place. There were cages inside, and rooms with a foot and a half of soundproofing on the walls so the screams wouldn't get out." Bennett's head wobbled a little as he stared at the screen.

"What did you do there?"

"That's where prisoners went before we shipped them south. That's where I worked sometimes. Hell, that's boring. Look, here's Li. First one of her I ever took."

The picture showed Kieu Li sitting on a stone bench in a courtyard. Frye noted the plantation mansion, lost to vines, in the background. Li had a worried look on her face, not sure how to react. Then a shot of her and Donnell. Then of her and a young Vietnamese man dressed in U.S. Army fatigues. He looked at the camera with a quiet arrogance.

"Huong Lam," said Bennett. "The man you asked about."

"Looks like a kid."

"Seventeen. Same as Li."

The next picture was of the three of them standing outside the cottage. They had their arms around each other. The jungle had practically choked the old colonial building. Frye could see a guitar propped against the wall.

Then a close-up of Li. Frye quickly saw the same things in her that Bennett must have: a simple beauty and dignity, a composure born of acceptance, a natural gentleness that emanated from her. He could see her strength, too, inseparable from her as water from a river or heat from fire. It's what she needed to get through—he thought—the psychic national currency. Spend what you need to survive, and save what you can. Li, at least, had enough of it.

"She tell about that place in her story to Smith?"

Frye nodded, transfixed by Li's face. "Sort of."

"Beautiful little place. Not so big as the Michelin Plantation or the Fil Hol. Right in the middle of Three Corps Tac Zone, which was squat in the middle of the Viet Cong. Fuckin' COSVN was less than a hundred miles northwest. It sat out in the middle of that jungle like a temple or something. Got run down after the French were kicked out, used for a bunch of different things. I used it to debrief Li. Was close enough for us all to get to, remote enough so we wouldn't get seen and shot at."

Frye looked at the slouching wall, clenched by vines. The fountain was in the foreground. Then a shot of Huong Lam, Bennett, and another Vietnamese man. Bennett had a bottle of champagne in his hand. Around Lam's neck was the silver wave necklace that Frye had made for his brother.

Bennett drank down half a glass of gin. "The other Vietnamese guy we called Tony. He was Lam's liaison. Never could get rid of him when there was a camera around. That necklace meant a lot to Lam, because he knew it meant a lot to me. What'd you make that thing out of, Chuck?"

"A quarter."

"Nice work. Must have taken forever to file out that little wave."

"Washington's head is the top of the curl."

"On patrol, Lam wrapped it in tape, so it wouldn't jingle against his crucifix. He was a . . . weird guy. He was, like, half civilized and half savage. I never saw anybody fight with such a vengeance as him. You couldn't tire him out. He'd take chances you wouldn't believe. If we found tunnels, he'd go down. Most of the Vietnamese, they were too scared of those things. Not even Tony would go down there. We found a new hole one time, outside An Cat, hidden under a bunch of brush. Li's intelligence told us where it was. We stood around for a minute while Lam got ready. He stripped down to just shirt and pants, took a knife in his teeth, a flashlight in his left hand and a nine-millimeter Smith in his right, and went in. We had tons of tunnel gadgets sent to us. Special shot-pistols, and headlamps like miners wear, radio transmitters that would strap to your back with the mike taped to your neck so your hands would be free. Lam never used that shit. All he had was a silencer for the pistol, because down there, a pistol shot could just about deafen you. He wouldn't take a radio because things were too intense to be talking back with us. He wouldn't smoke or drink or chew gum when he knew he was going down, because you really need your nose. Lam told me he could smell the Cong down there in the dark. Actually smell them. And he said he could feel them too, like sonar or something—he could feel their eyelids opening and closing, their muscles getting ready to move, their thoughts echoing off the tunnel walls."

Frye could feel it himself, the solid darkness closing around him like fingers of a huge fist, squeezing his fear together, compacting his terror like a press.

Bennett drank again. "Thirty seconds later we heard three muffled shots. That meant he'd found another trap door. He'd always fire off three quick rounds through it before he went in. Then, two more of his shots, and one of theirs, way louder. Contact. After he got deep enough, we couldn't hear much of anything. We'd just wait and hope he'd show again."

Bennett stared at the picture of Lam. "He always would. They'd booby-trap those tunnels like crazy. They'd use snakes and spiders, spears and stakes, one-shot traps that would take your face off. They'd set crossbows in the walls and a trip wire in front you couldn't see. They'd use fucking Coke cans to make grenades and fill them with rocks and broken glass. You set off one of those in a little tunnel and you were meat. One time he found three rats tied to a stake, and a vial and syringe not far away. He brought one of the animals out and we tested it— bubonic plague. The fucking VC version of germ warfare. Or they'd build a false wall and wait behind it. You got close enough, they'd whack you out with a fucking spear. They'd hide a claymore near the entrance 'cause they knew when someone went down, a bunch of us would stand around and listen and watch. When the tunnel rat went in, the Cong would detonate the mine from inside and blow off the people above ground. But Lam, he was hip to all that shit. He knew. Sure enough, he came out all bloody and grimy. He'd found three VC and wasted them all. Lam didn't say much more until later. He was too scared to talk. But when we got back and his nerves settled, he told me what went down. Turned out that time that there were four VC—all women. He'd taken out three and just couldn't waste the last one. She was backed against a wall, not even bothering to hide anymore because she didn't have a weapon and she knew he was gonna kill her. Lam just turned away and let her be. That's what I mean about him being half civilized, too. He'd be unbelievable cruel, then do something like that. Lam had his own channel. Hell, we talked about everything. Looking back, I know I told him some shit I shouldn't have. And he used it against us later."

Bennett drank again and considered the picture. "He fooled us all, right up to the end."

Another shot of the plantation, this one apparently taken by Houng Lam. Bennett and Crawley hugged Li, while a grinning Tony edged into the far side of the frame. The next picture was of Bennett and Li, crammed into a booth in a bar. Crawley sat beside her and three other soldiers were pressing into the shot, all drunken smiles. Frye noted a familiar face, far right.

"The Pink Night Club at the Catinat, Chuck. Helluva place. Li got a few gigs there. I got her an apartment on Tu Do Street in Saigon just a few weeks before I got blown up. Look at this one! That's Li and Elvis Phuong. Great singer, that fuckin' Elvis. He sings at the Wind sometimes. Li did a set with him and the band and Elvis backed her up. I thought she'd come unglued she was so nervous. Everybody loved her. She had that something about her. Now check this! There she is on stage."

Li stood, mike in hand. Frye could see the muscles in her neck straining beneath the pure white skin. She had on a black mini-skirt and a pair of matching boots.

"Nice, Benny. Burke Parsons, on the right?"

Bennett nodded and drank again, shaking his head. "Burke was CIA, so our paths crossed and we hung out some. He came and went. That was the spooks."

The next picture sent a chill of sadness through him. Bennett was leading Li to a dance floor, her hand in his, her face beaming up at him, his trousers pressed tight around his good strong legs.

Bennett stared at the picture a moment. "They still itch and ache sometimes," he said. "And my fucking knee gets sore. Remember the knee?"

"Football."

"Back then, I thought torn ligaments were a bummer"—more gin—"But I never complained, Chuck. And I'm not gonna start now."

"Maybe it would do some good."

"Fuck complaints, little brother. Fuck you and fuck me. Now here, this is the kitchen of our place on Tu Do."

Frye's heart sank as he looked at the screen. Li was sitting at a table with a cup of something raised to her lips, caught unaware, a look of surprise on her face. The apartment looked small and almost empty, washed in a rounded, yellow, distinctly eastern light. There was a vase with no flowers in it on the table in front of her. Frye felt an overwhelming sense of solitude in the shot—the solitude of a girl without her family, of a soldier far away from his, of a small room in a big city soon to fall. Two solitudes, really, vast and hemispheric as two halves of the earth, coming together for reasons more desperate than either of them could have known.

"Nice apartment," said Bennett. Frye watched him wipe his eyes with a fist. "Really nice little place to be. Cost me a fortune, but Pop sent money by the pound. You should have seen her, Chuck. Sitting on the bench at the plantation with a fucking guitar. She was just a girl. It was her innocence, how simply she accepted things. Innocence isn't right—more like faith. Yeah, faith, that was what she had."

Bennett drew carefully on the bottle. His eyes never left the screen. When he started talking again, it was to the picture. "Yeah, you should have seen her. She was everything I thought we were fighting for. She was young and beautiful as a girl could be. She'd sing all the fuckin' time and that voice was like heroin inside my veins. It made me feel warm and good inside. She had one of those faces that seem to have a light on behind it. Even when there wasn't any sun and it rained a week straight, she had a glow. It was unreal, but the things I felt coming alive in me when I talked to her, they were brand-new. It was like she was a perfect animal. A perfect human female animal, right there in front of me. Everything I thought that animal should be. We connected. She picked up English fast."

Bennett dropped the carousel controller and hooked his thumbs together, flapping his hands like wings. "She'd do like that when she saw me. Frye always came out 'Flye,' like a bird. I told her we could fly away from that war together someday. We did. We tried to."

"I see what you loved in her, Benny."

"No," Bennett said quietly. "You don't. She *was* Vietnam. Her parents came south in 'fifty-four because they were strong Catholics. Mom died of fever; they killed her father because he wouldn't shelter the Cong. You know what she wanted? She wanted to study music." Bennett examined his gin, tilted back the bottle and drank. "So there she was, like the rest of the goddamned country, trying to be left alone while the Viet Cong terrified them at night and we ran the place during the day. *She's why I'm here,* I thought. *These are the people we came here for. We're here to give them half a chance at running their own lives someday.*

Frye watched his brother lean back and stare for a long while at the ceiling.

"You tried."

Bennett reached clumsily under the couch cushion and brought out a .45. He almost tipped over, then righted himself and studied the barrel of the gun. "See this? I'm not afraid of this."

"Put it down. You're drunk."

Bennett clicked off the safety and looked down the barrel again.

"I got soaked in Agent Orange, Chuck, and I don't have cancer. I saw worse shit than you can dream up and I've never had a flashback I couldn't handle. I had enough pain for a whole city, but I don't shoot, pop, or snort. I drink because I always drank. I don't even collect the disability I got coming. You know why? Because I'm one tough stand-up motherfucker, and they can keep their dollars and send 'em to someone who needs it."

"Come on, Benny. Put it down."

Bennett gazed through Frye. "I got my legs blown off, that's all. But Chuck, I gotta tell you right now, if they kill her, I'm gonna blow my brains out too. That's no complaint, that's just what is. Without her, I'm a bunch of pieces left all over the globe. With her, I can still see why it happened and why it was worth it."

Bennett clicked back the hammer, hooked his thumb against the trigger and rested the gun in his lap, barrel pointing at his chin. "What more can I do, Chuck? What more? I keep looking, and she doesn't come home."

Frye reached out his hand. "Come on, brother," he said softly. "We're gonna get her. She's okay. It's going to come out all right, Benny. I promise. Then it'll be just like old times. We'll eat on the island on Thursdays and argue with Pop, and Mom'll be happy and Li can write some more songs on the Martin. Maybe you can meet this new girl—Cristobel—she's really good, Benny. The four of us could do something. Maybe we could get the family like it was in the old days. We'll be tight again. Come on, Benny. Debbie's gone. Don't you go too. That wouldn't be fair."

Frye reached out and touched his brother's hand. Slowly, he eased Bennett's thumb from the trigger guard, then brought the gun away. Bennett tipped over, burped, tried to sit back up and tipped over again. "What am I supposed to *do?*"

Frye and Donnnel worked his clothes off and got him to the shower. Bennett slumped in the corner and stared out, a defeated soldier, while the warm water ran down him.

# CHAPTER 20

ACK HOME, FRYE GOT INTO A pair of MegaTrunks and waxed his board. He made the ten-minute walk to Rockpile while the first light of morning coalesced in the east.

The hurricane surf had hit. He stood on the sand and watched the horizon, the plate-glass water, the gray waves marching in, precise as infantry. Each crashing mountain sent a tremor up his ankles and into his legs. Eight feet at least, he thought, and all muscle. Hard, vascular tubes, well shaped. The air filled with spray, and the sand vibrated. Frye watched two surfers carefully picking their waves. One took off and got launched from the lip—nothing but the long fall down for this man—his orange board trailing after him like a flame. The other thought better and backed off. More like ten feet, Frye saw now, and getting bigger. The beach trembled. The wide white noose of a riptide wavered out when the set ended.

He could still smell the death in his nostrils, on his skin, in the air around him, everywhere.

*What am I supposed to do?*

I don't know, Benny. If I did, I'd do it for you. But it's clear to me that you're over your head and so am I, and that things are going to get worse before they get better.

Frye sat on the damp beach, took a handful of sand, and let it run between his fingers. He wondered if he'd simply been there more, closer to Bennett, more involved with the family, more present, somehow this all wouldn't have happened. Ridiculous, he thought. But little things can make the difference. The road is paved by degrees, the thousand paths taken, or not. We steer by the second. Take your eyes off the road, you hit a cement mixer or cream a nun in a crosswalk. Take your pick. It's the small stuff that adds up, or doesn't. Something here prevents something there—a word, a gesture, an action.

And Frye knew that the last ten years of his life had been a slow retreat from his family, his wife, his own future. When you ignore enough problems, he thought, they become one problem. And the more you ignore it the faster it grows until you end up sitting on a cold beach, wondering if the one thing in your life you do well is going to kill you. More than anything, you hate yourself for being afraid.

I want back in. I can try.

He paddled out. Past the shorebreak, he looked south to Cristobel's faded blue apartments, which from this angle seemed to be spilling into the water. Brooks Street will be pumping, he thought, so will Salt Creek and Trestles. You have to admit it: Rockpile on a hurricane swell is one ugly break. A surfer waved; Frye waved back.

Sitting outside on his board now, he blew into his hands, tried to get the blood going. All he could feel was the damp chill of the tunnel, and the putrid cavern where Loc's brother lay. He shivered. The morning sky was gray and so was the water, and somewhere far to the west they met without a seam. The next set lined up against it. He lowered himself to the board and paddled hard, rising with the first wave. He was surprised how big it was. The next wave came close behind, bigger still. He scrambled up its face and pitched over on the far side, ready for another. Third time's charm, he thought, sliding for the sweet spot on the incoming mountain, finding it, pivoting his board and with three hard strokes of his arms, felt the wave's mass catch hold of him, take him up, then hesitate and offer him that one last opportunity to get out.

Frye looked down, felt the panic clustering at the base of his spine. He looked down at the miniaturized shore, the tiny hotel and blue apartments, the toy cars inching along Coast Highway a thousand feet below him. He looked down at the water sucking out, the beach receding. He felt the wave rising, rising, rising with him into the gray sky, gathering its aqueous tonnage for final release.

He made one last terrified assessment, then bailed.

Grabbing his board with both hands, he yanked it back toward the ocean as hard as he could. He plopped down to safety as the wave rose, hovered for a moment, then boomed ashore behind him. Somehow he made over the next wave of the set. He sat up on his board, heart thumping, arms weak and cold. The board dipped and bobbed. He could see his feet below, pale smudges in the dark water.

Frye could never remember feeling so isolated out here, so separate and temporary. It is not good to feel part of nothing.

He just sat there and watched the next wave coming in, his face flushed, feeling some part of himself—a portion of what he'd always been, a sense of substance and character, a feeling of singularity, at very least a passion that defined him if only to himself—passing him up with every untaken wave.

The clean-up wave formed ahead of him, the last and largest by far.

What he did next was partly out of spite, partly out of desperation, partly out of shame. It was the one thing he could think to do that was positive. He did it for Li and he did it for Cristobel and he did it for Bennett and he did it for himself. He did it as a funeral for the way he had been.

He pivoted, stroked twice, and dropped in.

The downward rush was exceptionally steep and fast, his board trying to jet ahead without him. He eased a rail into the flank of water and shot laterally, the wave lip smacking his head. Then he was in front of it, banking back down, body bent and arms out for balance, centered for speed. At the bottom he snapped his heels out and leaned in, shooting up again as the board rose instantly and he loosened his knees for the shock, climbing up the vertiginous wall, looking back to the big cylinder that gained quickly on him. Near the top he crouched and leveled off and let the heaving barrel come over him, then stood and slowed just a fraction to get far back into it, where the sand and the foam swirl furiously and the world condenses to a roar that you can feel all the way to your bones. Frye gently traced his hand along the wall of water that enclosed him, fingers thrumming liquid ribs, feet vibrating with his board, looking ahead as through a fluid telescope to where the wave was forming—this momentary heart of things—fresh and big and new out of the sea. In a moment of purest velocity, knees bent slightly and his fingertips brushing the cylinder, he stood there: reduced, washed, opinionless.

As usual at this point, Frye never knew what hit him.

All he did know was that he felt suddenly dark and pressurized, strangely removed now, with only a dull thundering somewhere overhead. No light. A rotating kind of motion, but not self-governed, as if he were a gear driven by other gears in some great liquid machine.

He tried to let himself float to the top but the grinding of the huge wave held him down. A few kicks toward bottom—just where is it now? Eyes open: a gritty swirl of shadow and half-light, shapes moving within shapes. Blow out some air and follow the bubbles up. But he was tumbling still, and the bubbles simply joined the turbulence and disappeared.

Then this wonderment of the senses: a feeling of falling but not necessarily down, maybe up or sideways or all directions at once; followed by a realization that something is missing here, some fundamental faculty linking the organism to gravity. He pushed off the bottom with a fear-driven heave, but there was no bottom. Lights arced through his head. He thought of saving the last of his breath to simply float upward, but the last of his breath was gone.

He thrashed against the darkness, a burst of energy as he strained for the surface and finally gulped a mouthful of sandy water. He could feel the scream from his system: what is this, Chuck? God, please no. Then the weakness coming, and a warmth with it, and the uneasy hypothesis that he was really just dreaming and about to waken and everything would be okay and Hyla would be there with hot chocolate and let him watch TV awhile. Another breath of water. He could sense his arms out ahead of him in the murk, paddling, turtlelike, trying to lead his head to air.

Then Hyla had hold of him. She was dragging him. She was barking like a dog.

Her face finally congealed before him, at odds with memory. Blond hair and long, nothing like mom. Why is she barking? Hands under my arms now, some dragging motion on sand. Faces. Legs. Puke, then breathe, in that order. Then a hot rush of sea water up from the lungs, burning nose, mouth, ears, eyes, pores. A wolfish creature bearing down, speaking in tongues. Someone up there slaps it away. More shapes, all in black. I am in alien hands. I am on my back. Chest goes up and down. Air is good. Life is good.

Of course. Cristobel. Surfers. Dunce.

He worked himself to hands and knees, chest heaving, vomiting between breaths. Dunce barked and shot in and out of his vision with each wretched outpouring. He could sense someone beside him: bare feet, jeans, a spill of light hair as a hand tried to steady his back. In the mid-distance he saw more legs, heard mumbled concern. "Whoa, he's like throbbin' lucky he's not totaled right now. Rad wipeout. Is that that Frye guy, or some tourist?"

Good God, he thought. Get me out of here.

Cristobel helped him up and guided him to where the sand meets the rocks. He settled down to the cool earth, still breathing heavily, lights still pinging around his skull. A moment later she returned with his board, both halves, which she leaned against a boulder. Dunce sat and studied him as Cristobel wrapped a towel around his shoulders. "I knew it," she said. "I felt it, strong."

He looked at her, hugging himself under the towel.

"I saw it. When you didn't come up I waded out. Blaster helped."

"Thanks," he said. His voice was helium-high. He watched another set forming outside and shuddered, then launched into a new fit of coughing.

She knelt beside him and tucked the towel close to his neck. Her smell cut straight through his brine-drenched senses, an aroma of woman and earth so solid you could stand on it. The onshore breeze stuck a batch of golden hair to his face as she leaned in close. "Can you make it to my place?"

A while later he stood uneasily, straightened his shoulders and breathed deeply, which sent him into another paroxysm of coughing that bent him in half. When he'd discharged what seemed at least half a gallon of ocean water, he smiled like death at Cristobel. "Let's go."

"What about that?"

Frye looked at his board, halved neatly and leaning on the rocks. "Public service reminder," he said, and offered her his hand.

Blaster led the way, his red scarf in a cavalryesque lilt to the east.

He sat in a sunlit rectangle on the floor, warming in the rays that came through the window. Jim was on a shoot in L.A. Blaster nuzzled against his leg, then turned over for a belly rub. Cristobel changed into dry shorts and a halter top, then went to the kitchen to make coffee. Frye regarded the dress she was working on, now hanging on a mannequin. He coughed. Cristobel's humming came to him from the kitchen. He had always liked a woman who hummed. He liked it so much he fell asleep.

When he woke again the sunlight had drifted from his face to his stomach. Lying still, he watched Cristobel's back and legs as she stood in front of the dress, as she then leaned forward to make some adjustment. Steam eased up from the floor a few feet away, and he rotated an eye for explanation: a coffee cup placed on the carpet, just far enough so he wouldn't knock it over. She had put a pillow under his head. He watched her hands now, slender but large-knuckled: one pinching the fabric, the other reaching forward, a pin ready. She was up on the balls of her feet, springy, like a basketball player. She moved forward for a closer look and smoothed the silk with her finger. She arched her back, cocked her head, and crossed her arms in an analytical pause, then turned to look at him. "Well, sleeping beauty, what do you think?"

"Perfect."

"Not much of a critic, are you?"

"I know what I like."

"It's not finished yet."

"It will be soon. Then you'll see what I mean."

She bit her lip gently, looked at the dress, then back to Frye. "I designed it myself."

She smiled, blushed a little. Blaster's tail knocked against the hardwood floor. "Every time I look down to Rockpile I see you going over."

"I'm glad you were there. You saved my life, Cristobel."

"Aw, shucks."

He sipped the coffee, leaned up on an elbow. "Now you're stuck with me."

"What's a girl to do?"

"Could come over here and lie in the sun."

She looked at the dress for a long moment, then at Frye. Blaster lumbered over, working his nose under one of her hands. She took a pillow and lay down beside him, a couple of feet away, braced on an elbow. She was back-lit by the sun. It made her hair even lighter as it dangled down in a loose braid. Frye looked long at her, and she looked back. "You look real beautiful to me," he said.

"I'm glad that's what you see."

Blaster tried to squeeze in between them; Cristobel shoved him away. He lay instead on the other side of her, resting his head in then narrow part of her waist, watching Frye with big round eyes, affable, moronic. "You've got an admirer."

"Isn't he a sweetheart?"

Frye shrugged. He had learned years ago that a man can't compete with a woman's pets. He reached out and touched her face.

She reddened. "You feel okay?"

He nodded. He could feel himself getting sucked into her dark brown eyes.

Suddenly she was telling him about fashion design, how it started off as something to do to win trophies at the local fair. She explained that her older brother had Little League and Pop Warner trophies all over the place, that her father had Toastmaster plaques, that her mother had a whole roomful of civic awards and citations. "I had this dresser in my room with nothing on it but one picture of my horse and one of Mickey Dolenz. I decided to fill it up with hardware like everybody else had. I started entering all the little fairs and contests in Mendocino County, then some down in Sacramento and San Francisco. Sure enough, I heaped that whole dresser full awards and ribbons. Then my brother became a hippie, so he tossed the trophies. And Dad had already won everything he could at Toastmasters so he quit. And Mom got sick of philanthropy so she stuck to the garden. I didn't want to lose a good thing, so I just kept on sewing. Later, I started designing my own clothes."

"You're smart to stick with it. Now you've got something that's yours."

Frye reached out and touched her face again. It flushed, but she kept looking at him. He brushed back her hair. He could sense her body tensing; her jaw went tight. She lifted a hand toward him. It hovered a moment, withdrew. She looked away, took a deep long breath. "This isn't anything like you think it is," she said. "There are layers of me to cut through."

"With a little luck, I'll cut in the right place."

She sighed and touched his face with her hand. "There's no such thing as luck. We get what we ask for."

"I feel lucky you were at Rockpile today. That you were there Monday morning when we met."

She looked at him oddly, then away. "Anyway, what about you? Always surf and stuff like that?"

Frye told her about the first time he'd paddled out on a surfboard, one that Bennett had made for him, a cute little thing just under five feet long, with his name written in flashy red letters across the deck. He was six. Bennett was eleven. "I couldn't stand on the damned thing, so I just slid around on my belly all morning, riding the whitewater in. After lunch we went back out. It was one of those hot fall days when the water's green and the waves are little and shaped perfect. Bennett said he wouldn't let me back to the beach unless I stood up and *rode* back. He helped me find the right place to take off. I fell a hundred times, then finally got up. I can see it just like it was. I'm crouching down like I'm going a hundred, arms out, absolutely stoked. We stayed out until the sun went down, and I had big rashes under my arms from the wetsuit."

"You'll never forget that day."

"No way." Frye went on to relate how that night Benny and his friends had taken him down to the water at the island and performed the ancient Hawaiian ritual that all new surfers were allowed to enjoy. They made him drink three swallows of his father's bourbon—part of the ceremony, they explained—then peed on him.

Cristobel laughed. Blaster looked up and panted knowingly. "What horrible little boys," she said.

"I was deeply moved. I had my swimsuit on, so I just waded out and washed off. I was laughing like a fool. Bourbon hits a kid hard."

Frye described his abortive college career, his attempts to major in geology, marine biology, English. Finally, he just flunked out and joined the surfing tour, to the horror of his father. He recalled Edison's letter of acknowledgment, which arrived while he was competing in the miserably cold waters of Australia and getting rather creamed by unfriendly locals, saying, "If you choose to kill your mind, son, then your body will surely follow. With love and disappointment, Father."

Cristobel frowned, then laughed again. "Sounds like my dad. They always want you to do what you want to do, as long as it's what *they* want you to do. They try. Mine was extra hard on Mike, my brother. So when Mike was shot down over there, it tore Dad up."

"Your folks still alive?"

She shook her head. "Just me now. Don't say you're sorry. I hate those words. Just put your hand on my face again, like you did."

Frye touched her. He scooted closer, but not too close. She smelled so good. She kept looking at him. For a long time he just held his face close to hers, smelling her breath and the richness of her skin. What do I smell like, he wondered, seawater? When he moved his lips to hers, she turned away. He kissed her ear instead. She pressed up close to him. She was shaking. "Something's starting. I don't want anything to start. That's not why I'm here."

"Yes, it is."

"But just hold on to me awhile, Chuck. Kind of light, like. I'm . . . I'm so damned glad you're alive and here with me."

He did, a long while, until his lower shoulder was asleep and the hand that stroked her head was heavy and tired. Twice he started to tell her about the tunnels and what he had found there, but he stopped, unwilling to bring that horror into Cristobel's sunlit living room. The rays rushed the window and made her hair warm. Blaster, his head still resting on the small of Cristobel's waist, looked up at Frye, yawned, and closed his eyes again.

Frye could hear the surf pounding outside, and through the corner of window he could see the lanky palms of Heisler Park drooping far in the distance. The sun hovered, an orange disc. For the first time in two days he felt warm. He was glad to be alive too, and to be here with her. Some things, he thought, are so good and simple.

Then she was kissing him, lightly at first, then deeper. She moved closer. A hand touched his neck.

Inside, Frye shrieked with delight.

She sat up, cross-legged now. Frye sat in front of her, legs apart, scooting close. "I hope you don't hate me for this someday," she said.

"I don't know what you mean."

"You don't. You really don't."

He slipped the straps of her top away and kissed her round dark shoulders. Her breasts were soft under his hands. When he pulled away the halter she breathed deeply and her nipples stood up and he took one between his teeth. She leaned back, hands braced behind her. She lifted her butt as he slid her shorts down, then tossed them onto the couch. Frye looked down at her nakedness, her lovely round body, the plain of tan on her stomach, the narrow white section of hip, then the dark wedge between smooth strong thighs. Blaster gave him a concerned look. Then Cristobel moved forward and put a hand up his leg, all the way to the sandy lining of his swimsuit. He helped her get it off. Their mouths locked and she moaned. She pulled away. "I don't know if I can do this." She touched him gently. "I see that you can."

"Oh, yes."

"Be slow."

Frye lowered her on her side and guided her hips toward him. The kiss got deeper and deeper, and he could feel the sunlight on his hand as he moved it across her shoulders and back, her butt and legs, down the outside, up the inside where, to Frye's mild astonishment, she was very much ready for this. "Oooh, *God*," she said.

He found her mouth again. He rolled her over and braced himself on his hands and knees.

Then she pulled away. "No."

"Yes."

When he tried to take her, her legs suddenly clenched, a corded flex that felt like steel. He tried to get a knee inside. "It's okay," he said. "Okay, sweet woman, okay."

Her head was tilted back. Tears ran up her face, into her ears and hair. "This is wrong," she whispered.

"This is right."

He could sense her will taking over. Her legs opened, her stomach quivered. The moment he touched her, Cristobel grabbed his arms and pushed off him, wriggling away. She worked herself up with the unsteadiness of a foal. She stood there in the sunlight, trying to cover her breasts. She looked down at Frye with her hair a disaster and tears rolling off her cheeks. "I hate this," she said. She turned and disappeared into the bathroom.

He sat there for a moment, his member aiming dolefully up at his own forehead, wondering what you do in a case like this. She was running water in the bathroom. He thought he heard sobs, too.

He went in without knocking and took her in his arms. She had already put on a silk robe. Frye took it off, and it melted to the floor. He held her close and rocked her like Hyla used to rock him, back and forth with his hands spread across her back and her face buried in his neck. "It's okay, Cris. Forget it. We'll do it when it's right. It's okay."

"I don't want to forget it, and it's never going to be right. I want you."

"Oh?"

He led her to the bedroom, a collection of purples and lavenders, a bright, sunny room. They fell onto the bed.

"What I want you to know," she said, "is that this isn't at all what I wanted to happen."

She was stroking him again. The idea struck him that Cristobel was a contradictory animal, but he was soon past the point of ideas altogether. Then she guided him in, slowly, a little shudder as he entered and buried himself deep as he could go, a perfectly tooled connection.

"Oh no," she said.

"Oh yes." He let her have the control. She was tentative at first. She lay back her head and closed her eyes, and Frye wondered what visions were exacting themselves on the backs of her eyelids. Her face was dotted with sweat. Her hair was all over the place. Then the ancient rhythm took over and Frye joined her,

222

chasing down that place in her where all the nerves converge, where the detonations begin, where the center explodes and reforms and sends out deltas of pleasure all the way to the fingertips. He could feel it gathering inside her, inside himself. There was nowhere else on Earth he'd rather be. He propped up her head with his hand and kissed her. When it came, she arched her back and cried out, and Frye joined her, shaking, planting everything he had to plant, shuddering while the quakes broke over him, electrocuted on his own nerves. Below him, petals of voltage opened and bloomed, muscles tightened, breathing stopped, sharp fingernails trailed down his back.

They lay there, locked in aftershock.

Then Cristobel took a deep breath, so deep Frye could feel her heart slamming away as her chest rose. She released. Her fingers relaxed. Her legs lowered to the bed.

Cristobel slept while Frye worked himself free and went to the telephone to call Westminster Hospital about visiting hours for Tuy Nha.

He looked at Cristobel sleeping in the bedroom and felt fatherly. He smiled, then stood there, browsing the sundry collection of odds and ends tacked to the bulletin board near the phone.

Funny, he thought, how when you like somebody, even their minor stuff seems important to you: coupons, phone numbers, two Florida postcards with alligators on them, an old photograph, some slick shots of Jim, looking very *GQ*.

The corner of the newspaper photo caught his eye, because he had seen it so many times before, because he knew exactly what it was.

It was thumbtacked up there, behind a city recreation schedule and a local nightclub listing. Less than an inch of it showed, but he knew what the rest of it looked like. He swung away the other papers and looked at himself, dressed in the ape costume, grinning like a fool, chasing the Mystery Maid toward the hedge of blooming hibiscus.

God, how I hate that thing, he thought.

He looked at Cristobel. And what are you doing with it?

*You're Chuck Frye, aren't you? I saw you in some contests . . .*

Maybe she thinks it's funny.

Maybe she saw it, thought I was cute, cut it out.

Maybe it's Jim's, not hers.

The hospital operator gave him visitor's hours. He hung up.

He was curious. He picked up Cristobel's address book and turned to F. No Frye. Nothing under C. He tried Z instead. There it was, CF, followed by his number. His address was under it.

She was still sleeping. Dunce regarded him blankly.

Does she have the MegaShop number too?

Under the Ms was no MegaShop number, but a regulation business card that said Mai Ngo Thanh Tong—Saigon Plaza.

He closed the book.

Cristobel was still asleep. He went in, pulled the pillow out from under her head and stood there. "What's that picture of me doing on your fridge?"

She swam back from dreamland. "Picture?"

"The ape deal. And how come you've got my number in your book? We just met on Monday morning, didn't we? A coincidence, right? Accident."

She frowned, backed against the head stand, pulled the bed spread over her. "Jesus, Chuck."

"Jesus, nothing. What gives?"

She looked at him hard, then down at the bed. When she looked back up, he could see the anger in her face. "You fuck me once, you think you own me?"

"I don't want to own you. I want to know what you're doing with my stats when we met three days ago."

She shook her head, a bitter smile forming at the corners of her mouth. "Why don't you just leave?"

"Not until I get some answers from you."

"Wanna hit me? Maybe I'll talk faster."

"No chance of that."

"What do you think, Chuck? That I wanted to seduce you? That I had it all planned ahead of time? Where to find you? What your number is? Where to find your house so I can bring flowers and a card?"

"Tell me the truth."

"I just did."

She looked down again, bit her lip. Frye watched a tear roll down her face. She wiped it away with the sheet. "I'm sorry," she said.

"For what?"

"For this." She looked at him, then out the window. She swallowed hard. "Well, that's it. You can go now."

"I'm listening."

"What do you want? A confession?"

"Sure."

"You're an arrogant bastard, aren't you?"

"I never looked at it that way. I just want to know what's going on. And what about that Saigon Plaza number?"

"Okay, you deserve that much. I . . . I did plan it. I wanted it. I've had that picture for months. I got your number and kept it in my book for a long time. I made it a point to be at Rockpile that morning. It wasn't the first time I was there." She wiped her face again. "I'd seen you there a hundred times. I watched you from my window first, then I got a pair of binoculars. You were a man, but you were far away and I could see you when I wanted. I could control you. You couldn't get too close. And believe me, that's a nice option after being . . . put upon. I could see you and have the distance, too." Cristobel sighed and looked at him. He couldn't quite believe this was happening. "Look in the closet, Chuck."

Frye slid open the door. A brand new MegaBoard rested inside, never used. The price tag was still on it. "I was hoping you'd be there when I went in. I did see you there a few times. Guess you didn't notice. Those rolled-up things down by my shoes—they're posters of you. And that Saigon Plaza number, that's the fabric store where I buy my silk."

"Oh." Frye felt as stupid now as he'd ever felt in his life.

"I actually couldn't wait for some excuse to come over to your house. I had it pictured as being sinful and full of . . . I don't know. I heard it was a cave. When I moved to this place after the . . . after what happened, I started hearing about you. I saw you in a contest down at Brooks. I knew you were married so I didn't do anything. I cut out the picture of you because—it was a picture of you." She sobbed, looking away. "I thought I'd taken everything down. I forgot that Mystery Maid thing. I'm just a stupid fucking little girl. You can go now, Chuck. I just wanted you, and now I guess I've had you. Once isn't quite enough, but it was still pretty sweet, wasn't it?"

Frye sat on the bed. Then he rolled over and took her in his arms. She was crying now, and he could feel the warm tears running down his neck. "I'm awful sorry."

"Go, please."

"I'm sorry. I shouldn't have—"

"So am I, Chuck. I can't tell you how sorry I am."

"Can we forget about this?"

"I'll try, if you will."

"Jesus. You saved my life. What I'd really like is to make love to you now."

She moved closer to him and touched his face with her hands. "Yes, please."

# CHAPTER 21

**T**WO FEDERAL MARSHALS WERE standing outside Tuy Nha's hospital room as Frye walked up. One checked his name off a list while the other studied his driver's license as if it were a rare manuscript. They rummaged through the gifts he'd brought.

Frye found Nha staring out a window, past a cart piled with flowers and cards. The room was small and white, and the smell of carnations floated on a clinical underlayer of hospital air. A television was suspended on the wall across from her bed. The picture on the screen was a soap opera; the sound was off.

She lay, propped with pillows, a blank notepad on her lap, a pen in her hand. She turned a face so pale and drained of life to Frye he wondered if she were dying. "Chuck," she said in a whisper.

He kissed her cheek, sat, and took her weightless hand in his. "Nha."

"It was very strange, Chuck. My thoughts came through my fingers, and I wrote your name. Then, your name came into my mouth and I spoke again. It hurt."

"I'm honored you asked for me."

A smile suggested itself, mostly in her eyes. "When I look out at night and see the stars, I think of him. Did you ever think how far away they are, the stars?"

"We're all in the same sky, Nha."

"So far to get there."

"There's no hurry. Here." Frye gave her the package he'd hastily wrapped in the cave-house.

Nha's fingers picked at the thing, failed. Frye opened it for her, placing the box beside her. She pulled out a silver wave necklace, taking the pendant in her palm and letting the chain dangle through her frail fingers. "It has magical powers," he said.

"Really?"

"No. I just thought you'd like it. I designed it. They were popular a few years back, when I was. The first one I ever made I sent to my brother when he was in Vietnam. It was supposed to protect him and remind him of home."

"Did it?"

"He gave it away, to tell the truth."

She smiled. He helped her put it on. She fiddled with it, smoothing her hospital smock to give it a good place to lie. "Do you think it's possible to do a brain transplant, Chuck? I'm sure it is dangerous but I would volunteer. Think, Chuck. Not a single memory. I would choose the brain of . . . let's see . . . a cow. Dull and warm and concerned with grass and calves."

"I'd like you better if you stayed a woman."

"But think, to be empty. Where your past is only an hour long, and your future is a concept you are ignorant of. Will you ask Dr. Levin if he'll make me a cow?"

Frye smiled at her, inwardly shocked at the deadness in her eyes, the way she moved so slowly, the way her body seemed to withdraw from its spirit as he watched. "No, Nha. He's going to leave you a person. If you were a cow, the necklace wouldn't fit."

"I can always rely on you for logic, Chuck."

"Here, I brought you these, too." He set a folder of some of his articles on her bed. Attached to each were his notes on the subject, interview stuff, notes to himself before writing. "I thought while you had some time you could read the preliminaries, then see the way they went into the articles. Maybe give you some idea of how you get a bunch of information on something, then whack it down to a size you can work with. For your writing, you know. The articles aren't especially good—in fact I got fired for one of them—but you can see the process."

She actually smiled this time, white teeth and pink lips. "You're putting me to work already, Chuck."

"I don't want you getting into trouble here. Idle hands, and all that."

"Well, I haven't been a complete vegetable. Here is for you." She gave him a folded sheet of yellow paper. He could see the imprint of her writing on it, the long delicate script. "You can read it now if you like to."

> One new star appeared last night
> High in the heaven, seen
> Only by eyes that knew its light
> Here, where once he walked
> Beneath that sky unknowing
> It was soon to be his home.
> And as I watched,
> Its tiny fingers spread to touch others
> Through darkness thicker
> Than a midnight snow,
> And together made a chain
> Of light untouchable to me below.

"It's beautiful. It's perfect."

"My poetry professor would say it reeks of sentiment."

"He's never written anything this good."

Detective Minh's face appeared in the doorway. Frye watched him smile, then disappear.

"He's been here every day," she said. "And so have the FBI. At first it was questions. Now, it just seems they are here to keep the reporters away. It was difficult to get them to let me see you, but I became emotional."

Frye sat beside her.

She sat up straighter, fingered the pendant. "Chuck, you must help me. I need you to help."

"Anything."

Nha looked out the window as she spoke now. "My mother

and sisters have not gone back into our house. So it is undis-
turbed. In the living room, there is an altar. Small and red, near
the piano."

"I remember it."

"Inside the altar, behind the fruit, there is something I want
you to take and destroy. Burn it for me. And please, do not ask
me to explain."

Frye considered, studying her pale profile against the pillow.

Nha reached for her purse beside the bed and lifted it with
some effort. The key she handed him had a piece of red yarn
attached. "It will open the patio door in the back yard. Please, be
careful."

Frye went through the Tuys' side gate, around to the back of the
house, and ducked under the yellow crime-scene ribbon. The late
afternoon sun beat against the drawn curtains. It was hot inside,
and everything looked the same as he remembered. He breathed
deeply and felt dizzy.

The shrine was just where it had been, with the same fruit and
incense. He knelt and pulled out an orange, an apple, a tangerine.

He whirled away and stood, hearing a sound from the kitchen.

Then the stillness descended again, the unperturbed silence of
the dead.

He knelt again and felt inside the altar. Nothing. Just a small
square space, rough wood, unpainted. He reached in farther and
felt it there, taped to the roof of the little shrine. The masking
tape rasped away and the canister fell into his palm.

Black plastic with a gray top. Inside, a strip of film negative.
He held it up to the faint light. Writing of some kind, eighteen
exposures in all. The print was too small to read.

He rolled the strip back into the container and slipped it into
his pocket, then replaced the fruit.

For a moment he stood in Xuan's study. He looked at the
blood-soaked sofa and desk. What in the world, he wondered,
could possibly be worth this?

In the good light of the cave-house, Frye studied the negatives
under his magnifying glass. It was typewriting, done on an old
machine, with the characters in poor alignment and the tops of
the t's and f's missing. The typist kept dropping the cap key

**2 3 0**

before completing the stroke, so the big letters hovered above the lines as if trying to float away.

The eighteen frames were of six pages that described a detailed monthly itinerary of Thach, a description and clumsy drawing of an apartment, and an aerial photograph of a military camp.

Frye read it through, twice. It seemed that Thach spent one week a month at home, and the other three at the compound. *Thach is not approachable at camp.* While at home, he remained inside the apartment almost all the time. He slept in a room in the west corner, bathed and shaved in a bathroom with a window looking south. *Thach not approachable during this time. The street outside is too busy. His door is always watched.*

Subordinates bought food each day at four in the afternoon, and Thach prepared it himself. He ate alone. The apartment was built around a courtyard, in which he read during the day when the weather was conducive. *Thach is not approachable at this time.* At night, he viewed films of the war, making extensive notes on a large pad. The writer speculated that he was working on a book. Thach made from fifteen to twenty phone calls each day, none lasting for more than two minutes. Twice a week while at his apartment, he received a prostitute. She was always the same girl, delivered always by the same taxi. She would stay for two hours, then leave. The writer noted that at least one of Thach's men was constantly posted outside the apartment door, and the others busied themselves with errands. One guard always slept there. At no time was Thach completely alone. *Recommend that Thach not be approached at home.*

The drive north, which Thach made early in the morning on the second Sunday of each month, was a distance just short of one hundred and fifty kilometers. One of his men would drive, while Thach sat in the passenger seat.

*Because of the acute angle in the road twenty-one kilometers from the Saigon city limit, Thach's vehicle must nearly stop in order to make turn. This turn is sixteen meters south of the An Loc Bridge. On the north shoulder of the road, thick underbrush and tall palms provide dense cover. Because Thach sits on the passenger side, he is exposed at this moment. When the trip is undertaken during favorable weather, the vehicle top is removed. He is exposed at kilometer twenty-one. He is approachable at this place and time. Resistance sympathy is high in this area now, both entry and escape would be possible. The road to Loc Ninh is not heavily traveled.*

2 3 1

Frye read the material again, taking mental note of the particulars, then burned it in his sink.

Thach, he thought, with your monster's face. Writer of books, user of whores. Recluse, traveler. Dispatcher of assassins. Target.

Frye was rinsing the ashes down his drain when someone knocked at his door. He looked through a side window to see Burke Parsons standing on his porch. Burke must have seen the blinds move: he cocked his head at Frye and waved.

Parsons thudded across Frye's living room floor in his cowboy boots, hat in hand. "Hope you don't mind me just bargin' in like this, Chuck. You know, back in Texas, you got a open door policy with your friends. It's a insult if they call you first."

"It's okay. I'm heading over to Mom's and Dad's for dinner in a while."

"I won't be but a minute. Reason I came is Rollie Dean Mack. I saw him after the fights that night and mentioned you. What I think is he didn't rightly know what he was doing when he yanked that advertising from the *Ledger.* That's what he acted like, anyhow. So I just told him I'd met you and what a good guy you were, and he seemed a little ashamed at blowing his stack and all. Anyway, he owed me one, so I called it in, and he said he'd be willing to start up those ads again if you'd just lay off his fighters and quit trying to interview him. I told him to just tell you himself, but he ain't ever gonna talk to you. Says he hates reporters. So I got volunteered. Makes him feel important when someone else does his work, I think."

Frye handed Burke a beer and sat down. "What's he want in return?"

Burke looked at him, a little off balance, it seemed. "In return? Well, nothing he spoke of. See, Chuck, this is old-boy network stuff. He owed me. So I just collected."

Frye thought it over. "Is he going to talk to Billingham?"

"Said he would. So you ought to be getting a call one of these days. That's assuming that the *Ledger* wants you back, Chuck."

Frye smiled. "Thanks, Burke. Now I guess I owe you one."

Parsons drank off half his beer and wiped his mouth with the back of his fist. "No hurt in being neighborly. Me and Lucia live down to Crescent Bay here in Laguna, just a mile or two from here. Lucia and Edison are working on that Paradiso, so I figured, why not help Chuck?"

"Lucia set for that next trip to Hanoi?"

"Been a change, Chuck. There's some news that's gonna make big headlines tonight. All the networks gonna carry it at seven. She talked to the *President* about this one. I think her travel plans are gonna change a bit now. You ought to tune in."

"What's the news?"

Burke smiled and spun his hat on a finger. "I don't want to spring any leaks on this one, much as I'd like to help you out. My sister's one hard-headed lady."

"I get it."

Parsons put on his hat and burped. "You know, Chuck, I worked with Bennett over in the Nam for a year, and we got to be friends. Back here in the States, we've still been at least acquaintances. But that sonofabitch is harder and harder to talk to these days. It's like you can't get nothing through to him. If you ever get the chance, could you make clear to him something that I've been trying to make clear for upwards of a week now?"

"What's that?"

"That I'll do what I can to help him. I've got myself. I've got some resources. I can get things done. I've told him that, but he just gets that thousand-yard stare. He don't listen."

"I'll tell him."

Parsons headed for the door. "I'm offering to help, is all. If Bennett wants, I'll stay a million miles away. Man's gotta have his privacy. You might just mention that to him, if you ever find him in a listening frame of mind."

"Will do, Burke. Thanks again."

"Let's just wait and see if Mack comes through. Don't believe a promise 'til it happens." Parsons tipped his hat. "See ya 'round."

At four, Hyla called to remind him about dinner that night. A few minutes before five he showered and headed for Frye Island.

# CHAPTER 22

**T**HE TRAFFIC WAS HEAVY ALL the way through Corona del Mar. The hurricane far to the south had sent not only its waves, but its warm humid air. As the evening gathered, a damp breeze rose from the south bearing a faint hint of the tropics with it.

The Newport Peninsula was still crowded with tourists and beach-goers, most of them heading away from town as the afternoon cooled into evening. The sun hung dull and heavy in the western gray. A band of kids waited at the bus stop—Boogie Boards and flippers, towels and skateboards. Evening glass at 19th Street, he thought: monster waves looming into the point, a few locals braving the sections for brief rides with abrupt endings.

He swung onto Balboa Boulevard and followed the narrow sidestreets toward the island.

The boyhood home, he thought, his mind filling with reruns of lawn croquet; surfing the 19th Street point; a fierce spanking from Edison when Frye had loaded his fourth-grade friends into the helicopter to fly them all to school one morning; Debbie's yellow trike; Hyla amidst the endless cocktail parties looking more beautiful than any movie star; Debbie drying his tooth-brush after he'd used it, just to get him in trouble when Hyla checked it; Bennett and him wrestling on the grass; Bennett and him trying to dig to China; Bennett and him stuffing a potato into the muffler of Edison's car and waiting in the junipers for the explosion that sent him diving for cover in fear of assassination; Bennett and him shaping boards; Bennett leaving for college, then the war; Bennett coming home on a gurney with no legs and a wild, far-away glint in his eyes.

From here to the cave-house, he thought: Time passes, people change, lives end.

He found his mother in the kitchen. The amount of time that Hyla spent in her kitchen, Frye knew, was tied to the larger workings in her life. The more helpless she felt, the more kitchen time. It was a busy sanctuary, filled with chores easily done with half a mind. Her smile was hollow. She had cut her hair. She took one look at him, touching the place where Minh had slapped him with the pistol. "Oh, *Chuck.* Did you get my happy birthday card?"

"Loved it."

"We'll celebrate tonight."

"Grand. Love the new 'do. Kind of a punk-mom look."

"People say I look like David Bowie, but I don't know who he is."

"His loss."

"Yes, I'm sure it is." She turned to the counter so Frye wouldn't see the lank exhaustion in her face.

He put a hand to her shoulder, but she leaned away from him and sucked down a quivering breath, forcing herself calm by an act of pure will. "Papa's in the cottage with the dogs." She gently aimed him down the hallway. Frye turned to watch as she went back into the kitchen and into the smell of roasting duck.

He walked across the lawn to his father's cottage, stopping for a moment to consider the sun beginning to set above the junipers, scant gray clouds easing across an orange-to-blue backdrop. Thunderstorm for sure, he thought: you can smell it.

As usual, the cottage door was locked. Frye knocked and waited. A moment later it opened and Edison stood in the door-way. His face seemed to sag, his gray hair stuck out like he'd just slept ten hours, his clothes were a mess. He had a martini glass in one hand and a felt-tip marker in the other. "Hello, son. Enter. I'm almost done with this."

Edison went to his blotter, threw a page back and studied the writing. It said, *"Ransom Demand by Tues. 1200 Hrs?"* Frye poured himself a drink. The springers yapped outside.

His father crossed out the question and looked up at Chuck. "I was wrong. No demand, and it's Thursday already. I must have been looking at this all wrong."

"It might still come."

"Statistically, this is bad news. It means—"

"I know what it means. I just don't believe it. Have you gotten anything new? Arbuckle find any more Dac Cong?"

Edison eyed him, nodded tiredly. "Nothing you need to know, son."

"So, the blackout's still on."

"Any good organization compartmentalizes its—"

"This is supposed to be a family, not the CIA."

Edison tossed his marker to the desk and sighed. Frye studied his father's big face, how receptive, how innocent it could look. "We just go 'round in circles, don't we, son?"

"Guess so."

Edison nodded. "It didn't happen just all at once, you know."

"It all goes back to the day that Debbie went down, doesn't it?"

Edison stood up, distractedly poured another martini. He looked at Frye with a combination of exasperation and sadness that Frye hadn't seen in years. "Please don't say that. No, son. It goes back to the days—and there were many of them, Chuck— when you chose a different direction than the family's. When you went your own way and left us to ours. A break like that, it doesn't come just all at once."

"It wasn't a different direction. It was a different path."

"You're splitting the atom, Chuck. You never wanted to be part of the Frye Ranch. I suppose I can understand that. I wasn't too adamant, was I? You never wanted to be around the family much either. Those were ten long years when you did the surf tour and ran that goddamned shop of yours. What'd I get from you then, a handful of postcards? Really, son, correct me if I'm wrong."

Frye looked out the window to the harbor and the big homes on the peninsula. "I always tried to tell you what was going on."

"I didn't know you got third place in Australia until somebody brought in a clipping three weeks later. I didn't know you got second in Hawaii until a month after it was over. I didn't know you were chasing women around at your own parties until I saw it in the goddamned *newspaper*, Chuck. I didn't even know that you and Linda were having trouble until her father told me. That's your idea of telling me what's going on?"

"You were against the tour, Pop."

"Does that mean I didn't care?"

Frye, for the first time in his life, was starting to see things from Edison's angle. "You were a son. You know how it is. You tell your dad what you think he'll be proud of."

"Chuck, there wasn't one damned thing I did in my life that my old man was proud of. I'm not complaining—I'm stating fact. Charles James Frye was one heartless sonofabitch. I thought that then, and I think it now." Edison sniffed his martini and drank. "He inherited the ranch from his dad, who probably wasn't much better. So I've been where you are. And I don't hesitate to say that I think surfing for a living is one helluva waste of talent, but that didn't mean I wasn't for your kicking butt and being the best goddamned surfer in the world, did it?"

Frye recalled Edison's letters: One cannot remain juvenile forever . . . We've lost one child to the water, please don't become another . . . With Love and Disappointment, Father.

"Whatever, Pop. We've all got funny ways of showing things."

"And as far as Debbie goes, well, son . . . I'm sorry and it wasn't your fault. I know the waves were big. I know she'd been out in them before. But *you* were out there with her. Not Benny, not me."

Edison looked at him. "Let me ask you something, Chuck. We haven't talked in a long time. It's been a while since you've given half a damn about what goes on at this island. Now we've had Li kidnapped, your mother is torn apart, the Feds are crawling all over me and the shit's hit the fan in a big way. All of a sudden you want to start throwing things in my face. I'm not perfect. I spent years trying to make you think that, maybe. But I gave up. Why are you digging back? Why now?"

Good question, he thought. For the moment, he was stumped. "I don't know."

"I think you do."

Frye looked back out the window. Self-analysis was never his long suit. But there comes a point, he thought, when things fly away faster than you can catch up. There comes a point where wings beat and feathers fall and your hands tremble with what's no longer in them. You sit there and watch and wish there was something you could have done. *Something.* "Things are disappearing. Debbie. Linda. Li. The way I was a few years ago. The way we were."

He thought of Xuan, of the Dark Men in the cavern, of Eddie Vo blown away on his own front porch. He thought of Debbie, dropping in on that monster, looking frail and tiny on the little board he'd made her, knees wobbling, her feet so tan and small, and that look on her face as she glanced at him that said: I'm a bit out of my league on this one, but I've seen you do it, so watch, just you watch . . .

"Anyway, I guess I'm trying to hold onto what's left."

Edison was silent for a long moment. "Amen to that, son."

"It's Benny, Pop. I think he's in more trouble than he's letting on. I think Li was taken . . . for leverage. That's why there's been no ransom demand."

Edison arched an eyebrow, then glanced toward his blotter on its stand. "I'm listening."

"Do you know about the CFV? The supplies they send overseas?"

"Of course I do."

"Do you know it's guns he's running?"

Edison shook his head, smiling. "That's ridiculous."

"Well, it's true. I watched them loading a chopper out on the Paradiso. Guns, Pop."

Edison stood, began pacing. "Go on."

"Do you know about Colonel Thach?"

"The fuck is he?"

Frye told him. The war. The assassination. The heads. Xuan. "There's just a handful of us who know what happened to him, Pop. The FBI's keeping it strictly to themselves."

Edison jabbed a poker into the dead fireplace, rearranging ashes and old coals. "Benny's running guns against Thach, and Li was part of the pipeline. And I'll bet that Thach was Dac Cong in the war."

Frye nodded.

Edison slammed his martini glass into the fireplace. "Wiggins has been dragging his feet all along. Not sharing his evidence with me was one thing, but holding out something like this? What's his reason?"

"The party line is that they're scared of letting people believe that Thach's men are here. They've only got one witness—the woman who sold the black cloth—and they're saying she's unreliable. Just because the dead gunman was Dac Cong in the war, doesn't mean he works for Thach."

"Maybe they're right. Little Saigon will close up tighter than it is already if people get in a panic about nothing. But I'll throttle Lansdale."

"It isn't Lansdale's bureau, Pop."

"This is not good . . ."

Frye waited for the follow-up, but that was all. Edison at his most intense, Frye had realized some years ago, was a man of few words. The rest of it was just sound and fury, his style, his way of letting off steam. He went to the big blotter fastened to the wall and picked up the felt pen, still dangling by its string. Under FBI (LANSDALE), he wrote "Bureau knows of Thach, keeping all info to itself. Why?" He stepped back, studied his note, then dropped the pen. "Chuck, I know what you were trying to say a few minutes ago. I want you to know I'll try to be a little more inclusive. Come here, I want to show you something."

Edison led him to the back room of the cottage, his work room. Among the drawing tables and stools was a model of the Paradiso, like Bennett's but more detailed. "It's the biggest thing we've ever done," he said. "The best. Bennett and I designed it from the start. A joint venture, if you will." He stood back and studied it. "Look at that, Chuck, forty-thousand acres of the best real estate in the world. It's just a hills and cattle now, but when we're done, it will be the best place on earth a man could live. None better, except maybe for this island."

Frye noted the custom homesites, the marina and hotels, the equestrian center and riding trails, golf course, lakes, the heliport, the village of shops. Edison himself had designed the electric trolley that would deliver hillside residents to the beach every half hour, and take them home when they were ready. It would run on solar-generated power.

"I haven't gone over the details with you, have I?"

"Not really."

"Well, there she is!"

Frye admired the relative simplicity of it all, the fact that people living in the Paradiso would have plenty of ground to themselves. Edison stood for a moment staring at the model, absorbed. He nodded. "I'm happy with it so far," he said. "Still a lot to do."

"You've got lots to be proud of."

"You'll be proud of it still, when I'm dead and gone." Edison sat back down and considered his son. "Going to take a lot of people to get it up and keep it going. All sorts of people, Chuck."

"It looks great, Pop."

Edison smiled faintly, sipped again from his drink.

"Cost a lot to get going?"

"Financing's the easy part. Easy, but complex. Everybody wants in on a project like this. The return is a sure thing. The trick is keeping control of it. Your brother and I have controlling interest, of course, so a lot of the capital is ours. So the Paradiso is ours too. I mean, it's all of ours, Chuck. It's the family's."

"Then what's Lucia Parsons's part?"

"Financing. That's all. She and Burke have oil money, and now they've got a place to put some of it." Edison studied the model again, wrote himself a quick note. "Lucia says there is big news tonight at seven. About the MIAs."

"I saw you two retiring to the Elite office at the hotel."

Edison drank, watching Frye over the glass. "And?"

"It was Rollie Dean Mack at Elite who got me fired."

"He wasn't there, if that makes you feel any better."

"What's Lucia doing with a key?"

"Elite Management has donated a lot to the MIA Committee. I think Burke knows Mack or something. It's just a key—who cares? Let's not start again, son."

"You and Lucia looked pretty friendly at the fights."

"That's just what we are. Friends. Partners." Edison checked his watch, then took a deep breath. "Chuck, I'll try to keep you better informed about what's going on. This is from Lansdale again, information the FBI won't tell us. They intercepted coded radio transmission Tuesday night. Again yesterday morning. Wiggins sent a tape to Fort Meade for decoding, and the gist of the message is that they've got Li and their plans for her are progressing as planned. The FBI doesn't know who sent it, who got it, or exactly where it came from. They had it narrowed down to somewhere Saigon Plaza, but the transmission ended before they could find the radio. Wiggins is set up to pinpoint it the next broadcast."

"Was it in Vietnamese?"

"It sure as hell was."

"So people outside of Little Saigon have a hand in it. Thach's people—I'm sure of it."

Edison glowered at his blotter again, as if it had betrayed him. "Thach," he muttered softly. In big letters he wrote, RADIO CONTACT WITH THACH? LOCATION OF TRANSMITTER.

"Thanks, Pop. For keeping me informed."

Edison nodded, his face softening. A smile began. Frye felt good. Then he realized that Edison wasn't even looking at him anymore. His father lurched up and swept past Frye to the cottage door. "Ah! There he is! Get in here, son."

Frye turned. Edison knelt down and hugged Bennett. From over Edison's shoulder, Frye could see his brother's expression. The eyes had a dark look, a look of helplessness, fear, violence.

Edison stood and waved to Frye. "Into the dining room, men! Dinner. Search and destroy!"

Frye assumed his battle station at the table: left of Edison, Hyla beside him, and Bennett across. He could remember sitting here for breakfast almost thirty years ago, in a tall yellow chair with a detachable tray, dumping his oatmeal on the floor to watch it hit. For a moment he conjured images of everyone, even the old woman who had cooked for them. Edison had grayed. Hyla had shrunk. Bennett had been blown in half. What about me? Taller, with the same urge to toss things off high places just to see them land. Every time I sit here, I feel like a kid again.

Mauro, the servant, poured the wine and served the food, as he had for two decades. Hyla raised her glass and paused, though everyone seemed to sense what was coming. They drank to Li. Frye watched his father at the head of the table, standing to carve the duck. The silver tray glittered in the light of a chandelier so high in the dining room altitude that Frye once plinked it with his Daisy to bring down solid evidence that it was really there. He had carried the shard, bright as a piece of sunlight, in his pocket for two days. Edison had given him a licking he still remembered. He looked up to see the broken crystal but it was impossible to locate now, as it had been then.

Edison finished carving. "Any word from Linda, Chuck?"

"None that I've heard."

"She'll come back. No woman leaves a Frye. It's simply never been done."

Frye looked at his mother, attempting sincerity. "We're talking off and on. Things'll work out."

"The bitch is bluffing, Chuck."

"Ed!"

"Hyla! You can't publicly humiliate your wife and expect gratitude, now can you? It will just take some time for Linda to come to her senses."

"Chuck has a new . . . companion, don't you, son?"

Frye felt a subtle yet growing urge to strangle his father right here at the dinner table. "Her name's Cristobel Strauss. We've seen each other a few times."

Hyla sat, shoulders a little hunched, her eyes big and imploring. "Oh?"

"You'd like her, Mom."

"You're a married man, Charles."

"I'm aware of that."

Frye drank more wine as a silence descended upon the table. The clink of silverware became unbearable. "Mega's going into women's wear," he said.

Hyla rose to the switch of topic. "Nice things for women, Chuck?"

"Meganice."

"I still think it sounds like a bomb, son," said Edison. "Megaton. Change the name is my advice, for your marketing department, if nothing else."

Frye watched Bennett wipe a small grin with his napkin. Mauro had filled his wine glass from the martini pitcher.

"Can't change the name, Pop. Mega is my motto."

Hyla motioned Mauro forward for more wine. She looked at Chuck with an expression of sadness so complete that he had to look away. She feels worse about Linda than I do. In the silence that followed, he could sense everyone's thoughts leaving him and moving across the table to his brother. Bennett busied himself with seconds and another glass of gin.

2 4 2

When dinner was finished, Hyla brought out the birthday cake, an elaborate chocolate affair dancing with candles. She sang. Edison smiled at his bride. Frye and Bennett ganged up on the blowing-out routine, which ended—as it had for years—with the candles coming back to life. Edison got still another laugh out of this shopworn trickery. Hyla raised her glass. "To the two best sons God could give a woman," she said. "There are better times ahead for both of you. Happy birthdays." She bowed her head and prayed out loud for guidance and help, forgiveness and redemption, the return of Li and Linda.

Mauro brought in a tray with packages on it, bright wrapping paper reflecting off the silver. Frye got a television wristwatch that Edison immediately swiped and started to fiddle with, and a foam insect guaranteed to grow to two hundred times its original size if you dropped it in water. The package said Gro-Bug. Frye realized with a minor thrill that the thing would hit sixteen feet at maturity, bigger than his whole kitchen. What if you could make a surfboard like that, like, carry it in your pocket until you need it? He pondered marketing gimmicks as Bennett opened his gifts—a television watch also, and a plastic scuba diver with pellets to make bubbles come out his mask. Mauro brought out a big snifter full of water, into which Bennett deployed the frogman. For a moment they all sat, watching the fizz rise. It seemed to go on forever.

Mauro served coffee. Edison checked his watch. "Hon, might we retire to the den? There's an important news item I think we all should see."

They sat around Edison's beloved big-screen TV. Hyla dimmed the lights, and Edison turned to ABC. The regular show had been preempted for a special network news report. Peter Jennings had the honors. Sitting beside him in the studio was Lucia Parsons. She looked like a million bucks. Jennings welcomed his viewers and said that the government of Vietnam had made an unprecedented "and perhaps historic" move: They had requested American air time to broadcast via satellite a live statement from the Vietnamese Council of State President, Truong Ky. Truong had said that the statement would be of special interest to the West. Jennings said that the President of the United States had personally called the network, urging that the broadcast be carried.

Jennings speculated that the topic was American POWs. He asked Lucia.

She nodded, almost serenely, Frye thought. "I think, Peter, that is exactly what President Truong has on his mind."

"Oh, my," said Hyla.

Edison stared gravely at the set.

Bennett sat on the couch, arms crossed and silent.

". . . as you know, and the MIA Committee has been lobbying the Vietnamese government through the Vietnamese people for nearly two years. I'll put it bluntly, Peter. We all hope, we're all just praying right now, that our labors have paid off."

Jennings noted that ABC would supply an English translation in voice-over during the address; then the image of Truong appeared.

The picture was hazy, drained of color. He was sitting at a simple desk, a bristle of microphones in front of him, a Vietnamese flag behind him. He blinked into the lights. He was slight, gray-haired, dour. Without smiling, shuffling paper or any other visible preliminaries, he started speaking. The voice-over was heavily accented.

"It has come to the attention of the Vietnamese people that certain American soldiers are alive in this country. They were located after exhaustive searches, in remote provinces. They were being detained by primitive tribes who did not know of our nation's victory and believed that we were still at war with America. It is the desire of the Vietnamese people that these men be free to return home, or go where they choose. The Vietnamese people are now making arrangements for this to happen. The Vietnamese people are a peace-loving nation. This we wish to demonstrate to the world community. We are not at odds with history. We wish to work with the peace-loving American people, through the MIA Committee, for the timely return of these men. Their exact number is not known. Negotiations will begin soon. We ask of America only one pre-condition to negotiation: to end all support for terrorist groups operating on Vietnamese soil. We can no longer tolerate American-supported violence in this sovereign state. As always, the Socialist Republic of Vietnam will struggle for a world of free peoples everywhere. We will welcome negotiators from the MIA Committee, and a minimum number of American Government representatives, in Hanoi. Our nation wishes to continue its role as a leader of peace and freedom throughout the world."

President Truong stared into the camera, then vanished, replaced by an excited Jennings and a tearful, smiling Lucia Parsons.

"Oh, Ed! She's done it."

"Goddamn, I knew she would!"

Bennett looked up at Chuck.

Frye shook his head and grinned. He hugged his mom. He felt happy, but more: a feeling of freedom and release, the lifting from his shoulders of a weight he never knew was there.

Jennings's voice reasserted itself: "Negotiations pending . . . just how many not stated . . . what condition these men are in . . . what steps if any did the United States Government take to facilitate this . . . unprecedented cooperation . . . unsure what President Troung is referring to, so far as American-sponsored 'terrorism' is concerned . . . much depends on Lucia Parsons's ability to deal with Hanoi . . . a day of celebration and joy . . . the healing of a nation's heart . . . upcoming comments from the president . . . back with Lucia Parsons in a moment . . . now this . . ."

Hyla stood up. "This calls for champagne! Mauro!"

They drank the bubbly and watched the follow-up in silence. Frye wondered at Lucia's composure, her easy grace in front of millions. Jennings asked her about the so-called "terrorism" that Truong had mentioned.

"Peter, I believe there are groups, some of them centered in Orange County, California, whose unstated purpose is to overthrow the government of Vietnam. I'm not an expert in this, but I've heard talk of these people. It's time for them to stop any kind of activity that could even be construed as 'terrorist,' so we can bring our men home. We can only implore them to desist."

Bennett swung out of the room.

"Benny?" asked Hyla. "More champagne?"

Frye followed him from the house, down the sloping green of the huge back yard, to the dock. Bennett started up Edison's Boston Whaler, choking the engine up high while he worked the lines from the dock cleats.

"Where to, Benny?"

"Get in."

# CHAPTER 23

THEY TOOK THE WHALER FROM Edison's dock, chugging across the dark water of the harbor. Mullet jumped and splashed around them, pale comets in the black. The air was warm, and Frye smelled Mexico in it. No stars. Rain any second, he thought. Hose us all down. He worked the engine and Bennett sat fore, facing him. Halfway between Newport Island and his father's, Frye cut the power.

Bennett fixed his gaze on Frye. "There are some things I want you to know, and to do. These aren't easy to talk about, Chuck. I'm not too good at that sometimes. First of all, I'm sorry for keeping you in the dark. I didn't want you involved in . . . this. In me. But things don't always work out the way you want."

"No."

"Chuck, when Li got taken, it was just like losing my legs. I felt this part of me going away and never coming back again. If she doesn't make it back, I'm not so sure I want to stay here."

"Move away, you mean?"

Bennett pulled. "Not exactly."

Frye caught his brother's expression in the dim moonlight, the shine to his eyes, the anxious lines on his forehead, the heavy downward pull of his mouth. "Don't do that, Benny."

Bennett worked out a cigarette and lit it. The smoke hovered, then vanished in a puff of breeze. "I wouldn't leave any messes, Chuck. No loose ends. If for some reason I don't make it out of all this, I want you to do what you can for Li. She's capable, but she needs direction. She's cut in on the Paradiso with me, but Pop might just gobble her right up."

"Okay. Sure." Frye sat back and gazed at a fisherman on a far dock, elbows tight to his body, hat drooping, pole bent to the water. "Is there some reason to think you're not going to make it?"

Bennett exhaled a cloud of smoke. "Things are very . . . questionable right now. DeCord is CIA. We've been getting clandestine money from the agency for three years. Six months ago DeCord cut us off. He said the administration had a change of heart. I didn't believe that."

"Then why?"

"You just heard it on TV. Hanoi's ready to deal on the MIAs. DeCord said there were high-level talks going on, and all their support was going to end. He didn't say talks with who, and he didn't say how high-level. Now I know. And he was adamant. He didn't just want me to find other funding, he wanted me to shut the whole thing down. Hanoi's got us by the balls again, and our Government is following them right into the corral."

"What did you tell him?"

"To take a flying fuck at the moon."

"So you recorded the last few payments to Nguyen in case DeCord tried to hang you for the whole thing. So you could prove the government was involved."

"Damn straight. That's why he wants that tape back so bad. That's why he took his pictures to Minh—to get the cops to do the dirty work, if it comes to that. Minh is just a simple cop, and he's honest, but they can use him. And that's why the guy called Lawrence arranged the break-in at your place. It's clear to me that Lawrence is just another spook running around Little Saigon, trying to cover for the government."

"A spook with General Dien in his pocket. It makes sense now."

"Chuck, that tape was my protection. The plan was to copy it, put both tapes in a safe deposit box ready to go out to the networks if anything happened to me. But everything came down so fast. I kept thinking: I'll do it tomorrow, I'll do it tomorrow. Well, tomorrow came, Li got ripped off, and the best thing I could do was shuffle off that tape to an innocent party—you. If Lawrence got the tape to DeCord, my parachute's got a big hole in it."

"If the government wanted the pipeline stopped—would they have taken out Li?"

Bennett shook his head. "They'd have taken out both of us. DeCord is protecting the agency, he's just doing his job. But they would never have taken Li like that. There are much simpler ways."

"Is Li a bit player, or the star?"

Bennett hunkered inside his coat, lighting a smoke. "DeCord paid us money here for basic operational expenses, but the bulk of it was wired straight to Switzerland. Li made the pickups in Zurich to pay off our people at that end. Those tapes she always took? They had songs and news and propaganda on them, but also code. Meeting places, drop locations, contacts inside Vietnam, times, dates, places. Plans to coordinate military strikes with terrorist moves were coded into the programs themselves—the order of the songs, the first letter of the titles—things like that. We set it all up ahead. Li didn't know what exactly was happening until she got there and played the tapes. That way, if they caught her, the whole operation wouldn't be gutted. Li wasn't just another part of the resistance—operationally, she was the key."

Frye tried to collate the information now, make some sense of the details with this new light on them. "Who knew I had that tape, besides you?"

"Donnell. Nguyen Hy. And Kim, the woman you took to the airstrip."

"Then one of them is a traitor?"

Bennett nodded. "One of them."

"What about Kim? If it was her, what happens to the Secret Army? Will she let them tail her in, expose the network?"

Bennett sighed. "She made Vientiane. She was supposed to connect with our people, go south through Thailand, then slip into Kampuchea. The guns we flew from the Paradiso would be waiting in a village controlled by the Khmer Rouge. We haven't heard anything, Chuck. Silence. We got confirmation that Thach was in place yesterday. That tells me Wiggins's story of Thach being under house arrest isn't true. But Kim's silence either means she's under the gun and holding her breath, or she's sold out and my people are being greased while we sit here."

Frye considered. "How much good does the Secret Army do? What do they accomplish?"

"Lots, Chuck. Programs broadcast on the Secret Radio, straight into Hanoi. Recruitment of the disenchanted. Gathering up the villagers who've been smashed down by the Communists. They blow a bridge, attack a depot. Harass the regulars."

"It doesn't seem like much."

Bennett looked at him. "It's how Ho Chi Minh started. We're how revolutions breed. We're how history gets written. That's why Hanoi throws the muscle at us. That's why they've cut Thach loose against us."

"The radio transmissions from Saigon Plaza. Are they talking to Thach?"

Bennett nodded. "That's my guess."

Frye applied a little gas, easing the Whaler into a gentle bank that took them into deeper water. They chugged into the harbor through a canal. Once past the peninsula bridge, Frye could see the lights of the big restaurants wavering on the water, hear the halyards of the big pleasure boats pinging against their masts in the breeze. A bunch of people on the Warehouse patio lifted their drinks and waved.

Bennett stared up at them, then at his brother. "From where we are right now, Thach is the key. If Kim is working for him, the entire Secret Army will be slaughtered."

"And you plan to kill him at kilometer twenty-one."

"How did you know that?"

Frye told him of Nha's request, of the film he developed. "I put it together with something you were saying in your office Tuesday night. On the phone."

Bennett sat upright, a smile on his face. "I should have enlisted you a long time ago, little brother. You're a good soldier." The smile retreated. "We've tried to get to him a half dozen times. No luck. We'll try again tomorrow night. Nine, our time."

"And if you succeed?"

"I can quit. At least for a while. I want our prisoners back too, if there are any. I suspect it's a game played by Hanoi—I don't think they've got any Americans there who don't want to be there. But I won't stand in the way of them, if there are."

Frye wondered again at this man in front of him, at his passions and secrets, his plans and campaigns. He's holding off the CIA with one hand and Thach with the other, trying to assassinate enemies halfway around the world. Benny, always your own agendas. You just never give up. You don't know when to stop. Down deep inside, it's the biggest thing we have in common.

Bennett's dark hair shifted in the breeze. For a moment he was still, clutching the gunwales in his hands, his stumps centered on the bench for balance. He looked up to the restaurant as the Whaler glided by. Pale lights washed across his face. In the long silence that followed, the first rain started to fall, resonant upon the boat. The harbor water began to boil. Bennett had the thousand-yard stare, all right.

"It was a night like this—rain coming down, and thick sweet air. Man, it was a hundred shades of green. Everything drooping and slow. You wouldn't believe what I'd been going through with Lam and Li. I knew that one of them was tight with Charlie. Our patrols were getting intercepted. The fucking villagers would clear out way ahead of time. Some of Li's information turned out wrong. But was it wrong when she gave it to us, or did it get wrong when she, or he, tipped the Cong? Which one? Lam or Li? Or was it both?"

Bennett looked up into the rain. The big drops slapped against the Whaler, a drumroll of water on aluminum. "I was in love with her, and he hated me for it. I could see it in his face. With Lam, you were either a friend, or he wanted to grease you. He didn't have anything in between. I'd never known a guy so . . . singleminded. You know who I wanted the traitor to be—but how could I know?" Bennett shook his head. "So I set up my own trap. I asked Li to move to base with me. I knew that if she did, it meant she was innocent. And I knew that if Lam saw her moving to me, he'd know I suspected him. He'd try something. Our little triangle was over, Chuck. And I hated to see it go. Back when it started, we had it all. We were friends, and we got things done. Li's information was the real stuff."

Frye eased the Whaler into deeper water. The warm rain had soaked him.

"The night she was supposed to show, I waited. I really didn't know what would happen. I was past thinking about it, past caring. When I saw her coming down the path, man, it was the best feeling in the world. She came through a stand of bamboo and stood a few yards from me. The jungle was black and shiny behind her. She had a guitar, a basket full of clothes, some cooking stuff, and this pack on her back. That was all. Her face was white. She was dripping wet. She stood there and I'll never forget what she said. 'Benny, there is something on me. Lam put it there, and said we must open it together.'"

Bennett lit another cigarette, cupping it in his hand. Frye watched his face glow orange.

"Fucking gift from Lam, right? So I helped her off with it. Real careful. I could tell by the weight that he'd packed in enough shit to blow a whole platoon away. I put it in an empty mortar pit, took her by the hand, and led her to a hootch I'd set up near the perimeter. I let her inside and helped her get arranged. The whole time I was thinking of Lam. He'd played the same game I had. He'd used Li. The difference was, I loved her enough to let her live, and he loved her enough to kill her. And me. So I got my 'sixteen, and eight men, and hauled ass to the trail by Lam's hut. I figured he had five minutes on us."

The rain changed gears now, a steady shower of big warm drops. Frye guided the Whaler into a loose turn, heading back toward the Island. The ocean water boiled harder, and a mist rose from the surface.

Frye looked at Bennett, who tossed away the cigarette, then steadied himself on the gunwhales.

"I couldn't believe it when I saw lamplight in his hootch. The sonofabitch was just taking his time, packing up a few things. Tony was nowhere around, so I knew that Lam had wasted him. I went in alone and brought him out. He looked surprised, all right. It was hard, Chuck. He stood there wearing that necklace that I'd given him, and I wondered how in hell he'd managed to use me like that. I'd trusted him, almost all the way. If I'd been a little more naïve, I'd have opened that pack and blown up half of Dong Zu. I started to say something, but no words came out.

He just looked at me, like he had no fucking idea what was about to go down. I ordered my men to take him out. I told my sergeant to sweat him, then waste him however they wanted. Then I got the demolition techs out and told them to get rid of the pack if it didn't go off in the next couple of hours."

Bennett huddled tighter inside his jacket. "I went back and sat with Li for a while in the new hootch. We made love for the first time. For her, it was the first time ever. I could feel the power going out of me, and into her, then coming back. She was mine. A while later, I heard a chopper lift off, and I knew what they were gonna do to him. Somehow, Li knew. She was crying. I couldn't fucking take it, Chuck. I left her there, went to the Officer's Club and drank half a bottle of Scotch in about half an hour.

"The guys came back a few minutes later. Two of them were laughing. No Lam. They said he wouldn't admit a thing. He kept saying he was fucking innocent. The Cong were tough, Chuck. I saw a guy go for almost an hour strapped to a table with electrodes on his balls, and all he said was 'No VC, no VC.' He just died there, trying to chew off his own lips." Bennett sighed. "Sudden Deceleration Trauma was what we called it. The joke was: It isn't the fall that kills you, it's the stop."

They were quiet all the way back to the dock. Frye climbed out and tied down to a cleat. He ran the fuel out of the carburetor and stowed the cushions under the benches.

"Why don't you just give up, Benny? The war's over."

Rain slanted through the dock lights, splattered the stanchions, tapped the sand. Frye walked slowly beside his brother.

"You feel something for Tuy Nha, don't you?"

"Well, sure—"

"Then you have a little of what I have. I married it, Chuck. It's part of me now. I love the way they love. The way they fight. The way they suffer and still fight. I love the way they look. When I woke up after the mine got me, she was the first thing I wanted to see. She was there for me, and she just plain wouldn't let me die, Chuck. And she still wanted me when I came out of that hospital more gone than ever. What I hate most is the fact we lost when we could have won. We were almost there. Maybe someday, we will win."

Bennett smiled through the rain. "When it comes down like this, it's just like over there. It takes me back. I love it. I hate it."

They moved across the small beach, Bennett laboring in the sand. Then up the lawn, a perfect green slope in the darkness. The yard lamps cast drizzly light toward the grass. "You go in one way and come out another, Chuck. You hope things'll balance someday. What you want to be able to do is look your own eyes in the mirror and not be totally ashamed of all the shit they've seen."

"Yeah."

"You'll never get it, because you weren't there." They approached the back door of the house. Bennett stopped on the porch. "Now Thach's people are fucking with my head. It's textbook PSYOPS. I got a plastic helicopter in the mail two days ago. After that, they left a GI Joe doll on my porch, with its head cut off. Three bottles of fucking champagne. Thach is ten thousand miles away, looking at a file on me, putting on his own electrodes. They called me again this morning. It was the same man who talked to me before they put Li on. They said to put two million dollars in two suitcases."

"That was all?"

"Further instructions to come."

"You tell Wiggins?"

"They know. I'll have the cash tomorrow."

"Why not call off the hit? Call off the Secret Army. It's what everybody wants. Maybe they'll let her go. Maybe they'll let our POWs go."

Bennett smiled. "There won't be any hit tomorrow night. We're going to take him alive at kilometer twenty-one. He'll either tell his men to let Li go, or they'll kill him. His life for hers. By nine P.M. tomorrow Li will either be free, or they'll both be dead."

# CHAPTER
# 24

THE STORM ENDED AS QUICKLY as it had begun. He parked at home and walked down to the festival grounds, where the Pageant of the Masters had been delayed. The city smelled of wet eucalyptus and ocean spray. As Cristobel said it would be, Frye's ticket was waiting for him at will-call.

He found his seat, a minor chill moving through him under his still-wet clothes. The tableau on stage before him was called "The Four Muses," said the program, and showed four gold-painted women posing in re-creation of a sixteenth-century French statuette. The women were suspended mid-air—even from the third row Frye could not see how—giving them a precarious, other-worldly quality. Breathing stopped, a low murmur rose from the crowd, breeze jiggled the rain-slick trees around the amphitheater.

Then the stage went dark, and the announcer's resonant baritone came through the speakers. Frye could see the golden bodies floating offstage in the darkness. Where do goddesses go when their workday is done?

"The Pageant of the Masters would like to take just a moment," said the announcer, "to pass along the good news to anyone who has not heard it yet. The MIA Committee, based in our own Laguna Beach, will be negotiating with Hanoi for American soldiers still remaining in Vietnam. The pageant extends its warmest congratulations to Lucia Parsons and her committee." There was a round of applause, cheers from the crowd. "Our next piece is based upon . . ."

He closed his eyes for a moment, and issued a vague prayer heavenward that they could get Li back. Benny's falling apart, he thought. What if his plan caves in? She was his purpose, and Benny always needed a purpose. Without that, he's just a storm of impulse, not containable by skin alone. What was it that Benny had said after he'd come out of the hospital in Maryland, back to California with his new wife, his new body, his new life? *She got me through this, brother. She's not just a woman. She's my god.*

His muse. The stage lights came on slowly, and he found himself staring at a life-size Remington bronze, the cowboy galloping his horse across some timeless plain, reigns in one hand, lasso in the other, hat brim flipped up by speed. Frye could almost hear hoofbeats. The crowd's inhale was palpable.

Momentarily transported by this illusion, Frye crossed his arms, sank down a bit in his seat, and tried his best to think nothing except whether this cowboy was going to catch his cow.

It was impossible to think of anything but Li. What are your chances, Benny, of pulling this off? Not very goddamned good. But what would work better? No wonder the FBI is keeping wraps on the Thach story, with the POWs on the line. Hanoi sends over a terrorist squad and—just in time—happens to discover American soldiers still alive. Some diplomacy.

The next thing Frye knew, the announcer was telling the apocryphal story of Susanna, wife of a prominent Jewish merchant, who went to her garden to bathe. Left alone by her servants, she was viewed by two elders, who approached and demanded her submission. If not, he explained, the elders would claim to have seen her in adultery with a young man—a charge which could get her stoned. Susanna refused, the elders barked their story to the local tribunal and she got the death penalty. Only the cleverness of Daniel, cross-examining the elders and finding two differing accounts, saved her from death. Susanna's virtue was triumphant. The tableau was a re-creation of a painting of Susanna at her bath, under the eyes of the scheming elders.

When the lights went on, Frye caught his breath and felt his heart dissolve in one instant. Cristobel stood at the garden pool, about to step from her robe, her head cocked slightly as if she'd just heard a rustle from the two men spying on her from the trees. It was the angle of her head that caught him, the long gentle plane from ear to shoulder, white in the light and set off by the blue water of the pool. Her hair was tied up loosely, a strand or two escaping down and across her face, almost hiding the eyes that looked to the ground, both innocent and suspecting at once. Something in the angle of her head caught Susanna's indecision and doubt. Her arms were already lowering the robe, her neck and shoulders already bare. Frye considered the sculpted roundness of her limbs, the uninterrupted perfection of her back, and a leg, barely visible where the loose white material gave way with Cristobel's step to the water. He barely noted the lurking men, the trees, the bench beside her on which rested three small vessels and a folded towel, or the two servant girls disappearing in the background toward a house. The breeze moved her robe, just slightly, and Frye saw her hair brush her cheek. The lady beside him whispered something, but he ignored her. He hated the sniveling, cretinous elders, though he felt like a third. *Any chance you'd like to go to bed with me?* He shifted in his seat. What odd compulsion had brought Cristobel to this tableau and its shadows of seduction, rape, betrayal? What's going through her mind right now, with a thousand elders' eyes fixed on her body?

For a moment he swore her gaze wandered across the seats to him, but that was silly. Her leg was imponderably lovely. Was she getting cold? His body felt light and his mind distant, as under hypnosis. I could sit here all night. But the lights began to dim and he watched in genuine sadness as Cristobel's form lost its clarity and dissolved, slowly vanishing into the dark.

He met her outside the stage door an hour later. Her hair was still up and she was wearing a loose blue dress, tied at the waist with a sash. Two men he assumed were the elders walked with her, and she said good night to them at the bottom of the steps. They looked at Frye with a protective air, then headed down the sidewalk different ways. Cristobel ran down the stairs, smiling, and threw her arms around him. "Can you believe what Lucia did? It's just the best thing I could have heard tonight."

"It sure is. My jaw dropped when I watched the news."

"I'm just so . . . there's no way to say. Did you like my piece in the show?"

"Not bad . . ."

She stopped and regarded him, askance. "The rain got our timing off and made everything slippery."

"It changed my life, really."

"Do you expect me to believe that?"

"Yes. Get some coffee?"

"I'd prefer a little motion. All that posing makes me want to move."

They walked up Broadway, slick with rain and littered with eucalyptus leaves. The storm had left in its wake a clear dry sky, with stars emerging deep in the west. Cars hissed along the boulevard. Frye noted that the savings-and-loan thermometer read seventy-one. Even from two long blocks away he could hear the rumbling surf, and when a big wave hit it sent tremors up the sidewalk and into his toes. They tickled.

"Feel that?" she asked.

"Oh, yes."

She took his arm. Frye felt an immense pride as he walked down Broadway with Cristobel, secretly desiring that anyone who'd ever wished him harm could be here for this march of triumph. He would be humble in victory, though: signing autographs, giving advice, laying on hands, and what have you. They crossed Coast Highway and headed up the boardwalk toward Heisler Park.

"Must be kind of hard playing Susanna, considering the recent past," he said.

Her arms stayed in his. "I showed up for the audition, and they offered me Susanna," she said. "I was shocked. Then I thought about it, read the story in the library, and decided it might be therapeutic. Kind of like you going out on a two-foot day, maybe. Just to get wet again."

"That's it. One step at a time. First night kind of rough?"

"I wanted to run. The applause helped. It's all a matter of getting comfortable with myself again. When something like that happens to a woman . . . well, I felt . . . unclean. Spoiled and dirty. Somehow you have to get the shame out of your head. Time helps. And putting your toes in the water again. And being made love to by you."

"You were beautiful. All I saw was you." Frye stopped and put his arms around her. "I'm sorry about what I did, what I said. Both times."

"I am, too. Sorry you found out I had this obsession about you. I was going to play this very cool. Now, I'm busted."

He kissed her. People on the sidewalk had to move around them, but Frye didn't care. I could get lost in this woman, he thought.

She broke away and looked him. "There's something dark in you right now, Chuck. What happened?"

They lay on his living room floor and let the warm breeze pass over them. She rested her head on his chest. Frye stared at the ceiling.

"You can't keep it all bunched up inside," she said.

"I know."

A moment later, he was spilling it. The Secret Army, the tape, the tunnels, Eddie and Loc, Minh and Wiggins, Hanoi's POW revelation, Bennett's transcontinental grudge match with Colonel Thach. He left out the details, in deference to his brother, his family, his own sense of what you tell someone and what you don't. "The biggest worry I had last Sunday evening was getting a job," he said.

"How come you always think you have to solve it all and fix everything? Seems to me you lay a lot of blame for things right on yourself. That's either foolishness or arrogance, Chuck. You know that?"

"Who the hell are you, Toni Grant?"

He felt the muscles in her jaw tighten. She lay still.

"Sorry," Frye said.

"I know it's there, Chuck. I can feel it. But what is it? What is it that eats at you so bad?"

He closed his eyes and felt her head on his chest and smelled her rain-damp hair. He listened to the cars whisking by on Laguna Canyon Road. He could hear the power lines buzzing below, aggravated by the rain. Then, the sounds seemed to fall an octave and all he heard was a faint ringing in his ears. He could see it. He could see her. He could hear the seagulls yapping overhead.

"I had a sister, Cris. Her name was Debbie and she was a sweet kid. Two years younger than me. Kind of skinny, built like me. Nice smile. Hair like straw. Freckles. Tomboy, I guess. I imagine that she'd have grown into a good woman."

Cristobel's fingers moved through his hair.

"We were close in a lot of ways. Closer than me and Benny, because he was five years older than me, and you know how older brothers are."

"I sure do. They ignore you."

"Yeah. Well, Benny taught me to surf and I taught Debbie. Other kids had little league or powder puff or whatever. We had waves. We were close enough to the beach, we could ride down the whole peninsula on our bikes and find where the break was best. All summer that's what we did. When school was in, we'd get up at six, surf an hour, then make it home for breakfast. After school, back out again if the wind hadn't picked up too much."

"Mike and I had horses. Same kind of thing."

"When I look back now, I can see she worshipped me. Me. I just tolerated her, but that's how brothers treat sisters. She'd always do what I was doing—wear the same kind of clothes, get her hair cut like mine, pick up the slang I got from my friends. I think the first word she learned was *bitchin'*. Hell, she asked Mom if she could get braces when she was old enough because I had the damned things."

Cristobel laughed. "For a while I thought Mike's pimples were really swell."

Frye could see her, peddling beside him on a red Stingray, dragging a surfboard behind her on the wheeled cart he'd made her. "When I went out on the big days, I wouldn't let her come. She'd scream and bitch and I'd make Mom keep her home. One day I came back from a six-foot morning at the River Jetty, and Debbie had spray-painted all over my surf posters. Then one day, the swell was up, and I saw Debbie's bike and board were gone. I went down to the point at Nineteenth Street. Ten foot, solid walls, sets lined up four and five at a time. The current was so strong I watched a guy paddle out at Seventeenth Street and before he got outside, he was four streets down—all the way to the pier. Man, it was awesome just to watch those things come in. Her bike was chained to the trash can and she was already heading out. She was eleven years old.

"So I went after her. I had to wait five minutes for the set to end just to paddle out. The whitewater was high enough to keep the goons from going in. There were photographers and a crowd there, just to watch. I got outside and looked back to shore. It felt like I was a mile out, the houses looked like something on a Monopoly board. It was twelve feet. I'd never seen it like that. Corky Caroll was out, and Rolf Arness—Matt Dillon's son. They still got pictures of that day up in some of the surf shops in Newport. Every place has its Big Wednesday, and that was ours."

"Big as Rockpile two mornings back?"

"It made Rockpile look like a swimming pool."

Frye shuddered. "I was thirteen. I'd been surfing the point since I was six. And I'll tell you, when I got out, I was scared. Debbie was thirty yards away, and I could see how white she was. I told her to go back in, so she paddled away further. The more I yelled, the less she paid any attention. Finally I got sick of screaming and missing waves, so I got my hair up and dropped in. It was second wave of the set, ten feet and I shredded that sucker all the way to shore. It's the kind of ride you don't forget. I still haven't. It was the first time I ever made *Surfer* magazine."

"Not the last."

Frye looked up at the ceiling. Cristobel slipped her hand inside his shirt and ran it over his chest.

"When I got back out, Debbie was still there. She was grinning like an idiot. My heart was doing backflips. Then I looked outside and the next set was lining up. Biggest of the day so far. We had to paddle like hell just to make it over the lead wave. Then two more. I looked across from me and watched the other guys paddling too—they looked like an army of ants riding sticks. Deb got outside faster. The next thing I knew she was dropping in on the cleanup wave. It was just too goddamned big. She stroked a couple of times. She looked at me, like, watch this.

"It lifted her up and she tried to stand, but she was going too fast and she pitched. It had her. It drove her down. She just kept falling, but she wasn't free of the thing, she was imbedded in it, this little girl in a black wetsuit stuck in the curl, trapped like a fly in amber. The board spiraled down after her. I sat there and waited. When you look at a big wave from the back, all you see are these big muscles of water bearing down, then you hear the boom, then you feel the world tremble, then you see the whitewater shooting up like a geyser. I kept waiting for it to bring her up. Five seconds? Ten? I don't know. What I do know is I was there in the middle of it, diving down with my eyes open and not seeing a thing except a green swirl everywhere I looked. Then coming up and screaming for help. Back down again. Then up. Then a bunch of guys diving down too, and lifeguards, and a few minutes later the rescue boat roaring up and almost capsizing when the next set hit."

Frye closed his eyes and saw it all again, clearly as the morning it had happened. He could feel the burn of the saltwater, the ache in this throat as he screamed and went down again, the cold sludge of sand under his fingertips as he clawed along the unyielding, treasureless bottom.

"They found her twenty minutes later, wrapped around the last piling of the pier."

They lay still. Frye listened to the cars below. He could hear Denise's stereo throbbing away down the hill. The curtains floated with the breeze.

"It wasn't your fault, Chuck."

"Maybe. Maybe not. But I was the last one with a chance to do something, and I didn't take it. I could have stopped her before she left home. I could have taken her board. I could have just chased her down and dragged her in. There were a million little things that might have prevented what happened. It never got said that way, but that's what mom and pop thought too. I could see it in their faces. After it happened, nothing was quite the same."

"You've never talked about it."

"Tried to a couple of times. Didn't want to grovel."

"That's not groveling, it's wrestling. You have to wrestle it until you pin it down and it leaves you alone. Is that why the water gets to you now? The dizzy spells you told me about?"

"I don't know. I thought it started when I banged my head a few months ago. I thought it was that, but the doctor says I'm fine. Now, under the water, or in a cave or tunnel. Even in my bed sometimes, when the covers are pulled up too tight—I just can't handle it."

"Sometimes, it just takes a long while to heal. Believe me."

"I believe you."

"I love you, Chuck Frye. I want to spend some time with you. Get under that skin of yours."

He looked at her, touched her face, looked into her dark brown eyes. "Those words sound good to me."

She led him to the bedroom and shut the door.

They were dozing when the phone rang. It was Shelly from Elite Management, who had stopped by the office to get a couple of "rilly good joints" she'd left in her desk. As she had driven away, Rollie Dean Mack had driven in. "He didn't see me, so I thought I'd call you. You still, like, wanna see him?"

Frye considered. "Sure I do. What kind of car does he drive?"

"Black Jaguar. Totally rad."

"Totally. Thanks, Shelly."

Cristobel pulled the blanket up, and snuggled close. "Who was that?"

Frye explained. Cristobel seemed to shrink away a little. "Something wrong?" he asked.

"No."

"Want to come with me?"

She checked her watch, then looked at Frye for a long moment. "I should go. I've got an early shift at the towers tomorrow."

"Suit yourself. You okay, Cris?"

She dressed quickly, slung her purse over her shoulder, and kissed him lightly on the cheek. "Can't you just get a job somewhere else? Quit screwing with this Mack character?"

"I liked my job. I liked the *Ledger.* And everybody else wants five years experience. I got one and a half. Besides, there's something strange going on at Elite. I'd like to know what. I could use another set of eyes and ears."

"No. But good luck."

The black Jaguar was out front, parked beside a long white Cadillac. The lights of Elite Management were on. Frye sat for a moment in his car, composing his story to Mack: I saw it as a dive, but I might have been wrong. I gave your fighters better coverage than anybody else did. Let's forget the piece on the welterweight. You reinstate your ads, and I'll get my job back.

What I might not ask, just yet, is why Lucia Parsons has the keys to your suite at the Sherrington, or why you never come to work.

He climbed the stairs and went to the door. He could hear a

voice inside, drawling away. Something about it was familiar. He stopped his fist just short of knocking, then moved to a side window. The blinds were cracked open just enough to see inside.

The lobby was empty. But through the open door he could see Burke Parsons, phone to his ear. Behind him sat General Dien, arms crossed.

But no Rollie Dean Mack.

Parsons hung up. The phone rang a second later. He answered, checked his watch, slammed down the phone, and stood. "Come on, General."

Frye flew down the stairs as fast and as lightly as he could. He realized he'd parked three cars away from the Jaguar.

He dodged around a corner and ran along the first-level suites. He pressed into a dark doorway, flattening against it as best he could.

Parsons and Dien moved quickly toward the lot. The General stopped beside Frye's car and said something. Burke got into the Jaguar and started it up. His voice echoed across the lot. "Come on, Dien. We don't have all fuckin' night, now do we?"

The general shuffled toward his Caddy. Frye watched the Jag back up, straighten, then bounce from the Elite Management parking lot onto Palisade. Dien's car followed.

Parsons, he thought. Of course you know Mack. Of course Lucia has a key to his suite at the Sherrington. Of course you could ask Mack a favor. You *are* Mack.

Frye sat in his living room for a few minutes, wondering why Burke Parsons had gotten him fired. No matter which way he turned it, he couldn't make sense of it.

The phone rang just after one A.M. Detective John Minh sounded exhausted. "I've been here since eight this morning," he said. "Did you hear about the banners?"

"What banners?"

"Draped all around Saigon Plaza sometime last night. They said 'Thach Watches,' 'Thach Knows,' 'Thach Sees.' I got there at nine and there must have been two hundred refugees milling around the plaza, staring at the things. By noon the place was deserted. Nobody but FBI. They got those banners down very quickly. No one's going out. Everybody thinks they've seen some old ghost from the war now. I've got a stack of reported sightings

263

a foot high—Viet Cong murderers, Dac Cong torturers, traitors of every description. Everybody's carrying a gun. Just after dark, an old Vietnamese shot someone trying to get into his house. It was his son, who'd forgotten his key. An hour after that I found the Dark Men and Ground Zero patroling their neighborhoods on foot. More guns on them than you could count. Tonight around ten, Loc tried to get into Dien's house. Dien's guards found him inside the fence and shot him down. They said he fired first. It's crazy up here. Now listen, Frye, I shouldn't have taken the time to look into this rape thing, but I got the answers you need. I checked with the police in Long Beach, Los Angeles, San Pedro, Wilmington, Seal Beach and Portugeuese Bend. L.A. county she-riffs, too. Nobody named Cristobel Strauss was raped up there. Not in the last ten years, anyway."

Frye's felt his heart accelerating. "Oh."

"Maybe she's a little crazy, Chuck."

"Maybe. Thanks."

He called Cristobel but the line was busy.

He went back out to the Cyclone.

The blue apartments were dark and the traffic on Coast Highway was thin. Frye parked in front of the bookstore and wondered just what he was going to say. The truth of it was, he didn't have any idea.

The house lights were dim. Frye looked through the window and saw nothing. Then, two silhouettes materialized on her deck that overlooked the water. He moved to the railing and peered around the corner. They stood on the deck, the water sparkling black behind them.

One was Cristobel, and the other was Burke.

He couldn't make out their words because of the surf rushing in below. He could see that Cristobel was sobbing. She was outlined against the ocean: face in her hands, hair spilling forward, back quivering. Parsons reached out and drew her to him. He lifted her chin with a finger and put his mouth on hers. Then a muted crack of flesh against flesh, and Burke's head snapped. Cristobel crossed her arms, and Parsons laughed.

The next set of waves drowned him out. Frye headed down the stairs and back to his car.

# CHAPTER 25

JUST AFTER SUNRISE FRYE clambered upward from a dream of dark water and headless bodies to the sound of someone moving across his living room. The old floor creaked; he could sense the weight and motion, the secretive tiptoe of the intruder.

He slipped from the damps sheets, pulled on a robe, and took Bennett's .45 from under the bed. Backing along the hallway, he heard something rustle in the kitchen. His heart thrashed like a sparrow in a shopping bag. He held the gun to his chest, sidled into the living room, and drew down on the woman just as she turned. The briefcase fell from her hand.

"Jesus, Chuck!"

"Linda."

"Don't kill me. It's just a divorce."

Frye lowered the weapon, hands shaking. "You shouldn't sneak up on people."

"I guess not. What the hell's wrong with you?"

He placed the .45 in the silverware drawer and slid it shut. "The pressures of modern life."

"Pressure was never your specialty. But why the gun?"

"I had a break-in." Frye felt cold, idiotic. He put on some water to boil and Linda went to the living room.

She sat on his lacerated couch. He watched her as he mixed the instant. Same auburn hair, same quick brown eyes, same sad mouth. She had a briefcase beside her. She lit a cigarette.

Frye sat down across from her. "You look good."

"Thanks, Chuck."

"Like New York?"

"It's not for everyone." Linda balanced the case on her legs now, swung open the top and pulled out a sheaf of legal papers. "It's preliminary stuff. I'm not asking for any material settlement."

"Half of nothing isn't much."

"No," she said quietly. "Anything of mine you want?"

"It's all still here. Take what you need."

"I'm settled in. It's yours."

"Ken there yet?"

"He moved out two weeks ago. Got a job with Kidder Peabody. What happened to the couch?"

"Medflies. How'd it go in Detox Mansion?"

"I'll never touch that shit again, if that's what you mean. Anton bailed on me when I checked in."

"I knew he would. They got him three weeks ago with half a kilo and two-hundred grand cash."

"I know. I saw him yesterday for a minute. He's at it again. I got out of there pretty fast."

"Time for a quickie, though?"

Linda shut the briefcase top, snapped the latches. "I could have had my lawyers send this over, Chuck. But I thought we could maybe be okay just for a few minutes. You gotta just realize how crazy it all was. Anton and I . . . I was in the grip."

"I'd have rather you paid him in cash."

"We didn't have any cash."

The cigarette burned down in the ashtray. Frye signed the papers.

Linda wiped a big tear away, but another formed to replace it. "Baby, we messed it up so bad."

"I know."

"It all happened so fast, and now I'm a million miles away, and I don't know anyone but Ken. I miss you, Chuck."

He moved to hold her, but she stood, briefcase sliding to the floor with a thud. "No. I'm gutting this one out. I just have to cut it off clean, Chucky. In New York I'm Linda Stowe, and I got a job and a flat, and there's nothing crazy inside me. Here, I'm just a mess of a girl." She wiped her eyes again, futilely. She looked down at him. "I know you loved me when I was a mess of a girl, but I couldn't keep that up. I got a life too, you know. Your idea was always to break things up just to watch the parts fly around. That white stuff got to me. You weren't supposed to let that happen. It hits different people different ways. Just because you could take it or leave it, didn't mean I could. Oh, hell, Chuck, we've been through this before. I should have let the lawyer do this."

Frye felt like killing himself. In the silence that followed, he knew that everything she said was true, but it was far less a comfort than either of them needed.

"Did you ever tell the cops who the Mystery Maid was?" she asked.

"Nobody."

"Not even your folks?"

"No."

"Swirk find out in that stupid contest of his?"

"Nobody'd tell him. We had good friends."

She sat back down, her composure thin as makeup. "Good. If Dad knew that was my ass all over the front page, he'd disown me. He really would."

"Your secret's safe."

"You know, Chuck, one of the things I wanted you to do was bring out the worst in me. Then when you did, I freaked. We were borderline depraved, some of the stuff we did."

"We had our moments."

She smiled through a smear of mascara and tears, a little wickedness in her, even now. Linda was always game, he thought. In the end, a little too game with her dealer, a few too many nights with the sun coming up and the blues rolling in to claim her like a cold, dark tide. In the end, we all skipped the fun and went straight to the weird. We were all just willing victims of the age. The whole spoiled, rich, gutless, fucked-up generation.

Strange, he thought, it's all part of another time now.

"You ever—?"

"No more."

"That's good. You were always stronger." Linda picked up her cigarette butt and shook her head. "I hate these things. One habit for another. Well, I'll go now. God's truth is I wanted to see you again. It's going to be a while, Chuck. When this is final, Ken and I are going—"

"I don't want to hear about it."

For one terrible moment he saw Linda steering her old convertible up the driveway, her hair flying and her Wayfarers on, saw her walking up to the cave-house looking so good, smiling at Denise. Then he saw her heading down a gray cold street in New York City, crying like she was now. There just has to be a better way, he thought, to treat the people we love. "I'm glad things are working out for you. In my own weird way, I'm always gonna love you, Linda."

"Me too. Got another girl?"

Frye thought of Cristobel. "Not exactly."

"I'm just shattered, about Li. Anything new?"

Frye told her everything he could, which wasn't much. No sense, he thought, getting someone else involved. He expressed confidence in the FBI and Minh, but she must have heard his insincerity.

She wiped away a tear. "What about all the kids she brings over from the camps?"

"I guess they'll have to wait."

"Is that why they took her, to stop that?"

"I don't think so."

A blade of anger flashed in Linda's lovely, red-rimmed eyes. "They should have thought about those children. She brought more of them over here than anyone else ever did. The time she took me to LAX to pick some up, it just took my heart away, these little rugrats pouring down the ramp and she was the one they ran to. She was the one they needed when they got here. The bastards who kidnapped her should have seen those faces. They might have thought twice about ruining all that. How are the last batch doing—Trinh and Ha and that little girl with the speech problem?"

"I think they're all okay."

Linda wiped her eyes with a tissue, then tossed it into the briefcase. "Li can make it through. She's like a nail wrapped in silk and perfume. Benny's probably taking this like a good Marine, isn't he?"

"That's Benny."

"That's the Fryes. You're all just goddamned Marines, when it comes down to the way you live your lives. Give my love to them anyway." She stood in the doorway, the bright morning sun and the tan hills of Laguna Canyon behind her shoulder. "Good-bye, Chuck. I wish . . . I wish we both could have settled for a little bit more."

"Me too. Good-bye, Linda."

Just before noon the phone rang. It was Julie at the Asian Wind. She was looking for Bennett. She'd called everywhere she could think of and couldn't find him. "He asked me to call him if General Dien did anything out of the ordinary. He has set up a meeting in my private room. He often does his business here. He has requested the room for a party of four, just one hour from now."

Frye hesitated a moment. "I don't know where Benny is."

"I'm not sure why he wanted me to keep an eye on the general. I only told him I would let him know. I trust your brother. The general, I do not."

"How good is that one-way window of yours?"

"How did you know about that?"

"I found it when I was in the dressing room."

"It's very good. The FBI installed it eight years ago, because they believed that Communist agents were using my club as a meeting place. The light fixture on the ceiling contains a listening device. They used it a few times, then quit coming in."

"Does Dien know about it?"

"Of course not. I've told no one that they were being spied on in my cabaret. I'd have taken it all out, but it would be expensive."

Frye thought again. "How about if I take Benny's place?"

"I wish you would."

"I'll be there in thirty minutes."

Frye sat on Li's dressing room chair. Julie reached into the wardrobe and pushed the button. The wall panel slid back to expose the window.

Julie fiddled with a tape recorder. "Why do you want me to record this, Chuck?"

"I don't know yet. I'm fishing, and I feel lucky."

"If the general hears it, he would take severe revenge on me."

"He's the last one who'll hear it."

Ten minutes later, the party started. First into the room was one of Julie's waiters, carrying menus. Then the general, followed by a thin, wolflike Asian in a gray suit.

"His name is Tòng," whispered Julie, "But he is called Willie. In Saigon before the fall, he sold women. He tried to sell me."

Then a chubby Vietnamese man, short, with the serene baby face often seen on deported religious leaders.

"Mr. Dun," she said. "He is in the narcotics business. He lives in San Francisco. They are gangsters."

Three young men in suits and sunglasses came in next. Each took a wall and crossed his arms; one carried a briefcase. Stanley Smith's *Gậy Trúc*, thought Frye, in living color—the Vietnamese Mafia down from San Francisco.

Julie excused herself, checked her makeup, then slipped quietly out of the room. The microphone picked up the shuffle of feet and bodies, the sliding of chairs on the floor.

The last one in was Burke Parsons, cowboy hat, grin and a newspaper in his hand. "Well, ain't this the cutest lil' o' room in Little Saigon? Dien, you know your way around here, I'll give you that." He looked straight at Frye, took off his hat, smoothed his hair.

Julie brought in a bottle of champagne and uncorked it. Willie the pimp rested a hand on her hip as she stood beside him. Dien jabbered something at her. She put the bottle back in its bucket, bowed slightly, and left.

The four principals sat, the three bodyguards stood at ease. After a round of small talk, attention drifted to Burke.

He raised his champagne glass and studied Willie, then Dun. "To success," he said. "Thanks for coming by. I know y'all are busy men, so I'll make this brief. You two gentlemen are in a good position. We're all in good positions. You know what we got here in Orange County? We got good weather, hard-working people, and more hard-working people just dying to get in and live here. We got L.A. an hour north, we got more beaches than all get-out, and there's plenty of money to keep the gears lubed up right."

Frye checked the tape recorder. The red light was on, the tape turning slowly behind the plastic window.

"Now, gents," Burke continued, "When you get a lot of people clamoring to live in the same place, you see your real-estate prices get high. I mean sky-high. This here county's one of *the* prime hunks of ground in the world right now, and a little bit costs a bunch. You get out to the coast, you're talking even higher."

"How much per acre?" asked Dun, his pudgy hand pouring tea.

Parsons laughed. "It don't sell by the acre, Dun, it sells by the foot. Varies. I drove past a crooked little patch of weeds in Laguna Beach yesterday, way up in the hills. Right on the road. Sixty by sixty. So slanted all you could build on it would be a billboard, and the askin' price was a hundred thousand. That comes to a hair under twenty-eight dollars a foot. And that's the lot, Mr. Dun—it ain't got nothin' on it but the for-sale sign."

Dun nodded while Willie lit a cigarette. Dien watched them over the top of his champagne glass.

"There's three things to remember here, gentlemen. One is that real estate's the most valuable commodity we got. Second is that it's getting more valuable as we sit here and drink. Third is that you don't just walk in and buy the kind of land I'm talking about at a K-Mart." Burke poured some more beer and leaned forward. "It takes more than just money to get it. Everyone's got money— Columbian coke heads, Japanese bankers, Iranian princes. Think any Californians' gonna sell them their coast? I'm not talking about a home here and a shop there, I'm talking about *bulk.* I'm talking consolidated acreage. Hell, you know what I'm talking about. I'm talking about the best investment property God ever made. I'm talking about the Laguna Paradiso."

Somehow, Frye thought, I knew that.

"It was in the paper today," said Willie. "Solar-powered trolley take people to beach."

Burke smiled and unfolded the newspaper he'd brought in. The front page of the business section had a feature on the Paradiso, sketches of the development, pictures of Edison and Bennett.

Dun smiled like a cherub. "How valuable is it, Mr. Parsons?"

Parsons leaned back. "Let me talk straight with you, Dun. You sell heroin. Well the Paradiso is better than a Burmese mountainside of poppies under government protection, a process plant, and a distribution network run by ex-CIA jocks. And you, Willie?

You sell women and, heh, related services. Both are high-end items. But, over time, the Paradiso will get you more per square foot than your best-looking whore, *and it don't wear out.* It just keeps gettin' more and more valuable. You don't even have to buy it fancy clothes, and it won't pocket money behind your back. A commercial-retail coastal venture in Southern California is the safest, surest bet there is. We've got tax-abatement incentives, a soft coastal commission, a board of supervisors that's plenty receptive to developers. We got people with money all over the place. They'll move into the Paradiso soon as the paint dries." Burke held up the paper again. "We're talking condos that start at eight-hundred grand. Homes at a million plus. That's *first phase.* A marina, shops, hotels. There's no risk, the profits are solid. If—and I repeat *if,* it's handled by the right people."

"What profit?" asked Dun.

"Fifty percent over five years."

Dun raised his pudgy hands. "I can get that at a bank, at the Sears Financial Network."

"On millions in twenty-dollar bills that smell like dope? Try it, Mr. Dun. I'm talking about a risk-free, fifty percent return on cash money. Say between you and Willie here—ten million going in—fifteen coming out. It's a lead-pipe cinch."

Julie and a parade of waiters came in, bearing lunch. She fired up the sterno grill in the middle of the table and placed a skillet filled with fish and vegetables on it. The waiters arranged the side dishes. Dien waved them off. Julie bowed again and left.

"Not only that, but you'll have the benefit of legitimacy—call it prestige. General Dien, can I speak frankly here about our arrangement?"

Dien nodded.

"The general has had the good sense to see the possibilities. He's helped his country all he can. He's raised a lot of money, and now he's found the smart thing to do with it. He's collected several million dollars from the refugees over the last five years to finance patriots trying to reclaim your homeland. The general's helped them out, but he's got some change left over. And he's realized something that I'd like you to consider. Right now the biggest piece of ground you could get on this coast would be a house somewhere, and the neighbors wouldn't even talk to you when you took out your trash. A year or two from now, people are going to warm up to you Vietnamese, and I mean all the way. Things'll change when we get our POWs back, when people here get used to you. So, as investors in Elite Management—that's me—you can get your money down and your foot in the door of Republic Investments—that's my sister. That's how you buy into the Paradiso." Burke paused, pointing his chopsticks at Willie and Mr. Dun. "Hell, in good time, you can do a project on your own and come to *us* for financing. Imagine that."

Imagine that, thought Frye. Burke's laundry service. Won't Benny and Pop like to know where their investors get the money.

"See," Burke said, leaning forward again, "the general knows that by the time he gets that kind of prestige in this county, he'll be in deep clover so far as *really* helping his people goes. I'm talking ways he couldn't have even dreamed of 'til now. I'm talking friends in business and government. I'm talking legitimate power, American-style. Getting it ain't easy, but once you got it, you can pretty much do anything you like with it."

Willie and Dun looked at each other. Burke leaned back in his chair. "Gentlemen, we've all worked too hard alone to stop now. Together, we can do very wonderful things. For all of us. But if you want the kind of success I'm talking about, you have to work inside the system. And gentlemen, I *am* the system."

They ate. Burke cleaned his plate in five minutes, then piled on another helping. "Anyway, gentlemen, that's my offer. Fifty percent over five, and we'll take cash. My lawyers will draw up the papers in a jiffy. You'd both be legally incorporated as partners in Elite Management, and you'd both sit on the board with me. I'll call the shots. I'm looking for ten million, round numbers. If you don't want a piece of the action, I'll go somewhere else. No shortage of backers for the Paradiso, I can tell you that."

"Then why come to us?" asked Willie.

"Your assets have the desired bulk and liquidity," said Burke. "In other words, you got cash and you got lots of it. And you'll appreciate the silent aspect of the partnership, I think. I don't want a bunch of whining bankers telling me how to run the Paradiso. You wouldn't have to worry about it. I won't *let* you worry about it. She's my baby, and I'll make her work."

"Correction," said Dun. "It is Bennett Frye's baby, is it not?"

Burke drank off the rest of his champagne. "Don't worry about Bennett Frye."

Dien settled back in his chair. "What Mr. Parsons has failed to boast about is that your ten million would give Republic Investment a controling interest in the Paradiso. He can arrange this limited stock purchase very quietly and quickly. It would leave the Fryes in a . . . diminished position."

"Behind Bennett Frye's back?" asked Dun.

"Bennett Frye has enough to worry about right now," said Parsons.

Dun smiled. "And your sister has made much progress with Hanoi, in getting them to locate the missing Americans. They are willing to talk now. You are right, Mr. Parsons, a new era is coming between our countries. Perhaps we can all work together for mutual understanding, and profit."

"Thank you, Mr. Dun."

He stood and shook Burke's hand. Willie did likewise. Their bodyguards moved to the door.

"You have a day to think this over," said Burke. "You can reach me through General Dien."

Frye watched them leave.

Dien and Parsons looked at each other.

"They'll go with you," said the general.

"They're not stupid. You got it all?"

Dien nodded. His man came to the table, set the briefcase on top and opened it. Frye could see the neat stacks of bills, all hundreds. Beside them were three small bags and half-dozen bars of gold. "The jewels have been appraised; the gold bars are certified. The documents are in the bags. The value here is one million four hundred thousand dollars. With what I gave you last week, the total is three million. Are all the papers in order?"

"My lawyers say it's a go. Your people would be proud of you, General. They thought they were buying back fucking Vietnam, but what they're really getting is the Laguna Paradiso."

"What *I'm* getting is the Paradiso, Mr. Parsons."

"We're both getting it. There's plenty to go around."

"Mr. Thieu will accompany you to your car, Mr. Parsons. So much petty theft in Little Saigon these days."

They laughed. They shook hands. Parsons closed the briefcase and followed Dien out.

Frye sat back on Julie's bed. She came in a few moments later, stopped the tape, and gave it to Frye. "I hope you found what you wanted."

"Not exactly. They say anything on the way out?"

"I heard one phrase Mr. Dun said to Willie. *Dịp may hiếm có. Mày nghĩ sao?*" Roughly translated it means 'A really big chance, what do you think?' "

They sat in the bedroom. Bennett shut the door and climbed onto the bed. It was dark and musty, a diluted wash of sunlight coming through the drawn curtains. His face receded into the shadows as Frye told him about "Rollie Dean Mack," and the meeting between Burke, Dien, and the investors. "I've got it on tape. And don't worry, I'm not going to lose it this time."

Bennett's face was locked, grim. "I always tried to keep Burke close, because I never really trusted him. I guess I didn't keep him close enough."

"What do we do?"

"We cut off Republic Investments as of right now, that's what we do. I'll tell Flaherty and the other attorneys not to tender any more shares of the Paradiso for the next week. Then I'll take care of Burke. There's no way I'm going to finance the Paradiso with the blood and sweat of the refugees."

"What about Dien?"

"Burke can throw the money back in his face if it's not good with me."

"Willie and Dun?"

"If Burke takes their cash and can't spend it, then they all get what they fucking deserve. See how Parsons likes having the Vietnamese mob after him."

"I got to thinking when I watched Burke and Dien. Remember the man that Loc said approached him about stealing the tape of DeCord and Nguyen? The description fits Parsons, except for a mustache he could have faked. And the tape was delivered to the general. I think Parsons was Lawrence, and I'll bet he delivered that tape to DeCord."

Bennett just looked at him.

"Will DeCord try to take you down for gunrunning? Parsons would love it—it would get you out of the way while he tries to sell the Paradiso out from under you. Lucia would love it—it would satisfy Hanoi."

"If I get Thach tonight, and he'll release Li, DeCord won't have to take me. I'll quit. I'll be done, Chuck."

"Then what?"

"I'll have my wife back, and Thach will be greased. That's all I want out of life right now. Michelsen and Toibin were ordered back to Los Angeles this morning."

"Why?"

"No explanation."

"It doesn't make sense."

"Especially when they knew I was instructed to get this." Bennett climbed off the bed, reached under it, and pulled out a suitcase. He flicked up the latches and opened it. The money was neatly stacked, bound by rubber bands. "Two million, total. The other half is in another suitcase under here."

A strange smile crossed Bennett's face. He checked his watch. "The timing is perfect. Thach's just where he's supposed to be. We'll have him in seven hours. In nine or ten, we'll have Li. I'll never even have to touch this money."

# CHAPTER 26

CRISTOBEL WAS SITTING ON HIS porch. She had a little package on her lap, gift-wrapped in lavender paper, a deep purple bow. "Hi, cutie," she said.

Frye felt his ears getting hot, a jolt of bad energy shooting up his spine. He stared at her, cracked a skullish smile. "Hi."

She followed him in. "What's wrong?"

"Not a thing."

"For you."

He opened the package. It was a daily planner for the year, with a good pen attached. "Nice," he said.

"I figured you could use it, Chuck. Interviews for jobs and stuff. I mean . . . what's wrong with you? Is that supposed to be a smile or—"

Frye took her face in his hand, hard. The planner fell to the floor. He grabbed an arm, dragged her to the couch, and pushed her down. "Then you'd know exactly where I'd be, wouldn't you? Was that the deal, Cris? Keep an eye on Chuck? Make sure he doesn't get too close to Rollie Dean Mack because there isn't any fucking Rollie Dean Mack?"

Her color drained, her eyes went hard.

Frye slammed the door and locked it. He kicked the planner across the floor. He pulled the purse from her hands and spilled it out. A .22 automatic bounced onto the couch cushion. He waved the little pistol at her. "What are you doing for Burke?"

She looked at him with absolute disbelief now, a dignity so deeply shocked it was all she could do just to behold him. "You're really crazy, you know that?"

"I saw you with Parsons last night, on your patio."

She breathed deeply, nodded, looked straight at him. "You better listen to me, Chuck, and listen really well. I met Burke Parsons at the fights with you. And I happened to goddamn *like* him at first. Last night, I finally told him to cool off. That's between us, not you. But Burke doesn't care what you do or when you do it, and I don't either. You're the last topic of conversation when we're together—I can guarantee you that. Don't flatter yourself. I attract men, and I can get rid of them when I need to. We were *talking*. Don't try to chain me up. And don't even dare try to tell me which men to see and which not to. I'm sick to death of you and your plots, Chuck. You don't own me. Fuck somebody else if you can't hack it. Fuck yourself."

"Did he send you to Rockpile that first morning? Was that your idea, or his?"

Cristobel looked at him, eyes clear and dark, jaw set. "You don't listen, do you? Getting to know you was my stupid idea, and it gets stupider by the second. I saw you out there in those waves, and I had to find out if what I thought was true. What a silly, dangerous, romantic, stupid bitch I am. After what happened to me in Long Beach, it made sense to admire from a distance. I should have kept it that way."

Frye could feel the rage bubbling far down inside himself, a sour potion coming quickly to boil. "Nothing happened in Long Beach, or any other beach. You made it up. You weren't raped. You weren't touched. I had a cop friend of mine check it out. Like or not, Cristobel, you came back clean."

"He's lying. It happened on August sixteenth of last year, just before one in the morning. I was drunk. I had a fight with—"

"You told me that already."

"I sat in the station while that lady took samples out of me, I found the men who did it in the line-up, I sat through sixty days of court while they put that guy away, I dream about that night every goddamned time I close my eyes."

"They never touched you. There weren't any men. You made it up."

She took a deep breath, stepped toward Frye, and slapped him hard across the face. "Don't you ever say that, Chuck."

Frye reached out to her blouse, took it firmly in his fist, and yanked it down. Buttons popped, the material flapped open.

She slapped him again.

"This how it was?"

He reached for her pants and she hit him harder this time, fist closed, knuckles ringing off his eyebrow. He caught her knee with his palm as it slammed upward toward his crotch, then spun her around and pushed her down to the floor. She sprawled, slid, gathered herself up, and charged him. Frye caught her first blow with one arm, her next with the other. She teetered off balance, and he shoved her over the back of the couch. Her shorts and panties came to her knees with one tug; he yanked them away, then forced her head into the cushions. He was a little afraid of how easy it was.

"Or was it more like this?"

She straightened and swung her empty leather purse. It hit him flush in the head, a whack that left his ear ringing and one eye screaming in pain. He pushed her into the bedroom. He could hear the lock clicking, her rapid breathing.

And he could smell himself, a wicked, high-pitched stink unlike anything he'd ever smelled before, a smell of attack and cruelty, a smell of rage. He lowered his shoulder, ran three steps, and blew the door right off its rusty old hinges.

She ran into the cave. Frye followed. There she was in the darkness, pale flesh retreating. He lunged toward her golden hair, following it like a beacon. Amazing, he thought, how weak her arms are when you get a good solid hold of those wrists.

She threw her knees at him, but he just angled forward and they caught him in the thigh. Crashing through his box of Christmas ornaments, they tumbled over to the cold damp earth.

Frye stood over her, a foot on her ankle, one of her wrists locked in his fist.

She was panting below him, hair on dark earth, sweat-slick body shining.

"This what it was like?"

"Kind of. They were rougher. Come on, Chuck. Finish it off."

He stepped off her, let go of her arm, and pulled down his pants. For a moment he considered his dick, limp as a sock in the half-light of the cave. He pulled his pants back up. "I don't understand this part of it. When you get this pissed, the last thing you want to do is fuck somebody. I guess I'm not the type."

"I didn't think you were. You don't have the nuts."

Frye was tempted to punch her in the face, but he was losing his sense of purpose. "This'll sound dumb, but I thought we had something good going," he said.

"We did."

"You got something I could love. But I wouldn't believe you if you said good morning."

She was silent for a moment. He could hear her breathing. When she spoke again, her voice was hard. "I hate you," she said.

He walked back to the living room, threw all her stuff into the purse, and heaved it onto the floor by the door.

She came out a few minutes later, an earth-smudged mess, blouse ruined, hair wild, eyes down. She found her shorts and stepped into them. A tear tapped onto the hardwood as she leaned over and lost her balance. Her knees were scraped. Her face was red.

She went to the door, picked up her purse and slung it over her shoulder.

"Why?"

"Why what?"

"What hold does he have on you?"

"The same as you—none at all." She looked at Frye, then wiped her face on the back of her hand. "What you believe now doesn't matter."

"Get out of my life."

She fiddled with the lock, swung open the door, and walked out.

Burke Parsons called five minutes later. "Haw Chuck, how's it hangin'?"

"Funny you should ask."

"Well, things are sure good here at this end. Lucia's back from

Washington and we're having a few good pals over for drinks. You and Cristo-hoosey wanna come by?"

"What for?"

"For drinks, like I said. Celebrate the MIAs and all. Just casual. Your ma and pa are coming. Bennett's wrapped up in something, but I thought you might as well join us. I got some news from Rollie Dean."

"Not interested."

Burke paused. "Chuck, truth of the matter is, I'd like to talk to you about something. Private like. I think there may be some misunderstandings I can straighten out."

"Like what?"

"I don't talk business on the phone, Chuck. Superstitous. All I can tell you is I got something you'll want to hear. I been involved in some stuff you might want in on. I ain't gonna beg you, boy, it ain't my style. We're in that little old mission-style deal down on Crescent Bay. You'll see the cars out front."

Frye figured it might be as good a time as any to tell his father that Burke was getting ready to screw him. "Why not?"

"See ya in half an hour, Chuck. Bring that girl now, if ya want to."

"Haven't seen her in a while."

"Hell, bring someone else. Imagine a guy like you's got plenty of arrows in the old quiver."

Parsons's house was a three-story Spanish style on Crescent Bay, with flower pots under the windows, iron grates over them, and brown tile on the roof. Frye noted his father's car on the street and Burke's black Jaguar in the driveway.

Lucia answered the door with a smile on her face and a glass of wine in her hand. She'd permed her hair since the show, and now the black locks fell in curls to her shoulders, over her forehead. "Come in, Chuck."

"Congratulations, Lucia."

"Thank you. It was worth every hour I put in. No Cristobel?"

"Apparently not."

She gave him a sly smile, then led him down a wide entryway done in Mexican tile, potted palms, a gurgling fountain that fed a wide pool. Gray, foot-long fish moved through the water with a langorous, automatic, side-to side rhythm. "Baby sharks," said Lucia. "Burke loves them. Ugly, aren't they?"

The hallway opened to the huge living room on the left and a dining room and kitchen to the right. Past Lucia's shoulder, Frye could see Edison and Hyla. And at a glance: General Dien, Senator Lansdale, Carole Burton, a local millionaire who'd made his fortune in car wax, the Orange County DA, a soap actress and her cleavage competing for Burke's attention, an Angels' first baseman who could hit for power, an insanely tanned TV evangelist who'd recently taken up residence in Laguna Beach.

It's just too crème de la crème for words, Frye thought. I could puke.

He took some champagne from a passing waiter and downed it.

Edison performed an elaborate greeting; Hyla hugged him and kissed his cheek. Lucia introduced him to a few people, then moved off to greet another guest.

"I guess Benny's got that rally to get ready for," said Hyla. "I wish he could have come. I think he needs a break or . . . something."

"He's all right, Momma."

"I hope so."

Edison glommed two glasses of champagne, presenting one to his wife. "Lucia's done a job, I'll say that for her."

"Burke's about to do a job on you," said Frye.

Edison drank. "How so, Chuck?"

"Come outside."

Burke appeared as if conjured, standing between Frye and his father now, a glass of champagne held out to Chuck. "Haw, Chuck. How do you like our digs?"

"Looks nice, Burke."

"This ain't but a bit of it. We got three stories here and a basement that'll blow your mind. Ed and Hyla's seen it all, but how about I give you a tour?"

Parsons guided him away with a grin. "I'll bring him back in two shakes, Hyla. Won't be time for me to get him in trouble."

"Oh, Burke."

"Lovely lady, your mom, Chuck. Real lovely."

He led Frye through a sliding glass door, across a patio with another fountain. A guest house stood at the far end of the yard, under a tall stand of banana trees. "That little place is where Lucia's staff works—around the clock, sometimes." They entered the west wing of the house. "This is my part. And I got the whole second floor and basement. Lucia's got the third."

"I didn't know you lived together."

"Works out good, on account of we're both gone a lot, but at different times."

Back inside, Frye could hear their footsteps echoing on the paver tiles. A wooden chandelier with big candles glowed overhead, a rounded doorway gave way to a library with ceilings a mile high and bookshelves all the way to the top. Burke had one of those sliding ladders attached to each shelf. There were four good leather recliners, each with a reading lamp next to it. Along one wall was a small bar, well-stocked. Burke waved him toward it, then reached over the counter and stood back. A section of the paneled wall eased out, to the low grinding sound of a motor. A light went on. Frye regarded the staircase leading down.

Burke smiled. "I'm gimmick-heavy, Chuck. It's my nature. Watch these steps now, kinda steep."

Frye followed him down.

"You know, Chuck, that Cristobel's one good-looking hunk of girl. Lucky find."

"I'm not sure how lucky it was, Burke."

Parsons turned to look at him. "She a dud in bed or something?"

"She's great in bed. We get near one, she starts a feeding frenzy."

Burke smiled. "Think that's true about blondes bein' dumb?"

"No."

"Me neither. But I sure like 'em that way. Blonde and dumb is a hard combination to beat."

The basement was one big space, divided only by poles supporting the ceiling, and lit by rows of industrial fluorescent lamps hung by chains. It felt like the parking structure for a department store, but without the cars—wide and cool with the light tapering off into dark planes and corners. Frye heard his footsteps echo as he stepped to the floor.

The left quarter of the room was covered with padding. There were two exercise bikes, two heavy bags, a speed bag, a Universal machine and a bunch of shiny weights in stands. The support pole by the speed bag was wrapped in padding to head height.

"The gym," said Burke. "I try to get in an hour a day, but usually it's more like two. I got pairs of everything for Lucia, but she don't go for this stuff."

Frye smacked the heavy bag on his way by.

"You spar?" asked Burke.

"No."

"It's fun."

"I get carried away sometimes. Same as Bennett does."

Burke gave him an assessing look. "How far you get carried is the question. Sparring and fighting are two different things. Check these."

A stand in the corner contained six Japanese fighting swords, some long, some short. Frye noted the long handles, the lacquered scabbards, the leather grips well-stained by sweat, the ornate pommels.

A fancy version of what was used on Tuy Xuan, thought Frye.

"Katana," said Burke. "Several thousand dollars' worth of Jap killing edge. I got them black market in Hong Kong during the war. Those two on the end were billed as genuine Sagami School, and they're not. But you know what, Frye?"

"No."

"It don't matter." Burke slid out the weapon. The layers of the temper line caught the light. "Waste of money, actually. I don't get more than a couple hours a week on 'em. The exercises bore the hell out of me, and there's nothing you can actually hit with these things. Cut that pole in half if you put your mind to it."

"Looks wicked."

Burke looked closely at a blemish on the blade, then straight at Frye. "Not 'less the man who's swinging it is. How come you been poking around Elite Management, Chuck?"

"I wanted to talk to Rollie Dean. Seen him lately?"

The padded floor was soft under Frye's feet. Burke set the weapon back in its scabbard. "Over there's the gun range, Chuck."

The bullet traps and targets were flush with the far wall. A bench was positioned about fifty feet away. A chain with clips on it ran from each trap all the way to the bench, powered by smallish motors to bring the targets back and forth. Frye noted that the trap walls, angled gently to guide in the bullets, were pocked with silver and gray. Two padded headsets rested on the bench, and several boxes of foam ear plugs. Burke tapped a file cabinet that stood beside the bench. "I got a weakness for side-arms, Chuck. When I got in the agency, they took advantage of it. I was good at what I did. You know, Chuck, in a way I'm just a good ol' boy. I like to sip my beer and watch the boxing match. I like a round of poker and a good rodeo. I can talk redneck with anybody's fucked his daughter. But there's another side of me that just don't care about some things that lots of other people care about. I want you to think on that for a second. Anyway, I'm into hardware. Pull out that drawer there, have yourself a peek."

The inside of the drawer was lined with felt. On the bottom was a wooden tray with two rows of handguns, upright, handles fitted perfectly to the wood, barrels resting on the felt bottom. Fifteen, Frye thought, maybe twenty.

"That's the big-caliber stuff, forty-fours and fives. Hell, I got a fifty-four magnum in there I killed a grizzly with up to Montana. Hit him in the snout at fifty yards and the thing did a back flip. Ended up with a bearskin rug without a head. Anyhow, below those are the medium-caliber ones, and the last drawer down has the derringers and subcompacts. You shoot?"

"Pop taught me to shoot trap. I was pretty good with his old .45, too."

"Pick up that Gold Cup, there. Clip is full. See how you can do at fifty feet."

Frye removed the Colt from its place, checked the magazine, jacked a round into the chamber. He flicked off the safety and aimed down the length of his arm at the white-on-black silhouette.

"Shoot for speed, Chuck. Bad guys are always fast."

Frye took a breath and let it out slowly—just as Edison had taught him—then squeezed off the first round. His ears rang, smoke rose into his eyes. The automatic bucked up, and when it leveled, he added six more.

Parsons laughed, hit a button, and the target slid toward him, pulleys squeaking. "You didn't even get paper with that first one," he said. "The other six all got on the white, though. That's fair shooting at fifty feet, but I'll tell you, it's that first one you want true. Usually, that's all you get."

"Your turn, Burke."

Burke shook his head. "We're not in the same league, Chuck. Not at this game, anyhow. Let me ask you something. I saw an old convertible parked at Elite Management last night. That was your Mercury, wasn't it?"

"Sure was."

"Then I guess you figured out by now that Rollie Dean Mack don't exactly work there, in the strict sense."

"That's what I gathered."

"World's a crazy place, ain't it?"

Frye shrugged, slid open the action, and put the pistol back in place.

"You know, Chuck . . . I feel awful bad about what happened between you and Elite. If I'd have been paying closer attention to things, you wouldn't have lost your job. But I'm too damned busy these days—really. Would you be willing to let me square things with Billingham and get you all set to write again?"

"I thought you were going to do that two days ago."

Parsons pushed the drawer shut. "Just between you and me, I was hoping you'd give up trying to find old Rollie. I didn't bank on you being so damned tenacious. You nosed around my business, and you blew my little cover, so there's no sense playing games with you anymore, Chuck. See, Elite's my business, but I don't like being the front man. I hate those bright lights—I'm best in a backup position. It's actually none of your concern why. Put it this way, if I was a Beatle, I'd want to be Ringo."

"But you'd still want to write the music."

Parsons smiled. "You got it. Can I get you your job back? I mean . . . do you want it or not?"

"Why'd you get me canned in the first place?"

"I thought I explained that. You just caught onto Rollie's cuff like a pit bull and wouldn't let go. Hell, I figured if you were gonna keep calling and writing, sooner or later you'd come around for an impromptu interview instead of a scheduled one. So I just took you off the case. See? I was right. And I'm glad you're not going to the paper tomorrow morning to write about there being no Rollie Dean Mack at Elite. That'd be bad for everyone. But I didn't figure you'd keep after him. Christ, Chuck, don't you ever just give up?"

Frye baited him. "All that to cover a crooked fight?"

"Oh, hell, the fights don't mean a thing to me. That's the one tiny legit thing I do at Elite, just to keep the door open. Chuck, I move a lot of money in and out of that place. Oil. Stocks and bonds. Real estate. You name it. Some of it's even legal. Elite's got divisions and groups and wings and holdings and subsidiaries you ain't even heard about and never will. And I'm every one of them. I move and shake. Sometimes I gotta do things that are gonna catch the public eye. That's when I let Rollie Dean and the rest of the other fellas handle it. I just do it in their names. Like I said, I don't like the spotlights. I wish to hell you'd a never tangled with Rollie, because I didn't want to lose him, and I didn't want to mess you up either, Chuck. Funny part is, my fighter plum got knocked out that night. There wasn't no fix of any kind in. I swear it. I got better things to do than fool around with nickel-and-dime boxing matches, for cryin' out loud."

"Why'd you put Cristobel up to watching me?"

"What in God's holy name are you talking about, Chuck?"

"You and Cris, on her porch last night."

Parsons blushed. Frye couldn't believe it.

"Gosh, you weren't supposed to be in on that one."

"I was. What were you doing there, Burke?"

Parsons shook his head, stared down at his boots. "I was only tryin' to get it wet, Chuck. Same as you. I have to admit one thing, and I ain't ashamed of it, mostly—I love poontang. I took one look at her at the fights that night and I just had to have her. I'd say I'm sorry, but I'm really not. And I'm still working on the bitch, too. Cristobel's the hardest piece of ass in the world to get. Last night I took her some flowers and sweet-talked her a little. I tried to kiss her up, but she didn't like that a bit. She had some rape trouble up to Long Beach, is all I can figure. Gun shy." For a moment Parsons looked at him with the exasperated good humor of a kid caught with a *Playboy*. "Hell, Chuck, you don't own that girl, but I'll lay off Crissy if she means that much to you. I got plenty other fields to plow. So far as her watching you, that just never occurred to me. Maybe it should have. Truth is, I don't trust anybody enough for that kind of work. Especially some bimbo I don't even know."

"Do what you want, Burke."

"Say no more. I can see I stepped out of line a bit with her. Hey, get over here and check out my critters. You'll really like these, and I caught most of them myself."

Frye stood before a huge glass cage. It was almost twenty feet long, six high and deep, with a eucalyptus branch lying in the middle. Half the floor space was a pond. The other half was all reptile, coiled upon itself like a rubber telephone pole, head resting, tongue easing in and out for leisurely whiffs of the atmosphere. The eyes were pale green, big as quarters, with elliptical pupils like a cat's. The scales along its jaw looked like tile.

*"Eunectes murinus,"* said Burke. "Anaconda. He's pushing twenty-six feet long and tips the scales about two-eighty."

"What do you feed him?"

"You don't want to know. Could eat a small man, though, if his shoulders weren't too broad. Or a woman, easy. Probably eat your average Vietnamese real quick like and still have room for dessert."

Frye looked at Parsons, who was studying the snake with a detached admiration. The animal began to move now, sliding against the glass with no visible means of locomotion. Frye felt the muscles in his back go cold.

"So what's your next move, Chuck, far as Elite Management goes?"

"I'm not really sure. Any ideas?"

Parsons laughed. "I like you, Chuck. You're the kinda fella'd drive a car salesman bugshit 'cause you'd never make an offer 'til you got one from him first. Now, if I were you, what I do about Elite would depend on what I'd done already."

"I haven't told anyone," he lied. "If that's what you're thinking. Not Benny. Not Pop. Nobody."

Parsons nodded along. "Now we're getting somewhere, Chuck. It's good you've kept this to yourself. That's good for starters. See, it's important in a situation like this that I stay mobile. I hate getting pinned down. What I find in this life is a whole bunch of snake pits that truly aren't worth sticking your hand into, 'less you like getting bit. Every now and then you find some sorry fella who does, but that ain't you, Chuck. If I were you, I'd take a no-harm, no-foul outlook. I'd let things alone. I'd forget any quirks you might have noticed about the way another man does his business." Burke led him past the anaconda's cage to a stack of three smaller terrariums. "Top cage is Gaboon viper, longest fangs in the world, up to an inch and a half each. Middle one is black mamba, fastest snake in the world and the meanest. Believe me. Bottom is a good ol' western diamondback, and that sucker weighs almost twenty-five pounds. Caught him myself, right outside El Paso. I used some snakes in the war when I questioned prisoners. Cong hated them. Couple of times, things got out of hand. Poor Charlie, he hated to see me comin' with a duffel bag and a putting iron. Putting iron makes a good snake-stick. Anyhow, you can get a feel for those snake dens of life I was talking about."

Frye bent down for a look at the rattler. It was big around as a softball, with a head like a slice of pie, and dark diamonds on a desert-bleached background.

Burke went to the next cage, smiled, and pointed. "That there is commonly held to be the baddest serpent of the land. King cobra, Chuck, *ophiophagus hannah.* They get to eighteen, twenty feet, but Charlotte here is only but twelve. Forty-thousand folks a year die of snakebite, and Charlotte's kind do their share of it. They're not aggressive, really—kind of lazy in fact. They're like me. You get 'em riled up, though, and look out! Here, I'll introduce you proper."

Burke pulled a pin from the cage top and swung it open. He tapped on the glass with the backs of his fingers and said something to the snake. Then he reached in and took her by the middle, hefting a coil up and dipping in his other hand to get more. The more he pulled and lifted, the longer the snake seemed to get. Then he stepped back, twelve feet of cobra sliding around his body as if it were a tree, its head free, tongue darting. "Charlotte," he said, "meet Chuck Frye." Burke grinned from behind a looping, pale green curl.

"Defanged?"

"Nope. She's loaded, just like my guns. But she's friendly. Here, like to hold her?"

"No thanks."

"Don't be shy, Chuck. Don't want to hurt her feelings now, do ya?"

Burke gathered the animal, its head still waving free through the air, and arranged her over Frye's shoulders. Frye felt his legs go heavy and his ears start to ring. The snake was cool, and he could feel the muscles inside it, precise, mechanical, effortlessly bunching and sliding over his own. He supported the last three feet of her with his left arm. Charlotte cranked her blunt, heavy head to him and looked him straight in the face.

"Now, Chuck, if Charlotte here were to zap you right in the snout, where she's aiming, you'd scream, untangle her, run up the stairs, and croak before you hit the patio."

The snake pointed her tongue at Frye, wiggled it, took it back.

A freight train roared through Frye's brain. He felt the sweat rolling down his back and sides.

I'm not going to show it, he thought. I'm not going to give Burke one bit of satisfaction in this.

When he looked at Parsons, it pleased him that what he felt strongest now was not fear, though he felt that too, but rather a clear, uncomplicated rage. It felt good inside him, somehow familiar, somehow new.

"I'm glad to know that, Burke."

"It's a neurotoxic venom—stops your heart and just about every other moving part you got. Turns your nervous system to soup. Over in Asia, an elephant steps on a big cobra, gets nipped, and falls over dead a minute later. That's power, Chuck. Over in the 'Nam now, I'd use vipers on account of their poison works slower and burns a helluva lot more. Eats up your flesh, muscles, the works. Man, I got some interrogation results with my little bag of snakes. And the same putter I'd play nine holes with in the mornings, too!"

Charlotte's head moved away, and Frye eased his hand under it for support. She reeled back and he saw the eyes coming at him, scales getting bigger, tongue out. On his shoulder, her head was light and cool and the scales slid against his neck like leather buttons.

"You couldn't do that with a pit viper, Chuck, on account of they sense the heat and zap it. Charlotte here's a more primitive model. She's slower too. Fast movement, though, she don't like one bit. That'll set her off, and she'll get mad as all get out and zap whatever she can hit."

"Guess at this point, it would be me."

Burke stepped forward with an opaque grin and tapped her head. He tapped it again.

The head rose, took on a certain fierce alert, and tracked Burke's hand as it moved away. Frye could feel his chest hitting cotton.

"Anyway, Chuck, the main reason I want to see you is just to say I can help you on the job. Now for my askin' price—I just want you to lay off snooping around my business at all hours of the goddamned night and basically stay the fuck out of my life. You forget about Rollie Dean. You got a problem with the way I make a living, that's too bad. I don't believe for one second you haven't squawked to Bennett or that blond airhead I'm trying to bang. I can understand that. What I'm asking is you just lay off and leave me and my sister alone and let the law take care of the law. I don't ask twice, Chuck. I got a good thing going and I ain't about to let you mess it up. What the hell good would it do? You just go back to work instead of paying so much attention to other peoples' business, and the world'll keep spinning like it's supposed to. Am I being clear on this here proposal?"

"Pretty damned."

"Think I'm asking too much?"

"Your timing is odd."

"How do you feel?"

"Tarzanesque."

Parsons waved his hand before Charlotte again, then studied Frye. "That's my best and final, Chuck. I think it's a good offer, a fair trade. Frankly, though, I can't figure you out. You're an unknown quantity, and that makes me and Charlotte a bit nervous. You're no idiot though, so I think you can see I'm being fair here."

Burke stepped forward again and fanned his hand in front of Charlotte's face. She reared, wavered, held still. Then she spread her hood—two phantasmagoric flaps rising from her neck, scales spreading against translucent skin, a milky white light showing through between the rows. Frye felt her weight shifting as she swayed. His arm was getting tired. A drop of sweat burned into his eye. Charlotte's head pivoted as Burke moved to the side, then behind Frye. She swayed, seemed to focus on Frye's mouth. She was two feet away. Her tail dug into his crotch.

"We got an understanding now, Chuck?"

"We do."

"I knew you'd do business. You're sensible after all. Rollie Dean you're just gonna forget about, right?"

"That's right."

"No word to anybody?"

"Not one."

"There are a number of points being made in this conversation,

Chuck, and it's important that you grasp them. The bottom line is, you mess with me, and you're betting a dollar to make a dime. It just plain ain't worth it."

Burke reappeared in the corner of his vision. Frye sensed a flash of movement and felt the snake's body tighten around his own. Parsons stood back, Charlotte's head in his hand now. He was laughing. "Like winding up a garden hose, Chuck!"

Burke stepped back, hauling the snake with him. Frye could feel her tail dragging across his pants, then up his belly as Burke pulled her off.

A moment later he was stuffing the last of the light green body back into the cage, still holding her head in his right fist. "Charlotte don't like going back in, so I gotta hold her like this. Actually, I don't trust the bitch. Every inch a woman, isn't she?"

"Not like any I know."

"You haven't been around enough." Burke snapped the cage top shut, looked at Frye, and wiped a hand across Frye's forehead. He looked at his fingertips. "Not bad, Chuck. Not any more than I'd have sweated. I hope you don't interpret any of that as a threat. There's a million ways to get things done in this world."

Frye felt his pulse evening, the numb fear draining from his legs. But still, what he felt most was this new anger, non-negotiable, uncluttered. "You only need one, if it works."

Parsons laughed, walking toward the stairs. "Amen to that, young man. You want to know something weird? That kind of shit does absolutely nothing to me. Nothing. To me, there's nothing inside when it comes to violence, except it's a tool. It's like clipping your nails. That, basically, is where I stand."

"I see."

They walked up the stairs, Parsons first. The library door swung open automatically, its motor groaning. Frye easily imagined yanking Burke down the stairs, letting him fall, and strangling him at the bottom. He laughed to himself. That, basically, is where I stand.

"What you grinnin' at, Chuck?"

"Thanks for the tour. Sensible household pets are hard to find."

"You ought to be here at feeding time, Chuck. It's just like hell, and you get to watch. Gonna stick around a while?"

"I've got a freedom rally to catch."

"Oh, that thing. Hope someone shows."

# CHAPTER 27

**S**AIGON PLAZA WAS SWELLING with Vietnamese when Frye arrived just before sunset. He couldn't believe it. Banners and flags flapped in the breeze, booths lined the perimeter of the roped-off parking lot, streams of dark heads flowed in from the streets. Three patrol cars waited near the plaza entrance. Two more had come into the lot.

He joined the flow of bodies moving in. The entrance ticket cost five dollars and said FREE VIETNAM in English, with Vietnamese writing on the other side. A cop frisked him on his way through. Frye could smell food cooking—a spicy aroma that immediately made him hungry. Squeezing through a temporary archway that served as the official portal, he looked up to see a huge poster of Li's face, her eyes focused, it seemed, on the setting sun.

Massive reproductions of Thach's ruined face hung beside those of Li, with DEATH TO THACH emblazoned below in red.

A stage had been built near the center of the plaza, bathed in bright lights and festooned with Vietnamese and American flags. The podium was draped with a sign in both languages: DESTROY COMMUNISM. LIBERATE VIETNAM. FREE LI. Frye studied the backdrop—

three versions of Li's face, all taken from her album covers. He could see Nguyen Hy, sharply dressed in white linen, directing some activity behind the microphone. Beside the stage stood two men in dark suits, their arms crossed. More Feds, Frye guessed. Two others lingered on the far side, another munched distractedly beside a food booth. He spotted Wiggins talking to an NBC reporter. There were rows of chairs set up on the asphalt, but not even half enough, he guessed. Already the booths were surrounded by people buying food. In one booth a bingolike game progressed, with dozens of players studying little cards with numbers on them. The barker was a short man, his stubby arm turning a wire cage filled with numbered cubes, his voice a ceaseless syllabic river.

Strange, he thought, but it's all so quiet here. Nothing more than a low murmur, and already a couple of thousand people. Most of them wore black. Their faces revealed nothing. They looked joyless but not anguished, full of purpose but without focus, eager with impacted patience. The lights bore down and the people waited.

A young woman slipped past Frye, glancing at him, and he could see the fear—a minor tension was all she gave away—just a flicker in her eyes. The barker pulled another winner. A middle-aged man stepped forward, ticket raised. He received an envelope, then backed again into the crowd. How few of that age you see here, Frye realized: a generation decimated by the war.

He bought skewers of Vietnamese sausage on a bed of noodles, and two oddish, green blocks of gel wrapped in plastic for dessert. The Committee to Free Vietnam booth was busy. Standing outside the office, workers handed out pamphlets, pointing at the collection of Secret-War-zone photographs, taking names and numbers. One of the girls recognized Frye and waved him over.

"You like Vietnamese food?" she asked.

"Real good," said Frye.

"All the money raised tonight goes to free Li," she said.

Frye noted the long table set up on the sidewalk. The CFV workers were taking donations, which went directly from the outstretched hands of the Vietnamese into a gray safe. Ones, tens, twenties, a small jade necklace, pearl earrings. An old woman offered fifty cents. Then she stood there with tears running down her face and worked a ring from her finger. She handed it over. "Li Frye," she said. *"Tự do hay là chết."*

The girl looked at Frye. "She say, 'Freedom or death.' "

She smiled faintly and pointed out a picture on the CFV display. It showed a fragment of the Secret Army, eight heavily armed men. They appeared to be in the jungle somewhere, a camp perhaps. Frye studied the intensity of their faces, wondering what chance they had. Eighteen years old, he guessed, twenty? What spirit moved them into the jungle, against impossible odds, toward a martyrdom so puny it would be forgotten before their blood was dry? Maybe not, he thought: maybe all these people here would remember. That's where Li comes in. Keeping the memory alive. The memory tender.

"Secret Army," she said, still pointing.

"They're so young."

"Passion is not for the old. They are in Ben Cat, then in Bien Hoa, then in Saigon itself. No one can find them. They destroyed the bridge at Long Binh ten days ago. After that, they destroyed thirty-seven Communists near Cu Chi. Then, into the jungle, like a panther."

"How many of them are there?"

"Many. They are feared. They sneak into Saigon to meet with the resistance. They move across the border into Kampuchea. The Khmer Rouge help them, because they hate the Vietnamese. They steal supplies and disappear."

She looked at him placidly. "For freedom. Please give."

Frye nodded and dug out twenty bucks. Down to twelve dollars and change, he thought: I gotta get a job. He wandered toward the stage, where Nguyen was making a sound check. Hy looked down, grinned, and pointed to a small trailer parked behind the stage.

Donnell Crawley stood outside it, arms crossed, dark glasses on. He shook Frye's hand and almost crushed it. "He's inside," said Donnell. "Things are going pretty good, I think."

"I can't believe the turnout."

"Didn't surprise me. These Vietnamese got a lot of heart."

He found Bennett sitting in the trailer, a cordless telephone on his lap. He was wearing a suit and his prosthetic legs. His crutches leaned against a small refrigerator. Frye sat down. The trailer was hot and the windows were closed.

"What did Burke Parsons say?"

"He told me to lay off or he'd sick his snake on me."

"He pulled that shit in 'Nam, too. I hope you agreed."

Frye nodded.

"Good. How about Lucia? Beaming after her big moment in Washington?"

"Burke did all the talking."

"I used to think it was Lucia who wore the pants in that family. Now I'm starting to wonder. The dumber Burke plays, the smarter he seems." Bennett leveled a calm, hateful gaze at Frye. "He'll never buy into the Paradiso with refugee money, Chuck. I promise you that."

The telephone buzzed. Bennett raised his hand for silence, breathed deeply, then picked up the receiver.

"Frye."

A long pause. Bennett looked at him.

"Use Tran Khe, he's a better driver, and he knows the house. I want word immediately after the pickup. *Immediately.*"

Frye checked his watch. Bennett wrote something on a notepad that was open on his lap. A minute went by, then two. Bennett sat still, just his chest moving slowly, the telephone held to his ear.

A moment later he hung up. "Thach just left his apartment. In twenty minutes, we'll have him."

"Is it Kim you were talking to?"

"Kim is in a safe house outside Saigon, getting it from the field by radio. She codes it out to resistance radio in Trang Bang, then they leapfrog it from village to village, all the way to Cambodia. The Khmer relay to Phnom Penh, where they've got telephone to Hong Kong. Our people in Hong Kong have access to secure British lines, and our man in London is good." Bennett smiled. "He works in a travel agency. The rest is easy—London to New York to San Francisco to here. Pay phones. If the radios are all working right and the operators are good, it takes seven minutes to get word from Kim to me. If one thing goes wrong, it can take hours."

"Does the CIA listen in?"

"Sure they do. Up until three months ago, we used some of

their people for relay. NSA has us wrapped, but it takes time when you use different pay phones at this end. They've got us, it just takes a while to find us. They're an hour behind, at least."

Nguyen came into the trailer. "On schedule?"

"He's on schedule, Hy."

"Any chance I'll get to make the announcement tonight?"

A sly grin passed over Bennett's face, but he forced it away. "One step at a time."

Nguyen nodded, then headed back out for the stage. Frye watched him through the window, shaking hands with Pat Arbuckle, who looked on with an air of bemused superiority. Crawley grasped a huge speaker cabinet to his chest and walked it closer to the stage front. A CBS news crew had cornered Minh, freezing him in bright light. A sound man held a boom over his head while the reporter pressed a microphone to his face. The chairs were already filled, and people without seats were pressing toward the stage for a good view. Willie and Dun entered, surrounded by bodyguards. Albert Wiggins loitered near a noodle stand.

"Amazing, isn't it, Chuck, how much they love her—the old and young, the good, the bad, and everyone in between? They need her almost as much as I do. It's important to me that these people don't buckle under. When they show up here tonight, it's like telling Hanoi that freedom won't die. It's a hard thing for them to do, because they're scared. Kidnapping. Murder. Fear. The cops and FBI in front of them, Hanoi behind them. A little island of people locked inside the strongest country on earth. They've got balls."

Then Nguyen Hy took the stage to a rousing hand of applause. He welcomed everyone, first in Vietnamese, then English. He said that freedom would never perish, and neither would America or Vietnam. "We have come here to pledge our support to those great countries, and for the Voice of Freedom—Li Frye!"

The crowd cheered; the applause rose. The band struck up a number, which he recognized as one of Li's—"Freedom's Bones." It was an instrumental version, her voice replaced by an electric guitar. Frye could see her face on the banners, lilting in the breeze.

He listened to Nguyen's fevered voice again. Hy said that the kidnapping was executed by Communist agents of Hanoi, enemies of freedom, Moscow-fed animals out to destroy the Vietnamese people. The crowd listened quietly, then stirred. The band started up again, another Li Frye song. Nguyen exhorted the people to support the cause of freedom. His arms were raised heavenward, his hands open as if to draw blessing directly out of the sky.

Frye saw Albert Wiggins standing near the CBS news van, scanning the plaza balconies with binoculars. The reporter was talking with one of the CFV girls. Bennett wiped the sweat from his forehead, then stood clumsily on his crutches. "I'm on for about two minutes," he said. "If the phone rings, come get me. Don't answer it. Don't touch it."

Through the trailer window, Frye watched his brother labor up the back steps of the stage as Nguyen introduced him. A fresh peal of applause rose as Bennett stepped into the bright lights and, balancing with difficulty, raised his hands. Frye could hear Bennett's voice, loud and clear over the microphone. He thanked them for being there. He told them that courage didn't exist without fear. He told them that Li was here in spirit, and that her body and her laughter and her voice would be with them again soon. "You are full of power and grace," he said. "Never give up."

He stood there as the band played "Star Spangled Banner," then turned from a surge of applause and headed toward the trailer. Frye helped him through the door and onto the small bed. Bennett's face was dripping sweat, and his pupils were big. He loosened his necktie, brought the phone to his lap, and checked his watch. "Any minute, Chuck."

Frye could hear Nguyen, his voice rising, the clapping and shouts, swells of approval. He could see an old man dragging an effigy of Vietnamese President Truong Ky up a center aisle toward the stage. It was dressed in black pajamas with red hammers and sickles all over them.

The crowd came to its feet as the old man moved toward the podium. Nguyen paused and watched.

The phone was buzzing. Bennett lifted two crossed fingers to Frye, held them in the air, then picked up the handset. Through the trailer window, Frye could see Nguyen now, standing on the stage as the old man shuffled the last twenty feet toward him. A dozen celebrants had stood to form a loose gauntlet as they passed by. They yelled and spit on the dummy, its stuffed head bobbing toward Hy, spittle wobbling through stage light toward the effigy. The old man covered himself from the barrage. The crowd was chanting, *Thà Chết không làm nô lệ, thà chết không làm nô lệ . . .* When Frye turned back to Bennett, his brother's crossed fingers were still in the air, but his face had gone pale. He stared straight at Frye. He was nodding.

Nguyen hoisted the dummy onto the stage, to a ferocious chorus of cheers. He held it by the neck, out at arm's length, waving the face toward the seats.

"We will resist! We will unify Vietnam! We will struggle until freedom is ours!"

Bennett gently put down the phone. He looked at his brother with something that Frye had never seen before. It took him a moment to realize what it was. It was fear.

Frye could scarcely hear what Bennett said next. The crowd hit a frenzy as Nguyen prepared to decapitate the dummy with a plastic sword. Bennett spoke softly. "Thach knew about kilometer twenty-one. He was ready for us."

Frye reached down to help Bennett off the bed. He glanced outside as Hy lifted the dummy for execution. Something went wrong with the stage lights. For a fractional second, Hy and the doll were so brightly lit, blanched in a flash of white so pure that Frye's eyes burned.

Then they were blown apart by a concussive orange blast, emanating from the head of the effigy. The trailer rocked, and Frye slammed against the side. Nguyen's outstretched arm, his shoulder, and his head disassembled in a bright shower that sprayed all directions at once. His knees straightened, his torso jerked back and collapsed. The plastic sword shot skyward. The dummy jumped into the air, as if yanked by invisible wires. The people in the first rows turned to run.

As the crowd's cheers turned to wails, Frye struggled outside. Crawley had already dragged Hy off the stage and onto the ground. The cops were converging, sidearms drawn, ordering everyone down, but the people streamed around them toward Bolsa. Frye watched Bennett join the surging mass.

Half a dozen bodies lay scattered by the first row of seats, some moving, some screaming, some inert. The network newsmen were still taping. Westminster police and FBI agents ran around, guns drawn, looking for someone to arrest. A hundred feet from the exit, a group of refugees had caught the old man. Frye watched him vanish in the dark mob, fists pounding away at the gray, sinking head.

He ripped off his coat and pressed it onto an old Vietnamese woman who was laying face up on the asphalt, her chest smoking. He looked for Bennett, but couldn't find him. Someone beside him started moaning. He could see Crawley carrying a boy toward the stage, limp head and feet cascading over his arms. The CFV girl tried to tie a Vietnamese flag around a man's bleeding thigh while a woman stood over him and wailed. An FBI man, pistol in one hand and a radio in the other, screamed at two others, who seemed lost for purpose. Then Frye spotted Bennett climbing into his van. Minh was on stage with Wiggins now, trying to sound assured as he spoke into the microphone, telling the people to proceed in an orderly exit toward the boulevard. Frye lifted his coat, took one look at the crater in the woman's chest, and covered her face. A camera man steadied his lens at Frye and told him to pull the coat away. For a moment Frye just knelt there and watched Bennett's van drive away, barging through the crowd to the avenue.

He helped Donnell get Hy to a paramedic van, but there wasn't enough of Nguyen left to have any hope for. He ran for the Cyclone. It took him five minutes to force his way across the lot and onto the street. He sped down Bolsa toward Bennett's house, lights and sirens flashing past.

The door was standing open and the lights were on, but the van was gone. Frye parked in the driveway and went in. The house was quiet. His ears rang and he was breathing hard. The television emitted a pale, hissing static. "Benny?" He checked the kitchen, then Donnell's cottage. Where would you go, what's more important than a dying friend? Why did you cut and run, Benny? As he stood in the back yard, Frye began to understand. It could only be one thing. The kidnap of Thach didn't just backfire; it backfired exactly the way somebody had planned it. They had not only told Bennett that his operation had collapsed, but told him something about Li.

In the bedroom, he stooped down and looked under the bed for the suitcases of money. They were gone. Lying on the floor were Bennett's crutches and suit.

How do you know where to go, Benny? I was in the trailer

while they talked to you, and there wasn't enough time to set up the details of a trade. You didn't write anything down. You had no instructions. But you came here, took the money, left the television and lights on, the door open, and you ran. You didn't know where you'd be going when you got here, but when you left, you did. *The instructions were here. They left instructions here, while you were at the rally.*

He walked into the living room. The static snow of the TV hissed quietly. The red PLAY letters indicated the VCR was on. Frye hit rewind and listened to the tape whine. When it stopped, he hit play. Li appeared on the screen. She looked exhausted, with dark pouches under her eyes, her face pale, her hair filthy. "Benny, I am all right. I love you so. They will release me to you if you bring the two million dollars they asked for and follow their instructions. If not, they kill me tonight."

Someone offscreen pushed the barrel of a shotgun into her mouth. She sat there, staring out at Frye with her lips around the steel, tears running down her cheeks as a man's voice gave instructions.

"Bennett, you must put the money in two suitcases and put them in your van. You must drive to the phone booth at U.S. Gas, at Division Street and Palmdale Avenue in Palmdale. Answer the phone at exactly ten forty-five P.M. You must not contact the police or FBI, or allow them to follow you in any way. We will watch you carefully. You must bring only the money. You must be alone. Do not be a fool and bring weapons."

Frye felt his heart sink, then come back racing. He checked his watch. It was just after nine.

The Westminster Police lines were jammed. The FBI offices in Santa Ana were closed. A Los Angeles agent named Burns took the phone booth location, the plate numbers and description of the van and driver, the address and phone from which Frye was calling, then ordered him to stay exactly where he was.

Frye stayed exactly where he was for almost two seconds, then gave up. He found a .45 in Bennett's drawer, shoved it into his pants, and headed back to the Cyclone.

# CHAPTER 28

**H**E REMEMBERED THE WAY TO Palmdale from his journey with Kim to the Lower Mojave Airstrip. She had taken him the long way, so he took the 605 to the Interstate, then bore north, through Los Angeles, holding his speed to seventy. Once past the city he flogged it to eighty plus, letting the old V-8 eat the highway, watching his rearview, feeling the air go dry and hot as he entered the high desert. Palmdale Boulevard crossed Division Street just a few blocks from the freeway. He spotted the Lucky Star Chinese Restaurant and U.S. Gas on the corner. It was ten thirty-nine. Bennett's van was parked in front of the phone booth. His brother paced outside it. Two Vietnamese men stood and watched.

Frye parked a block short, cut the engine and waited. No sign that Burns's agents were here. Just the watchers, hands in their coat pockets, still as statues. A thermometer readout from a savings and loan across the street said eighty-six degrees. Hot breeze blew in his car window. The Cyclone's engine popped and hissed. Frye checked the clip in the .45. Seven shots, and he knew Bennett never kept one in the chamber. He held the thing in his hand, then slid it under the seat. At 10:45, a withered old man shuffled toward the phone booth. The two guards shooed him away. The man turned, shaking his head, and trudged into the darkness. Frye saw Bennett push into the booth, reach up, and take the receiver. He nodded twice, slammed the phone back in place and shoved his way out. His escorts were already in their white pickup truck.

Highway 14 was a ribbon of moonlight winding through the desert. The wind grew stronger, pressing against the Merc, stiffening the steering wheel in Frye's hands. He stayed four cars behind the truck until there were no longer four cars to stay behind, then dropped back, killed his headlights, and followed. He prayed to his rearview for Burns and the cavalry, but saw nothing behind him except the night and slow truckers, and nothing ahead but a brother delivering a fortune to men who would take it and kill him.

Bennett stopped in Lancaster and waited outside a pay phone at a K-Mart. His escorts parked beside his van, but didn't get out. Frye watched from the dark recesses of an parking lot across the intersection. At 11:02, Bennett answered the phone, took his instructions and climbed back into the van. Then back onto Highway 14 to Rosamond Boulevard; Frye knew for certain where Bennett was being led.

It was the same route now that Kin had shown him: five miles east down the boulevard, then north on the wide dirt road marked by the sign for the Sidewinder Mine. He dropped far back, let Bennett and the truck make the turn far ahead of him, then cruised past the turnoff—just another desert rat meandering home after a beer or two with the boys.

A half mile down, he turned around, pulled to the side of the road and waited. How long would it take Benny to go a mile north on the dirt road, pass through the gate, and travel the last five hundred yards west, across the arroyo to the airstrip? Five minutes? Less? He rolled down his window and listened. Except for the firm gusting of the wind, the night was silent. On the other side of the highway, the dry lake bed stretched flat and pale. No cars, no aircraft overhead. No FBI, he thought: We're on our own.

At the rock pile he cut his lights and let the moon guide him down the wide dirt road. He drove past the gate, continued on another hundred yards, and parked. He put the .45 in his belt, left the hood up to indicate distress, then climbed the chain link fence, plopped down on the other side, and headed toward the airway on foot.

The rocks were treacherous, but the moonlight showed him the way. He climbed a gentle hill, crunched down the other side, then followed a long wash toward the terminal. The next rise was high and steep enough to hide behind. He lay on the warm sand and peered over the crest to the airfield. It was just as before, flimsy and beaten and apparently deserted. But now a naked bulb burned at the entrance of the Quonset hangar, and Bennett's van was parked beside two pickup trucks in front. The terminal was dark. Behind it, just to the side of the dark slouching tower, a helicopter waited. Looks like an old Bell—Frye thought—a company craft for lifting executives above the traffic. As he watched, the hangar door opened and a Vietnamese man stepped into the raw light of the bulb. He slid shut the door, adjusted the strap of his automatic rifle, then lit a cigarette.

The back of the hangar seemed his only option. He ducked back down the embankment and looped out. A sandy gully took him almost all the way around the compound, while the wind puffed, echoed in his ears, shot sand at his ankles. Above him the stars blinked clear and sharp. From behind an outcropping of sandstone, he looked at the back end of the hangar. A dull light emanated from where windows had once been. No guard. The corrugated sliding door had long since fallen from its track and now stood at a tilt, its runners jammed into a low bank of wind-blown desert sand. No way to approach under cover. He stood, took a deep breath, crept from the rocks, and loped down a long wash that left him crouched behind a yucca plant, fifty yards from the helicopter. Another measured run and he was kneeling beside the chopper cabin, his heart pounding hard, his skin dry and hot, his right hand wrapped around Bennett's pistol.

The hangar was thirty yards away. He crawled across, beneath the sightline of the windows, and brought himself to rest against the old building. The wind eddied, throwing dust and sand at the metal. A branch scratched at the siding. He moved to a window and stood. In the dark foreground he could make out the shape of an old prop plane, then the outlines of crates and boxes. But past them was a cone of light cast from overhead, widening down from the high ceiling. Dust wavered in the beam, which rocked gently in a draft. The light spread to a circle on the floor and Bennett sat on a chair in the middle of it. A guard stood behind him with a machine gun, the two suitcases of money at his feet. Bennett said something in Vietnamese, and the guard snapped something back. As Frye looked at Bennett stranded in the light, alone in a chair in the middle this great nowhere, he felt a rage course through him. I'm too far away, he thought. Too far to hear, too far to shoot, too far to do anything but watch. Do they really have Li here, or did they just drag Benny all this way to take his money and bury him in the desert? His heart was thumping so loud he wondered if the guard could hear it.

He crawled back to the defunct sliding door and squeezed into the hangar beside the old plane. The cement floor was dusty but quiet. He moved slowly under the wing of the aircraft, then dodged behind a stack of old ammo boxes. Outside, the wind slapped against the walls. Frye watched the guard look in his direction, then turn back to Bennett. Fifty feet away, he guessed: I could take him out with one shot. *You didn't even get paper on the first one. It's the first one you want true . . . usually that's all you get.*

Shapes were moving just outside the light. Frye saw the guard stand at attention. Then the echo of footsteps slowly approaching Bennett, and a tapping sound. A young Vietnamese man dressed in green fatigues stepped into the light, looked at Bennett, then eased back into the shadows. Bennett looked up. Frye could see the stunned disbelief on his brother's face as he squinted into the darkness. Two more steps, slow steps, punctuated by the tapping sound again. The profile of a man formed. With one last step he entered the light, a stooped figure leaning on an ebony cane, a face twisted beyond recognition. He wore dark glasses. Thach and Bennett stared at each other for a long, long moment.

Frye's body went bone-cold. He couldn't take his eyes off Thach's molten face—the way the cheeks and nose and mouth fused together, as if welded by some skilless artisan using the last scraps of creation. Thach wore an army shirt and pants, a black belt and boots, an officer's holster, a batch of medals on his bulky, misshapen chest. He continued to stare down at Bennett, who stared back. Frye did too. The .45 seemed impossibly heavy and useless. Then Thach lifted a hand from his cane, just slightly, and motioned to someone behind him. Li stepped into the light, wrists bound tightly, ankles linked by a foot of rope, guided by a soldier with one hand on her arm and the other on his rifle. She wore the black pajamas of a Vietnamese peasant. Bennett started off his chair, but the guard stepped forward and drove him back with his gun butt. The man with Li cinched her close to him. Thach looked at the suitcases of money, then back to Bennett. When he spoke, his voice sounded artificially induced. "Your wife and I have had many long discussions these last days. I expected to find a strong woman in Li Frye, and I was correct. I had hoped to show her the truth of history, and of nature, but she is too far lost to your lies to ever see the truth. You were thorough, Lieutenant. Our attempts to re-educate her have not been a success."

Li stood motionless. Again Bennett tried to go to her, and again the guard jammed him back with his weapon.

Thach turned to the darkness and waved again. The guard that Frye had seen outside now pulled a small table and chair to the edge of the light. Thach maneuvered himself behind it and sat down. "We have some formalities to complete before our transaction can be made." The guard placed a sheaf of papers on the table. Thach removed his dark shades, removed a pair of reading glasses from his pocket, wrapped the cables carefully over what remained of his ears, and read. "On July second, nineteen-seventy-two, you ordered South Vietnamese Army sergeant Huong Lam interrogated as a traitor, then executed?"

Bennett sat forward, still looking at Li as if she were the only person left on earth. As she gazed back at him, Frye tried to identify the strange expression on her face. She looked exhausted, almost resigned, but still with hope. What had Thach *done* to her?

"Lieutenant Frye, please answer."

Bennett gave his name, rank and serial number.

Thach shuffled the papers, then looked at him. "I must tell you, lieutenant, that the war is over. You lost. The sooner you give me answers, the sooner we will finish."

Bennett was still staring at Li. "Yes, I ordered Huong Lam interrogated and killed."

"Huong was a man you had worked with for nearly a year, a

man you had come to suspect was a traitor to the American war effort?"

Bennett nodded.

Li was looking at Thach now, as if paralyzed by the face and the disembodied voice.

"On the night you took this woman, she came to you with a pack on her back. Huong Lam had given it to her. What was in it?"

Bennett looked at Li.

"Answer, lieutenant."

"He gave Li a bomb. He strapped it to her back and told her to take it to me. He said we should open it together."

Li looked at Bennett expectantly.

Thach wrote something down. "Tell her, Lieutenant Frye, what your men found in the pack given to Li by Huong Lam."

Bennett started off his chair again but the guard lifted his gun butt. Bennett ducked, covering up with his elbows. Frye saw the guard's disdainful frown, the disappointment that he'd already beaten the fight out of his plaything. His brother sank back into the seat. Frye's grip tightened on the automatic.

Bennett looked at Li. "She knows. It was a bomb, a frag grenade made from three dead mortar rounds."

Thach rose slowly from the table and tapped his way to Bennett. He stooped, bringing his face close, and removed his glasses. Bennett sat, frozen by Thach as a mouse is frozen by a rattlesnake. Then, slowly, Bennett leaned forward. Their faces almost touched. Bennett's hand rose slowly, as if to touch Thach's cheek, but hovered there, unable to complete the motion. Bennett spoke in a whisper. "No."

Thach's face twisted into something like a smile. He stood straight. "What is wrong, Lieutenant? You look like a man who is seeing ghosts."

*"Lam."*

"Bennett."

"Lam . . . you fell, you—"

"I was thrown. Let us not distort the truth as we have distorted each other. I am still thrown from your Huey a thousand times a night."

"Lam," whispered Bennett.

"Lam died in the sky as he fell to earth. He died in the trees that tore his face. He died in the mud where he lay while the rats ate him. He died in the tunnel where they did not set his wounds because he could never live. You killed him."

Thach brought up a hand, looped something off his neck, and tossed it toward Bennett. It landed on the floor and Frye knew in an instant what it was: the silver wave necklace he'd made and sent to Benny all those years ago.

Bennett breathed deeply, his eyes moving from Thach to Li, then back to Thach again.

Li stood still, staring at Thach as the colonel approached her. Frye could see the tears glistening on her cheeks.

"Lam," she said. *"Lam."*

Thach took her face in his hand and turned it to Bennett. "Tell us, Bennett, what you found in the pack that I prepared for you two to open together."

Thach yanked Li up close to Bennett, still clenching her face in his hand. "This must come from you. I've waited many years for the chance to hear you say that one word. Li would not believe me. Tell her now, what I packed for you to open together. Tell me what I was tortured for, what I was thrown from the gunship for."

"Champagne," said Bennett quietly. "Three bottles of French champagne."

Thach released her. She didn't move.

"And what else?" asked Thach.

"A note that said, 'Friend, you have won.' "

Li looked at Bennett imploringly. She seemed to diminish into the pajamas. "Benny . . . no. It was a bomb."

Bennett's voice was low. "I didn't *know.* I didn't know, until after. It wasn't until my men tried to defuse it that I knew what had really gone down. I was drinking in the officers' club that night. I was drinking because a friend betrayed me. Then the ordnance team came in and tossed the pack onto the bar. They were laughing. I just stared at those bottles and realized what I'd done. I thought you had betrayed us, Lam. And I thought you tried to kill me for taking Li away. Go back, Lam. Go back to that night and ask yourself what you would have done."

Bennett wiped his face, then steadied himself him the chair. He looked up at Thach. "When I saw the champagne, I went to Tony

308

and tore apart his hootch. He had code books, maps. He was our traitor, all along. I can't tell you how many times I've prayed for your soul, and prayed I could bring you back. Jesus Christ, my prayers were answered."

Thach looked at each of them. Frye saw a strange amusement in his face. "Ah, Tony. I suspected him. I wondered if he were an idiot. I nearly shot him once, simply on instinct. Months later, when I found out what valuable work he had done for us, I was glad I didn't. I'm sure you Americans did a good enough job of that, Lieutenant."

Thach balanced himself on his cane and peered for a moment up into the light. Frye beheld his ruined face, then his brother's. When Thach turned again to Bennett, his eyes were fierce. "What made you believe I would betray you? I fought for you. I nearly died, many times, for you. I brought Kieu Li to you. I led your men against my own people. What made you believe that I would not give up a woman to you?"

"Christ, Lam, you'd been with the Viet Cong once. Our intelligence was leaking worse every week, and I knew you loved her. I saw the look in your eyes when you watched us. If you could have been me that night, you would have figured it exactly the way I did. What in hell else would I think, when you strap a heavy pack on her and tell her to open it with me? Why else would you be packing up to head north when I found you?"

"You were afraid of me?"

"You're goddamned right I was."

Thach seemed to consider this. He finally turned to Li. "But, you. I gave you a path to follow, a channel for your passion. I let you see what was happening to our country. I treated you with respect. I protected you. I came to you in the marketplace of An Cat and walked you home at night. I loved you, and you saw it, too. Why did you ever believe I could betray you?"

Li looked down. "Because, Lam, you were fierce, more fierce than anyone I knew. When I told you that I was going to an American soldier, it wasn't hatred I saw, it was something quieter, something far worse. Your look connected with . . . with a part of what I was feeling. And your voice, when you tied that thing to my back. Not for a moment did I imagine that you would let me go to Bennett."

Frye watched as Li stood, wrists and ankles bound. She looked at Thach and held his gaze. "Deep in my heart, I didn't want you to let me go. Deep in my heart, I felt that what I was doing was wrong. I loved you as I could never love an American. I told you that a hundred times! But didn't you feel how impossible it all was? That was the war, Lam. There were only two sides. Some part of me wanted to stay with you, but parts of people can't stay behind. And there was no room in my heart for that doubt, just as there was no room in yours for what I was doing. I was terrified, but I was happy that you would want to kill me. I . . . *needed* to believe it."

"Why?"

Li breathed deeply. "Because it made me free of you."

Thach looked at her. "You were always so simple, Kieu Li. You still are." He drew close to her again, bringing his face close to hers. "The truth is, that when I saw the love pass between you two, it sickened me. It still does."

Frye saw the slickness on the colonel's face, the blotches of sweat that had soaked through his shirt. Thach's breath was coming faster now. Frye saw one of the guards glance at the other. Then Thach reached out with his cane and poked Bennett's chest. "In these last days, I have told Li the truth many times. But she would rather believe you. You have occupied her, Lieutenant, like your army occupied my country. You have kept her a child. I have helped reeducate thousands, and none has been so completely . . . shaped as Li. You should have much pride in her. And much shame."

Li struggled against her rope, glaring at Thach. "I've listened to my own heart since I was seventeen years old, Lam. *You* have only listened to others. *You* are the child, not I. You surrendered in your fight for freedom because you saw yourself as a man betrayed. What of our countrymen, Lam? What of those who fought on against the greater terrors that the Communists unleashed?"

"Such words mean nothing to a man falling through space to his death."

Frye watched now as Colonel Thach hobbled back to his table and sat down. His breath was fast, exhaled from his twisted nose with a labored hiss. For a moment he seemed lost in his papers. "I have always wanted to bring these truths into the open. Those days are still very clear in my memory. In a sense, they matter

310

little. What are intentions and beliefs? What are reasons and motives? They are things we attach later to our actions. Only the action matters. All else is convenient falsehood."

Bennett shifted in his chair. "How did you live through it, Lam?"

Thach looked at him. "The *mam* grove was high. The water was deep because of monsoon. The fall was broken first by leaves, then branches, then the swamp. The Communists took me into the tunnel to die, but I lived. The darkness became my ally. When I woke and saw my new face, I knew that Lam had died. I hated that face. I knew I would stay in the tunnels so no one would see it. So I would never see it. And with a crippled leg I could still crawl, no slower than anyone else. All I knew for certain was that you had betrayed my trust, the same way I knew your country would betray mine. My faith in America was my faith in you, Bennett." Thach stopped and shook his head. "You are right, I was more foolish even than you, Lieu Li. And almost as innocent."

"So you turned."

Thach smiled again. Frye could see a grim pride showing in his eyes. "Communism. Democracy. We both know by now that they are only words. They are two fat old women, fighting over a bowl of rice. I turned to my race, Lieutenant, to my people. I turned to my mirror and asked how this had happened. I turned to myself."

"How did you do it? How did you get to this country?"

"With much planning and waiting. With help from many comrades in your country. When I first heard the songs on your Secret Radio, I was almost certain it was Li. I found later that this 'Voice of Freedom' was married to an American. My suspicions were correct. Much planning, Lieutenant, much waiting."

"How long did Kim work for you?"

"Four years. She has family in Vietnam. She was easy to use. The false intelligence she sent you from Vietnam was very effective. Look how easily you were fooled. I knew the people in Little Saigon would believe I was here. But you Americans would never believe it. I used your arrogance as a weapon against you. I used the tunnels under Saigon Plaza because they are my element. Kim supplied the words."

"And the Dark Men?"

Thach stood slowly. "They asked no questions and wanted little money. They are frightened children."

"Why did you bring us here? Why the airstrip?"

"With Xuan gone and your network crippled, it was a secure place. Nothing is so safe as an enemy camp with no enemy left. Before coming here, we held Li in Los Angeles. We have sympathetic friends there."

"You won, Colonel. You've slaughtered the resistance, haven't you?"

Thach shook his head. "I have one hundred and twelve people from your network. They will be tried for treason. Only one remains, and you are going to reveal his identity to us. We know he is highly placed in Hanoi, and we must move with caution. One of his code names is Nathan, is it not, Lieutenant? Nathan, who guides you to our positions, describes our strength, misinforms our leaders. Nathan, for your country's first spy? Yes, I can see already that I am correct."

Thach's breathing seemed to accelerate again. Frye watched the sweat run down his face. "Look at all I have accomplished. I have destroyed the resistance and the Voice of Freedom. I have removed the irritating Tuy Xuan. I have shown the people of Little Saigon how small and helpless they are. And I have you, Lieutenant."

Bennett bowed his head. A moment later he looked to the suitcases, then to Thach. "I brought your money. Take it, and let us go."

"Your money is a filthy thing, Lieutenant. I demanded it to satisfy my allies in this campaign. I have no need for it myself."

"Then we're finished."

Thach picked up the pen and papers from his desk and brought them to Bennett. "Almost. What we discussed earlier is written here. Also, a statement that you are responsible for organizing a Secret Army in Vietnam. That your government financed it. A list of the accomplishments of the army is included. The bridges they have destroyed, the factories they have sabotaged, the men and women they have assassinated. You will find the information to be accurate. Read it. Sign it."

"What for?"

"For me, Lieutenant. And to satisfy my superiors. I cannot tell you how rewarding it has been to see you confess. It is something

I will want to have with me forever. Even I am tired of hatred. I am almost finished. I kept you from Li for all these days so you would know what it is like to have your love taken away, so you could know how Huong felt. And also, to give me time to convince Li that she should come home with me, confess her betrayals, and work again for the good of her people. At this I may have failed. I knew it would be difficult. But I do have another plan for her, and for you, Lieutenant."

"Never," Li spat out. "Never."

"I'm not going to sign that thing."

Thach seemed to know all along that Bennett would refuse, but for a moment, Frye thought he saw something like confusion on the colonel's face. "Why? After all that happened, why did you continue to make war?"

Bennett looked at Thach. "For the people I knew who fought and died for something they believed in. For Li. For myself. For Huong Lam, what do you think of that?"

"And you, Li? For fifteen years you have continued to fight. Your Secret Army has brought death and destruction to the new republic. You fly from rich America to the jungles to deliver codes and instructions. I have photographs of you bearing arms over the mountains of Thailand into Kampuchea. I have watched your progress across our maps in the basement of the defense ministry, marching through the jungle with your pathetic little army. I have imagined the way you must hold the M-sixteen in your thin, beautiful arms. I have hours of tape on which you sing, then plead with my countrymen to join you. Why?"

Li struggled against her bonds. Frye saw her aiming at Thach a frightening, untethered wrath. "I did it for the same reasons I told you a thousand times in the last days. Because the Communists kill the spirit. Because they turn men like Lam into men like you. Think back to the days at the plantation and An Cat, to the young soldier you were. What made your eyes clear then, and your heart strong? What gave you your courage? The promise of freedom! Is there still a Vietnam where that can happen? All you are is a state machine now—soldiers take away the poetry of peasants before the ink is dry and see if the verses help the government."

Thach looked at Bennett, then Li. "I am very tempted to shoot you both now. But that was not my intention."

"Then take your victories and money, and let us go," said Bennett.

Thach returned to his desk and set down the papers. "I now arrest you both in the name of the Socialist Republic of Vietnam. The charges are inciting treason, conspiracy to overthrow the government, and murder. You will return with me, through Mexico and Cuba, to be tried with the rest of your resistance force. You will confirm to us the identity of Nathan."

Bennett hurled himself off the chair, but the guard slammed him again with the butt of his weapon. Bennett covered up, hands raised. The guard lifted his gun for another jab, but stopped, shook his head with scorn, then backed off. Frye held him in the sight of his .45.

Bennett lowered his hands. "You're crazy, Thach. You can't try us. Your own government will shoot you and send us back here in a week."

"Maybe. But we have arranged for you to be apprehended in the jungle near Ben Cat. You will be identified by your own people. You will sign confessions, of course. At a time that Hanoi is releasing American soldiers, news of your capture will soon be lost. You will see how quickly the U.S. Government washes its hands of you, as they do of their CIA pilots in Nicaragua. That is their choice. You have made war on us, Lieutenant and Li, ever since the war ended. You have tried to assassinate me. While we try to handle the problem of Kampuchea, you send arms against us. While we try to feed our people, you destroy bridges and waterworks. While we try to build a peace, you bring death. My government may indeed execute me someday, Lieutenant, but my campaign will be complete. I will have ended the war. They can do with you what they believe is right. You must have known that you would someday have to answer for yourselves."

"No. Not Li."

"You think you were her salvation, Lieutenant. But you cannot save her now. She goes back with us, to the same fate."

Frye kept the sight of the .45 on the guard beside Bennett, centered on the man's chest. Three men, he thought, and Thach. Automatic weapons. Even if I'm lucky, I can only get two. It's a mismatch. I could kill the light. I could kill the chopper. What happened to Burns?

He watched Bennett, balancing himself uneasily on his fists.

"Let Li stay. I'll go with you, sign what you want. What good can you get from her that you can't get from me alone? I did what I did to you because I made a mistake. It was a war, Lam. See if you can do any better now. Take me. Your vengeance for my betrayal. My legs for your face. Fucking hang me in Hanoi if that's what you want. I'm not going to beg. Just let her go."

"I won't stay here without you, Benny."

"You sure as hell will."

Thach appeared to ponder. He gazed up toward the light bulb. His distended chest was heaving. Frye saw that the two guards were standing closer together now, that he could take them both in two shots. He steadied his aim on the man nearest Bennett. Thach stepped in front of him.

Maybe, Frye thought, I should take Thach first.

"I will offer you a solution," Thach said. "You identify Nathan to me now, with satisfactory particulars, and I will let Li go. You, Lieutenant, will still return with me."

Li writhed against her ropes. "No, Benny!"

Bennett stood as if frozen. Frye could almost see the gears turning inside his head. Bennett looked at Li, then Thach. The colonel's body was turned to Frye now, a full target, standing still.

"Choose, Lieutenant. Nathan for Li. Li for Nathan."

Li tried to break from her guard, but he held her fast by the arm. "They can kill me, Benny, but not what we have done. Don't say a word. Don't kill what we have accomplished."

Thach stepped forward. "You will tell when we go back and probably die in the process. Identify him now. Save your wife from the firing squad. Who do you love more, Bennett? Your wife, or the hopeless ideas she promotes? Choose."

Thach balanced on his cane and looked down at Bennett. His face was pale, shining with sweat. Frye could hear the soft hiss of his breathing. He shook his head, motioned in Frye's direction, and stepped toward his table. *"Bỏ chúng vào trực thăng"* he said.

"Let her go!" screamed Bennett. "Lam, let her go!"

Thach lifted his cane toward the helicopter and the men began to move.

Bennett charged toward Thach, but the guard stepped forward again and drove his gun butt into Bennett's chest. Frye was amazed at the speed with which Bennett's hands locked around the gun and yanked it away. The guard's head jerked back as the blast echoed through the hangar. When Li's guard leveled his automatic, Frye shot him in the chest, rocking him back as his gun clattered to the floor. Frye saw the bright muzzle flash of the third guard's weapon, heard the rounds sucking past his head, felt the wooden splinters of the boxes spraying into his face as the rounds split them apart. Li drove at him, head lowered. Frye dove to the ground, rolled into the open, and fired off two rounds as fast as he could. The off-balance soldier spun and landed face down. Bennett sat in the cone of light, his weapon raised toward Thach. The colonel stood just on the edge of darkness, resting on his cane, his pistol drawn and aimed down at Bennett. Later, Frye would realize that some acknowledgement took place between them there, some admission that this was the only true end to which it all could come. Then a quick, vicious volley, each one firing orange comets into the other while Frye tried to sight around Li. Thach's cane flew. Bennett shuddered with each impact. But they both kept firing and punching holes in each other while ropes of blood lurched and wobbled into the light and Li screamed and Frye wondered how they could stay alive enough to kill each other anymore. Then, just as he had a clear shot, it was over, and the terrible quiet descended. The colonel lay on his back. Li was hovering over Bennett. Frye stood amidst the haze of gunsmoke, confronted by a silence more complete than he had ever known, a stillness into which everything was sucked, inhaled, consumed. The air was heavy with the particulate stink of powder. The lamp beam swung gently as the smoke rose into the light. Outside, the wind gusted.

Still be with us, brother. Please.

As Frye came close he could hear his brother's little gasps, quick and shallow as if taken at high altitude. He untied Li's wrists and ankles. Bennett was on his back. Thach lay fallen in the shadows.

Bennett looked up. The peace in his eyes bore no relation to the rapid lifting and falling of his chest. Li knelt beside him. Bennett blinked, moved his eyes slowly from his brother to his wife, blinked again. That was all.

Li placed a hand on either side of his face and lowered her head to his chest.

Frye knelt there a long while, shivering cold in the hot night air. He still had Bennett's .45 in his hand. He picked up the silver wave necklace he'd given to Bennett, that Bennett had given to Lam, that Thach had given back, passed from one hand to the other like a gift of death. Li had begun to keen—a high, faint moan that seemed to come from everywhere in the room at once.

He finally stood, moving as in a dream, stuffing the .45 into his belt. Li was wailing louder now. She turned to him, then looked at the weapon that lay beside her, her eyes a pit of desperation so deep and complete and understandable that he wondered if she would ever really see out of them again. He lifted her gently from the floor. "Come with me."

She looked at him, then back to the gun. He guided her toward the hangar door, then off across the desert toward his car.

It was the longest walk of his life.

They drove the dirt road back, following the tracks of Bennett's van. The wind howled, driving sand against the Mercury, easing him to the right. Fifty yards from the hangar, Frye heard the engine of the helicopter groan faintly to life against the wind.

The rotors began to move, and its lights shot into the darkness. As Frye swung his car toward it, he could see Thach hunched awkwardly in the cockpit, working the controls. Frye slid to a stop in the sand, tumbled out, and pulled the automatic from his belt. He drew down and fired, the gun barrel swaying with the wind. A swirling cloud of sand engulfed the chopper, then dispersed. Frye fired again. The rotors spun and the lights shone off into the darkness, but now the cockpit was empty. He pushed Li behind the car and told her to stay.

Frye approached the 'copter's door from behind, on the passenger's side. Above him, the blades were slowing. He stood by the door, struck momentarily by the idea that all he wanted to do here was kill this man; it was all that mattered now, all he could think about. Two shots, he thought: I've got two left.

He steadied the gun before him, jumped to the door, and aimed through the window. Inside, red lights blipped, instruments gave their bright read-outs, the harness swayed free in the vacant, blood-smeared pilot's station. Through the open door on the far side, he could see Thach, a hundred feet away already, laboring over a hillock, then disappearing in a cloud of dust and wind.

He ran back to the car and found Li right where he had left her.

She looked up at him, a hint of clarity in her eyes now. "I'll stay here. Good luck, *em*. He can't go far."

This time, he's mine, Frye thought. He got a flashlight from the trunk of his car, then leaned into the wind after Thach.

He made the hill in a matter of seconds. It overlooked a wide arroyo, pale in the middle, peopled on its flanks by the shapes of yucca that materialized, then faded back into the darkness. Frye saw movement at the rim of the gully, a lurching motion that became fainter the harder he looked at it. He's shot and bleeding, Frye thought. He's crippled. *I know where he's going.*

Frye plodded into the heavy sand of the wash and followed. He saw Thach twice more—flashes of motion in the dark—and each time, he was a little closer. Where the gully bent north, Frye marched on, using his flashlight. Thach's blood, dark and heavy as old oil, led up the embankment and out of the channel. Frye scrambled up the loose side of the arroyo and followed the shiny trail to the foot of a steep hill.

The old wooden framework was partially collapsed, sagging around the cavern entrance. Sheets of decayed plywood, used once to block the hole, were torn down and strewn around it. Obscenities were spray-painted on a huge boulder that sat at the mouth. Beneath the words and the graffiti, Frye could make out the words SIDEWINDER MINE—DANGER! NO TRESPASSING.

As he stood and looked into the black hole, he could feel the pressure gathering upon him, the slow squeeze of walls and darkness, the frantic terror of enclosure. Everything of Frye, from his heart to his fingertips, told him no. Everything except that voice deep in the center of himself, the voice that had led him to some of the very worst moments of his life, the voice that would simply never take no as an answer, on principle, on faith. Thach's blood shone on the stones, glimmering in the beam of the flashlight.

For Benny, he thought. For Li. For me.

He took a deep breath, felt a clammy chill break over his scalp, and ducked inside. Five steps in, and the world went silent. The air was cool, damp, heavy. With the flashlight he could see twenty feet ahead at best, to where the cavern narrowed and turned to the right. The floor was gravel—dark and ferric—that shifted and crunched as he made his way to the turn. His face was cold now, his body beginning to shiver with the sweat that oozed through his clothes. He rounded the corner.

The shaft led down to another bend that went left. The silence deepened; the echoes of the gravel under his feet rose against the walls and seemed to both follow and precede his steps at the same time. He sat, quietly as he could and pulled off his shoes.

The rocks bit into his feet, but, stepping deliberately and slowly, Frye found he could move with hardly a sound. Or was it just his heart roaring in his ears that drowned the lesser noise, that same pressurized howl he felt when he went under in the waves and the world locked around him like a coffin?

He looked back toward the entrance, but saw only blackness. He was almost to the next turn when he first heard the breathing: fast, shallow, wet. His hands tightened on the gun and flashlight, his back shuddered in a spasm of nerves. At the turn, the sound came louder, nearly synchronized with his own rapid breath. He brought himself to the corner and waited, gun raised, stinking of death and of a fear beyond death, wondering why things get funneled down to such narrows, to such irrevocable moments. It was your choice, he thought. You could be a thousand miles away if you wanted to be, washing your hands, forseeing reasonable futures, tending curable wounds. The simple awful truth is that somehow, this is where you set out to end up. Sometimes the best thing you can do is the worst thing you can imagine.

He stepped out, flashlight held up and away from his body, aiming down the short barrel of the .45 at Thach. The man was sprawled against a rock wall, legs out, trunk propped up, head back. The eyes were open in the ruined face. His shirt was torn away. His left hand was jammed up under a thick, protective vest that had slowed the high-velocity bullets, but not stopped them. His right hand lay on his lap, clutching a pistol. Thach blinked, coughed, moved his head slightly.

Finish it, Frye thought. Finish what your brother started twenty years ago. He could feel the darkness moving in around him. His vision blurred. His breathing matched Thach's, as if both were geared to the same engine.

The colonel coughed again. His voice was faint, drowned. "Who are you?"

"His brother."

Thach groaned, closed his eyes, then stared up at Frye.

Their breathing was still locked together—meshed, one. Frye couldn't break the rhythm, then he didn't want to, as if it were something to hold onto, some stabilizer in a body that without it would disintegrate. "Who are your allies in Little Saigon?"

The colonel shook his head, coughing lightly. His eyes regarded Frye from the twisted, bloody face, but there was something satisfied, almost amused in them.

"Who are they?"

"I won." Thach stared down at his pistol as across some unpassable distance. His hand began to move. Frye inhaled slowly, deeply, disengaging himself from Thach's breathing. Then he was falling. Up? Down? A swirl of vertigo and pressure, a dissasembly, a melting away. He felt the gun slipping from his hand. He braced himself on the mine wall. The scene before him broke into kaleidoscopic shards that rotated, rearranged themselves, fractured again. And in the center of it all: Thach's face, a moving hand, a bloody finger slipping inside a trigger guard, a barrel rising slowly toward him as Frye steadied the .45 and blew Thach forever out of this world and into the next.

For a long while, Frye stood there. Slowly, the walls receded. The pounding in his ears began to fade away. His breathing slowed, and his focus started to sharpen again. As he looked down he saw not one man lying before him, but two. He saw Huong Lam, the kid who brought Li to Bennett, the kid who sent three bottles of French champagne to a man he admired too much in war to oppose in love. He looked again and saw Thach, the monster who had cut down Tuy Xuan and Bennett and countless others. And finally, he saw Charles Edison Frye, who, like Lam and Thach and Bennett, had become just another willing drinker of the same endless bloody cup.

He dug the silver wave necklace from his pocket and tossed it onto Thach's chest.

# CHAPTER
# 29

**F**RYE ISLAND. HYLA WEPT AND Edison stormed. Frye could look neither of them in the face. The family doctor, a stout Swede named Nordstrom, filled everyone but Frye with sedatives. Edison called Lansdale and bellowed nonsense. Frye called Minh, Wiggins, and the Newport Beach surf report. To the first two he gave the location of the slaughter. He almost called Cristobel.

Li, still wearing her peasant pajamas, walked into the den and shut the door. Frye could see her through the glass of the French doors, first spitting her tranquilizers into a wastebasket, then taking up the telephone, her face downcast. She made eight calls. Then she motioned Frye in, and they sat next to each other on the sofa. Her eyes were dull as sun-baked glass. She took his hand. "Xuan, too," she said. "And Nguyen Hy. And even Eddie Vo."

Frye listened, removed again from himself while Li talked, the names of the dead slamming into him like speeding trucks. Her hands were cold and tight.

"What I wish to do is die," she said. "But I can't do that. There is a debt to the living. The first thing one learns in war is that sometimes death is a luxury."

"Who are Thach's allies here?"

"He said nothing about them."

"He had help."

Li breathed deeply and sat back. "Communist agents, buried deep in the life of Little Saigon. I don't know who they are. They have been very careful over the years."

"What about Dien?"

"I suspected him for a long time. It is possible. But it's possible too that he is simply a profiteer, an aging thief."

"Someone is going to come for that ransom money."

"You should leave it here."

"Then they'll come here to get it. I don't want those people in my mother's house."

"That much cash is like a magnet. You will attract them."

Frye realized fully that the suitcases in the trunk of his car were a portable curse, a beacon for the killers who had helped Thach plan his mission. It's their payment, he thought: Thach didn't do it for profit, not even for two million bucks.

Li told him what had happened in the last six days—being taken underground at the Dream Reader, coming up blindfolded somewhere else, a two-hour ride in the trunk of a car with ropes and a gag cutting into her flesh, then the endless days of Thach's interrogation, the dirt and thirst in the closet where they kept her.

"Why didn't you recognize him until tonight?"

"I never really saw him," she said. "He was always in partial darkness, or wearing sunglasses. The light was painful to his eyes. It was so strange. He began by questioning me about the resistance positions, but he didn't really seem to care. He gave up so easily. At the time I thought I was wearing him down, but now I know that Kim would be supplying him with all this information soon. So he talked of Saigon and An Cat, and prodded me into memories. He was very curious about Lam and Bennett and me. He wanted to know every detail of the meetings. Most of all, he wanted to know how I felt about the two men. Who I loved more, and why, and how I came to my decision to go to Bennett. More than once, I wondered if this man could be Lam. But it seemed impossible. For days I sat there on the stool in the dark, remembering."

Li squeezed his hand and looked up with her dull eyes. "I acted as I believed, Chuck. And if Bennett told me a lie to kill my love of Lam, then it was a lie that I believed even before he spoke it."

Then Li hugged herself and bowed over. She began to sway gently. Frye watched the tears hit the black cotton of her pants. From across the living room, Edison and Hyla looked in through the French doors.

Frye took a long shower, then sat with his mother and father and Li for a while. No one said anything. An hour later, he walked out to the dock. The night was cool now and a thin fog hovered over the water. The house lights across the bay shone through, magnified, dulled. Hyla's keening issued from the bedroom.

He could feel his brother inside himself, tangible, actual. He could remember it all perfectly, every look and every word that Bennett had given him. I can feel you, Benny, he thought, I can almost see you. Like right there, just fifty yards off the dock here when we caught that blue shark and tried to stuff it with newspaper. When we made those wings out of wood and Mom's dress and you tried them out from the roof and broke your ankles. The way you looked when you were mad, eyes all big and the pupils little and, you fucker, you'd heave me down and stuff sand in my mouth or hit me in the stomach so hard I'd gasp for breath while you laughed and gasped along with me. The way you'd get even madder if any other kid but you tried to do that to me. I remember the way you looked in that Little League uniform, the way you got the socks to stay up and look like the pros, the way you batted like Yasztremski. The way you pitched the playoff game with your left arm in a cast and still got a three-hitter against Orange. I remember the way you looked for the proms, with those stupid sideburns halfway down to your chin. I remember the way you rode that big old board in storm surf and got your picture in *Surfer* magazine. I remember the way you went and fought. They didn't even have to draft you. I remember the way you stood up for me at my wedding, even though you didn't have much left to stand on. I see now that you lost more than your legs over there, you lost part of your heart too, and that's the wound that wouldn't heal, that's what was hardest to live without. I can see how you tried. And I see now the way you never gave up trying to make it all mean something, the way you just plain wouldn't stop until there was nothing left, and that's what it came down to brother, nothing left of you at all.

He tried to gather his thoughts, piece together the collusion that had sent Bennett alone to his death. Surely, thought Frye, Burns sat on the information. As surely as Toibin and Michelsen were called off at the eleventh hour. The Feds are probably up in Mojave right now, clearing out the bodies, tidying up the scene. They'll leave a Vietnamese or two, drum up some identification for them, and make it look like a ransom drop gone wrong. Thach's body will disappear forever. And they'll sit hard on me and Li to keep our mouths shut. How hard?

Five minutes later, the white belly of a chopper lowered from the darkness to the helipad. Frye watched Special Agent Wiggins and Senator Lansdale duck the blades and hurry toward the house. Not long after that, the two men, with Li in tow, headed for the cottage. Wiggins broke away and headed toward Frye.

He stood on the dock, just a few feet away. "We're awfully sorry about Bennett," he said.

"I'll bet you are."

"Chuck, we'd like to talk to you now. First you alone, then Li, then the two of you together. It's very important."

Frye stood up and tried to walk past him. Wiggins caught his arm. "I can put you under protective arrest, if I have to."

"Please don't." Frye turned and hit Wiggins as hard as he could, an uppercut just under the sternum. The punch started down in his toes. He was amazed how far his fist went in. The special agent huffed and his hands flew out, beating like the wings of a landing bird as he fell backward into the water.

Frye went to the cottage, peered through a window and saw Lansdale explaining something to Li, his hands out for emphasis, an imploring look on his face. She glanced up at Frye, and he was sure she was about to break down.

Back in the main house, he found Edison lurking near a window, trying to see into the cottage. He looked at Frye forlornly.

"They're hurting Li, Pop. Why don't you throw them off your property? Or at least sit in so you can hear the lies they'll want her to tell about your son."

Edison hesitated, then breathed deeply, slammed open the door, and marched across the lawn toward his cottage. The dogs started yapping. Wiggins slogged to intercept him, but Edison just bellowed and walked past. Frye had never loved his father so much in all his life.

The cave-house was dark and empty.

*Your money is filthy to me . . . I demanded it satisfy my allies in this campaign.*

Frye thought: What I have to do now is deal with the final mover and shaker. He'll come for the ransom cash. Thach didn't want it, but he tried to collect it for his partner. Now I've got it, safe in the cave beside a box of Christmas ornaments. And anyone who would orchestrate all this will certainly come for the payoff. Why didn't I know that it was Dien, all along? The connections here, and in Vietnam. The greed. The tape of De-Cord. The showpiece shooting at the Wind, to move suspicion from him. The millions of dollars he leeched from his believers, so he could sink them into the Laguna Paradiso. Organizing the terror of his own city, to drum up more resistance, raise more money. And the final scam: Help Thach kidnap Li, then cash out. When his money isn't at the airstrip, he'll know something went wrong. When he finds out I'm alive, he'll come.

It doesn't matter, he thought. I'll be ready.

Frye checked the time on the wall clock, then put a blank tape into his cassette recorder and slid it under a newspaper on the coffee table. He checked the clip in the .45 that Bennett had given him, jacked a round into the chamber, and flicked off the safety. Carefully, he placed it under the couch cushion, handle out.

He got his old shotgun from under the bed, took it outside and sawed off most of the barrel with a hacksaw he used to cut out surfboards. He removed the plug, pushed one round into the ejection port, then four more into the magazine. He took it back to the cave and placed it in the box of Christmas stuff. The two suitcases sat behind the box.

He wandered. He checked his Grow-Bug: it was up to five inches now. He made coffee, took a cup back to the sofa, sat down, and waited.

It was one of those nights when you hear everything, whether you want to or not: the electricity buzzing in the power lines outside, the individual swish of each car on the road below, the

325

ticking of the clock that you never once heard tick in the five years it's been there. He breathed deeply but it didn't do any good.

I'm safer here than anywhere else, he thought. Except the island, and I won't have them coming onto the island for the money. I'm on my own ground. There's no time to bring Donnell here, and Pop needs Arbuckle. Minh, if I could even trust him, would be out of jurisdiction. And I wouldn't believe the Feds if they said hello.

Why not stay with the Laguna cops, let Dien come and go, and find no one here and his ransom money gone? I'll tell you why, because I'm past the point of being a good citizen. Was never cut out for it anyway. Because it's time and evidence and lawyers and courts and plea bargains and reduced sentences and early paroles and what I truly feel the need for here is some tangible satisfaction.

He was sitting on the couch with a fresh cup when he heard the car coming up his driveway, saw the headlights slide against the walls, then die. Outside, an engine shut off, a door opened and closed. Exactly twenty-three minutes from the time I got here, he saw: he must have been waiting on the Canyon Road. Was it Wiggins who tipped him, or "Burns"? Does it matter? With a shaking hand he found the tape recorder and switched it on. He rearranged the newspapers. He touched the handle of the .45, concealed well within the cushion of the couch. Footsteps. A knock.

"Door's open."

To Frye's disbelief, it was Burke Parsons who peered in, looked around, and shut the door behind him. He was tan and fit, with a white shirt open to his chest, a blue blazer and a pair of expensive jeans. "Hello, Chuck. My money was gone, and so were you, so I figured something went wrong. I thought you'd be here sooner."

Frye just stared. Burke. "I was with Mom and Dad."

Burke walked slowly toward him, hands out a little, palms up, an innocent man. "That must have been real hard."

"Worst day of my life, Burke."

Parsons stood beside the chair across from him. "You're awfully cool right now, Chuck. Where's the gun?"

"No guns."

Burke pulled a big automatic from his coat pocket and leveled it at Frye's chest. "Don't mind if I have a quick look, do you?"

"Go right ahead."

Parsons waved him up. Frye stood while Burke patted him down, twice. "All I can say is I'm about done with you Fryes. Not that it hasn't been a pleasure all along. What I need from you is my ransom money and I'll just be on my way."

Burke stepped back and looked at Frye. For a moment he stood there, and Frye could see that he was listening, watching, smelling, sensing. His brow furrowed. "Something's wrong here, Chuck. I just know it."

Burke smiled, kept the pistol aimed at Frye while he bent over and ran his hand under the couch cushion.

On his second pass, he brought out Bennett's .45. "Well what do you know, Chuck."

Frye sat down.

"Now, you have my money?"

"What money?"

Parsons studied him again, his face darkening. "Something's still wrong, Chuck. What is it? You ask too many questions, and you ask them too fast. Do I smell a tape recorder? Isn't that what I should expect from a reporter type?"

He leaned over the coffee table and poked through the mess of newspapers with the tip of his gun. He smiled, flipped the papers off the machine, pushed the stop button, then the eject switch. He pocketed the tape. "You're not exactly bright sometimes, Chuck. But I gotta hand it to you for perseverance."

Where's that feeling now, Frye wondered, the one I had down in Burke's basement when I thought I could kill him?

All he felt was numb.

"Chuck, what I really want out of this is my money. You do have my money, don't you?"

Frye nodded.

"When Thach's men didn't deliver, I just knew you were the reason, Chuck. You've got a helluva talent for getting in my way. Of course, I can't have you telling what happened, so I'm in a tough position here. Basically, I have to kill you, 'less I can think of some reasonable alternative."

"You set this whole thing up?"

"Me and old Thach, or Huong Lam, or whatever the fuck he called himself."

"Dien?"

"Naw. Dien and me just do business. He wasn't in on the kidnapping. Hell, he almost stopped it that night at the Wind, didn't he?"

"Why'd you do it?"

Burke sat down, placed the gun on the coffee table in front of him. "Why *not*'s a better question. It was one of those opportunities that just fall in your lap. See, Thach and Lucia talked on one of her early trips to the 'Nam. He told her the story of his big historic tank battle, how he got his face shot off and still saved his company. When she got to know him a little better, and he told what really happened, about Huong Lam, the whole deal. Those gooks trust my sister, Chuck, I don't know what it is about her. Lucia told me and I thought: Bingo. I *know* that guy. So I got to thinking, sent word to him through Lucia, and we started communicating. He remembered me. He remembered what a dipshit I always thought Bennett was. He'd already heard Li on the Secret Radio, and he was burning to nail Bennett and his pipeline. He already had Kim in his pocket. It was slow, but over time, it got clear what we could do with a little . . . creativity. Thach got a little more creative than I did, though, that's for sure. Original plan was to off your brother and Li, but Thach decided he wanted to take them back with him. I told him it wouldn't work, but by that time I'd made up my mind to grease him anyhow. For my part, hell, it was just a way to make my ransom money and get Bennett out of Lucia's way."

"Out of the way?"

"Well, Hanoi sure wasn't gonna deal for the POWs with some legless American shipping guns over, now were they? Early on, they told Lucia that one condition of release was to stop the Secret Army. That's why she talked to Thach in the first place— because he was the counter-terrorism pro. And, of course, your pig-head brother wouldn't stop, even when DeCord cut off his government scholarship. So I said to myself, self, you can help Thach raise some hell over here, make a big pile of money, *and* do your patriotic duty to get those POWs home, if you stick up Bennett and wreck his pipeline. After that, it was just a matter of planning it all out."

"So you used the Dark Men and framed Eddie?"

"Sho'nuff. They're young and violent. We knew Minh would suspect Vo, and when he ducked out of the Wind, it didn't help the kid any. When the FBI shot him, that was great good luck. We'd planned all along to plant the evidence in his house. Perfect. All we needed from Vo was a little time to make Bennett sweat— that was one of Thach's ideas. And, of course, to get the ransom stuff set up proper. I put on a mustache and dressed like a gigolo to do business as Lawrence."

Burke picked up his pistol, studied it with a philosophical air, put it back down. "Chuck, the times they are a-changin'. Uncle Sam and Hanoi'll be in bed together before you know it—POWs out, diplomatic thaw, the same old story. That's gonna happen soon enough, you know. But we got thousands of refugees here, burning up 'cause they got no homeland left. We got guys like Benny who still just can't believe the United States couldn't win a war. We got enough free-floating residual hatred these days to start up our own hell. That's all energy, Chuck, needing to be channeled. In just a few short months, it'll be gone. The war will really be over. Well, I saw a chance to make a killing while the nerves were still raw, and I took it."

Frye could feel the rage gathering, rising up inside himself. It seemed to be coming from Burke, some psychic osmosis. Keep feeding it, he thought: it feels good. "You'd help Thach kill Bennett and Xuan and Li. You let him bomb Nguyen Hy and half a dozen innocent people. What kind of a man are you?"

"I'm a good man, Chuck. A patriot. Of course, I'd have killed Thach before he got a chance to go back home."

"Why kill your partner?"

Burke looked at Frye as if he were a fool. "To make sure the POWs get back! Uncle Sam isn't going to deal with Hanoi while one of their colonels is running amok over here, any more than Hanoi's going to set POWs free while Bennett was running guns. Talk about a situation that needed fixing. It was like turning loose the dogs to eat the cats, then shootin' the dogs. And I *am* a patriot, Chuck. DeCord couldn't stop the pipeline without killing your brother, and the CIA may be low, but they're not that low. Besides, Benny had DeCord on tape, making payments. And the FBI couldn't find Thach without help, so Burke Parsons came to the rescue."

"Our government knew Thach was here?"

"As of about two days ago. A select few knew it. At first, everyone thought Thach was quarrantined in Hanoi for his political trouble. He was. Then he disappeared. Hanoi stalled a few days to figure out where he'd gone, but when Li got taken and Xuan's head rolled, they knew damn well where he'd gone. They didn't want that maniac on the loose. See, Hanoi's going to collect close to two million bucks for each POW they let go. That's one of those diplomatic conditions Lucia hasn't discussed with the American people. Hanoi loves those dollars. So about eighteen hours ago, they let it be known that Thach was gone and probably here. I told DeCord I could find Thach faster than he could. I suppose I left him with the idea that I'd grease him fast and keep it quiet."

"What was in it for you?"

"I got rid of a murderous Commie bastard for one thing. I got three hundred grand 'operational expenses' coming from the agency. And I closed down the Secret Army once and for all. Actually, Bennett did most of it for me. But I'm the hero, Chuck!" Burke grinned, then rotated his head quickly, seeming to assess everything in the apartment in one glance.

"If you knew where Thach was, why didn't DeCord just throw your ass in jail?"

Parsons shrugged, smiled. "Because I played it cool, Chuck. I never told him I *knew* where Thach was. I said I'd find out what I could with my connections in Little Saigon. But mainly I just took a page from your brother's book and blackmailed 'em. I showed DeCord the tape of him paying Nguyen. He couldn't touch me. Still can't. Why should he? Thach is dead, the Secret Army's wiped out and the POWs can come home. I'm a good guy, Chuck. I made this country a better place to live."

"DeCord got the administration to call off the FBI and just let Bennett walk into a trap at the airstrip?"

Burke's brow furrowed. "That's what I told him would work best. If he let Thach take out Bennett, then I take out Thach, we could keep it all real quiet. No cops. Minimum Feds. No reporters. No nothing. Couple of bureau gophers already planted IDs on Thach's guys. Then they'll set the place on fire. When it's all said and done, Bennett got shot trying to ransom his wife from slant gangsters. Press will love it. Clean. Look how right I was."

Parsons eyes narrowed. "You do have my money, don't you, Chuck?"

"I've got it."

Parsons smiled.

"What about me, Burke?"

Burke leaned forward, arching an eyebrow. "Chuck, I got to admit, I've never seen anybody nosy, stubborn, dumb, and clever as you. If you hadn't written that crap about my fighter, I'd have left you alone. But I'm kinda sensitive about people snoopin' around Elite. So I hired Cristobel for a little kiss and tell. Just in case you got motivated and started poking around Little Saigon when we bagged Li—like you poked around my business. Crissy kept me posted on what you were doing, and everything was fine. But then you trail Bennett to the airstrip, take the money, and come home with it. Jesus, boy, don't you ever just give up and quit? I tried to cover every angle, Chuck. I've been working on this for three years, so no expense was too great. Now you can see why that two million ransom is only what I've earned."

"And you've been playing up to my father and brother for three years, getting your foot in the Paradiso."

"Once Lucia tumbled with Edison, we couldn't lose. Your old man rolled her in the hay a couple of times and thought she was the perfect girl next door. Horny old goat. Anyway, it was three years of hard work, so you can see what that two million means to me. You know something, it's the old-money people like you Fryes that sucked the life out of this country. Now it's a new ballgame. People like me who came from dirt-poor nothing are going to raise this country back up to where she was. Me and Lucia never had any oil money. We had to scrape together the rent. That ain't right, salt of the earth folks like us struggling through life while the government helps all these 'disadvantaged' types. Mess with me, and you'll get disadvantaged real quick. Fuckin' Vietnamese, anyway. This isn't their country. This is *my* country. All men were created equal, but a lot's changed since then."

Frye regarded Burke's dark eyes, his curly brown hair, white even teeth. "I'm trying to figure out how a man like you can do what he does."

Burke's face went matter-of-fact. "I just do what I gotta do, Chuck, same as anyone else. I work on a bigger scale, is all."

3 3 1

Frye smiled, wondering if Burke could see the hatred behind it. His heart was racing now. "Count the bodies, Burke. There's the kidnapper from the Wind, two Dark Men, Xuan, Eddie, Hy, Thach, Bennett. There's a hundred-plus freedom fighters in Vietnam and the network. You killed all those people just for a resort and a bunch of money. How do you shave that face in the morning?"

Parsons was frowning, shaking his head like Edison used to do: Dumb kid, won't you ever understand? "I told you once, Chuck, back there at my target range. I plain old don't care about some things that other folks make such a big deal about. I have no opinions at all about killing people. Far as my face goes and shaving it, well, hell, I like my face."

Parsons picked up the gun with one hand and reached into his pocket with the other. He screwed on a silencer and stood. "Let's get the money now, Chuck. Time for me to be rollin' down the road."

Frye worked himself up from the couch. He expected his legs to be heavy and useless, but they felt strong and ready. He could imagine where the shotgun was, precisely where he had positioned it, and he could see, as clearly as he'd ever seen anything, what he would do with it. He could hear every movement, smell every smell. His eyes seemed to gather in details he'd never noticed. He looked at Burke, thinking: Your ass is mine. "Money's in the cave."

Parsons smiled, looked quickly around again, then moved to Frye. "You're a big strong boy, aren't you, Chuck? You ought to relax a little."

Frye never saw the pistol move, he just felt the bony crunch as it hit the side of his head. He knew he was on his knees. He saw the floor moving, rectangles of hardwood floating, mixing, reforming.

Parsons hit him again. The next thing he knew, Burke had yanked him up by the shirt collar. Frye felt himself swaying, trying to keep his legs under him.

"I don't like all this quiet." Frye watched him push one of Li's tapes into the little portable player and turn the volume up. He waved the pistol toward the bedroom. "You first, Chuck. Move quick, I'll shoot you right between the shoulder blades."

Frye stumbled into the bedroom. He braced himself against the doorjamb, stopped, looked back at Burke. There were three or four of him, all moving in perfect unison. They waved guns at him.

Frye's heart started roaring now, sending tidal waves into his ears. He moved into the cave. The light from the bedroom was weak. "Back there," he heard himself say, "in that box."

Parsons looked hard at him. "You get it out, Chuck. You got so many tricks here tonight, I plum don't trust you no more."

For some reason, Frye thought this was perfect. Then he remembered the .12-gauge he'd hidden there. Yes, he thought, this is going according to plan. When he took his next step, Parsons caught him by his shirt.

"You moved too fast, Chuck. That changed my mind. I think I'll just fetch it myself."

"It's booby-trapped."

"Don't expect me to believe that now, do you?"

"It's not here. It's somewhere else."

"Getting desperate, Chuck? Don't do that. It's unbecoming. Well, this is it. Head or heart? Nobody's gonna ever find your body, 'cept the sharks, so I'd vote head."

Frye turned to face him. "The money's at the MegaShop."

"The money's either on Frye Island or right here. If it's on the island, I'll deal with that. But either way, you're gonna be dead in less than two seconds."

Burke sighed.

Frye pivoted and lunged toward the box.

The pistol went off, louder and from a slightly different direction than Frye expected. He waited for the rip of pain, but it didn't come. Then Parsons tripped clumsily, like a drunk man. The gun spilled from his hand as he caught himself on all fours. "Shit," he muttered.

Cristobel stepped into the cave from the bedroom, her small automatic held out. Frye kicked Burke's weapon away, then pulled the shotgun from the box.

Parsons worked himself up from the floor unsteadily, hands pressed against his stomach, blood running over his fingers. His hair was tousled, his eyes dim, his skin gray. He looked like a man who just woke up. He considered Cristobel, first with irritation, then disappointment. He stared at Frye and offered a wouldn't-you-know-it shake of the head. "What a dumb-ass way to lose this one," he said quietly. "That stupid bitch."

He wobbled, reached into his jacket, and had a derringer halfway out when Frye shot him as close to dead-center as he could get, which from that distance was close indeed. Parsons went everywhere, but most of him slammed into the cave wall and crumpled into a heap. The air drizzled warmly.

Frye jacked another round into the chamber and walked to Cristobel.

She backed out, eyes wide, face pale. She dropped the pistol. Frye looked at her, and she looked back with an expression of fear and disgust almost as deep as his own. Her voice was quiet, sickened. "Everything I told you was a lie."

Frye turned off the music. Cristobel went into the bathroom. When she came out, she leaned against the living room wall and stared at him. She looked white as the paint. "Burke used me to watch you. I didn't know why, not at first. When things got clear, it was too late. The rape story was just to put you off, because I had no intention of making love to you."

"Why? Money?"

She shook her head. "My brother didn't die over in Vietnam, Chuck. Not officially. He was just missing. Burke found out he was alive. He played me a tape of Mike talking to Lucia. Said he could get Lucia to spring Mike first, when Hanoi started letting them come home. When I started getting scared, he also said she could get Hanoi to leave him in prison until he died. I did what he wanted."

Frye looked into her dead brown eyes.

"I'm sorry," she said. "But I couldn't let him get away with this. I'm so fucking sorry. I'd have told you sooner, but I was afraid of what he'd do to me. I know you saw through me—" Her tears ran fast, but she still looked straight at him. "I was so glad you saw through me, Chuck, but I wasn't going to crack. I just wasn't. He had me fooled a while. Then real scared. I didn't know what he'd do. Until I realized he was going to kill you, Mike came first. Everything I did was for my brother. Everything except when I made love to you."

She cried silently as she looked at Frye. Slowly, by sheer force

334

of will, Cristobel recomposed herself. "I did that for me. Funny part is, I'd fallen in love with you. I lay in bed that night knowing I'm in love with a man I'm cheating on and lying to and setting up for God knows what. I'd never treated a person worse than I treated you. It doesn't mean anything now. It means less than anything."

She turned, walked toward the door, stopped. "Tell the cops I did it, I don't care. I'm actually proud I shot that sonofabitch. I had a lot to live for a couple of days ago. Right now, all I want is to see Mike again." She looked down for a long moment, as if in prayer. When she looked back up at him, Frye saw how far gone she really was. "I'd get something on that head of yours, it's bleeding an awful lot."

"Stay."

"I'm sorry, Chuck. You're a pretty good man."

Frye watched her go—a single body moving down a dark tunnel, surrounded on all sides by relentless steel—no exits, no yields, no turns, no options, no comebacks, no light at the end of it . . . just footsteps, golden hair, echoes.

He went back to the cave and dug Burke's house keys from his sopping pocket.

Then he carried the shotgun to his car, placed it on the seat beside him, and drove to Lucia's house.

# CHAPTER 30

THE PORCH LIGHT WAS ON and the doormat said THE PARSONS— WELCOME! Frye opened the lock and then the deadbolt, and stepped in. A light shone from the kitchen. In the hallway he could see the thin shadows of the palms on the walls and hear the bubbling murmur of the shark pond. He moved lightly over the tile, then into the living room, where a single torchière widened its light to the ceiling. *I've got the second floor, Lucia's got the third. She does her work in the guest house.*

Through the sliding glass door, Frye saw the guest quarters in the back, hidden under the banana trees: lights on, a few of Lucia's tireless minions laboring over paperwork. He climbed. His head throbbed, but his mind had cleared. The first flight of stairs ended at a short hallway—Burke's rooms, he thought—and the second began at the other end of it. As he started up, Frye could see a light above, and hear someone moving across the floor. At the top, he stayed close to the hallway walls, taking the last few steps quietly as he could. From inside the bedroom came the sound of a woman humming, the buzz of a long zipper being locked. The stock of the old Remington was warm and slippery in his hand.

Through the bedroom door he saw her, dressed in a black silk robe, her hair loose and flowing, organizing the contents of a suitcase that lay open on the bed. The Pacific sparkled through the window behind her, turned to purple-black by the moon and window glass. She spoke over her shoulder. "That you, Burke? Paul?"

Frye stepped in. Lucia gasped sharply, straightened. "Chuck? Burke's out now, he's—"

"I know where he is."

"You talked to him tonight?"

"Mainly he talked to me."

"You men come to some agreement about things?"

"Yes. We decided you owe me three million dollars that Dien stole from his people. I'm here to get it."

Frye moved toward her and Lucia backed up. Then she reached slowly to the lamp and clicked it on. "Is that what I think it is all over your shirt?"

He looked down, nodding.

"I'd have never thought you could do that, Chuck."

"Burke didn't either. Get me Dien's money, Lucia, or I'm going to do something extravagant."

She looked at him a little defiantly, then sat on the bed. One big tear rolled down her face. She wiped it with the end of the robe sash. When she lowered her face into her hands, black hair cascaded down. "What did you do to him, Chuck?"

"It kind of got down to one of us or the other."

She looked up with an anguished face. "You just keep living through things."

"Funny, isn't it?"

"Not really." She sobbed into her hands again. Finally, she stood. Her chin shook. "Does it matter that I loved him? More than as just a brother?"

"Let's weep."

Lucia seemed to study him. "You got something real cold in you, Chuck. Part of Edison rubbed off, whether you know it or not."

"Get me the money. I'm sick of you."

"It's in the safe down in the basement, with his snakes."

Frye waved the shotgun toward the stairs. "You first, Lucia."

"I've got a plane to catch in twenty minutes. I'm not going to miss it."

Frye grabbed her robe and shoved her to the door. "March."

She gave him a hopeless look, then led him out of the bedroom, down the stairs and into the library. She flicked on a light and groped a moment for the hidden switch. The wall panel swung out and the light went on. She shivered, then started down.

Their footsteps echoed in the big room. The heavy bags cast fat shadows on the padded floor. Frye could see the anaconda, six feet of it resting on the glass, interrupted on its nocturnal prowl. Lucia stopped, turned to him, and shivered again, wrapping her arms around herself. She nodded at the safe, wiped her eyes. "The key's under Charlotte's water dish."

"The cobra?"

"Nobody else here with that name."

"Get it out."

She shook her head and stared at him. "Chuck, you could pay me, beat me, slander me, or steal my money, but you couldn't get me to put my hand in that cage. Never." She was trembling now, and her eyes were big. "There's a nine-iron that Burke used to fish her out with sometimes. It's leaning on the wall over there."

He went to the cage. Charlotte's head shifted; an eye beheld Frye. The water dish showed beneath one of her curls, a wedge of light blue against her pale green scales. Suddenly, her hood spread and she hissed. Even through the glass he could hear her—a big, pressurized sound like air being let from a balloon. Frye's heart was in his mouth.

Charlotte stared him down, swaying, uncharmed.

The shotgun blast took half the cage with it, a splintered hurricane of glass, blood, scales. Charlotte slapped in the debris, loops and coils everywhere, a muscular, headless frenzy. He fished her out by the tail and dropped her to the floor.

The key was under the dish. It slid easily into the safe, and Frye brought Dien's briefcases full of cash, gold, and jewelry onto the floor in front of him. "You knew about all of this, didn't you, Ms. Ambassador? You helped him set it up."

"I did what I had to get our men back."

"There were a thousand easier ways. Ways that wouldn't have killed my brother and a lot of other people."

Lucia wiped her eyes again with the belt, then crossed her arms. "Burke threw in a couple of things that I . . . wasn't expecting. I didn't know he helped bring Colonel Thach here. I didn't know he was behind the kidnapping until a couple of days after it happened. When Burke's plan went into motion, the best policy option was to see it through, rather than try to stop it. There comes a point when you go with what works."

"What about the Paradiso?"

"That was something we had our eyes on for years. There really isn't anything illegal about it, Chuck. Dien's money is legitimate investment capital so far as I'm concerned. Your father cut us in as partners. It just took a little convincing."

"You fucked him."

Lucia checked her watch. "That helped."

Frye found the video tape that Loc had stolen out of his apartment. He put it in one briefcase along with the loot.

Then Lucia brought her hands to her face and broke down. Her shoulders heaved, the robe jiggled. Her sobbing started loud and kept getting louder. Frye could see the tears dripping off her wrists. He stood there for a minute until the storm passed. When she had gathered herself back together, she gave him an odd look, and shook her head. "Do whatever you want, Chuck. I'm being picked up in ten minutes for a flight to Washington. I don't intend to miss it. I've got men to bring home."

She turned and climbed the stairs.

In the bedroom, Frye watched her pack. She moved mechanically, efficiently. "You can't possibly be thinking of having me arrested."

"It's pretty damned possible."

"If you do, Hanoi will shut down and start stalling again. You can bet on it. Those men of ours will sit there longer, rot a little more. Basically, Chuck, you can take me, or you can let the prisoners come home. You can't have both. Think about it."

"I am."

Frye looked down on the guest house. Two of Lucia's young workers had set their luggage on the porch. One checked her watch, looked up toward the bedroom. Thank God for Burke's soundproof playroom, he thought.

Lucia yanked a dress from her closet and deftly worked it into a hanging bag. She glanced at the alarm clock. "Chuck, God rules up above, and people like me rule here. If you try to stop me, you'll only ruin a very good thing. The concerns you have are just too . . . small. In the big scheme of things, little people get hurt. It's really just simple math. And if you can put a stop to bringing back our men, then you've got to take a good hard look at your own soul. You ready to do that?"

"You might think you're a moral giant, Lucia, but to me you're just a whore. If I don't get what I want out of you I'll have your ass in jail before this night's over."

"You might get a good case, but I'd get a better judge. I've got three intelligence agencies and two cabinet members behind me. I'm subpoena-proof. So why not be smart? Let the men come home. Forget what happened. Take what you want, while you've got hands to grab with. Grow up. You've got the goods to be like your father is, or like I am. You've got what it takes." She faced him, hands on her hips, one long leg revealed by the slit in the robe. She smiled. "Do you?"

For a moment, Frye was actually tempted. "Paul DeCord will want to talk to Burke soon. What time is he due here?"

"He's due now. He'll take us out to the airport. Why?"

"There are some things I need from him. I'm going to get them one way or another."

"Going to kill him too?"

"If I have to." He looked down on Lucia's underlings, waiting outside the cottage. Idealists, he thought. Humanitarians. Suckers.

"You're as dangerous as the rest of them, Chuck. In your own way."

Frye studied her lovely face. He looked at the king-sized bed, the two night stands and reading lamps, the pair of cowboy boots on the floor by the far side. "How long have you and Burke been sleeping together?"

Lucia sat down. She looked at him with superiority, but the tears rolled down her face anyway. She wiped them away with her robe sleeve. "The first time, we were twelve."

"Why?"

"Then, just because it felt so good, and he was so beautiful. Later, because it was just our little thing. It's like being a vampire.

You just don't go back to the regular world." She looked at him, a hint of invitation in her eyes. She slid out of the robe, turned her back to him, bent her perfect ass his way, and worked on a pair of panty hose. Next a wool skirt, a blouse, black pumps, a suitcoat. She checked her watch, then locked her suitcase.

"What's in all this for you, Lucia?"

"I'm going to ease right into the district congressional seat when it comes up vacant next time, that's what's in it for me. After the first POWs come home, I'm going to be front-page everything. Cover of *Time, Life,* you name it. My recognition factor will be off the charts, so I'm going to use it."

"Isn't all that Texas oil money enough for you?"

"We only spent a year there. No oil money at all. Burke copped the cowboy talk and look because it gave him a part to play. He was as solid an actor as DeNiro, believe me. When he joined up in 'sixty-eight, military intelligence got him for a couple of years. Later, the CIA bought his contract."

She gave Frye a distant look, wiped a tear off her cheek. "I was really torn up when he left for Vietnam. I started learning the language so I might be a little closer to what he was doing. I loved him in every way a woman can love a man. We're not really bad folks, Chuck. We're just . . . different."

Frye said nothing. All he could think about was Bennett.

Lucia zipped shut an overnight case, then gave Frye a sad look. "Know something? A big reason I did all this is because it was my way of doing something good. You need to do something decent once in a while, when you do what I did with my brother. I think we're born with certain souls, same was we're born with certain eyes and ears. So I just tried to stack up some good acts to balance out mine. Deep inside, I have the soul of a mudshark. God, you wouldn't believe how cold it can get."

Frye looked out to the cottage as a white Lincoln rolled up and parked. Paul DeCord hustled out, opened the trunk, then headed for a side door.

Frye walked her down, his shotgun in one hand, a clump of Lucia's black hair in the other. He made her carry the two brief-cases of booty. She cracked the door and DeCord squeezed through. Frye intercepted him by the collar of his tennis shirt and rammed the muzzle into his throat. "You're under arrest," he said.

He pushed DeCord ahead of him and kept the gun on both of them as he marched them back to the living room. He made them sit next to each other on the couch.

DeCord rubbed his throat, darkly eyeing Frye. "Where's Burke?"

"I shot him, so your clean-up committee is out of action. Now, it's Uncle Same versus the people, and I'm the people."

"What do you want?"

"I want to live. And I want Li to live."

DeCord nodded. "Why shouldn't you?"

"Because Burke's idea was to waste us, and you went along with it. That was the old program."

"And you've got a new one."

"I've got a tape of the payments you made to Hy. I've already made copies," he lied. "I've packed them and addressed them to the networks, the attorney general, and the president. And if anything happens to me, or Li, or my family, the lawyers will get them out of the safe deposit boxes and mail them. *Anything.* If my father has a car accident, I'm going to blame you. If my mother gets mugged in a shopping center some night, I'm going to blame you. If Li has people following her around Little Saigon, I'll blame you. If I wake up in a bad mood, I'm going to blame you, and the tapes go out. I never want to see your face again, DeCord. Or hers, except when she brings the prisoners home."

DeCord glared at him, then nodded hopefully.

"The alternative is I can call the cops right now and they'll take Lucia down for conspiracy to kidnap, murder, fraud. Your deal with Hanoi will go straight to hell."

"Don't let that happen, Chuck," said DeCord. "It's all ready. I know a lot of things have gone—"

"And I want a prisoner named Michael Strauss to be the first one off that plane, if it ever comes in. That's what I want out of all this."

Lucia nodded.

DeCord stood. "You've got your deal. I promise we'll forget about you and what you know. I'll have our attorneys put it in writing, and yours can approve it. I promise the U.S. government will use its power to protect you and Li under any circumstances. But those promises don't mean a thing if we don't bring the

POWs home. Don't send out those tapes, Chuck. Don't write about this. Just let me and Lucia get this thing done."

Frye stepped forward, put the shotgun barrel under Paul De-Cord's chin, and eased him back down onto the sofa. DeCord closed his eyes as Frye pressed the weapon harder against his neck. The two MIA Committee workers—an eager young man and a pretty woman who had permed her hair to look like Lucia's—hustled into the living room from the sliding glass door. They froze, lips open and eyes wide. With the barrel of the .12 gauge, he pried DeCord's chin toward them. Frye looked at the volunteers and Lucia, then at DeCord's watering eyes, then down at his blood-splattered T-shirt.

"You've got your deal, Chuck," DeCord slurred.

Frye pushed the weapon harder into his neck. "I'd rather have my brother."

He stepped away, took the briefcases, and backed out of Lucia's house into the warm Laguna night.

Frye parked along Coast Highway at Main Beach and walked along the sand to the old blue apartments. He could feel his heart breaking. Above him were sky and a fractional moon that plainly didn't care.

Cristobel met him at the door. "I hoped you'd end up here sooner or later."

He looked at her. She may as well have come from another planet.

When she held him her arms were good and strong, and he could feel her body shaking against his own.

"They killed him."

"I know."

"They killed him."

"Chuck."

"Don't let go of me now."

"No, I won't."

He came apart.

# CHAPTER 31

**A** FEW DAYS LATER, EDISON captained the *Absolute* out of Newport Harbor, followed by a Coast Guard escort and a flotilla of little boats with photographers on them. Edison promptly lost them all when he got outside the warning buoys, gunning the twin diesels to thirty knots and heading west. Frye stood next to his father as they sped to sea, the sun hot through the black wool of his suit coat. Looking back to the deck he saw Hyla and Li and Crawley: three dark figures sitting amidst the polished teak and gleaming white of the ship.

Far out, Edison cut the engines, then he and his father joined the others. Hyla read from Psalms and Matthew. Crawley added something he had written. Edison wept. Li tilted the urn, and Bennett finally mingled with the ocean he had once loved, wisps of dust consumed by a gray Pacific.

Frye sat in the cottage with his father that night. Edison poured two big snifters of brandy that neither of them touched. He began, several times, to say something, but after each start he seemed to lose interest and stared instead at the dead fireplace. Edison's favorite dog sat at his feet. Finally he looked at his son, then around the room. "You're in line for all this now, son. We should talk about it. Do you even want it?"

"I don't think so."

"You said you wanted back in."

"I want in. I don't want the stuff."

"Big job, running Frye Ranch."

"I'm not the one to do it. But I'd sure like to feel I was welcome."

"There hasn't been a day in your life you weren't welcome here."

Frye thought back. "It was a good place to be, Pop."

Edison looked at his brandy. "I know there were things I could have done differently. What I thought was best might not have been. I made some mistakes. Can you forgive me?"

"You never did anything that needs my forgiving."

His father breathed deeply. "I know I locked you out, son. Bennett was always so easy—I'd just point him the way I thought he should go, and he'd take right off. It's an honor when a son listens to a father. It made me feel . . . like what I'd done was worth something. Like I had something to offer that was good. Debbie was my only daughter, and I let her wrap me around her little finger. I loved being able to spoil her. But you, Chuck, you had your own notions. You kind of scared me. You made me doubt myself, and I'd never done that before. I blamed you for her, I admit that. Deep inside, I did. And every step you took away from what I wanted you to be, I felt like it was a step away from me. If there's anything I should have done differently, it was to realize that my job on planet Earth wasn't to make you into a little Edison Frye. I guess a part of me wanted a couple of sons to be just like me. Maybe I figured if you were like me, you wouldn't see what a hard-headed unforgiving old bastard I really was."

"That's one of the things I loved about you, Pop. Running against you was like running against an ocean. It made me strong. I love you for it."

Frye watched his father battle back the tears. His chin quivered, then stilled. He drank the brandy in one gulp. "Thank you for what you did, Chuck. For the Paradiso."

"Let's start over, Pop."

"I'd really like to do that, son."

"Do one thing for me. Love your wife instead of somebody else. She could use some right now."

"I know. I will. I do."

Long after Edison had gone to bed, Frye sat up with his mother in the big house. They made a fire because neither of them could seem to get warm, and finished off the bottle of brandy. It was the first time Frye had ever seen Hyla drunk. For some reason, they kept remembering little stupid things that were funny. All of those things had happened a long time ago. The silences between their quiet laughter were longer than the laughter itself, and Frye knew that neither of them was fooling the other.

He lay in his old room the rest of the night, staring out the window.

There were official matters, though the first of them hadn't seemed very official at all. Paul DeCord and three men in coveralls had showed up at the cave-house just after he returned from Cristobel's. They bagged Burke's body. They removed the blood stains from the cave with a light blue organic solution, the plastic bottle of which actually said FDA APPROVED. One of the agents noted that it was great on melted surfboard wax. They used a portable vacuum with incredible suction to remove trace evidence. They washed and waxed his hardwood floor. When everything was just as it had been, they used a small bellows-like article to apply a fresh layer of dust in the disturbed places. Frye gave him Cristobel's gun, which DeCord assured him would be destroyed forthwith.

DeCord gave him an envelope stuffed with money and a wink too clandestine for words. "Silence," he said.

Frye threw it back. DeCord shrugged and headed out the door. They came and went within an hour. It was magic.

Lucia, Frye found out later, had been on a CIA jet to Washington thirty minutes after he left her.

Frye collected Dien's suitcases from the cave and drove to Bennett's house.

Li was helping Donnell Crawley pack his things. Frye watched them, each with a pasteboard box, heading toward his old pickup truck.

Li's smile was minor, drained, as he walked up. She hugged him and kissed his cheek.

"I'm glad you're staying," he said.

"Where else would I go?"

"Memories are tough."

"No memories is worse."

"What about the resistance?"

She looked at him a long while. "I'll continue. It's all I know."

"You still want the leading role?"

She nodded, wavy black hair catching the sun. It looked almost blue. "Our fight will never end."

Frye looked at the meager possessions in Donnell's truck: a little black-and-white TV, a radio, the bed and sheets, a bunch of potted plants, flatware, clothes.

Li looked at him. "I couldn't express my thoughts on the boat yesterday," she said. "But what I wanted to say was that he was the kindest man I ever knew. Even in the war, he had kindness in him. He tried to preserve it, and he knew he was losing it. When I began to know Bennett, it was like a new world I didn't know was there. He had passion, too. Maybe too much. What he did to Lam . . . it was a sin that God tricked him into committing. I don't know why. A test? I forgive him, Chuck. But he never forgave himself."

Frye walked around to the cottage, where Donnell was packing. He helped him with some boxes, a trunk, then a dozen or so plants from the yard. Donnell placed them carefully on the truck bed, then spread some blankets to keep them from sliding around. Frye watched his big hands make the gentle arrangements. "Going home, Donnell?"

Crawley wiped his forehead, nodded.

"Sure you don't want to stay?"

"I never liked it here."

"What kept you?"

Crawley considered. "Lots of people thought it was Bennett takin' care of me because of my brains, but that wasn't the whole story. I was lookin' after him too. Now he's dead and I'm going home."

Frye carried another pot to the van and set it in. "Thanks, Donnell."

"I couldn't see him carrying all that on himself, Chuck. Benny was the kind of guy who thought everything was his doing." Crawley leaned against the bumper and folded his arms across his chest. He looked at the ground. "I couldn't let him believe that. We was all responsible. It was me actually threw Huong from that chopper. That was one of my jobs. It's one of those things you don't feel good about, even if it's your country they say you're doing it for. If I'da killed him proper, Benny'd still be here right now. We'd be drinking beers or something. I think what I can realistically do now is just forget. It's time for me to go on to the next thing."

The silence got long. Frye finally said the only thing he really felt was true. "You did good, Donnell."

Crawley looked bemused. "Don't think I'll ever really believe that."

"I do."

"You weren't there."

"It doesn't matter. I know."

"Thanks anyways." Crawley shook his hand. "You gonna write all this up and get famous?"

"I don't know yet. Got some offers, though."

"Might be a good thing, since he was your brother. Anybody else just get the story all wrong. Papers don't seem much interested anyway."

Donnell got into the van and started it up. "I got a long drive. Take care of Li, now. Take care of yourself too. Good luck in the contest."

"Will do."

"Well, 'bye, Chuck."

The Committee to Free Vietnam headquarters was busy. Frye pulled up and parked, eyeing the group of young Vietnamese hustling about.

Tuy Nha came out, smiled, and hugged him. She had lost weight and her skin was pale. For the first time, she looks like a woman and not a girl, Frye thought. She looked at him and for a brief moment their silence said what words never could: something about Bennett and Xuan, about loss and the stars at night, about going on. There wasn't really much that was sayable. The silver wave necklace he'd given her in the hospital now shined against her breast.

"Billingham at the *Ledger* gave me back my job," Frye said. "He said he owed me one, so I told him to hire you, too. Rewrite desk to start. You'd learn fast. Lousy money. Interested?"

She looked down, then up again. "I am. Thank you, Chuck." A young man walked past them, and she smiled at him. The young man smiled back.

"I've got the money. Have you figured out a way to get it back to who gave it in the first place?"

She nodded. "We have a good lawyer, and time. Many people have come forward to claim what is theirs."

They leaned against the Cyclone. "What about the network?" Frye asked.

Nha sighed. "If even one POW comes home Friday, there will be a new era. Maybe it is time to stop fighting for what we don't have, and start building what we do have. Maybe it is time to fight harder. Is it really possible to go back? I don't know. We never knew. It's a time now to think."

Frye opened the trunk, then swung open the tops of the suitcases.

Nha looked from Frye to the money and jewels, then back to Frye. She smiled oddly, eyes glimmering, and Frye saw in them something of his brother's passion, a look telling him that Nha was and always would be a follower of her own agendas.

A moment later, a dark limousine rolled up. It stopped and a back window lowered. General Dien's withered face looked out with curiosity, and, Frye thought, maybe longing too. You didn't lose it, you old bastard. You sold it. Then the glass rose and the car slid away.

"I'd put that somewhere safe if I were you."

"I will," said Nha.

Detective John Minh was sitting in his cubicle when Frye walked in. It was late in the evening, three days after Bennett had been buried, the week of the scheduled release of American POWs from Vietnam. Minh had sounded subdued on the phone.

"Those three bodies they found up in Mojave weren't locals. I can't prove it, but I know they weren't."

Frye said nothing.

Minh stood up and poured two cups of coffee. "I'm sorry, Chuck. I suppose that doesn't mean much now. I knew your brother had a lot going on, but I didn't know how much until a day ago. I got curious about all the refugees he and Li sponsored into this country. I wondered where they all went, whose property they were paying rent on, how they were living. I knew Bennett was into real estate, so I did a little legwork, a little paperwork, too. He owned thirty-five homes in Little Saigon. Made the payments on every one of them himself. That's thirty-five families he set up here and never charged them a cent. He paid the utilities and insurance too—everything."

"I didn't know that."

"I thought it was all just guns and supplies. I talked with the president of the Vietnamese Scholarship Fund of Orange County yesterday. Bennett had willed them money in the event of his death. One *million* dollars."

Minh looked out his small window. Frye saw sadness in the detective's eyes. "When the FBI started giving me directions, I thought I'd take orders like a good cop. But later, when they started pushing me to arrest Vo, clamp down on Bennett's gun-running, and denied even the possibility that Thach's men were behind it all, I got suspicious. John, they said, we need you for disclosure control at the back end of this operation. John, the bureau is keeping an eye on you for possible federal work in the future. How would an assignment with the Asian Task Force sound to you? I had two legitimate sightings of Thach's men! I had others worth checking out. But the bureau sat on me, did the interviews themselves, and nothing happened. I let them run over me, Frye, and that makes me angry. I'll never let it happen again. Ever."

Minh lit a smoke. "What I wanted to do here in Little Saigon was see this little refugee community have a chance at fitting in. I wanted to keep the gangs in check and to make the people feel free to live and do their business. And I wanted the department to let me recruit some young Vietnamese men to help accomplish that."

Minh handed Frye three personnel request forms, each describing police department positions now open. They called for Vietnamese men and women with good English language skills, two years of education, and a desire to uphold the law.

"Congratulations."

Minh studied him. "When the FBI let Bennett walk into an ambush up in the desert, I decided they were covering up. You wouldn't happen to know what, would you?"

"No."

"You ever see him?"

"Who?"

"Thach."

"Far as I know, he's under house-arrest in Hanoi."

Minh looked at him doubtfully, then stood. "Thanks."

Frye shook his hand and walked out.

Lucia Parsons spent a well-chronicled week in Hanoi. Negotiations fell apart, then came back together; impasse was reached, then surmounted; the Vietnamese walked away from the bargaining table twice, and so did she. The final deal was struck. Unspecified amounts of "reconstruction aid" were reportedly agreed upon. House Bill 88231 passed overwhelmingly by both houses in an emergency session. The men would be freed in a "phased release." News analysts speculated that diplomatic concessions to Hanoi were in the balance, though just what they were, no one was sure. Hanoi hinted that withdrawal from Kampuchea was inevitable. Administration spokesmen remained enthused, mum.

That Friday, an air force jet from Honolulu scraped down at Orange County John Wayne Airport, which people felt was either appropriate or ironic, depending their political bent.

Frye, wearing his new press pass, worked his way through the vast crowd and managed to get close to the ramp leading off the plane. A red carpet had been laid from the steps to a roped-off section of the runway, where the president of the United States waited amidst very heavy security.

Beside that was another area for VIPs. Frye scanned the dignitaries and spotted Cristobel's golden head of hair. He waited while the air force jet taxied into place and the crowd began cheering.

A moment later, the first POW came down the stairs. He was a thin, slow-moving man whose alien gaze suggested a lifetime spent on another planet. He wore a crisp, tan uniform. He was alone. He saluted the president and waved to the roaring crowd.

Lucia joined him and the president. She sported a gray suit and hat, and she stood as straight-backed and impressively as any of the color guard. She shook hands with the frail man, then with the president, who took her hand and raised it to the crowd. The applause was robust.

Two men in dark suits escorted Cristobel toward the man. He looked long at her, then opened his arms, and stepped forward.

Cristobel and Mike Strauss hugged a good long time. Frye watched the sun bounce off her shoulders while Mike's hands clutched her back. The crowd roared even louder.

No one else got off the plane. Lucia explained that afternoon on TV that the POWs—twenty-seven in all—would be released one per week if the United States continued in good faith to abide by Hanoi's conditions. Said conditions were not so much explained as simply referred to.

Frye listened to Mike Strauss's speech. He said, "I thank you. I thank God. I never forgot you. If I could explain how it feels to be back on American soil, I would try, but I'm afraid I couldn't do it. Thank you all for never forgetting us." Then he faltered, and his face broke into a smile. He and Cristobel disappeared into a waiting limousine.

Frye watched all this with a sense of abstraction and unreality, the same feeling that had been with him since Huong Lam had walked into the hangar in Mojave. He was there, but not there, mind and body somehow separate, a tenant in himself. He cut out early and missed the president's address. Frye hated crowds.

A day before the Masters Invitational started, a south swell rose from Mexico. Frye stood on shore and struggled into the orange vest. He was number four. He picked a seventy-inch thruster and ground on a fresh layer of MegaWax. Just after sunrise his heat was called and the other five surfers hit the water. Frye watched the big gray waves rolling in beneath a purple blanket of clouds. The crowd was a good one, even this early. Amazing, he thought, that people want to watch this.

Even more amazing was the arrival of Edison and Hyla. Frye was about to head out when he heard his name called and turned to see his father. Edison was holding tight to Hyla's hand, hustling her across the damp morning sand, an arm raised in greeting, his gray hair wild and long. Even from this distance, thought Frye, he looks so much older.

"Gonna win, Chuck?" he panted.

"I'll try."

"Get first, or I wasted my time and gas."

"Oh, Ed." Hyla smiled. Frye detected a hint of genuine happiness in it.

Bill Antioch was there, pissed that Frye had missed the surf movie of which he was the star and had failed again to stimulate retail sales interest in the Mega line. Shelly Morris clung to his arm, drawn to stern businessman Bill.

The heat went by quickly, as they always do: scrambling for position on the waves that look like point-getters, trying to keep the stupid vests from riding up and choking you. Frye stayed to the outside in hopes of getting a big one. Finally he did, a magnificent six-foot right all to himself. He played it out, a little conservatively, rising to the top to snap off the lip, charging down for a turn at the bottom, then a long quick streak with his fingers on the flank of the wave. When it sectioned, he hung on and broke through, riding out the last of it, crouching in a tiny tube exactly his size. He could hear the applause as he paddled back out.

About halfway through, he kind of forgot what he was doing. The sun had peeked out to spray its rays through a cloud wall in the east: the kind of scene you get on complimentary bank calendars with a line from the national anthem under it. Frye decided that this was certainly a good time to count blessings, and he did. So many of them right up there on shore, he thought, watching this silly stuff. He looked back and saw Cristobel standing with Edison and Hyla now, her hair a golden patch against the gray sand. As he sat on his board and scanned the horizon for the next set, he realized that he wasn't afraid anymore, that the old terror had simply fallen away. Making room for new ones, he thought. Stronger in the broken places. Count that as a blessing, too.

Something inside him was big and fragile, huge and tender, and he could feel it right on the edge of exploding, on the verge of spontaneous combustion. A flutter, a shifting of things, a long moment of waiting. Then a feeling that there was new territory out there, a world of things beyond what he had felt before and what had gone before. You close your eyes and jump, he thought, grab for anything that might apply on the long way down.

He sat on his board and waited. He looked back to shore again.

And something else kept trying to get through to him, something that Bennett had taught him in a thousand ways but never quite managed to learn himself, something about forgetting what's gone and holding for dear life onto what's left. If you're one of the lucky left standing, it's the least you can do. Forget the losses; exaggerate the wins. Maybe not exactly how Benny would have put it. There will be time to think it through. Time. We've all got some of that left, thank God. That's all there is, between the living and the dead. I'll see you soon enough, sweet sister Debbie. You too, Benny. Sorry, I'm just not in a hurry to get there right now.

Remember, forget. Nice wave coming outside, paddle right over. Remember, forget. This thing has ten points and my name written all over it. MegaGood. Slide right in now. Comin' your way, Cris.

Anyhow, he got second.

# About the Author

T. Jefferson Parker is an award-winning journalist, and author of the bestselling *Laguna Heat.* He lives in Laguna Beach, California, where he is working on his next novel.

086251

Parker, T. Jefferson
Little Saigon

S.G. - 88